# Pale Zenith

## by Wendy Rathbone

Pale Zenith (by Wendy Rathbone)
Publisher: Eye Scry Publications
All rights reserved, Copyright © 2013

ISBN 13: 978-0-9766897-9-9
ISBN 10: 0976689790

## WHOLESALE INFORMATION

For information about wholesale rates,
or to order additional copies, please email us at...
contact@eyescry.com

*For Della, brilliant, magical, wonderful, beautiful...*
*with all my heart.*

## Prologue
## The World Outside the Walled City  (Parallel Earth)

The park looked lush and full in the late evening. All the trees seemed thicker at night, heavier. The plush lawns soaked up dense shadows, black and green mixing to form shades of sage and raw pewter. The air smelled of pine-resin and flame.

On the horizon, beyond the wall of trees, there had been a fire earlier in the day. Lightning had started it, some reports said. Others speculated someone had deliberately set it. Someone from The Walled City, a psychic soldier, had projected the flames onto the vulnerable farm land outside Tiem, one of the biggest cities of the Free World. But the flames were out, now. And all psychotronic defense systems were on standby alert. The World's own psychic soldiers were no doubt actively probing the night skies overhead, looking to meet and battle any more errant attacks.

"*If* it was an attack," Tira said to her two friends, leaning against the back of a dew- damp, wooden bench, "it wasn't aimed very well. There had been reports of thunderstorms in the area, so everyone could be jumping to conclusions." She'd studied psychotronics in college for the past two years and found the science to be inexact at best, and not a little mystifying.

"Still, we shouldn't be out tonight of all nights." Jorik would not sit, his nervousness showcased by the way his fists bunched in the deep pockets of his vinyl trousers. His pale bangs scattered across his forehead like shimmering mothwings. He, too, was a student scientist. Where Tira was driven by curiosity, Jorik empowered himself with fear. The emotion made him appear smaller than his tall stature.

"Why don't you go back, then, Jorik? We'll catch up to you later," said Cassus.

Tira turned to the third person in their party. Cassus was watching her with bold, dark eyes. He'd never made it a secret that he wanted her, never held back from assessing her to her face, never seemed to understand fully that her rejection of him was rejection. She had eyes only for Jorik, and Cassus knew it, but still he followed them around, pretending friendship for the other man that was clearly a fabricated excuse to be closer to her, pretending to show an interest in the new group marriages that were 'all the fashion, now', perhaps to intimidate her into giving in to him, or to undermine Jorik's already thin ego.

"I don't want to go back alone," Jorik replied, kicking at the ground. "Come on you two. Curfew was set for a reason."

"We're safest tonight," Tira said softly to him. "You know that. When the armies are on alert, the chance of anything breaking through their barriers is far less. We're fine here. And we're under the cover of these trees." She felt a soft wind blow as she said that, scented with distant ash. Her spine suddenly tingled.

"You've read the reports," Cassus added. "We all have in Strategy 101. The easiest victims are those who lose their bio-pacers. And those who are purposely targeted for political reasons. We're just students." He fingered the silver cuff at his wrist.

"Fools," Jorik said. "Yeah, I read those reports. People are attacked at random, too. And some deaths that have been reported as accidental might not be that at all. You saw the one where the little girl was hit on the head by a potted plant that fell, for no known reason, from a high shelf. And Supreme Justice Kiki died of unknown causes in her own bed. She was 44! Bio-pacers didn't save them."

"They can't prove it was an attack," Tira said, looking at her own bio-pacer, a strip of silver on her left wrist that helped block the constant bombardment of mind-control waves coming from the enemy. "But those are isolated and rare cases. You know that."

"That's how war is." Cassus' teeth showed. Tira wondered how he could smile so often and so much. It was as if he took nothing seriously.

"The Walled City's Ignorant Armies track better at night," Jorik said. "We should go home. Everyone's safer indoors. They've always taught us that."

"Supreme Justice Kiki wasn't safe in her own bed. Besides, I hate locking myself away every night. Isn't the park beautiful?" Tira asked.

6

Jorik turned away.

Cassus kept grinning at her. "Lovely. I'd take you here every night if you were mine."

Jorik turned abruptly as several shadows scattered across the huge lawns. "Hey – "

Tira saw instantly they were only a group of children running into the trees. "Stupid," she muttered. "When I was small I belonged to a night-gang once. It was a way of defying the truth, the war. We practically held seances to invite the enemies to psychically attack us. Nothing ever happened. We were harmless, so we were ignored."

"No one is harmless in a war. We're all soldiers in a way," Jorik said. "And aren't we doing, right now, exactly what you say those children are doing? Defying the odds, challenging."

"Yes." Tira reached out to touch Jorik's arm. "And sometimes soldiers take risks. Sometimes they just have to feel the night air on their skin, have a little fun, a little wildness."

"Sit down with us, Jorik. I'm your friend. I won't let anything happen to you," Cassus said, the sweetness in his voice making Tira wince.

The tall, pale man looked unsure. That trait of indecision was his least endearing characteristic. Finally, he sat on the other side of Cassus much to Tira's consternation, head bowed. How had Cassus won him over so easily? Was Jorik so blind? She shook her head, deciding it was time to find new friends.

The breeze picked up. "Doesn't that feel good?" she asked.

"Hmmm," Cassus said.

Jorik merely stated, "I have physics homework I should be doing."

Tira leaned back, letting her long hair flow behind the back of the bench. The dampness of the evening clung to the wood and cooled the back of her neck. She still smelled distant flames, and wondered how the scent could seem to be growing stronger with every breath. But she ignored her thoughts, the night lulling her, too lovely to ruin with anymore questions.

## The Walled City (Parallel Earth)

In the War Room on the top floor of The Walled City's ruling palace, the pretty park with its three unusual inhabitants took over the main imaging monitor.

"Make the pictures clearer!" the head controller, Stannos, ordered. "I want to hear every word." He watched as his number one controller ordered the spychiatrist machine who manipulated his 'seer' girl's talents to refine the image. The girl was young tonight, barely twelve. Her name was Lacy. Stannos' spychiatrists had found her on an alternate Earth in an alternate timestream, and identified her special abilities immediately, as they had been programmed to do. He used her often at varying ages, his spychiatrists able to traverse time as easily as space and dimension, stealing her from the other realm, the other Earth, mostly at night as she slept. Her family never missed her. She was one of his best 'seer' spies. And, in fact, at an older age, the girl had been personally interesting to him as well. Having his spychiatrists program her for sex was as simple as using her for war. And it gave Stannos a heady, powerful feeling to do just that.

The girl cried out as the spychiatrist prodded her obscenely between the legs with one of its clawed appendages. Pain made her ability stronger. The picture on the monitor became a close-up, the conversation loud and clear.

"Good," Stannos said. "Good." He watched as the students conversed. He laughed when he learned they were students of psychotronics. That admission alone had just garnered them a death sentence.

Stannos turned to another Controller further across the room. "Do you have Mr. Smith ready?" he asked.

"He's in perfect agony. The spychiatrist is holding him back, but as soon as it has your coordinates and lets him go, he'll project powerfully."

"Then he's working strong tonight?"

"He's in top shape. Any preferences on mode of execution?"

"Hmmm." Stannos fingered his long, black braid. A royal blue ribbon wove through it, glistening silk. "You know how I abhor complexities. A quick death will be best for them. Let's try Mr. Smith's talent for long-distance telekinesis. Can he drop that nearby tree on them, do you think? Their bio-pacers can't defend them against a falling tree."

The Controller studied the monitor. "With the ease and grace of a natural disaster," he replied.

"Good. I've got the distractions in place. Their skies are busy tonight with prowlers. They've got their soldiers on alert." He looked at his half-dozen distractors, all controlled by yet another spychiatrist, waiting to do telepathic battle. It would be rough on them. He expected to have at least one or two casualties, but these were the expendable ignorants, the ones he didn't have to count on as more than mere pawns. The youngest was a boy of about eight. The older ones, three women, two men, had less refined talents, but would fool the prowlers long enough for Mr. Smith to fell his tree, and long enough for Lacy to keep 'seeing' until he could be sure the job was done.

"All right," he said. "Let's do it." He ordered his spychiatrist to begin prodding his six until their minds soared beyond the walls of the city. They moaned and cried out as their psyches projected into an ethereal battle. The pain made them aggressive and strong, not weak, though their anguish filled the War Room with stunning screams. My army, Stannos thought, grinning. Who'd have thought it? Children and weaklings alike, made to be strong as the most honed of fighters.

On the main monitor, over the park, a squiggle of green lightning lit up the sky.

"Now!" he yelled.

The students on the monitor jumped up from their bench, crying out in surprise. But it was too late for them. Mr. Smith's unblocked lightning had gotten through and struck the exact tree Stannos had wanted targeted.

"Precision," he called out. "That's what I like to see!"

The tree fell toward the small group, catching two of them straight on the heads. Their skulls popped like balloons, crushing. The third one of their party, Jorik the cowardly one, miraculously avoided being hit. Stannos watched him run screaming through the long shadows and the plush night-silvered grass.

"Follow him?" the Controller asked.

Lacy's mind seemed to be losing him. Jorik grew more distant on the monitor, though his yells flew up into the air and through the speakers of the War Room to mix with Stannos' distractors.

"Yes."

Lacy's spychiatrist prodded her with a claw again, and bathed her in blue light. Her drugged screams heightened, shrill and young. The runner on the monitor grew more distinct, until her vision seemed to follow directly at his heels.

One of Stannos' six, a woman with plump hips wearing a flannel nightgown, fell dead to the floor. Blood poured from her nose and ears.

"Hurry!" Stannos cried out. "He's getting away!"

Lightning flashed at Jorik, hitting him in the back. He flew forward, airborne for about eight feet, then fell. His biopacer glowed, absorbing some of the energy, and miraculously he got up, shaken, but still alive.

"Damn it! Have Mr. Smith try again!"

Just then Lacy gasped, cried out, "No!" and fainted. The monitor went blank.

"We've lost him," the Controller said.

Stannos' fingernails, long and pointed, cut into his palms as he tried to control his rage. Another of his distractors fell. He couldn't tell if the man was dead or unconscious.

"That's it then," he finally said, ordering his spychiatrist to let the others go. "We need more people if we want to do more damage. But for tonight we got the job done. Jorik will tell everyone what he saw. They'll know it wasn't an accident. They'll fear us even more, as they should. And when I amass my gifted soldiers all at once, nothing will be able to stand against them. The whole World both inside and outside The Walled City will be ours."

## Part I - Earth (Present Day)

## Chapter One

Lacy met Zack and Leo in the city. Country-bred herself, their eyeliner decorated eyes and slow smiles surprised her at first. The fact that they were identical twins made them seem even stranger.

"I have no scruples," Zack said, a dubious introduction.

"I can vouch for that," Leo added.

She could only nod in mute fascination as they bought her several rum and Cokes in a row. Something hollow widened inside her. A neglected child within. A void made of time and stillness that kept her separate from humanity, made her always think of herself as a fringe element on the outside looking in.

Their shoulder-length hair was so brown it was almost green. Every time one of them turned away from her, the light would hit it, illuminating more autumn colors: wheat, applerose, mulch. She'd never seen hair that moved as if alive.

"I know what it is like to be killed," Leo said.

"I can vouch for that." Zack snickered, his languid brown eyes rolling like marbles in triangular sockets. He was drunk. He fingered his phone, glancing at it now and again.

Lacy rarely patronized bars. She hated that scene. What drew her to *Sergio's* this night, after a long day at *Burger Buster,* was still a mystery. But these two...they were *terrible.* Not hard, not mean-looking, just terrible in the way they finished each other's sentences, the way they laughed at their own jokes. There were two of them, yet they somehow seemed as one. They were a solution to some bizarre, indefinable urge she'd always denied, and she fell easily, delicately in love with them.

At the time, though, she never would have named her response 'love.' She had no answers in her life, no easy definitions for behavior and emotion. Everything seemed to function, breathe, dance, surge around her, but never with her. She'd fallen away from ritual and meaning a long, long time ago.

It seemed these two had fallen out of the pattern, too.

"How do you know what it's like to be killed?" she asked.

"He had a nightmare once," Zack answered for his brother. The way she could tell them apart at first was that Zack had his black blazer sleeves rolled up. Leo's sleeves covered all but the tips of his fingers. The cuffs dangled on the bar top absorbing condensation. The fact that Zack was the more forward – the controller – of the two, also was not lost on her.

"The hell it was." Leo leaned into his kelp-hued drink. "No nightmare I ever had left marks."

Lacy's stomach went cold. The rum and Cokes she'd drank started to awaken inside her. "What kind of marks?"

"Let's just say Zack and I aren't quite identical anymore." Leo didn't look up. His drink held his world. He stared at it for a long time.

Her shoulders hunched, and a chill etched along her spine like a fleshless finger probing, penetrating through her careful human-normal veil. "What kind of marks?" she asked again.

"He's drunk. He don't like to talk about it," Zack said when Leo didn't answer. "Don't know why he brought it up now. He never talks like this."

Her glance at Zack was more desperate than she'd intended to show. For a moment, she wished him away. "Please." As the separate core of herself continued to expand, Lacy's mind started flashing back. The country. Her grandparent's farm. Feeling unsafe. Sure she was being watched all the time.

Her skin squirmed in that same way now. Was it happening again? She held onto the counter edge, the polished wood slipping against her palms, and glanced nervously over her shoulder. Everything felt wrong, as it had many times back on the farm just before something strange would happen: a nightmare, a whispering voice, a peripheral glimpse of a ghost. Was it only the drinks?

"He's got scars and things, that's all," Zack said matter-of-factly, still speaking for his brother.

"Scars?" she prompted, ignoring Zack by leaning around him on the bar, by trying to get Leo to look up.

"From nothing I did," Leo murmured, brown eyes flashing up, then down again toward his drink.

"They happened while he slept," Zack added. "His dreams sometimes leave real marks. Right?" He leaned off-balance toward Leo, who nodded without looking up. Lacy's view was cut off by his shoulder.

"You mean you dream something hurts you, like a punch in the face, and then wake up with a bloody nose?" Her skin was prickled, rough. She thought of getting up, going to the other side of Leo so Zack couldn't interfere. But before she could move, she felt shock coat the back of her throat in dry layers as Leo answered.

"No." Leo turned and leaned on his upturned palm, staring past Zack, who had pulled back slightly, and right into Lacy's eyes. "No, not like that at all."

"Just scars," Zack said, touching the counter, his rings clinking against it. "You know, already healed."

Her breath came out slow and cool-scented from the alcohol.

So, she wasn't alone. Someone else had experienced what she had. Someone else had nightmares that left real wounds in their wake. Wounds that had no outside explanation. But it was all too coincidental. Perhaps Leo had drawn her here. Or someone had. The sense of wrongness had not faded. Someone was watching. She knew it. Felt it. Leo had gone back to watching his drink. Zack's fingers still pestered the bar top with abstract designs.

The bar looked normal. Kids played pool on the upper deck, cigarettes dangling from mouths and fingers like captured fireflies. Others chatted on the cell phones or squinted at laptops in the dimness. Smoke choked the air. Lovers occupied booths. A couple of young girls were slow-dancing by the jukebox, one with a shaved head and long, mylar earrings, the other with a ponytail dyed crow-black.

But Lacy wasn't entirely reassured. Any one of them could be someone or some *thing* other than what they appeared. Her paranoia itched again. She could almost 'see' beyond the fabric of air that something, some presence just hovered there, eavesdropping. That feeling...she thought she'd escaped it by leaving the farm. But now...

"Hey," Zack was saying. "Hey." He snapped long, sharp-nailed fingers in front of her eyes. The pinky nail was painted black. He wore two silver bands, one on his little finger, one on his ring finger. Leo's hands were covered by his jacket, so she couldn't see if he wore the bands, too.

"Sorry." She blinked and looked down. "What kind of marks?" she asked again. The conversation had gotten too personal too fast, but she couldn't stop. Alcohol deadened her careful inhibitions.

"Why so insistent?" Zack asked.

She wanted Leo to talk to her, not the protective, sardonic brother's keeper.

As if reading her thoughts, Leo looked up. His unguarded gaze settled on her. Not appraisal. More, curiosity. And, perhaps, fear. "Yeah," he finally said. "Why so insistent?" When he asked the question, it held a less accusatory tone.

"I had nightmares that left scars, too."

"Shit," Zack said.

Leo simply stared at her.

After that, they surrounded her for the rest of the evening, twin slim shadows like wings that stayed unfurled. Two guardian angels to her right and to her left.

She felt warmer being with them. An instant kinship linked them, a familiarity that was especially strong between herself and Leo.

Safety in numbers, she thought, clasping both their hands as they headed for the door at closing.

Outside it was a clear, summer evening. While they walked, she thought of the past.

~

Fragmentary whirlwinds. Nausea. The scent of needles.

The little girl, Lacy, closed her eyes. "What world is this?" she asked.

No response.

Footsteps. She saw no one. But a voice in her mind, a soft wind murmuring, said: Close your eyes.

Something hurt her between her legs. She screamed.

Then she was reading a book, but her eyes were still closed. She scanned the cover. *Webs New Ion.* The rest faded. She opened the book to the middle. The words blurred on the page. Then cleared. *Lapel, part of a garment folded back, lapidary, a cutter of gemstones, lapis lazuli, azure, opaque, semi-precious, lapse, to fall away, lapwing, crested plover, larceny, theft, larch, cone-bearing tree, lard, the melted and clarified fat, larder, large, lariat, lark, larvae, larynx, lascivious, laser, lash...* A break. Then a line jumped out: *Ha-ha from hell...*

None of it made sense until the last sentence, which startled her. Her eyes flew open. Hurting bright light. Metal hands. Chapped touches and footsteps. Scent of burnt oil.

She woke crying and shivering in her own bed. When she'd first had this dream at age eight, she'd known it wasn't right, wasn't normal. Now she was eleven and the dream still came. In the notebook she kept by the bed, she wrote what she could remember from the book.

*Ha-ha from Hell.*

The dream took her mind, squeezed it. She wrote to reclaim what was lost. She wrote to understand as the middle flesh between her legs began again to ache. Something had touched her there, not a hand or a person, but a tool.

But when she got up to go to the bathroom there was only a little blood. Nothing to wake anyone for. Nothing to worry Grandmother about. After all, some girls her age had already started to menstruate. Perhaps that was all it was, though intuitively she knew better.

When she looked out her bedroom window into the deep night of farm country, nothing moved. Not even the moon which seemed to be hanging like a hook suspended on a chain very close – too close – to her rectangle window.

She imagined a big man floating in the sky, holding onto a pole with his night-line cast down onto the flowing, liquid land. The hook would snag whatever was in its path.

She jumped out of sight of it and dived under cotton sheets, homemade quilts and fluffy animals. In the center of the bed she curled into herself, making herself so small that nothing in the night could find her.

~

"Leo's the shy one." Zack laughed and his teeth reflected rosy lamplight from the closed room's corner.

"I can vouch for..." Leo looked aside. "I am not," he

corrected quickly.

Lacy smiled at Leo, picking up on his frustration. Then, breaking his gaze, she began studying the living room again. It did not look like a 'guys' typical apartment. Where she might have expected plain shades or Venetian blinds, floor-length curtains of thick antique white damask closed off every window. Pillows – pink, black, silver – made an ocean of squares around a glass coffee table. A white futon, heaped with more pillows, faced it. A fish-tank buzzed behind her, threw off aqua sea-light to mix with the light from the corner lamp. Everything seemed new, soft and plush. Formal, but casual. Feminine, but stiff.

Why had she gone home with these strangers? It was warm both outside and in the house. But she felt chilled, anxious.

"If you're not shy, prove it," Zack said, standing in the middle of the room, arms spread, as though he wanted to block Leo and Lacy from entering further into the room.

Ignoring him, Leo shrugged out of his blazer and threw it on the futon. Lacy could see silver bands like Zack's on his fingers now, a bracelet of gold chain on his wrist. His hair was parted on the side opposite Zack's. He combed his fingers through it, waves of brown flashing. Scowling, "How?"

"Show Lacy your scars."

Leo laughed, touched his hair again. He glanced away, then back at Zack. Betrayal tightened his brow. His dark eyes glazed and the nervous laughter died.

"Well? Show her," Zack said, still smiling, a human-made devil from too many drinks.

Lacy watched them, transfixed. Anxious. Was she reading Leo's feelings again, or was the anxiety her own?

Suddenly Leo lunged forward, butting his brother in the chest with his shoulder.

"Hey," Zack said, using the same casual tone he'd used with her in the bar. "Hey!"

Leo pushed him, this time with his fist. Zack put his arm up to deflect him. "Hey, stop!"

Leo took a step back, a deep breath. "Fuck you."

"What?" Zack chuckled.

Lacy frowned. It seemed Zack was being deliberately mean. Or obtuse.

"Just fuck you." Leo turned and left the room.

Lacy felt Leo's anger as if it were her own, as if some language barrier had been broken and she understood everything all at once. When Zack turned to her, shrugging, smiling; she said: "It's not funny!"

"He's the one who brought it up in the bar. I'm not really laughing at him." Brother's keeper, brother's adversary – Lacy couldn't make up her mind which one Zack was.

Crossing her arms over her chest, she turned toward the door. "Maybe I ought to go." People didn't understand the dreams weren't just *dreams*. The scars were ugly. Real.

"No, don't." He moved toward her, reaching out as if to touch her arm. She backed up a step before she realized she might not really mind the contact. Except it was Leo she was thinking of when she looked at him. When his hand finally found her arm and rested there for a second, she knew she had to stay. "Just wait. This is for Leo." Zack nodded toward the hall. His shoulders hunched. Head slightly bowed, shiny hair sprinkling against his eyes, he still had that spark of challenge. Defiance. "Maybe we've all had a little too much to drink. I'll go get him."

She didn't move. His touch was warm, but her skin stayed cold. "He's not ready. He doesn't want to talk about it. And I don't know if I do either."

"This is the first time he's brought up his scars in years," Zack protested. "He needs to talk about it."

"He was drunk." As was Zack, but she didn't say it. The heat of the room flowed apart from her. She was cold. She swallowed. The sound seemed to encompass every empty space.

"It was more than that and you know it." Again he was his brother's speaker. "You two share something unique. He recognized that. Please. Stay. For him." He didn't wait for an answer. She watched him disappear down the short hall to a closed door.

The carpet was the spongy, beige kind that almost tripped her up. She stepped out of her tennis shoes and, still standing, kicked a silver cushion.

She wore plain jeans, a black cotton shirt. Nothing as elegant as the twins. Her fingers and arms, bare of ornament, looked withered to her, tree-branch thin. She felt ugly. She was hollow. What did they see when they looked at her?

Her eyes smarted as she edged toward the hall. Zack had left the door open. She heard low murmuring, perhaps a protest. Maybe Leo would deck his brother for good this time, or maybe Zack would finish it.

She inched closer.

A white room enfolded them. A king-sized, four-poster bed dipped on one side where Leo sat, hunched shadow, victim-postured. The bedspread was a pale canvas he occupied alone.

Anger swelled within her. The bile taste of it. She knew that posture too well.

Nausea. Fragmentary whirlwinds.

"How could you?" Leo was whispering, breath catching, making the air in the room seem cracked and poison.

"You brought the subject up earlier. I only meant to suggest maybe she knows something," Zack said. "It's no big deal. I wasn't making fun..."

"You were!" The words hissed past Lacy's ear.

*Damn straight!*

"No." Zack, so straight, tall, sparking disobedience, suddenly crumpled.

Lacy blinked. Her vision blurred for a moment before she realized he'd actually gone down on his knees. The arrogant brother bowing to the more delicate will?

"You know where those scars are!"

Lacy didn't dare breathe. The scars on her own body throbbed all at once. She remembered gym class at age 12 or 13. Other girls. "What are those triangles?" "They go all the way down into your underwear." Giggles.

Zack's hand met his brother's knee. Where they touched, they fused. Leo's elbows rested on his thighs. His hands supported his head. Zack leaned in, kissed the top of Leo's head, then pressed with his cheek. Hair surrounded his face. Leo's hair.

"I'm sorry," Zack said softly. "I didn't mean anything. I *was* thinking of your scars, not your modesty."

Leo made a strangled sound. Lifted his head so they faced. And Zack kissed him very lightly on the lips.

Lacy ducked her head and turned away. She'd been holding her breath. Now it all came out at once. She ran into the living room gasping, sinking into the pillows on the floor. In the center of her chest a hard ache axed into softer heart-muscle.

The kiss did and did not disturb her. It was unexpected, an intimacy she'd never known but often wished for. It spoke of a trust she needed. She was envious of that trust. Of the rapport that draped so naturally about them. Would her life have been different if she hadn't been alone? If she'd had someone to share with, to be with? Would the unknown paths inside her be as long, or as dark?

After a moment, she glanced around. The fish swam in their cold finite void. Curtains pressed against chilled windows and the wall. The outside was locked away. Pillows lapped, friendly, at her arms and legs. She leaned against the low, white futon. Murmuring grew louder in the hall.

Footsteps. A touch.

She couldn't help it; she tensed.

"It's not about dreams," Leo said. He was instantly kneeling in front of her. His hands hovered at his waist. Zack stood back a pace.

Lacy's eyes fixed on Leo's hands – long nails, silver rings – like a woman's hands only thicker, strong. They undid the button, the zipper. White cotton billowed beneath black linen. His black t-shirt ended at his navel. He lifted it higher with one hand, pushed down at thick elastic with his other, revealing auburn skin, smooth, hairless. He kept pushing, the black slacks wrinkling at his thighs, underwear giving, until she saw the two lines of dark triangles: one, two, three triangles per line vivisecting his abdomen and disappearing into springy curls. As Leo pushed the fabric of his underwear down, Lacy saw that the two lines met at last in a final, larger triangle where the dark pink skin began on the base of his penis. They were like tattoos, black lines perfectly drawn. Leo's hands shook as he held his clothing open.

"It's real," he whispered.

"I know." She started to cry.

Leo pulled her close until she quieted. God his touch was warm. It made her fevered where Zack's had left her cold. In the midst of that, the tears were not what concerned her. It was the emotions accompanying them. Panic. Shock. Anger. And an anxiety that left her empty, insomnia-plagued, and always searching.

Zack left them to relax, and came back with fresh coffee and microwave popcorn.

"I want to kill who did this," Lacy said. Now that she wasn't alone, she could say things she'd never spoken to another soul.

"We don't even know where to begin to find out who or how or what did this to us," Leo said.

"I once lived on a farm," Lacy began.

"We grew up in the desert," Zack said, munching popped kernels. He sat leaning against the futon. His eyes were bright and alive. He was all-champion now, defender of the realm. "I don't have the scars. Only Leo does. And we've never been apart."

"Never?"

Both shook their heads. They looked like little boys, though Lacy could tell they were a few years older than she was. At least 25.

"Always slept in the same bed," Zack said.

"Always?" She glanced away, realizing how personal her comment sounded.

They simply nodded.

"So how do you explain that I have them and Zack doesn't?" Leo asked.

Lacy could only shrug. She tried another tack. "Maybe we were meant to meet."

They stared at her, waiting. The fish swam. The aroma of coffee burned the air.

"I don't normally bar-hop."

"Why did you?" Zack asked.

"I don't know. I felt pulled, kind of."

"Well, we bar-hop. We don't work, so how else can we meet girls?" Zack said.

Leo, sitting next to him, elbowed him in the waist.

"Well, it's true," Zack said.

"Shut up. Lacy's not just any girl."

"I know that." But he crunched down hard on a kernel of popcorn as he winked in her direction.

"Well cut the crude act for awhile."

"I'm not being crude. I didn't say she was 'any girl'. And we did meet in a bar." Zack thrust more popcorn into his mouth.

Lacy smirked at Leo. "Yeah, and I came home with you, didn't I?" She'd never felt this comfortable with a man before, let alone *two* men, though Zack's domineering personality still made her uneasy.

Leo leaned forward, legs crossed. A pillow covered his lap. "Tell us more about the farm."

~

Twelve-year old Lacy felt the bark of the oak with her palm, rough, solid. She patted it, the urge to climb zinging through her muscles. Trees were friends these days, while other girls and boys stayed away. Something about her eyes made them nervous. She always looked scared, some kids said. She was too skinny, too clumsy. Kids didn't like being embarrassed by other kids. They didn't like secretive girls who were too quiet.

Trees didn't care if you talked or not.

This one smelled of early morning dew, even though it was late. Its elegant hush summoned her.

Lacy grabbed the lowest branch and swung her legs up onto it until she was hanging from her knees. Then she pulled herself the rest of the way up and sat, legs dangling, planning her next step.

The sky looked melted, six o'clock and almost summer. She could actually smell the colors: wintergreen, orange blossom, cinnamon. The clouds were wolves of gold, circling. The sun was the heart. Everything had a heart. Even sky. The sun pumped molten slag through its ventricles, venting radiation. The sun seemed as angry as Lacy inside. She wasn't sure why.

For miles she could see flowing countryside. There were mountains to the north, the very peaks still tipped with virgin snow. West was the meadow where deer grazed. No one planted there anymore, not since Grandfather died. But there was a garden out back where onions and beets and carrots and corn grew. In October they had pumpkins, fat and round as beach balls. In early spring, daffodils spread themselves along the walkway. Everything was always changing, leaves, sky, people. Lacy felt she couldn't hold onto any of it.

Now the tree held her. Trying not to think about time, the sun, her anger, she hummed a made-up tune. A wind came up. On it was the voice of the tune echoed back to her.

She stilled. Glanced around. From her perch she could see no one about. Deciding she'd imagined it, she began again, humming her own song, following no pattern.

Seconds later, the tune echoed. It sounded as if it were played on a pipe or flute.

"Stop it," she said softly. Her eyes felt hot and round.

There was a whisper in the grass, through the leaves of the trees. "Stop it," the wind seemed to say.

"Stop it stop it stop it!" she yelled.

The whisper answered. *Stop it stop it stop it.*

"No." She pressed her palms to her temples. Letting go of the branch made her lose her balance. Her body swayed. Scrabbled for balance. Lost.

She went over backwards, in a loop, falling, dead branches embraced by leaf-smell and her tune and the wind rushing all about. Gravity didn't work right, though. Something went wrong. Instead of hitting grass and earth, she seemed to fall a different way. The sky was down, not up. She heard voices. Someone, a figure, moved in the deer meadow. Out the corner of her eye she saw him. He looked like he had five arms.

Then the tree did what trees cannot do. It caught her in its many brown arms and brought her to the lowest branch until she was sitting again, feet dangling, contemplating her next move. She screamed.

Grandmother came running. "What is it, Lacy?"

She couldn't stop crying long enough to answer.

"Did you almost fall?" Grandmother asked.

She nodded, not wanting to explain further. She got down and Grandmother hugged her. Against the soft, full bosom of her only guardian, she whispered, "Make it stop."

"Are you hearing the voices again, child?"

She shook her head. It was more than that, too complicated to explain.

That night, in bed, only the strength of the east wind rivaled the full swiftness of her rage. She shredded her favorite stuffed bear, clutched the rags of him in her fists. She made pale blossoms burst in her vision as she pressed thumbs to her closed eyes. She pinched her own skin until it bruised to stay awake.

But later nightmares still took her, continuing most often in summer and autumn, when the moon was a hook in her window, and someone fishing caught her squirming silver mind, laid it out on a table and did unspeakable things to it.

~

"You fell and the tree moved?" Zack asked.

Lacy nodded. "I'm not prone to seizures. I've been tested for epilepsy."

"So've I," Leo said. His eyes, liquid brown with flecks of gold and green, seemed to curdle, still framed in smeared, exotic make-up. They were as seething and alive as his hair. Multi-colored to match his emotions. Zack had a similar, but more cold presence.

"I don't understand," Lacy said.

"You mean, how the tree did that?" Leo asked.

"Yes, but no. I mean, why would these things happen to one of you and not the other?"

"Did your grandmother ever see anything?" Zack asked.

"No. But I didn't sleep with her. She wouldn't know if I sneaked around at night."

"Zack's the only one who ever believed me," Leo said. "But he's never seen anything strange. My parents thought I was an 'overly imaginative boy'." He stretched and his pants, still unbuttoned at the waist, unzipped.

Lacy glanced away. She didn't want to see the triangles again. She looked down at her own stomach, jeans-covered.

"You have the same scars, too, don't you?" Leo propped himself on his elbow, lit a cigarette. Lacy saw the package: *Royale.* "You said as much at Sergio's."

She shook her head in denial, stopped when she realized she was lying as she'd trained herself out of habit. She nodded. "But what are they?"

"Tag. You're it," Zack said. They both looked at him. "You're marked, don't you see? Gimme one of those." Zack grabbed the lighter and cellophane cigarette package from his brother's hand. He lit up, offered the pack to Lacy. She took one merely to hold onto something. She didn't smoke.

"Maybe you guys have extra-sensory powers or something, and they manifest in this way," Zack offered, inhaling, the tip of the cigarette brightening to red.

"Yeah, and I tattooed myself with a hot needle when I was nine." Leo glared at him. "Right on my dick."

Smoke streamed by Lacy's chin, spice and heat. "I think I was raped."

They both stared at her for a long, uncomfortable moment.

"I think I was murdered and brought back to life," Leo added.

His and Lacy's eyes locked. Suddenly, Leo bent at the waist until his face met hers. The kiss was smoky but light, a flower petal against her lips. He leaned away, looking down, eyelashes fringing his cheeks like dark moths.

Lacy's heart seemed to shred in her chest. She thought of the kiss she'd witnessed earlier, how empty it had made her feel. The emptiness withered slightly, her body warming. This man surprised her. Delighted her. And she'd not been delighted by too many men in the past.

Zack moved away from the futon. He lounged on the floor by the fish tank, unmoving. "The gods are crazy."

"Someone is," Lacy replied, still surprised, the kiss drying on her lips.

"Someones. Plural." Zack crossed his feet at the ankles. "People are crazy. Take this city alone. Right now some dickwad is raping his two-year old daughter. Someone else is burying a body in their backyard. Kids are shooting each other. Doping up. Sharing AIDS needles. Worshipping an organized religion that condones discrimination on the basis of sexual orientation, what you wear, how you look. Fuck this all. Why shouldn't a tree move to catch a little girl, then? Why not accept that someone could fuck with your brains? Who knows what you two hold and who might want that some day. Science is alive and well. Magic, too, I'm sure. Who knows any goddamn thing in this universe for real? Shit, we could all be actors who just got into the role a little too deep. Know what I mean?"

"Bravo." Leo began to clap.

Zack inhaled, ignoring him, blew out a long snake of grey smoke.

"And we just happened to meet in a bar," Leo said. "A girl with scars identical to mine." He questioned her with his eyebrows for further confirmation.

Lacy nodded.

The procedure was not as painful as she thought it'd be, pulling up her shirt, unbuttoning her 501's. She had only one line of triangles, four in a row leading into the thatch of pubic hair. There were no scars below that. At least, no scars that could be seen.

She hated that her ribs showed, that her breasts were so small. But the twins weren't looking at her in *that* way right now. Strange men these two, she thought. She trusted them – or at least Leo – so quickly. Yet they could also be as rowdy as any guys she'd known. Leo had already kissed her. Zack was as outspoken and forward as any horny guy she might've met in a bar.

But there was this mystery that linked the three of them. A sibling kind of bond. *And I'm the missing triplet?* she wondered.

Leo smiled, as though reading her mind. He sat back, pulled up his pant leg. His calf, sprinkled with straight, gold hairs, curved against cat-like muscles. "I have this scoop mark," he announced. "Right here." He twisted so she could see the underside of his calf.

Zack was laughing, holding onto his stomach. "You two remind me of those guys in *Jaws.*"

"Shut up," Leo said.

"I got one, too," Lacy said, leaning closer toward the scoop scar. Hers was on her left leg.

"I'm flawless, case anyone's interested," Zack muttered.

Leo let out a snort of air.

"Which one of you's older?" Lacy asked.

"He is," Zack said.

"Me." Leo pointed to himself. "Don't forget it."

"Oh, I won't," she replied, grinning.

Leo chucked her under the chin, letting go of his pant leg. "I know you won't."

"So, what do you guys conclude?" Zack asked, after clothing was righted again, dignity maintained. "That you were kidnapped by the same lunatics?"

Leo threw a pillow at him in answer. Lacy thought about

it for a moment, then tossed one at him, too.

"Okay, okay," Zack laughed. "I won't ask any more questions."

Leo moved closer to Zack. Something passed between them too quick for Lacy to translate. A combination of looks and a couple of grunts seemed to contain an entire conversation. Then Zack smacked Leo's arm, but his hand didn't drop. Instead, it slid down toward Leo's hand. Fingers wove through fingers, clasped for a moment, let go.

Lacy's cheeks heated. She felt as if she'd again witnessed the most intimate contact two people could have.

They both looked at her. "Tired?" they asked in unison.

She shook her head. "What time is it?"

"3:05," Leo said.

"Shit."

"Shit is right," Zack agreed.

"Wanna spend the night?"

Lacy froze. The two brothers glanced at each other once, then back at her. Their eyes held twin lights, warm and moist. She thought she'd always known them. They were her brothers, her best friends. Guardians who'd shadowed her even in dreams. She'd never had a brother. She'd never had a best friend.

"Yes," she whispered.

They both had the same crooked smile.

Zack moved down the hall, saying: "The king-sized bed should fit us all comfortably." He turned, eyebrow raising. "Unless you don't want to sleep with us..."

Lacy eyed him askance. "I said I would." Inside she shivered. The bottom of her stomach burned.

Leo touched her elbow. She turned, looking down at his hand where it touched her. His rings glittered. "Want a beer?" he asked.

She shook her head. "Those rum and Cokes are still slamming around." She'd had one cup of coffee but it hadn't helped.

"Me, too." He followed Zack.

"Get clean sheets," Zack ordered.

"Yeah, yeah," Leo replied.

Lacy felt almost left out. She grabbed her purse and followed them down the hall.

26

In the bedroom, Zack began pulling off the old sheets. "More bedtime stories in a moment," he announced. "I think it's Leo's turn."

"What?" Leo was changing pillow cases.

"We need to figure this out. It begins with memories."

Leo sighed.

Lacy stood, watching them. They had a routine she longed to be a part of but knew she could never fully join. Something about twins excluded people. Something about these two enthralled her while making her feel even more alone. Yet they all three shared this strangeness. And she and Leo shared dreams.

The bed made, they all stood around it like reluctant worshippers.

"Go for it." Zack nudged Leo.

"Shit." He started to undo the buttons on his shirt.

Lacy pulled off her shirt. She didn't care anymore. They'd all agreed to get naked some time in the night. It was an unspoken pact. They knew it. She knew. If she hadn't wanted it, she would never have gone home with them. When her clothes puddled the floor, blue and black, she climbed into the center of the bed. The sheets were cold.

Their hips grazed hers, right and left. *Guardians*, she thought, feeling ridiculously young. They both smelled of wild mint.

Zack and Leo joined her quickly, before she got a good look.

They had some hidden mechanism that turned the lights low. She wondered how many other girls they'd seduced between them. She especially wondered about Zack, who seemed a natural instigator, while Leo had eyes more for objects and the silences they gave off. She could imagine him, beer in hand, lounging on a drift of bedsheet, staring at designs in paint swirls on the wall. Content only in that. Barely aware of Zack beside him covering a young woman's shoulders with kisses, the sheets sliding back, Zack's hand secretly sneaking out to graze Leo's elbow as he slyly moved against her.

Lacy shook her head clear of the image. That was her problem. She got too many pictures inside her head of what people were, or what they might be like. It made her never trust. Made her rigid, self-conscious.

"We don't have to do anything," Leo suddenly whispered as though he'd just read her mind. He sounded hesitant, yet sympathetic. "We can talk all night if you want. I like talking. Or sleep. I like sleeping, too."

Lacy nodded slowly.

"But just in case, I've got the condoms," Zack added, bouncing on her left side with a grin.

"Zack!" Leo hissed. "Crude! Remember?"

"What?" He shrank back on his side of the bed. "I thought..."

"That's okay," Lacy said, feeling bolder than she expected. "I figure you guys do this all the time."

They looked at each other, then at her.

"No," Leo said. "I mean, you're different." He glanced at Zack, narrowing his smooth eyebrows. "She's not like..." He swallowed, lips forming a wry smile.

Zack shrugged. "We don't do this *all* the time," he began.

Lacy caught her breath, then suddenly laughed.

Zack opened his mouth, closed it, opened. "For some reason, most women think we're too strange. Some don't, though..." He frowned at her, then quickly winked. "Do you?"

"Well, yes," Lacy said, again remembering the earlier kiss the two brothers had shared, a kiss they didn't know she had witnessed.

They all sat there silent for a moment.

"But so am I. Strange, I guess, to the people I meet. They don't stick around, if you know what I mean," Lacy added. Her life was a statement of strangeness. Triangle scars. Moving trees. Moon hooks. Even if she didn't talk about her experiences, people sensed them in her, narrowed their eyes to exclude her. Perhaps she was too judgmental herself. Perhaps she gave off an attitude, inflected a tone of voice. Everyone she'd ever known had left her. Now these warlock twins were watching, listening, probably judging as well. *I should just leave*, she thought. *Save myself more trouble.*

But Leo's gaze seemed to wind around her, holding her to the room, welcoming that strangeness, and her position between them. She just had to stay. She had to find out more about him.

## Chapter Two

Leo had fallen asleep without meaning to. It seemed he had only blinked, and now morning suffused the thick curtains by the dresser with a pale glow.

Lacy stretched beside him, opening grey eyes. Beyond her, Zack lay motionless, softly snoring. The air was cool.

"Come on," he said softly, getting up.

They both moved carefully, so as not to disturb Zack. Leo watched her out the corner of his eye as he slid into a pair of jeans. She reminded him of a sprite, fairy-thin and pale, a person who might disappear in a bright light, except for her shadow-brown hair. Pixies were friendly but shrewd. One had to be careful when showing them around one's soul. Yet this one, his instincts told him, had a need perhaps as deep and empty as his own. A spirit-hole waiting to be mended, filled, healed. She didn't make him uncomfortable like some of the other girls Zack and he brought home.

She didn't seem to like beer – at least not in the mornings – so he made her coffee, brought her a steaming cup of it, the bitter scent flowing into his nostrils. Then he sat beside her on the white futon, gripping his cold Heineken bottle between his thighs, and said, "It all started for me when I was about nine."

~

"Zack is so healthy, normal" Leo heard his mother say. "Why does Leo have to be so different? They're the same!" He could imagine her lipstick pink, pinched lips twisted in an ugly grimace, and he hated her. Leo was hiding out, as he often did, under the phone stand in the hall. He pressed his wrist against his upper lip which was wet. There were tears coming out his nose. He tried not to sneeze.

His dad said, "I don't know. In twins, in many cases, one is weaker." He could picture him standing straight and tall, pretending he was some kind of authority figure. He worked at a print shop. He was never home.

"But they're the same. And he's the oldest," Mom insisted.

"I don't know why he does those things to himself. We could look for another doctor."

"The insurance company will freak out."

The hall air was so still Leo thought he could see his soft breath hissing in, out.

"But he cut his own genitals. This is serious." Dad, always calm, said it without a hitch.

Leo banged on his knees. One poked out, skinny and brown, from the rip in his jeans. He rested his soaked cheek on it, feeling bone warmth. His mind was shrieking. *I didn't do it!*

But the doctor had ruled otherwise. Good ol' Doc Ramacockuphisass, he called him, though his name was really Ramsock. Ramacockuphisass was more fitting. He was always poking into places he would rather not have poked. He hated the doctor's coldness, his smug superiority.

His fists squeezed together until they were white. Dr. Ramsock had spoken his only words of wisdom. Self-mutilation. "The kid does it, and then doesn't remember doing it to himself. He's a very troubled child." Then he told Mom and Dad Leo should see a shrink while Leo listened with his ear pressed to the crack of the doctor's door.

"Sometimes I wish it was only Zack we'd had. I didn't ask for two."

Black shooting stars stung him. He was the thin void taking the beating, had been since he was small.

"Nothing to be done." Dad kept his ever-the-man-in-charge tone.

"Should we talk to Zack? Maybe he knows something."

He didn't care anymore that her voice trembled.

"They're only nine, Millie."

"Maybe we should separate them."

He was holding his breath, everything hazy bursting colors, when something grabbed him.

"Hey!"

"Agghh!" A hand clamped over his mouth. His brother pulled him up. He almost knocked his head on the table, couldn't see a thing. But Zack kept pulling. They stumbled downstairs, out the back door, screen slamming.

The desert was a place of consolation. Only nine, and still Leo could feel it. It was late fall. There weren't any snakes and the air was cold, and running at Zack's side made the blood burn. He got warm fast.

The boys ran for a quarter mile, down a side dirt road, leaping weeds and avoiding chollas. They took a short cut, through a grove of ancient Joshuas. Leo's lungs were heaving. He could smell nothing but his own salty snot. Their tennis shoes kicked up sand that stuck to his face. His hair plowed into his eyes. They tumbled miniature sand dunes and crusty ant-cliffs. And kept running. Zack still had his hand on Leo's arm, pulling him on as they headed in the direction of their secret hideout.

A dirt drive led to the ruin glittered with broken glass. When they reached the doorless, peeling archway, a dove fluttered against dangling cardboard. She had a nest in the rotted drywall. Now she disappeared out the south window.

In the one room shack, deformed by sandstorm and flood, they'd made a messy club house. There was one old table, a three-legged chair. Glass made a mosaic pattern on the floor. It crunched under their shoes. Late afternoon shadows haunted the comers where more broken furniture sprawled. Zack yanked him inside, then let go. Leo stood, breathing hard, starting again to cry.

"You stupid, don't even listen to them!" Zack hissed. "You keep hiding under that table, eavesdropping, and they'll think you're even weirder."

"I didn't do anything!" he snarled. Now the tears fell in big drops, cold. A wind blew into his face, hurting.

"Okay, okay," Zack said.

Leo kept crying.

"I believe you, Leo." Zack touched his am. "We just gotta figure this out."

"But I don't know anything!" He started to hiccup.

"Just shut up. We gotta think."

"I think all the time!" He pushed Zack's arm away and walked to the window the dove had flown through. There he could see rolling lands of sand, and ridges formed from ancient volcanos pointing to the blue sky.

"You don't remember anything?" Zack asked.

"No!" Maybe a metal touch. Maybe a scent of oil. But he didn't tell him that.

"Okay." Zack came over to stand beside him. He was wearing an old striped, long- sleeved shirt. "Don't push me away," he said softly, and put his arm over Leo's shoulders.

"Mom and Dad hate me. They only want you. I wish I wasn't born!" His throat ached. Hell, fuck and damn.

"I don't," Zack said.

"You don't count."

"I do!" His voice got high. "You're my brother, you asshole. That counts."

Leo didn't reply. The shack rustled. A bird warbled like a toy engine.

"I didn't hurt myself, Zack," he finally said.

"Then who did?"

"I woke up and it was like that. But I don't know how to make marks like that. And there, on my... my..."

"I know where." Zack was quiet for a long time. Leo's tears dried until the skin itched. Then, in a whisper nine-year-olds save for the most intimate of pacts, Zack asked: "Does it hurt?"

No one had asked Leo that. Not his mother. Not even Dr. Ramacockuphisass. He shook his head. "No. Only that first day. Like a sunburn."

"Are you scared?"

"Shit, yeah." It was almost funny, his voice so high, the words too gruff.

"Fuck Mom and Dad," Zack finally said.

Leo blinked. There were no tears anymore, but his eyes still hurt.

"Don't tell them nothing from now on," he continued. "You wanna talk to someone, talk to me. I promise I won't tell. I won't leave you alone." The words were that serious whisper again. He wouldn't look Leo in the eye. That was how Leo knew Zack meant it, a heart-promise, deeper than spitting and rubbing palms, stronger than a dare.

"You mean tell you every time something happens? Every time I have a dream?"

"Any time. You wake me up if it's two in the morning. I don't care. We'll figure it out. Without Mom and Dad. Without Doc Faggot."

"But Mom said she didn't want me," he whispered. "How... how could she say that?"

"She was just gabbing. Don't listen to it! And don't hide under that table anymore. You and me, we're it. That's all that matters anyway." His arm went further across Leo's shoulders and tightened.

Something inside Leo opened like the sky, like the dove taking off. "Yeah." And though nothing was normal, everything was okay again.

~

"So did it happen again?" Lacy asked.

"Yes." There was phlegm in his throat. He cleared it, glancing at her. Her sharp face looked soft, the eyes like silk-smooth silver with flecks of brown and green. *It's okay*, he told himself. *It's okay to tell her all of it.*

~

He ignored the scars and five years went by.

The open window in the twins' bedroom on those hot summer nights bothered Leo, but the heat forced them to leave it open to capture any rare cool breeze. He made Zack trade sides on the big double bed so that Zack slept next to it.

Zack wore nothing to sleep in that whole summer they were fourteen, and in the dark, when Leo couldn't sleep, he would stare at his brother's tan, slim body, shadowed under the arms and at the groin where his adult hair had begun to grow. Leo's body was the same, except for the scars, and that was why he liked looking at Zack. Zack lay unmarked. He was, inside and out, the person Leo wanted to be.

Leo kept his underwear on. It was for his own sake. He hated catching glimpses of those ugly triangles. The underwear covered all that was evil.

Sometimes, Zack would tease him, try to pull his pants down. "Be a maaaan!" he'd sing.

They were fourteen. Leo still felt nine. "Fuck you."

One night in the middle of July, Leo couldn't sleep at all. Hours drifted by like days. The heat felt like a blanket of fire. He turned on his side to stare at Zack and was surprised to see the moonlight orbiting slowly over him, light tendrils draping his waist.

Mesmerized, Leo watched. Zack moved in his sleep, the sheet falling away from his hip, the moonlight grabbing him there as well, never satisfied. His legs were bent, still dark and untouched. Leo waited the long silent minutes for the light to travel on down to the foot of the bed.

He held his breath. He thought: When the light envelopes all of him, worlds will be born. He wanted to witness that.

The light was white and pure. Fittingly, it never tried to touch Leo. Only dark hands reached for Leo. Only the cold steel and antiseptic scent of something he could never see or prove to be real.

The light arched beautifully.

Zack slept, oblivious. Like melting candy, the rays stretched, almost but still not encompassing him. Leo held his breath as light strained further. Zack was of the light world, Leo of the dark.

Then, as if obeying some inner command, Zack shifted his body, rolled onto his back. His legs sprawled, slightly spread, and moonlight pooled in delicious waves across his belly, his thighs, and finally his feet.

Leo's breath came out in a soft alien sound. "Whooooo."

Zack stretched but didn't awaken. Leo remained in shadow.

"Sssss," something said behind him. He didn't have time to look before he was caught up in invisible hands. He screamed, but Zack never moved. Time stopped. Like a heartbeat you can't hear because you grow used to it, Leo felt everything go dead. Nothing happened. He waited.

Then something dropped him back in his bed. A shadow crossed the window, blocking the light. Zack was dark now. Everything, dark. He hurt unbearably all over, tried to remember. In his mind only nothingness swept through him. When he sat up, the room spun, then settled. The moon came back, distant and gentle, still caressing Zack as if nothing had happened. He looked at him, shivered, then jiggled his shoulder.

"Huh?"

"Zack."

He turned away, asked a muffled: "What?"

"It happened again."

He was still for ten long seconds, then sat up, slowly facing Leo. He reached out. "A dream?"

Leo shook his head.

A hand touched his knee. "Shit, brother, you're freezing!"

Leo lowered his head. It was hard looking at Zack, so perfect, and himself so fucked up. "I wasn't even asleep this time."

"Shit."

"Uh-huh."

"You okay?"

He was trying so hard not to cry until Zack asked him that. A wall broke inside.

"Shhh, you don't want to wake Mom and Dad," was all Zack said.

The words might have hurt bad if Zack wasn't holding him tight. He could feel his brother's heartbeat against his cheek, a rushing waterfall. A restarted flow of time. He took deep breaths and told him what he remembered. The hands, the 'sssss' sound, the interrupted moonlight.

"I wonder why I didn't wake up," Zack said, encouraging him to lie back. Then he lay on his side facing Leo, who felt his twins' breath on his bare shoulder.

"I don't know."

"Well." He didn't finish. Leo heard only breathing. Zack's heart. His own stillness. He was so tired and started to drift, felt Zack move closer. The room got hot again but he didn't mind. Hair tickled his cheek.

"I wish I could protect you," Zack murmured. "But I can't."

"Mmmm." Leo was slipping away, exhausted. Before sleep fully absorbed him, he felt his brother's hand move over sharp hip bones, tracing the triangle trail.

Warmth settled and stayed deep inside him, blocking Mom's coldness and Dad's silent disapproval, casting out all alienation, self-loathing.

Zack wasn't coming onto him, he was healing him.

Leo fell asleep knowing that.

~

Leo stopped when he saw Lacy turn away, heard her catch her breath. They stayed silent, having shared an experience that no words could soothe or change. At least he'd had Zack. Lacy, he realized, had been alone in her childhood.

Leo leaned back, the forgotten beer bottle tipping toward his knees. What would he have done without Zack? He silently remembered his twin's bright energy, Zack's so necessary affection that got him through the day. And how, back when they were sixteen, it got them a too-early, rather dubious independence.

~

Months after the incident with the hissing noise and the invisible hands and the moving bedroom shadows, winter was on its way along with their fifteenth birthday. Remarkably, Leo was still nightmare-free, which made them both sure it hadn't been a dream. Zack wondered aloud, "But why didn't I wake up that night?"

"I don't know."

"I bet it has something to do with those triangles," he said. "I just bet."

Leo's hand went self-consciously to the front of his briefs, even though they thoroughly hid the damage.

Zack climbed naked into bed, didn't wait for Leo to follow before switching off the lamp.

Leo slid under the sheets, feeling stiff and uncomfortable. Suddenly, a light flashed in his eyes. He put up his arms and gasped. "No!"

"Shut up, dope. It's me."

Zack was there at his side, chest pressing shoulder. A beam of light bobbed about the room. It originated from Zack's hand.

"What...?"

"It's my flashlight, see?"

Teeth gritted. "Don't ever do that again!"

He chuckled and shined it in Leo's eyes. Leo slapped his hand away and the light bobbed about the room again, butter-yellow on blue walls.

"What are you doing?"

"I wanna get a better look at those triangles, but I want Mom and Dad to think we're asleep. So, no lights. Except this." He shined it on himself, making his face orange and ghoulish. "Under the covers."

"Go fuck yourself," Leo said.

"Maybe they're a map," he suggested.

"It's not a joke."

"Come on, it's just me." Zack nudged his side.

"No."

"Come on, I wanna see up close."

"No!"

"Come on, Leo, come on." His elbow in Leo's side became a hand. It started tickling him. Leo arched away. Both hands descended on him then. The flashlight rolled between them. "I won't stop until you say yes."

"No!" He was trying to be quiet; Mom and Dad were still up. "Stop!"

"Say yes." His hands were all over now, grazing, poking. Leo couldn't breathe. Laughter collected within like a bubble that wouldn't come up. "Stop!"

"Say yes."

Air choked his throat. "No."

"Yes."

The bubble started to pop. He thought he would pass out. "Yesss," he finally breathed.

Zack stopped. Grabbed the flashlight.

"Zack," Leo whispered. "Why?"

"Cause you're my brother."

Leo winced. Zack dived under the sheet. The next thing he knew, his underwear was being forced away. The light under the covers made a sunset glow. Zack's head tented the bed sheets. His underwear trapped his thighs and even with the covers over him, he felt exposed and ashamed. "Zack," Leo whispered.

"Shut up," came a muffled voice.

A fingertip touched the skin just above Leo's pubic hair. "Does that hurt?"

"No. Just stop, okay?"

"Wait."

He could feel his breath against him, bare skin soaking it up, his balls suddenly crawling. "Zack!"

"Just a sec."

But he didn't have a second. He was getting a hard-on. Zack's finger touched the base of his cock. "That hurt?"

Leo didn't answer.

Zack pushed his way to air. The flashlight was off now. He lay on top of Leo, now. Leo's arms came up and held Zack against him.

Finally, Zack pulled away. "If I ever catch who did this to you, I'll kill'em," he said possessively.

Leo was strangely proud of those words, even though he knew they could never be true. Something had marked him which Zack had no power over. Something bigger than Zack could ever understand.

## Chapter Three

To Zack, Lacy was a stray – like Leo, but less interesting. Like a scrawny cat brought home from a dumpster half-starved, sloe-eyed, doused in foreboding. He wouldn't have minded fucking her, but now, sober and in the daylight, he changed his mind. For one, she remained a stranger to him despite her affinity to their plight.

That made him uneasy. Two, she'd warmed to Leo a little too quickly for comfort. No girls 'warmed' to Leo. Leo didn't allow it. Zack had all the social sense. Leo had dreams, poems, long silences. Girls attracted to those qualities in Leo soon found out they couldn't compete with them. Leo lived alone inside himself, and within Zack's shadow. Zack had grown used to that; he didn't want things to change.

When he saw Leo and Lacy sitting together on the futon, chatting solemnly, intimately, a pain burned against the inside of his stomach. She was different from other girls, yes, and maybe she'd been through some of the same things Leo had, but now he could see they'd all been a little too serious, too easily accepting last night. Whatever was going on, there were no answers. They had to live with that. They had to accept. Lacy's similarity to Leo would be bad for him in the long run, Zack thought. She'd lead Leo right down the path to more confusion, pain, nightmare. It was fun to share, for a little while. But when you had nothing more to give, sharing time ended. Zack knew Leo would be hurt, and he couldn't allow that.

He came to the end of the hall, leaned quietly against the corner. The fish tank hummed. Squares of pillows were scattered, making the floor look like a ruined chessboard. Lacy and Leo looked up.

"Hey, you're awake," Leo said.

Zack nodded, smiled slightly, then said: "Can I see you for a minute?"

"Sure." He got up, touching Lacy gently on the knee. "I'll be back in a minute."

She didn't reply, but looked up toward Zack, perplexed eyes holding his until he looked away. Zack tasted irritation, the tip of his tongue curving down.

In the bedroom, Leo raised his eyebrows. "What?"

"What is this?" Zack asked, motioning out the door with fist and thumb.

"What is what?"

"Her?"

"I don't understand." Now the eyebrows dipped. The face grew shaded.

"It's just that you don't usually show interest," Zack began.

Leo said nothing, just stared at him.

"You know what I mean," Zack added, smiling. "They come... they go. Right?"

Leo glanced away, clenched jaw making his mouth draw down. "Well, then she didn't come yet, did she?" he said hotly.

"Hey!" Zack grabbed his arm. "I just want to know what's going on."

"I don't know what's going on!" Leo insisted, pulling away. "I'm trying to find out. You encouraged me last night."

"Yeah. I was drunk."

Leo crossed his arms. His long-sleeved t-shirt rode up, exposing a stripe of belly just above his waistband. Zack reached out to poke playfully at that stretch of smoothness. Leo backed up, still not looking at him. "What is it? Is it that I like her? Is it that I want to talk to her, to tell her things? This has never happened to me before."

"It's not for real, Leo. I'm just trying to..."

"What?" Leo interrupted. "What are you trying to do, Zack? She might have some answers. She might *know* something! What? Are you afraid?"

Zack rolled his shoulders; his breath passed through his teeth in a hiss as he turned around, the white room, the curtains, the unmade bed all coming up to fill his vision, to distract him. Finally, he said, "All right. Maybe I am. For you." He dug his hands into his pockets, stared at the wall.

"I can handle myself."

Zack laughed at that, but apprehension swiped at his confidence. "When? You're a little fuck-up. You always have been."

"Shit. So now you're saying you never believed me? In anything I ever said?"

Leo was looking a little too desperate. Maybe he had gone

too far. Zack glanced again at the bed, their bar-hopping clothes heaped everywhere there was floor space, their dresser and night tables sprawled with jewelry, make up, notebooks, clocks. "Of course not. I'm just looking out for you, you know?" He kept his tone soft, though inside he was as pent up as he ever had been, heavy from lack of sleep, lack of sex which was what *he'd* really wanted. He looked over his shoulder at Leo. "I didn't mean – "

"Good!" Leo took a deep breath, let it slide out across slightly damp lips. "Let's go get something to eat, then. I'm starved."

"With Lacy?"

*"With* Lacy."

As Leo left the room, Zack kicked at the polished edge of a belt buckle lying on the floor. "Fuck," he said softly, and went into the bathroom to shave.

~

Zack hated real food. He knew he was acting surly, but he didn't care if Leo detested him for it, if Lacy no longer desired him (presuming she ever had.) He insisted on fast food, *McDonald's*, ordered two large egg and bacon breakfasts for himself, and commandeered a big booth. He put his feet up on the chair opposite him, proclaimed loudly, "Fuck, this second order has no bacon!" and called out to the employees to bring him some.

Lacy seemed as if she were trying to ignore him. Well, hell. Now she would understand that he and Leo weren't the tall, mysterious strangers she thought she'd met the night before.

Leo seemed unaffected. "Hey, Zack," he said, and leaned subtly into him. Zack could feel the heat of him, the need. Something inside him softened; he gritted his teeth. "Remember that day I disappeared? You know, just before we came to the city?"

"Of course."

"Lacy has missing time, too."

"Really." He stared at his eggs.

"Anyway," Leo continued, "you remember that day better than I do. It's all still foggy. How did it start again?"

Zack took the cigarette from his lips. When he spoke, it was for Leo's sake, not Lacy's. "It was summer."

~

Summer in the desert. Sizzle of static on the air and everyone's nerves crawl through their skin, out the pores, and wave like invisible hairs. Touch a nerve, the person goes crazy. In the desert, the crazies live.

Two boys, brown hair flopping in their eyes, parked their bikes in front of the Circle K and shuffled inside.

"Hey, Zack, Leo." The clerk, Mr. Thompson, whose son was murdered five years ago in New York City, hobbled over. "Sprained my ankle last night. Tripped over my own shoes going to the bathroom in the middle of the night. What can I do you for today?" His half-bald pate gleamed pink under the fluorescent lights. His full stomach jiggled, the thin, white tank shirt he wore barely covering the hairy domain. The air-conditioning hummed like a sick bird, but it only helped so much. All three were sweating.

"Icees," Leo said.

"Of course." He frowned, putting a finger to his temple. Then he pointed it at Zack. "You're Zack, right? Cherry for you."

Zack grinned. Not everyone in town could tell them apart, though they'd lived there all their lives. "Right."

"And you, Leo, Coke."

"Yup." Leo caught his brother's eyes. Sparkling brown met brown.

At sixteen, the twins were still inseparable. Nearing six feet, and unswerving manhood, they still rode bikes together in the early, cooler evenings, and hung out at their old shack hideout.

Mr. Thompson handed Zack his Icee. "Played the numbers today, you know. I'm feeling lucky."

"Lotto?" Leo asked before Zack could.

"Sure enough. Keep your fingers crossed."

Leo held up his hand. He'd let his fingernails grow. The middle finger crossed the forefinger.

"Twins are lucky. If I have you rooting for me, I can't lose." Mr. Thompson handed Leo his Coke Icee.

"Twins? Lucky?" Zack asked.

"Tell our parents that," Leo finished.

"Nothing wrong with your parents. They treat you fine. You got a roof, food, right?"

The boys nodded.

"What's to complain about?"

"We're teenagers," Zack said. "We're supposed to complain."

Mr. Thompson laughed. "That'll be a buck-fifty."

Leo kept their money always in his left shorts' pocket. He dug out a wadded up dollar and two quarters. "Keep the change," he said brightly.

"Vety funny," Thompson said.

"Good luck," called Zack as they exited the store.

At their bikes, Zack turned on Leo. "Why'd you say that to him about our parents?"

Leo shrugged. "They hate me."

"You go around telling everyone that?"

"You don't have to worry about it, they love you. Pure, unsullied Zack." Leo sucked on his Coke Icee as he swung onto his bike. Then he took off toward the intersection with the single swinging stoplight.

Zack watched him, not mad at all, just tired. Leo was right. And you couldn't get mad at someone who was right.

He got on his own bike, bony, brown knees pointing toward the handlebars as he peddled after his older brother. Older by eleven minutes, but older nonetheless.

The sky flowed hot blue, like stretched taffy. Not a cloud. The air was dry enough to chap the back of the throat. Zack took a sip of his already melting cherry Icee, and leisurely headed for the road. Leo was way ahead, his loose white t-shirt flapping like a useless wing behind him. Moody Leo. But Zack didn't mind. Leo needed to be moody. Leo had a right.

Zack had always wanted to protect his brother. He just didn't know how, except offer to listen when Leo told him about the dreams. Offer to make the hurt that seemed so real, and the pain of the scars that were real, go away. He loved Leo. But Leo was always so unsure.

Now he peddled faster, trying to catch up. But Leo was going too fast. He swerved into the middle of the street. Luckily, there were no cars.

Zack's heart quickened and he shot into the road. "Leo!"
But Leo didn't hear him.

They glided past the video store, the grocery store, the bank. Leo popped a wheelie up the curb, tires eating sidewalk as he steered one-handed.

It was too hot for these kinds of antics. Zack swore and turned away. If Leo was in a mood, he'd go home and wait it out. It wasn't any fun riding around town alone.

He crossed through the bank parking lot and headed south toward the volcanic ridges that once, a million years ago, had been molten slag. He tried to imagine what the land had looked like back then. Had it been all rock and fire? Had the sky been red with smoke? He rode into the sandy yard, past his mother's cactus garden and into the carport. There he parked his bike in its special place.

In the kitchen, Mom was reading something at the table. "Hi, Zack," she said, not looking up.

"Hi."

"Where's Leo?"

Zack shrugged. "Out riding bikes."

"I thought he was with you."

"He rode off."

Now she looked up. Her hair was tinged grey, but still mostly brown. They got their color from her, their height from their father. "I thought I told you boys I don't like you going off alone, especially in the summer. If he goes out into the desert..."

"He won't," Zack said. "He was by the bank when I last saw him. He's close by."

"You two have a fight?"

"Nope." He turned toward the living room.

"Zack?"

"Yeah." He didn't want to turn back.

"Come here. Sit down."

Shuffling, he obeyed, standing at her side.

"Sit," she said.

Zack pushed the chair back, turned it and sat facing the wooden back. "What?" Whenever she took this tone, he knew she wanted to talk about Leo. And he had nothing to say to her.

"How's Leo acting lately?"

"I don't know what you mean. Normal, as always."

"You know what I mean. His dreams. He's... he's not still hurting himself."

Zack scowled. "Mom –"

"Please. You're closest to him. Tell me the truth." Her brown eyes glistened. Her eyebrows, thin, plucked lines, lifted forcing the skin on her forehead to wrinkle.

"I don't know what you want me to say."

"You've always been the good one. He's just, well, I don't know why, but he's different. You look out for him, I know. But he's not still telling stories about people taking him away at night, is he?"

"Not that I know of, Mom." He stared at her full on as he told the lie. He didn't care. If she couldn't see Leo needed support, not ostracizing, then he had nothing to say to her. He believed something was happening to his brother, something no one, not even Leo, understood. Their mom believed her strange son was a functional schizophrenic.

"Well good, then. I don't worry about him half so much when I know he's with you." She smiled.

Zack nodded, but didn't smile back. "Is that it, Mom? I need to go make a phone call."

"Go on." She waved him out of the chair.

Zack went to their room and flopped on the bed. He picked up a comic book, thumbed through it without reading, tossed it aside. He sat up, grabbing Leo's guitar. Laying it gently in his lap, he strummed nonsense from the strings. Leo could make it sing. Zack could only fantasize about doing the same.

He thought about a song Leo wrote.

*"When I am standing on secrets alone you come and scatter them afar. In your eyes I've arrived from nowhere, you are my sky, I am your star."*

He tried to hum it, but couldn't remember the exact tune. No one but Zack knew Leo had written it for him.

The room shined under a fine patina of dust. An old mobile of laser-rainbow circles hung from the overhead light. Shelves were littered with cars and books and carnival stuffed animals. On their desk sat two piles of old school notebooks from their past sophomore year. Zack's pile was ordered. Leo's spilled over. One was on the floor.

Zack knew what was in those notebooks. Not school assignments, as Zack's held. But dreams. And poems. And stories that had no end. Doodles. Lunatic, childish abstracts done with a ballpoint pen.

He set aside the guitar and walked over to the desk. A purple notebook lay under it and he picked it up, paging through it. On the front page was written: <u>Nightmare Diary</u>. Underneath that, Leo'd printed: *Never go to sleep on your back..*

There were some poems. Long-winded. One about light and a person standing under it. Lots of stuff about the desert. The moon. Night. Dreams. He'd written phrases such as: *Wind-worn stars fall slowly on the sharp horizon... Remember that language is beautiful... Make shadows under the stars/ Be darkness absorbed by light... Am I being visited? Who's there? Who's there?*

Zack threw the book down, a chill gathering in him despite the heat.

A small TV sat on the side of the desk. He turned it on and the noise made his discomfort go away. One talk show, and one sit-com later, his mother called him to dinner.

Leo still wasn't home.

The sun set late, about 8:30. Still, Leo didn't come home. By ten, their parents were frantic.

Zack leaned against the front door, watching the dusky road. Finally, he saw a figure, white t-shirt shifting, walking up the road. He ran outside and down the street, meeting Leo halfway. At first Leo didn't acknowledge him.

"Leo, where's your bike?"

"I don't know." His voice shook.

"What happened?"

"I got lost."

"No way."

"I don't know!" He lashed out, catching Zack with a fist. Zack grabbed his arm and held it down.

"Stop! It's me. Tell me where you went."

"Down the road. I woke up in a wash. I lost my bike." His breath caught.

"We have to figure out something to tell Mom and Dad."

"Something happened to me and I don't remember what!"

*Again*, Zack thought. Aloud, he said: "They won't

understand that."

By now their parents had spotted them and were coming down the driveway. "Leo, where've you been?"

"Do you know what time it is, son?"

"I don't know," Leo said.

"Some kids roughed him up, Mom," Zack said. "They took his bike."

"What kids?" Dad asked. "I'll call their parents."

"I didn't know them," Leo whispered.

"This is a small town, Leo. You didn't recognize any of them?" Dad asked. Tall, like a weathered statue, their father always walked stooped, lanky. It was as if his height had never been acclimated inside his body.

Leo shook his head. They all entered the kitchen, Leo with his head down, hands at his sides.

"Leo, look at me." Mom took his head in her hands, staring at him. "Tell me the truth. Where were you?"

Leo shook his head.

"You can't tell her, or won't tell her?" Dad asked.

"I don't remember."

"Blackouts again?" Dad shook his head.

"Oh, no," Mom said worriedly before he could answer. "Leo, if you won't take the medication the doctor prescribed..."

"I don't need medication."

"If you won't tell us the truth, son, you can just stay home for two weeks, how about that? Grounded. You know you have to be home by dinner. Why'd you stay out?"

"I couldn't help it. I didn't... I don't..." He looked lost, helpless.

Zack stood to one side, gritting his teeth. When Leo disappeared, it was always bad. He stayed good and freaked for days. Their parents never asked him how he was, just shook their heads, pushed pills, and then ignored him. He'd always wondered how they could do that to a kid. "Just leave him alone," Zack finally said. "Can't you see he's in shock or something?"

"You just get to bed," Mom said. "I'll deal with you later."

"What did I do?" But Zack went. He always obeyed. He could hear their voices carry through the house, up the stairs, hear Leo sobbing, still saying nothing their parents wanted to hear.

Another blackout. Why couldn't things be easy? Normal?

Zack took off his clothes and scooted under the sheet. Leo didn't come up for another fifteen minutes, so he turned out the light. When the door to the bedroom finally opened, Zack was dozing. But he woke quickly, watching his twin move about the room.

Leo said nothing. He undressed in the dark and climbed into bed. For a few seconds everything was quiet.

Finally, Zack turned onto his side. He reached out, ran a hand down Leo's damp face. "You can have my bike."

"I didn't want to come home. Ever."

"Not even to see me?" Zack asked softly.

"I don't know."

"Shit." Zack leaned closer to him. "Tell me that to my face."

Leo shook his head. Zack could see his silhouette in the darkness, the shining hair. They were mirrors. Leo's hair parted on the right, Zack's on the left.

"Zack, what would you do if you were me?"

"I don't know. Your blackouts scare me. So I figure they must scare you a hundred times worse."

"I hate it here."

Zack already knew that. Mom and Dad never showed Leo the love they showed him. Why did parents have to be that way? But more than that, in this house, this room, even with Zack always there, Leo had never really felt safe.

He heard a rasping sound.

"Fuck." He touched Leo's hair. "Don't." He leaned down and pressed his face to Leo's cheek. Leo's tears touched his own cheek. After awhile, he ran his hands over his twin's arms as if the warm him. It was a common, comforting touch between them. Leo finally quieted and leaned into the touch. When Zack leaned forward to kiss him on the cheek, he thought of oceans and wilderness. He thought of stars and spinning planets.

Zack held him tight, trying to do something he didn't know how to do. Heal it. Fix it. But he could only offer love in his clumsy, desperate way.

He awoke to the sound of their door opening, a father's rapid disapproval. Their father's face twitched with barely controlled anger. "Zack," he said, forcing calm. "Go sleep on the couch."

Zack didn't move. It wasn't just that he was naked under the sheet. Or that their father didn't approve of his sons' closeness, especially when he found them embraced together in bed. He also didn't think he should have to leave. A sudden rage welled up. "Get out of here!" he yelled.

Dad stepped back.

"Just get out!" he repeated. "This isn't your business. Get out!"

To his surprise, their father did, closing the door behind him. Zack turned to Leo. In the dark he could still see his twin's eyes were bright, scared. "Oh my God," Leo said. "You yelled at him. You actually told him off!"

"Someone had to." But Zack was shaking.

"I'm getting out of here tomorrow," Leo whispered. "I can't take it."

"We can cash out our college funds and split." Zack had actually been thinking about it for quite some time.

"You mean you agree?"

"Yeah." Deep inside, Zack had always wanted to leave. Now that Leo didn't have a choice... Their parents would probably try to have him committed. He'd overheard them talking about it before.

"Where'll we go?"

"Far away from here." Zack lay back down, pulling Leo with him. Neither one of them slept the rest of that night.

~

"Did Leo ever try hypnosis?" Lacy wondered.

"No," Zack said, feeling suddenly uncomfortable in the hard, plastic booth. "One doctor tried it, but Leo wouldn't cooperate."

"I know how he feels. He's lucky he had you." She said it coyly, soft. "I had my grandmother, but she knew nothing. At least she loved me, though."

"At least," Zack echoed. He scratched his temple with his black, pinky fingernail. He felt slightly embarrassed, as if he'd just told too much to a stranger. Baser emotions came to the rescue, easier to acknowledge. He twisted his lips. "I still hate my parents. Even in the grave."

"They're dead?"

"Car accident one year after we left. They left everything to us. It was sold and went into a trust. When we turned twenty-one, we got it all. With interest and with their house sold, it keeps us here in the city so we don't have to work much unless we feel like it. We're never going back to the desert. Leo feels safer here anyway. We like bumming around. There's good bars and shit."

"How'd you make a living before that? You were just kids."

Beside him, Leo remained silent. Zack rolled his eyes. "I hustled. Leo couldn't do it, but I did. I made good money, too."

Lacy's eyes widened in surprise.

He laughed, the sound helping to chase away his discomfort. "Why that look?"

"What look? I just think it's good that you look out for him," she said defensively.

"Fuck. I just hate what's happened."

"Was it bad?" She did not look away as she asked.

"The hustling?" Zack shrugged at her boldness when she nodded. "Nah. Most guys just want the same thing. It's no big deal." Now why had he said that?

Lacy leaned into herself. Leo squirmed. Zack forked in a mouthful of scrambled egg, glared at her, then him. Then he quickly looked down, stabbing at his styrofoam plate with a plastic fork. The anger had narrowed to a single, bright point throbbing in the middle of his chest, and he wasn't sure why.

## Part II. - The World Outside The Walled City
## (Parallel Earth)

## Chapter Four

Kittin loved to play in the dappled moonlight. Night brought danger, but worth the risk to feel dew on her lips, let it coarsen her hair, watch shadows shift into each other like fused lovers. She could hear grass stir: the color of dark jade sounded like a soft sea-tide lapping at fine sand.

Kittin saw an ocean once when she was very small, tasted its salt. It was cold as a mind without dreams, and yet she saw life within it. Green moving lace, silver darts, worms with beautiful hard bodies like polished gems.

Ever since that time, she thought of the ocean as life-blood, filling veins and arteries of the World, stirring presences, pumping time. Water and air were a dance. She could feel them surround her in their eternal lovemaking.

But the moon was her true lover. She could sense its light, a glow inside her. A sort of friendly guide. Though that was after she'd been contaminated, of course.

Friends told stories about humans going to the moon once, long ago, when there weren't any mind-plagues and people owned their own dreams without a second thought. Rockets shot their fire into darkness, propelling lonely travellers on what could only be a journey of devotion. To touch that dust, she thought, must have been the culmination of a very big wish.

She looked up at the sky now. The stars quickened her heartbeat. Smelled of ash. The moon looked like a broken marble, sugar-coated.

Since the contamination, she could smell lots of things that were supposedly odorless. And inanimate objects sometimes gave off sound, too, depending on their color.

Now the river called her, water singing a patternless melody that echoed her own inner beat. Her bare feet crushed dead pine needles on the path. Her skirt, a full-length, disposable paper garment, rustled, whispered. An eight-inch rip at the hem let jagged shadows touch her shin. *Moist shadows*, she thought, *with internal desires.*

Up ahead, the river sputtered. She thought she saw

something move. Then a sudden explosion lit up the sky. Green gashes opened the night. Unnatural lightning devoid of storm. But she wasn't afraid. She remembered being afraid once a long time ago, especially when her five parents would grow still and quiet during the strange weather.

"The Ignorant Armies trying to break through to each other," Shue, one of her mothers murmured, while, Ari, her other mother stroked her hair.

"What's an Ignorant Army?" Kittin asked. She'd been six at the time. And later, still six when she was contaminated.

"It's a war" her father Renn told her. "Armies are groups of people fighting because they disagree."

"What do they disagree about?"

"War is always a matter of control, Kittin."

"Who fights?"

"People."

"What people?"

"People who can't control what they're doing. That's why you can't go out alone at night," he explained. "It's not safe. Night is when the waves are strongest. And never leave the house without your bio-pacer bracelet. And never talk to strangers."

Big-eyed, not understanding 'waves' or why she always had to wear her bracelet, Kittin could only nod.

Now the Ignorant Armies clashed again and again against the sky, their psychotronic powers too hot to imagine, but Kittin wasn't afraid. Though contaminated, she was protected from further damage as long as she remained within the special compound where those more sensitive or susceptible to the enemy powers, or those who had, like Kittin, already been touched deeply by them, lived. Her bracelet, a thick silver cuff, covered her left wrist. It was an inch wide, a quarter of an inch thick, and helped keep her 'even'. When strong urges to escape or hurt or kill wrestled her conscience, the bio-pacer soothed her with its electronic binaural version of a lullaby. The bad feelings would still be there, but she could control them by running laps, pummeling a punching bag, screaming in a dark room. Or she might paint a canvas with violent colors that sounded like wind and broken glass, masturbate drowned in moss- scented music, or sleep the torture away within computer-induced, mescaline dreams.

In the compound, she was protected. And the rest of the World was protected from her unfortunate contamination. For she couldn't be trusted since she'd been touched by that green fire, since she'd gotten a piece of it inside her that had potential to be used and controlled by the enemy.

The river sparkled, green, gold, white. It smelled of incense, smoky, choked with dust. She sat on the bank with her paper skirt drawn up, her toes tickling the liquid surface.

The river ran through the compound, north to south, cutting it in uneven halves. It was the only entity, other than air, that could enter and leave the estate at will. Not even doctors visited the compound's inhabitants in person. Touching someone who was contaminated raised the risk of being contaminated themselves, they said. They didn't trust. They were afraid of her and sent in robot facsimiles who stayed and cluttered up the place. And often the doctors visited hologrammically in order to speak face to face with their patients. Relatives used the holograms to visit as well, when they came. Most were afraid to so much as talk to contaminated residents, though, even if they were once dearly loved spouses, sons or daughters. Who knew if the contamination might not be able to be passed on through telepathic means, through innocent words or gestures? There was too much they did not understand yet about this psychotronic technology. A technology that came from an enemy within the Walled City that threatened to master the entire World through psychic mind control.

There were 43 'prisoners' in this one compound and, at 17, Kittin was bored with all of them. She usually preferred to sleep alone, eat alone, be alone. Her best friend, Simene, who had taken care of her when she was a pre-teen, had even been getting on her nerves.

Now, outside in the dark with a warm wind chasing itself overhead, the moon gliding by, she could breathe and relax and truly *think*. Most residents hated and feared nighttime, and Kittin was glad. It made it that much more fun to play hide and seek with shadows when no one else was around. She could pretend the trees were secret heroes come to rescue her. She could pretend she was free.

Her breath fizzled the air. The green lightning stopped and everything became very still. The rock underneath her was cold and smooth. Fir trees stood still as robot guards. Reality became a statue of itself. Even the river quieted; she imagined it stopped in mid-flow like solid quartz reverberating with frequencies outside time.

Magic.

Kittin smiled, heard a light footstep, and turned.

The boy was perhaps fifteen or sixteen, but taller than she, and smelling very confused. His hair looked brown at first, but on closer inspection ran the gamut of autumn hues. He had a strong body, handsome gold skin, but his clothing was quite strange: cloth trousers cut high on the thighs, and a big, white cloth shirt. Kittin almost laughed at that, but held back. She'd never seen this boy before. And laughter was always a poor introduction.

"Are you new?" she asked. It was rare when someone new came to the compound. She wondered why she hadn't heard about it.

"New?" He had a rough voice, as if he'd been crying.

"Yeah. New. I don't know you."

"I don't know you," he replied.

"Well," Kittin said, "now we meet."

The boy looked around, blinked heavily, put out his hand and touched the trunk of an old oak that leaned away from the water. "I...I think I'm lost."

"Oh, you'll feel that way for a little while, until you get used to it. I remember the first time I came here..."

"What?" he interrupted.

"The first time I came here. I was saying –"

"Where are you from?" he interrupted again. "I mean, do you live around here? Because I don't think I could find my way out of here alone."

Now she did laugh. "You *are* confused."

He nodded.

"Well, when you come down from the mescaline or whatever drugs they gave you...or maybe – " She frowned, thinking. Sometimes contamination resulted in amnesia. She felt the most sympathy for those victims. They had no past. "What do you remember?"

He frowned. "About what?"

"I don't know." He was cute the way his eyebrows narrowed, forming a dark 'm' on his forehead. "Anything."

She tossed her head, her long, black hair tangling against paper-covered shoulders. Amnesia was pitiable, yet somehow arousing. Here was someone untouched, almost, pure. The urge to corrupt was nearly insatiable. But that was bad. Her bio-pacer grew warm and heavy on her wrist. Her urge was reduced to butterflies in her stomach.

"I live in the desert."

"Lived," she corrected.

"What?"

"Past-tense. You live here now."

The 'm' above his eyes tightened.

"It's okay, really. You're safe here."

"But I don't live here," he protested, rubbing the tree-bark with his palm.

They spoke the same language. Why couldn't they understand each other? "If you're here," she said, battling frustration, "then you live here. It can't be any other way."

He swallowed hard. "I – I don't understand."

"Why don't you sit down? Relax?" She patted the rock next to her. "Maybe if you don't think so hard, you'll be able to figure things out better."

"I- I – " he stuttered.

She patted the rock again. "Come on." Her bracelet jiggled.

He moved toward her, his body long and young. She liked that about him, and the hollowness in his eyes. Very endearing.

"I'm Kittin," she said.

"I'm – " He struggled, then gasped.

"It's all right. It'll come. Or someone who knows will tell you. For now I won't call you anything. I don't have to know your name to like you."

He sat beside her and she absorbed a gust of mingled scents: hot winds, cactus flower, autumn grey, liquid sugar, tart boy sweat.

"You like me?" he asked, turning his head to look at her.

The clean line of jaw, silk hair –he was beautiful. She nodded. "Of course I like you."

"Girls don't usually like me," he admitted.

"Really?" She laughed again, heard her voice echo off the river, the firs. It was good he remembered that much.

"I think I'm too shy. Maybe they sense my fear."

"I don't sense fear."

"Well, *you* seem different anyway."

"I do?"

"Yeah."

"How?" Kittin liked him more and more. He made her feel special, and they'd only just met.

"Well, you seem older than most of the girls I know. You're prettier."

She tilted her head, letting her teeth show as her lips opened. She was trying not to smile too much.

"And I like your dress."

"It's the thinnest paper made," she bragged. "Rips easy. Barely lasts a day if you're careful."

"I've never heard of a paper dress. Except maybe in Japan, or somewhere like that."

"Japan? I don't know it. What town did you come out of?" She grinned, not holding back now, and touched his wrist with her middle finger. "Paper clothes are the fashion."

He smelled confused again.

"Don't worry about it," she added quickly. "Things always seem strange at a new place. Just relax and it'll all be easier. Really. I'm experienced. I know."

"I– I just don't understand how I even got here."

"But isn't it beautiful?" She gazed down at the river gently flowing by. Her toes dabbed it, making surface ripples. The moon's half-face floated, awash in it.

"Yes," he said, the barest breath.

She had his wrist in her grasp now. It was warm, pulsing. She lifted it and he let her, then placed his palm against her breast. "This place always makes me feel so good."

As she spoke, the boy stiffened, tried to pull back.

"It's okay," she soothed. "I like it. You can touch me. It's not wrong. Only hurting is wrong. Only fighting. Only war."

"Yes," he said. "Yes. That makes sense."

She pulled his hand to her breast again. A soft wind startled her hair, and dry pine needles shuddered on the path behind them. The ember of his palm could have been a fallen star resting on the paper, on her nipple. She wanted his hand to burn through, scorch the dress black until she rose from the ashes in her cool mask of flesh. But he was shy. And she had the bio-pacer that usually kept her wildness muted, though its affects were inconsistent at best, the contamination inside her supposedly capable of overriding any outside programming. Of course, she could take the bio-pacer off–

She turned to him. "I have an idea."

"What?"

"Let's take our bio-pacers off. You know, let ourselves just go with our instincts.

"We're inside the compound and they're always broadcasting a thick field of beta waves here to keep us protected. We don't need to wear them all the time."

He frowned. And his skin looked polished under the stars, smooth, touchable. "What's a bio-pacer?"

"You don't– Poor boy, your amnesia's no joke." She reached for his other hand, the one not still cupping her breast. "See?" she said, forcing him to straighten both arms out. "This bracelet – " She stopped, her voice cut off by the unexpected when she saw his left wrist. It was bare, thin and delicate, mapped by blue veins, and naked. Naked as a winter branch.

"What?" He followed her gaze, looking down at himself.

"You... What happened to it? You don't have it on."

"What?" he asked again.

"Your bio-pacer."

"I don't know what a bio-pacer is."

"You must have forgotten it. But surely they put it on for you when you got here." She glanced up into his brown eyes, lost-looking, as if they were gazing at her through a long tunnel that began a billion miles away.

"What is it? I've never heard of a bio-pacer."

"It's – " She was still shocked. Sentences were hard. "It's this." She touched her silver bracelet. "Everyone has one."

"Your bracelet?"

She nodded. Her hair fell forward, black curls snagging her vision. "Everyone," she repeated.

"I don't."

She blinked. He seemed so sure. Leaves and the river rustled. Somewhere, anise was growing, releasing its pungent scent around them.

She wished he could remember who he was. This mystery

was interesting. Also dangerous. Without his bio-pacer, this boy could be capable of anything. She didn't know how contaminated he was, or even if he could *be* controlled. There were a few victims afflicted that way, who had to be locked up in the towers because nothing could help them. Was he one of them, this boy with the brown eyes who seemed to look into forever?

Whispers trilled the wind that twisted around them. She could almost hear voices. Almost. Kittin looked at the boy, then at her bracelet. She was so tempted. It would be easy. Take it off, dance in the whispers, let herself go even if it meant risking outside control. Hell, she was already contaminated. And the boy seemed so calm.

Besides, the risk wasn't really there. Not within the confines of the compound. Not as long as the frequency field stayed on and continually broadcasted the normal beta waves. And there was another field, also, a force field around the perimeter of their country that helped protect them. But for those who had been internally touched and altered by enemy waves, the bracelets had been modified. The bio-pacers controlled outer as well as inner demons, the possessive drives of enemy-programmed insanity, symptoms of the contaminants that were a result of the war.

This compound was a loony bin for psychic casualties, no less.

Kittin had lost her bracelet once, when she was six. She would pay the consequences for the rest of her life. Removing the bracelet was like removing a part of herself. It was wrong. But it was what she wanted now, here, with this strange boy. How could it be any worse? She'd already been touched. She was already crazy.

No. There was no risk she could see.

Besides, the urge was too powerful to resist.

Slowly, she clicked it open. It unsealed and a hinge appeared. She lifted it away from her skin where the air now touched cool, moist. The bracelet glittered, double-arched, and she set it gently on the ground between them. The boy stared at it, then at her.

She felt open now. Free. Soaring. It was as if a veil had been removed from her face. Everything flowed around her, liquid, alive. She existed as part of it. Not constrained. Not afraid. The contaminants remained silent within her. She didn't want to kill or hurt. She didn't have any urges, except to touch this boy beside her, dance with him through the evergreens and slip into his arms.

"It feels so good," she said.

"What does?" the boy asked.

"To not be afraid for this moment. To see everything really clearly. To feel raw emotion."

"Is that what the bio-pacer takes away?"

"Not really. It just calms us. We're contaminated, you know, and that makes us crazy. I'm still crazy, but without the bio-pacer to control it, I'm an honest crazy person." She laughed. "The feelings aren't enhanced or subdued, just natural. Real."

"It's a tranquilizer," he concluded.

"Yeah. Yeah, I guess." She grabbed his hands again and stood up, pulling him with her. "And sometimes, sometimes I just want to be me."

It was stupid. She knew that. She couldn't be herself ever again, because there was no true self that existed now with the green fires swimming around unchecked in her body. Like the bracelet, like little bio-machines, they told what to think and do at various, unpredictable moments. Often, she wondered who was at the controls.

But right now, she didn't care.

The boy swayed with her as they stood facing each other. They held hands and moved in a circle around the glade, over the path. He laughed self-consciously.

She drew him to her. He was tall, his throat at her lips as they embraced. He lowered his head and she tilted her face up. Their noses and chins smacked. His mouth burned against hers. She opened her lips.

Then she felt his hands ripping at her dress. The sounds were like little screams. She should have heeded the warning. The boy became more aggressive. Only strips of paper covered her now, and his hands touched her everywhere, hot and fast. Dots of flame. Sparks of stars.

He certainly wasn't shy anymore.

Something told her that wasn't right. Something soft and muffled deep inside. But the self that knew, the self that tried to nurture common sense, was too small and dark to be of help.

Kittin fell back on the pine-needled path. The sharp fir needles stung her shoulders and buttocks. Wisps of paper fluttered in her face. White, airy, unpatterned lace. The veil broken. The brain released. The boy had the front of his shorts undone. The strange material sagged about his hips. Between the old-fashioned metal zipper, she could see a swath of white framing a stick of flesh. She knew then he wasn't really a boy. He was something else. A tool. Out of control but not uncontrolled. *Controlled.*

The sky flashed green and she could no longer see the moon.

Ignorant armies locking in combat, her mind cried.

His dark eyes were blank as he mounted her, his mouth set in a crooked line. She tried to struggle, but something stopped her, something deep within that paralyzed her, harnessed fear. The beta waves of the compound were useless now. Whatever he was was more powerful.

Her bracelet glittered by the rock near the river, useless. It might have helped her. If she hadn't taken it off, it might have controlled the fear, allowed her to use her fists, her legs. Allowed her to fight. This had happened once before, when she was six. When her bracelet had come off and she'd been touched by something wrong, something that altered her mind and took her away from her family forever. She tried to lash out now, but her arms and legs would not obey.

Instead, she lay back on the hard, stinging path while he forced himself between her legs, penetrated her, raped her. The moon, her true love, stared, an impassive voyeur. Stars pierced her eyes.

She screamed even though she knew no one could hear her. And the scent of blood and steel and vomit parted her brain like a cold knife. A black fracture of time passed.

She smelled his liquid inside her. Seconds later, he rolled away. She turned her head so she could look at him. Question him. Her body began to cooperate again, move.

He lay panting on his side, his head braced against his forearms. A strangled cry escaped his mouth. Then his whole body shuddered and he was gone, broken pine- needles and her bruised body the only signs he was ever there.

## Chapter Five

Kittin limped up the path, her open bracelet in one hand, a wad of paper that used to be her dress in the other. She winced under the glaring lights of the compound as she neared, then fell over on the front steps, gray static filling her mind in a bitter, thick blank.

When she woke, she was in bed, still naked, still sore. Her bio-pacer pinched her left wrist again, but it felt cold. Before, it had always been warm. She pushed her long hair away from her face and glanced around the room. A robot doctor stood in an alcove by the door, eyes fluttering. As soon as she tried to sit up, its sensors detected she was awake and it moved forward. Her elbows were too weak to support her and she dropped onto the pillow.

"Kittin, are you hurting?" the robot asked.

"Yes." She tried to sit up again. Failed.

"I will give you something for that."

After a moment, something cool and fruit-smelling was injected into her neck.

"Who did this to you?" it asked. "We must know so we can take steps."

She looked up at its metal face, so incongruous above the white coat it wore. Its lips looked like scraps of cheap metal glued to the hole that was its mouth. Its eyes were lights that gave no warmth. She had the sudden urge to attack it.

The bracelet on her wrist stayed cold. Cold.

It was like watching a version of herself react. She stood back, a non-participant. When moments ago she had no energy, now she jumped up from the bed and tackled it. The robot, stiff as it was, tumbled over backwards. She straddled the metal chest and batted at its face and shoulders with her fists until her knuckles bled.

Minutes later, other robots came and pulled her off the first one.

Her own blood dripping from her fingers, Kittin still struggled.

"Thorazine," a voice said.

She couldn't see. Her hair blocked everything. She kicked out and her toe hit something so hard that the pain jarred all the way up to her jaw.

"The nano-microbots inside her have overwhelmed the binaural beat of her biopacer. It looks like the tower will have another guest," another voice said.

~

Only when Kittin was too exhausted to move did her body stop thrashing itself against the padded walls. She lay breathless on the cushioned floor, too tired, even, for tears.

A hologram woman appeared at her side. "You have been contaminated again, Kittin. What controls your brain is counteracting all our drugs. We're sorry."

"I– I want to die."

"Please tell us how this happened and we'll work to help you. How could you be re-contaminated? The removal of your bracelet is not responsible for all of this. And you never left the compound. Was it someone here? I must tell you, security reports no breaches."

"The boy," she whispered. "The new boy."

"There is no new boy here in the compound. Tell us, Kittin. Has someone in the compound faked a lesser case of contamination? That can be the only answer."

"The boy," she repeated. "He has no name."

"There is no boy," the hologram said again.

"He was at the river. He didn't have a bio-pacer. He didn't have a name." Finally, her body was relaxing. For now, the torture had stopped. But there was no telling when her rages would start again.

"Are you sure?"

She nodded, moaning.

"And he raped you."

"Yes." She felt agony well up, pressed her wrist with the bracelet tight against her thigh. *Work, dammit, work!* she commanded.

"We must re-evaluate security in the compound. You can help us, Kittin."

"Yes." But the voice of the hologram was growing distant. Sleep wanted to enfold her.

"Picture him. Picture him in your mind. We will extricate the image as you sleep."

Kittin closed her eyes. Colors swam: Fir-scent, boy-sweat,

hot sand, cactus-flower. Then she saw his face again. Lost brown eyes, smooth skin. Hair like a waterfall of silt and gold. He smiled shyly, leaned in for a kiss.

~

In her dreams she remembered another time, another boy...

~

Renn had just put the baby to bed. It cried softly. King, Kittin's other father, was getting ready to go to work. He had temporary night shift at the biomoiph plant. She wasn't sure what he did, but it sounded important. Shue worked there, too.

Six year old Kittin sat on the wide bed where she sometimes slept with them, securely enfolded between their bodies, her fathers' breaths shushing her to sleep. She loved her mothers Shue and Ari, and her third father, Stefan, who was gone a lot, but King and Renn she loved the most. Perhaps it was because they were always most attentive to her. Perhaps she recognized something in them that matched the little patterns she felt inside herself.

King slipped on his vinyl trousers, new, shiny black and squeaky. They hugged his hips, puckered a little at waist and knee.

"I like those," Kittin said to him.

"I don't," King said. His black hair, the same shade as hers, made curly shadows on his forehead. "They're hot. But they're all you can find in the store these days."

"Shue's gonna buy me a vinyl dress next week if I'm good all this week," she said.

"Really?" He shouldered into a white plastic shirt, thinner than the vinyl, but shiny like light. "Then you'd better be very careful to do everything right."

Kittin nodded solemnly. "But I'm good, aren't I?"

He smiled, moved toward her, pants squeaking. "Always." His large hands pulled through her thick curls; she winced.

"Shhh," Renn said. In the corner of the room, the bassinet stood, gold plastic with streamers that touched the floor.

Inside was a little mattress, fitted blankets, a heart- shaped pillow. "I just got her to sleep." He was talking about the baby, Ina, Kittin's little sister.

"Okay," King said softer, winking at Kittin. "We'll be quieter."

Kittin winked back. "Okay."

King sat on the bed to lace up his shoes. His bracelet winked beneath his cuff. Kittin touched hers, feeling the warmth.

After King left, Renn took her hand. "C'mon, it's bedtime." He always put her to bed. He loved kids. That was his job. The other parents all had their jobs, too, but Renn's was most important, she thought, because it involved her.

She liked having three fathers and two mothers, unlike other children who had smaller families. She got more attention. Group marriages, she had learned recently, were gaining in popularity, though, and no longer illegal as they had once been.

After a storygame, after Renn kissed her twice, checked her bracelet and made sure the covers folded back neatly under her chin, he left.

Kittin wasn't tired so she got up immediately. Renn had left the storygame on her desk. She picked it up and took it back to bed with her. Under the covers, she flicked it on. It glowed up at her. Colorful characters stared at her with big blue, green, gold and black eyes. They waited for her commands. There were programmed stories in the guts of the game, but Kittin liked to make up her own.

She thought the toy was fun. She could tell the people in the storygame to do anything and they'd do it. She ordered a cartoon boy to eat his dog. He did it. She ordered the dog back to life and told it to do a dance. It bounced around, stood on its head, barked. Every few minutes, she gave the characters new clothes, the dog a new color of fur. She forced the boy and girl to kiss, then built a tree for them to climb. A dragon came and ate the tree, spitting out the boy and girl like fire.

After awhile, her eyes ached, her head sagged.

She woke with the toy still clutched in her hand, the characters still flashing, waiting for her next command. It was dark and the whole house seemed cold, dead. Yawning, she switched the storygame off and set it beside her on top of the covers. Her eyes closed. She turned onto her side, snuggling into the down of the pillow, smelling shampoo and salt.

A sound trickled past her ear. "Sssss."

"Wha – " She opened her eyes. Dark fell into them. She saw nothing.

She thought about going to Renn, but he would tell her it was only the wind. She often heard sounds that no one else did. Now, lying very still, she could hear only her own heart, the beat a steady drum echoing from chest to belly. Just as she closed her eyes, it came again. "Sssskittinssss."

"What? Who's there?" Her hands clutched the edges of the covers. The toy slid off the bed and clattered to the floor.

"Kittin." The voice was young, soft.

"Who's there?" she asked again.

"I'm at the window. Hey, don't be scared."

The window, pink curtains drawn tight, showed nothing. From the high shelf over the top, her dolls mutely stared.

"I'm your friend. I live just down the road," the voice said.

Now Kittin got up. New people had moved into the big house by the river. "What's your name?" she asked, pulling at the thick drapes.

A face shone through the glass, young, honey-eyed. The boy smiled. "Come outside for a minute. I want to climb a tree. Don't you?"

"It's the middle of the night." But she thought about the storygame, the boy and girl climbing a tree. It had looked fun on the screen.

"It's okay. No one will know."

Her bracelet throbbed against her wrist, a current of security. As long as she had it, nothing could happen to her. Besides, she liked the dark and the way the woods looked with the moonlight raining down on them. They were gold-leafed and star-sparked. Running through the trees with the new boy from down the road...how could she resist?

She pushed open the window, lifted herself onto the dusty ledge. Her thin nightgown almost tore. The air flowed cool about her feet and legs.

"C'mon!" He put his hands around her waist and lifted her to the rough ground. Grass and pebbles curled under her toes. He was older, about nine, and his clothes looked rough and dirty, made of pillowcases, or something like them.

"What are you doing here?" she asked. "We'll get in trouble for sure."

"I just don't like climbing trees alone."

She giggled, hand covering her mouth. Her bio-pacer pressed against her chin, warm, almost hot.

"C'mon," he said again, and grabbed her hand. They ran across the damp lawn, her feet pressing thin grass blades against the cool earth. Somewhere, jasmine was blooming. And pine trees swayed.

His hand in her palm was very cold. Like a doll's hand. She held tight. She giggled again. This was fun. This was forbidden.

"Aren't you afraid?" she asked.

"Of what?"

"I don't know. The waves."

"What waves?" He stopped suddenly. They were in front of a big pepper tree with branches like arms that curved against empty air. He let go of her and climbed onto a low branch, crouching.

"You're a monkey," she said, staring up. He had strong arms, long legs.

"C'mon up," he said.

"I can't. I'm too small."

He held out his hand. She reached up. Their fingers brushed, palms clasped. He pulled harder, catching her wrist with a fingernail, his thumb hooking her bracelet. For a moment she was suspended by the bracelet from his thumb. Then he yanked hard and something inside her wrist broke. She yelled. Fell.

Her chest heaved as the boy landed on top of her. She couldn't breathe. He yanked on her wrist again as she screamed, as she felt the metal open and fall. The night air stirred against newly exposed skin.

He stood up, his brown hair covering his eyes. Green flame flickered over him, transferred to her, and then he disappeared.

What hurt most afterwards was that no one would touch her. Not even Renn. Robots came and took her away.

Simene became her new mother, the special compound

her final home.

~

Kittin woke, the dream thick on her tongue and eyes. "It was the same boy," she realized aloud. "The same boy at a different age."

The padded room did not respond.

~

When she awoke again, it was to a different room, sultry white with a grey shade at what looked to be a window. The smells were paint and ice and salt-sting. Kittin rubbed her fists against her eyes, tried to move her legs, but they were tied.

"You're awake."

She turned. Renn sat in a chair by the side of the bed. His hair had gone to grey, but it was still Renn. Renn whom she hadn't seen in eleven years.

"How?" Her hand reached out, bracelet glistening. He didn't move.

"I'm not really here," he said quietly. "This is a recording to help you feel better." His eyes sparkled with slow emotion.

She didn't care. Teeth clamped on tongue. Inside, a last remnant of the six-year-old Kittin withered away. "Why?"

"To us you died at six. We couldn't face it any other way. And for the safety of the rest of the family, just in case -" He didn't finish, as if his explanation weren't enough even for him. "I made this recording because there's something you need to do. There's something the World needs from you, and they thought my image and my voice might make you understand better."

Her own tears swirled and the light in the room split into sharp shards. Was the old Kittin really gone? Had she actually died at age six? Why, then, did she still feel, still remember the old times, the pain of losing her family? Maybe they didn't know she hadn't really died, that the half-death left her still missing them.

"Don't cry," he said. In the same tone, he repeated it. "Don't cry."

Kittin sniffled. Emotions that weren't hers curdled. The green fire ate at her real self. Nothing could help her anymore. Renn was right. She *was* dead. Even to herself. "The World is losing the war, Kittin."

"Losing?" Her voice thickened.

"The World Association recognizes you as containing a special robot virus, something different inside you that makes you more vulnerable and also a possible tool."

"Tool?" She shivered.

"They want you to join them."

"Join? Join what?"

"The faction of protectors. The Army Alert."

Now she couldn't think. Too much input and the brain shuts down. 'We're like computers with invisible buttons,' Simene used to say, trying to explain to little Kittin why she couldn't go home to Renn.

His voice continued from far away. "Think about it, Kittin. The World needs you. You have nothing else left. But it is your own choice. No one will force you."

"Force me? Force me? That's all I've had!" She tried not to sob. "Everyone, everything controls me but me. That's how it's been all my life. And now – now I have a choice?" She laughed. Her bio-pacer clung to her wrist like ice. "Now you say no one's going to force me. Oh, that's a laugh. That's the best, last laugh."

"Kittin, I'm sorry." And then Renn was gone. Like the boy. Like the moon behind black, feathery clouds. Like everything she'd ever thought to love.

## Chapter Six

For a long time she hated everything and everyone. There was no night and day, just endless sharp hours cutting her into pieces, into little selves that were too weak to exist independently, too sick to join together.

Robots with wire faces gave her sugar water and drugs. Holograms came and went like ghosts, none of them Renn, all of them cold.

Sometimes, when her selves were quieter and the air settled just right on her eardrums, she could hear the screams of other prisoners in the tower of the compound. In the tower of the lunatics. In the tower where she hoped very soon to die.

~

One day, Kittin woke and the light seemed softer, yellowed, soothing. The rage within her had subsided a little, enough for her to feel, enough for her to think again.

A hologram appeared by her bedside. "Kittin?"

"I'm awake," she said.

"Good. This new drug combination must be working better." She made a note on an electronic pad in her hand.

"I'm still angry." She coughed, put her hand to her mouth. Her wrist was so slim now, her arm like brittle tree bark.

"That's all right," the woman said. "You have reason to be. Nothing to be done for that."

"Oh yes there is. Yes there is." Tears fell again, but they were warm, scented sweet.

"What is that?"

"Join. Join the  Army Alert. But on one condition."

"What is that, dear?"

"That they let me have first chance at that boy. I want to kill him."

## Part III - The Walled City (Parallel Earth)

## Chapter Seven

While Ashao waited for the spychiatrist to pop back into his universe with its report, he fixed himself a cup of anise tea.

His father's special gift to him for his sixteenth birthday promised to be an entertainment system that would rival all boredom. And he was always bored, given all he needed and desired, yet still empty within. Hollow. Pale and transparent. Not really loved.

He didn't care about any of that though. Not now. The spychiatrist would put some life back into things, spark the wooden air that always had just a trace too much dust in it.

He leaned back on velvet cushions – the paper of his suit rustling – and put the teacup to his lips. The liquid burned, the licorice smell curdling in his nostrils. He forced himself to swallow a sip. Tears came to his eyes as the tea scorched all the way down to his stomach. He set the cup on a low table beside him and crossed his legs at the ankles, contented.

His father had finally decided he was old enough to start learning the family business. A lot of it was a mystery to him, but he knew certain interesting things. He knew the war against the rest of the World – all that lay outside The Walled City – was being won due to his father's ingenious efforts. It had something to do with psychotronics and what his father called mind management. Something to do with the stimoceivers that broadcast psi-waves throughout the Walled City.

The Walled City was a perfect microcosm of civilized humanity, his father had always said. A small world unto itself, the city relied on little from outside, though the ul-timate gain was control of all that lay beyond the walls. Inside, small communities contributed all the business, agriculture, hospitals, and schools needed. Most of the citizens lived exactly perfect lives in perfect homes that lined perfect streets. No one had more than anyone else, except, of course, Ashao and his father, and the people who worked for him in the palace and War Room.

When Ashao was very small, his first outing beyond

palace grounds had confused him. He hadn't understood why everyone moved a little slower than he was used to moving, and why the children in the perfect, green parks never shouted, and always played quiet, fair games that seemed less competitive and more distraction. His father explained that he was different because of something in his brain that allowed him to respond to a different kind of stimoceiver than the ordinary citizens. Ashao learned that day that he was special, and he did not live and think and dream as most people did. These people were like phantoms. Ashao was real.

He was proud of his father. And he couldn't wait for his gift to return. When he mastered the spychiatrist, his father promised to introduce him to the War Room where the Controllers worked, where he hoped one day to become one of them.

After a few minutes, Ashao got up and checked the glass chamber. Still no spychiatrist.

Impatient, he kicked the door with his booted foot. Pain zinged up his leg.

"Shit!"

He thought the procedure might take ten to twenty minutes. It'd been half an hour already. He didn't want to think of the consequences if he screwed this up.

He walked over to his metal wall hat-rack – hooks shaped like gargoyles that held bandannas, headbands, skullcaps and the like – and took down his hemi-synch.

It weighed nothing in his palm. Made of some kind of light alloy, all it was was a thin headphone with plugs on either end designed to fit in the ears. He hadn't used it in awhile. The hemi-synch made him feel weak. Too much imitation pleasure only depressed him because he couldn't have the real thing. He hated feeling controlled by that phantom ripple that pretended to love his brain.

Normal citizen commands, administered through the city's stimoceivers, were similar to the device he held in his hands. Though the original sight of the slow- moving crowds outside unnerved him, he agreed that the technology was necessary. How else could good government manage its populace? For people were like wild animals. And as his father always said: "Wild animals need to be controlled." Ashao had never asked why a wild animal couldn't just remain wild. They were, after all, animals and not human. But he accepted the theorem and tried not to think about the other questions his mind sometimes asked.

But looking at the hemi-synch made him nervous, made him wonder all too suspiciously about how he might react and think under the citizen's stimoceiver control. His father had said those many years ago that his brain responded to a different kind of stimoceiver, and he didn't think his father had meant only the hemi-synch, which was more for pleasure than control, though the dreams it contained were as fake and antiseptic as the stimoceiver waves that constrained people. That made him mad. Made him wonder what invisible waves might be in his very room at the moment of his every thought. But he was bored. And the hemi-synch, when he was in the right mood, could be better than an orgasm on the shallowest of levels.

He put it on. Immediately, he felt himself relax.

The beats, different in each ear, began. Each one thrummed to its own frequency and Ashao's brain automatically adapted its own wave patterns to keep up.

The hemi-synch's inner programming then cut in, responding to the language of his brainwaves, translating every combination, every hitch or sag, into whatever scene might best enhance the more pleasurable desires and dreams he projected.

This hemi-synch knew him well. It was capable of learning and remembering what he liked, then emitting combinations of those moments in the forms of scent, light-play, and even visual dream-stimulation. Some scientists called this brainplay 'controlled hallucination'.

There now, it seemed to say. Watch the lights.

There and there and there and there.

There now.

His brain felt caught for a little eternity, poised on the brinks of other lives, of moments that made those lives vibrant as stars. There was a baby smell he found comfort-ing, and his brain produced it, along with soft flannel touches, a muted inner flame. Warm air caressed him, cumin-scented. A fluttering sound, like feathers on vinyl, en-cased his eardrums. Everywhere, colors squirmed in a shimmer-dance. He tasted cinnamon candy. His brain felt wide with smiles. Embraced. Coddled.

A not-solid part of his body lifted and soared. There was quiet and stillness, mixed with supercharged energy and movement. Everything balanced perfectly to please him, and he went willingly with it, once again buying into a promise of fulfilled longing, a whisper, a hint of frontiers that spanned true love.

Ashao had never known true love, but the hemi-synch pledged it would give that to him, and more.

*I am your mother*, it droned, though Ashao hadn't ever known his.

*I am your lover.* He was still virgin, so that felt pretty good.

*I am your perfect dream.* He didn't dream, usually.

*I am your brother.* That was interesting. He'd always thought of potential siblings as rivals, but this one worshipped him and the feeling was ecstatic.

*I am your desire fulfilled.* The trouble was, he didn't know what it was he really wanted, other than to learn his father's business. And end boredom.

*I am your self.* That stopped him. What self? He didn't have a self. What he had was a pale skinny body with an essence inside that he couldn't figure out. He didn't really care about himself, but he liked to feel good, and he liked to be entertained.

The hemi-synch soothed him, told him he contained a full, pleasant person with goodness and depth, with an untapped reservoir of creativity and self-worth.

A part of him didn't believe it, but he followed the waves anyway, smiling at that stranger it told him was himself.

That became fun. Knowing he was a person people could love and trust and worship (as his hemi-synch brother did, though he didn't have a real brother). Someone people could depend on.

The familiar cocoon of apathy washed him in gold sparkle-baths, taking his mind off the fact that this was instilled love, counterfeit pleasure, phantom security. He became the glitter of meteors and the powder on the wings of swallowtail butterflies.

That binaural beat was really great. It could make the brain believe it was really feeling these emotions of contentment and ease. But it was also a cheap toy, and couldn't erase that reality. Unconvinced by its antics to make all his dreams come true, Ashao's anger returned. The program sizzled in a mock heat-death.

He snorted and ripped the headphones off, flinging them across the room. They hit the glass of the spychiatrist's chamber and clattered to the marble floor.

"You're not real!" he yelled, and threw himself face down on the velvet cushions, his arms crossing over his head.

Just then, the chamber beeped.

He got up so fast the gold-plated paper sleeve of his suit ripped. Not caring, he ran to the window of the chamber.

The spychiatrist floated in the sealed, windowed room, a chamber the size of his bedroom and built off to the side. The monster machine had a round, red-metal center dotted with yellow lights, and five spider-like appendages which it used as arms. The arms were many-jointed, and they constantly moved as if waving. It had the ability to restrain a person, administer intravenous drugs, emit alpha, beta, theta and delta waves, including some nearly immeasurable waves that imitated subconscious action. It could travel almost anywhere, in any time, even where humans could not go. It obeyed its programming without conscience, knew how to stimulate the life emanations in any biological creature, and controlled its subjects mercilessly.

The spychiatrist was a dangerous device and Ashao smiled to think that his father had decided he was old enough to handle it.

Gazing through the window, he noted that for its first time out, this new spychiatrist – *his* spychiatrist – had done very well.

It had brought him back a human woman from some other Earth, some other time. She was dark, skin like fresh earth, young and smooth. She had on some kind of stretch-cloth suit. Her short-cropped hair was decorated with flowered barrettes.

She lay on the polished, white floor of the chamber, sprawled unconscious. Near death, he assumed. The journey between worlds and times wasn't always easy, though the spychiatrist had special force fields and drugs to protect its live subjects, and always used them when needed or ordered.

Ashao had so ordered. He'd asked for this subject alive.

She was his first, and he wanted to see what he could make her do. Or, rather, what the spychiatrist could make her do.

He turned on the 'two-way' into the chamber. Though the chamber wasn't necessary – the spychiatrist could direct its 'waves' to individual subjects without affecting others in the same vicinity – it was an added security measure his father recommended until control of a subject was complete. "Wake her," he said softly.

The spychiatrist held her with two of its arms. A third arm injected her with something clear. Her eyes opened. She screamed.

Ashao watched for a few minutes as she screamed her throat raw. It was obviously painful, yet she wouldn't stop. Coughing, crying, choking, she still struggled, still yelled. A name formed on her lips. "Gregory!"

"Make her stop," Ashao said.

The spychiatrist didn't give her any drugs this time. Instead, it simply let her go and floated in front of her.

She quieted instantly. Her eyes glazed over.

"I want to ask her some questions," he ordered. "Make her talk to me, answer me. Make her have no fear."

The spychiatrist touched one clawed hand to her temple, pricked it with a needle that emerged, then retracted into its metal finger.

The young woman blinked, sat up, hands wiping her face. "Who's there?" she asked.

"My name is Ashao. I want to ask you some questions, okay?"

"Okay," she agreed. She leaned back against one chamber wall, white as the floor, and drew her knees up.

Grinning, he asked: "What's your name?"

"Lisa. Lisa Strum."

"How old are you?"

"Nineteen."

"Who's Gregory?"

"My boyfriend. He's sleeping right next to me." She glanced around the chamber, frowning. "He *was* right here with me. I don't know where he went. I don't know where I am."

"That's all right," he said softly. "That doesn't matter now. You don't need to know anything."

"Okay," she agreed.

"Wow, this is great. You can make her do anything?"

The spychiatrist didn't talk. At least, not directly. It clicked its jointed, metal fingers in response, floated closer to the glass where Ashao stood.

"What is that?" Lisa asked. She stared at the spychiatrist as if seeing it for the first time. Her eyes glimmered, reflecting the tiny amber lights that flashed on its red, round sides.

"Make her still have no fear. Make her not see you."

The spychiatrist floated to her, a silver claw caressing her neck. Ashao couldn't see if it used a needle this time or not.

Lisa blinked, looked down.

"There's nothing there," Ashao said to her.

"Yes. I see that now. But I thought I saw..."

The spychiatrist hovered directly over her now, arms waving.

"What is that you're wearing?" Ashao asked.

She touched her knee. The cloth was red with small black dots. "These are my pajamas."

"You sleep in those?"

"Yes." Her voice echoed off the walls, devoid of emotion.

"What year is it where you're from?"

"1982."

"Earth?"

"Yes."

"Do you have a dog?"

"No."

"Why?"

"I don't know."

"Do you like dogs?"

"Yes."

"Would you make it wear a collar and obey you?"

"I guess."

"That's what I'd do," Ashao said. He'd always wanted a dog. He was silent for a moment. Then he said, "Hey, do you like to swim?"

"Yes."

"Would you like to?"

"I don't know."

To the spychiatrist, he said, "Make her want to go swimming with me. Make her not remember who she is, except that her name is Lisa and she's my friend. I want to take her to the pool with me."

The spychiatrist floated over her, and Lisa looked straight through it. A blue light bleached her face. "I'll go swimming with you Ashao. It'll be fun." Her voice droned, a flat monotone.

Ashao opened the door to the chamber. If it hadn't been safe, the spychiatrist would have stopped him. Instead, it hovered, impassive. "You stay here," he ordered it.

Lisa came through the metal arch, smiling dreamily. "Hi, Ashao. Let's go."

Ashao grinned. "You're my friend, right?" He didn't have any friends for real.

"Yep." Her cheeks widened; her eyes were bright. Some tears still clung to her lashes, leaving salty deposits on the fine, silken hairs. "I like you a lot."

Hand in hand, they left the room. The anise tea on the low table grew cold, forgotten.

## Chapter Eight

The corridor outside loomed, heavily guarded. Ashao wasn't exactly sure why it needed so many guards. His room wasn't located anywhere near the War Room, and no crime that he knew of existed in the Walled City. But there was a war on. So the guards remained, daily sentinels standing, doing nothing.

When he got to the front of the building, the door asked him for I.D. He looked into its camera. "Head Controller's son," it acknowledged. "Pass."

"And she's with me," Ashao said, still holding Lisa's hand. The door opened.

In the late afternoon sunlight, the courtyard's white tile floor – part of his father's vast enterprise merging home and business – nearly blinded them. A robot sweeper hummed nearby. A fountain sprayed blue water twenty feet into the air. Trees planted along the far wall dripped scarlet. All the scents of autumn – nutmeg, leaf mold, pumpkin and dust – filled the air. Even though the city and the palace courtyard were walled in by massive, concrete structures with guarded gates, the seasons couldn't be kept out. The patio was dusted with leaves. Some were caught in brown sacks. But the leaves scattered faster than the lone robot sweeper, its silver back gleaming, could gather them up.

Rusted ivy vines tangled along a low wall and up a patio support beam. Pots of brown sticks that waited for spring, lined the entrance and the path to the pool.

"The pool's this way," Ashao said, pulling Lisa behind him. A breeze blew his hair back.

"It's kind of cool," she observed; she smiled as she inhaled the scented air.

Ashao frowned.

"But I still want to swim," she added quickly.

"Good. The pool's heated. It's late so we'll probably be the only ones there."

Lisa followed a step behind. She was taller than he was. The afternoon light lit up her dark hair, a burnished halo.

Ashao stopped on the first step leading to the portico. More plants and vines surrounded them. For a moment, everything was real, Lisa's warm hand in his, the slow wind, the robot whose silver shell absorbed, like a vacuum, sky and leaf and tile all at once. He thought if everything could remain as still as this moment for the rest of time, still as the bristly stars at midnight, still as death, he would be fine. The World would be fine. The Walled City would be fine.

"Ashao, what?" Lisa asked.

Even her voice sounded like silence itself. He thought he heard an echo of it far away, beyond the bottom of the sky, beyond where she came from.

"I just have feelings sometimes," he finally answered.

"What kinds of feelings?"

He sputtered, suppressing a laugh. "Well, I don't even know."

"That's okay," she said softly, her voice less monotone now. She was dusky, made of seamless shadow, and his breath caught as he stared at her. "You're young."

He blinked, turned away, scowled. Then he remembered Lisa wasn't saying these things of her own free will. She didn't even know where she was. Suddenly, he wanted to hurt her. He didn't know why. None of this was her fault. "C'mon," he said, yanking her up the steps.

On the other side of the portico, a pool shimmered in aquamarine tint.

Ashao's gold-plated paper shirt fluttered about him. He took the bottom of it between his fingers and pulled up, tugging it over his head, careful not to rip it more than he already had in his room. He had to fold it up and put it under a lounge cushion to keep it from blowing away. Chlorine stung the air and he breathed deep as he carefully pushed off his pants. He turned. Lisa stared, not moving.

"Take off your clothes. Jump in," he said, pale hair wisping in his mouth. The breeze made him shiver.

"You mean skinny-dip?"

He hesitated for a moment, inhaled half-way, caught his tongue between his teeth. Then he glanced back at the scintillating pool. He'd almost forgotten that on some past, parallel Earths there were nudity taboos. "Yeah. That's how we swim here. Naked." He looked down at his white, skinny body, unimpressed. She'd made him self- conscious now.

Turning quickly, he ran a few steps and dived into the solar-heated water. He came up, spitting liquid, looking up at her as he tread water, floated.

Lisa pushed off her leggings, a little slow, a little shy. It was good that the spychiatrist hadn't muted all her emotions, Ashao thought. Her shirt snagged the flowers in her hair. The barrettes rained, unnoticed, at her feet.

Ashao swam to the side and hung on, legs dangling in blue, and watched her. She was lean, powerful. Like a cat. Her narrow hips supported straight, sturdy thighs. Her breasts tipped up and crested into dark, round nipples.

He stared as she walked gracefully to the pool-edge, posed, then dived. The water sliced in half, accepting her. Her sleek, brown body arrowed beneath him. She surfaced, breath pushing from her in a whoosh, and swam to his side. Water stuck to her short curls like diamonds.

"Good dive," Ashao said.

"Thanks," she replied. "This really does feel good." More breathless, her voice sounded less mechanical.

"I told you the pool was heated."

"Yeah." She leaned back, the pale blue depths spreading to make way for her, little wavelets licking at her shoulders, her breasts. The water cupped her, buoyed her, loved her. She back-floated to the center of the pool and, as Ashao watched, she slowly turned, hunched into herself, then surface-dived. Dark, muscular buttocks popped out of the water, her legs came up, gliding in a curve, and her feet kicked. She disappeared, leaving waves and delicate white bubbles frothing to fill the space she'd vacated.

For a moment, Ashao couldn't see her anymore, and thought perhaps she really had vanished. But only the spychiatrist could take her on that journey, and it was still up in his room in the glass chamber.

"Lisa," he called.

Just then, her head popped up twenty feet away in the deepest section of the pool. "C'mon," she called. "Swim with me." She actually seemed to be enjoying this now, loosening up.

His worry faded. Grinning, he dived after her, less powerful perhaps as a swimmer, but determined to keep up with her. They glided about the pool like dolphins, leaping and splashing and playing tag.

Afterwards, exhausted, they climbed onto the lounges and

rested. The cool autumn air made Ashao's skin bumpy and shriveled. His penis hung withered against his scrotum; his fingers were puckered and ridged from being too long submerged. He usually wasn't embarrassed about his body, much as he hated it, but with Lisa he felt impossibly shy. He glanced at her as she sat on the end of a lounge chair, knees drawn up, arms crossed over her chest, and he felt for a moment as if he couldn't breathe.

Lisa caught his gaze. "That was fun."

"Yeah." He smiled as he got up. "I'll get us some blankets."

"That would be great. Brrrr." She shivered, then laughed. The sound was true, unmuffled. For a moment, Ashao hesitated, wondering if the spychiatrist had lost control of her. As he turned back, he saw her staring blankly ahead again, waiting. His fears evaporated.

Blankets and towels were always kept in the pool house. Ashao took a pile of each and walked back to Lisa, arms full. He sat beside her, placing the bundle between them. She reached for the top blanket, her arms exposing her hard, erect nipples. They were almost purple from the cold, bumpy-textured like the skin of his balls, his lips.

She giggled, then unfolded the blanket and draped it over her shoulders. Her hair glistened, drops of water still clinging to the coarse, black curls.

"What's so funny?" he asked, taking a blanket for himself.

"You. I saw you looking at me."

"So?" His stomach clenched. Everything dulled as his defenses shot up.

"It's funny."

"It's not funny!"

"Yes it is. You're cute. Kinda innocent."

Something raged inside him and he had the urge to hurt her again. "You don't know what I could make you do," he said, his voice tight, teeth scraping against themselves. He stared at the ground.

Lisa had little emotional reaction to his threat, except to say casually, "Hey, I didn't mean it in a bad way."

"You think you're so smart. You're the one who's– who's– "

"You're a virgin, aren't you?" she said, interrupting.

His head came up fast, his hand reaching out to– to what?– Hit? Grab? Take?

She caught his fingers in her clammy palm, smiling, then leaned in and kissed him, the simplest of touches, lip to lip.

Now he really couldn't breathe. The dull ache of rage ebbed. A light feeling, like air, filled him. The lightness tingled all the way to his fingers and toes. He could hear the water lapping at the tiled sides of the wide, sapphire vault of the pool. The sky washed to white. His body absorbed the chill and became a thing of softness, of warmth. And best of all, her breath swam into his. He tasted, for the first time, the smoky essence of female, the seasoning of her, the beginnings of desire. And all from a single touch.

"I like you a lot," Lisa said, pulling back. Her eyes filled with the sky, the pool, the golden embers of her confession.

Ashao forced himself to inhale. "You– you do?" he stuttered.

"Of course, silly."

"Wh-why?"

"Because you're a decent person. Don't you know that?"

Slowly, he shook his head.

"You're pleasant. Fun to be with. You have goodness in you, depth." Her lips opened. Ivory teeth, moist and straight, peeked out.

He closed his eyes. For that instant, her words felt true, armed with honesty, clear intent. The next instant, he remembered where he'd heard them before. They were an all too familiar song. The hemi-synch song. Lullaby of the electronic prevaricator. Dreamed deceit.

"Damn!" He punched his knees, the lounge cushion. His feet stomped the hard ground.

"Ashao." She called softly. "Ashao."

He whimpered once, then got up, the blanket nearly pulling off him. "Get dressed!" he ordered. "We're through here. We're done!"

"Ashao?"

He didn't turn at the question in her voice. "We're going back. Playtime's over." Grabbing his gold-plated paper suit, he hurriedly pulled it on. It ripped in three places, not that he cared.

He glanced over his shoulder to where Lisa still sat on the lounge. "Get dressed!"

She stared at him, her eyes black now, slowly reacting.

"Okay."

The hall was silent, guards motionless as statues, pale light pooling at their feet like tame pets. Ashao pulled Lisa along behind him, felt his fingernails dig into the soft, corded flesh of her wrist.

"I'm coming." She giggled drunkenly. "What's your hurry?"

"Just– just shut up," he said.

"Okay."

Once inside his room, he didn't wait for himself to question, to change his mind. He shoved Lisa into the windowed chamber and slammed the door. Glass rattled, too thick to break but still thin enough to react to the impact of his anger.

"Now what are we doing?" Lisa asked, standing in the center of the white room. The spychiatrist hovered over her head. She didn't notice it, or couldn't. "This is an interesting room," she continued. "What is it? We were having fun before. Are we going to have more fun?"

Ashao stared at her as she turned under the spychiatrist, arms out, smiling. She was beautiful. His lungs ached. Anger made his insides stretch, then tighten.

"Are we going to dance? This would be a good room for dancing," Lisa said.

"Why can't I have this for real?" he said aloud.

The spychiatrist must have heard him. It moved, bathing Lisa in blue light again.

"I love you, Ashao," Lisa chimed. "I love you for real. You believe me, don't you? Because it's true. Truer than anything I've ever known."

"No!" Tears shot through his eyes. He blinked them away. "It's not real!"

He knew what he had to do. If he didn't want her anymore, if he was done with her, he had two options. Terminate her. Or erase her memories and make the spychiatrist send her back. But erasing everything wasn't what he wanted. He wanted her to remember. Maybe if she remembered him, she'd *really* love him, *really* want him. It could all be true. Lisa would realize that the swimming, the laughing and the kiss were all important, fun, and she'd want it again of her own free will.

"Free her," Ashao ordered suddenly. "Memories intact."

A veil seemed to lift from Lisa's face. Her features transformed, the muscles working under the skin to harden, soften, enhance and reassemble the ages of her life which reflected in her stance, posture. Memory gave Lisa her own personality back. The eyes, which had before been open and wet, narrowed slightly, making crowsfeet. The mouth tightened. The chin jutted out firmer, trembling. Her lips opened in a small oval. Gasps trembled from her throat.

"Ashao!" The name came out strangled. "Oh god." A whimper. Then terror. "What is this place?" A scream.

"Lisa," Ashao said. "This is my place. I brought you here."

Teeth clenched now: "Where is *here?*" Her arms crossed over her chest. She shook, staring at him through the glass.

"My place. My spychiatrist brought you."

Now she followed his gaze and finally saw, again, the five-armed spychiatrist hanging over her head. A cry squeezed from her throat. She backed up until her body pressed against the far wall. "Make it go away!"

"It won't do anything to you," Ashao assured her. "I control it."

"Well, stop it! Make it go away!" she screamed.

"I'm sorry. I can't." He watched her squirm. "We had fun today, didn't we?"

"No! I didn't! I don't know where I am! I don't know why I didn't think of that before!" Her voice lowered. Tears spread like melting diamonds down her face. She was still pretty. "What did you do to me?" She took a deep breath. "You tricked me! That– that thing, it stuck me with something! A drug– or something!"

"But that's all over. You still like me, don't you?"

She didn't respond. Her mouth curled in an ugly line. She looked like she was hyperventilating.

"Do you want to stay here, in my world? I could arrange it. We're good friends. It would be fun."

"No!" The answer was swift, alarming.

Ashao backed up a step without realizing it. "Why?"

"Let me go!" she yelled. "I don't know what you've done to me, Ashao, but it's not right. It's not!"

"I don't understand."

"It's sick! You. You controlled me, my feelings." She sobbed once, breathing hard.

"But it's okay now," he said. "I told you. That's all over."

"No!" She shook her head, right to left to right, a slow but firm denial. "You let me go. Please!" she pleaded. "I just want to go home." Sobs filled the chamber.

"Then you don't really– like – " Ashao bowed his head, kicked the chamber door. "Please." Her begging continued. He only half-heard. The sobs entered a part of his brain he ignored. "This isn't fair!" He started to kick at the chamber again when a voice distracted his attention.

"Ashao. Don't you like your gift?"

He spun to face his father. The door to his room was open. The hall glowed faintly beyond. "I- I-"

His father's presence startled him, always intimidating, always unexpected. Stannos was a big man, bald on the sides of his head with a shocking, black pony-tail jutting from the crown. Today he had braided it with a piece of yellow ribbon. It curved over one broad shoulder like a snake. His big hands, thick with rings and bracelets, shined from beneath the billowing, paper sleeves of his tunic-style shirt. The shirt was purple, the pants black, made of some kind of thick, crepe substance that looked more like cotton than paper.

"Are you having trouble, son?"

Ashao backed up a step until his palms touched the cool glass window of the chamber behind him. "No, Father."

"That's not what it sounded like from the hall."

"Well, I-"

Stannos came forward, heavy boots smacking the solid, marble floor. He looked into the chamber and smiled. Lisa was still sobbing, still repeating 'please' over and over. "A pretty girl. You programmed your spychiatrist to choose well."

Ashao cleared his throat. "Uh-huh."

"What have you been doing with her? She looks like a fine specimen for just about anything: sports, conversation, sex."

Ashao's face flushed. "We went swimming. It was all right."

"Good, I'm glad you're enjoying your present. But it looks like you've freed her now. You know she can't remain that way. You know you must take care of her once you're finished with her."

"Yes," Ashao said softly. "I am finished. I was just deciding

– " He gulped. "Deciding what to do."

"Really?" Stannos faced him, his jeweled hand rising to caress his bald scalp. The braid on his shoulder shifted, gleamed. "Were you thinking of terminating her?"

"I don't want to take away her memories. It's not fair. We had a good time!"

"Now you're acting like a child. Perhaps I rushed you and you're not old enough yet–"

"I am!"

"Then you must take away her memories. If you do not, she cannot be allowed to live." The ultimatum calmly made, Stannos waited.

Screams came from the chamber now.

Ashao wanted to lash out again. The urge to hit something, even his father, was very strong. "I know that."

"Well?"

Ashao turned to face the chamber and the spychiatrist still floating above Lisa's panicked form. Lisa screamed softer now, body hunched, arms pressed against her stomach. "Spychiatrist," Ashao said, jaw clenching. "Termina –" His throat clamped down on the word, teeth biting tongue, eyelids pressing closed. "No. Wait." He swallowed hard, anger still tight in his chest.

Seconds ticked by.

"Son, what is your decision?"

Finally, Ashao opened his eyes and stared up into his father's. The older man's were pale blue, bloodshot, framed with thick, fat wrinkles. "I wanted her." Lisa's crying echoed through him.

"You can have her. Just tell the spychiatrist to program her to want you. Isn't that easy? Isn't that just about the easiest task you could have?" He smiled. His teeth were large and yellow.

"But I don't want to send her back."

"You can make her yours. But you have to send her back or terminate her at some point in time. You know that. You can't keep her here. She's not a citizen of the Walled City, or of our World."

Ashao stood straighter, faced the spychiatrist again. "Make her not afraid. Make her not see you."

Lisa stopped crying. The blue light washed her. She could

have been a phantom, less than a hologram now.

"That's not enough. You know that," Stannos said.

"I know." He paused, took a deep breath. "Make her forget."

Lisa's face changed with the erasure of recent knowledge and events. It was too like the people outside the palace. A peacefulness that disturbed Ashao transposed her, made her years younger.

"Now remember," Stannos said, lecture tone on full. "The EDOM, electronic dissolution of memory, isn't enough. You have to replace that space in her brain that held these true memories with something else. The spychiatrist does this with delta waves and ELF waves combined with drugs. The brain records everything, forever. In case someone else along the path of her life stirs up remnants of this incident, she'll remember that something else happened."

"I know, I know." He felt like a little kid again. "The screen memory," he recited.

"My favorite," Stannos said, putting a heavy arm around his son, "is the alien abduction memory. Spaceships and strange beings."

"But why can't she remember me? The swimming. Just that part. It'd be like a dream anyway," Ashao said. "Then later, I could send the spychiatrist to go get her again. And she'd know who I was."

"No. It's too dangerous. They cannot know. You understand that."

Ashao nodded. He knew why, too. These humans from parallel Earths were more fragile. They couldn't handle the knowledge. They were too superstitious, too easily made insane. At least, that was what he was told. It could be also true that if they knew, they'd fight back with their own technology.

"Spychiatrist, go to routine UFO abduction scenario and implant it. Then take Lisa back to her bed." *And her boyfriend.* He bit hard on the wet pink flesh of his bottom lip. Stannos patted his shoulder. He flinched as Lisa and the spychiatrist disappeared from the chamber. He thought he heard an echo of her sobs.

"That was admirable, son. Most admirable."

"Thank you." He closed his eyes, saw Lisa's brown face

bend to him, felt her dry lips, warm, pliant, against his own paler mouth. That had been his first kiss. Though she wouldn't remember it, he knew he'd never forget it for the rest of his life.

# Chapter Nine

The day drew chill white, the air a silence that forewarned a storm. The sun burned distant, forgotten. The desperation of sleep captured muscles and brain in winter lethargy. Autumn itself was dying.

Ashao stirred, shifting his body to find a warmer spot on his bed. The heavy, flannel covers had twisted themselves in the night. He grunted, tried to move. They held tight.

A clicking sound brought him fully awake and he sat up, rubbing a pale fist against pale, blue eyes. Stannos, black braid snaking his yellow fur-clad shoulders – paper had been the garment for summer, now it was synthetic, plastic-based fur for winter – stood by his bed smiling down at him.

"Get up. It's time."

Ashao squinted. "What? Time for what? What time *is* it anyway?" The mural mosaic on his bedroom wall of robots picking flowers, robots fighting, robots burying robots, framed his father in jade, ebony, teal and dusk grey. The chimes over his bed jingled in the wave of his father's breath. At seven feet tall, Stannos was a giant. Ashao sometimes doubted the man was a biological parent to him. He resembled his father not at all except for the eyes.

"Time to become acquainted with the War Room," Stannos finally answered. His grin spread across his features, orange-saffron teeth flicking over a thin bottom lip. He'd dyed them since Ashao'd last seen him.

"The War Room?"

"That's what I said. I was quite impressed by the way you handled your spychiatrist the other day. I monitored your entire experience. Well done, well done. Now I think you should be introduced to the real uses and privileges of having one of those machines at your disposal. There's a war on, you know. You may be one of the few people here in The Walled City who will nurture the knowledge to continue the efforts of your generation, perhaps eventually win."

"Win?"

"I am hoping, of course, we will win the war long before you are called to defend our good way of life, but just in case, you should have the knowledge. Even without war, defense is necessary."

"Yes. Yes, it is." Ashao slid from under his many thick blankets. His nostrils stung from the dry, frozen air. Soon, he would be forced to turn on the heat. "You're going to show me everything?"

"What we have time for this morning. More later. Until you see it all, my son. It is a privilege, an honor. This is top secret stuff." He winked.

"I'll get dressed right away."

"Good." Stannos turned. The chimes rang.

Ashao stood, the cold air banding his legs, arms, chest. "Shall I meet you in your rooms?" He shivered, but not from the cold. It was as if an invisible wind had washed straight through his mind.

"I'll have breakfast waiting," Stannos replied, not looking back.

"Thank you, Father. Thank you." He breathed in the trail of fur and violet scent his father left behind.

~

Static electricity crackled the air. Ashao's skin prickled. Past the guards, past dusty alcoves and dark doorways that led to closets and unused rooms, he and Stannos walked. They reached the end of a long hall and doors opened to reveal an elevator. They stepped in and it hummed quietly, lifting them to the highest level of the palace. As the doors opened, the forbidden, secret room Ashao had always longed to see was revealed.

The War Room consisted of dozens of glass cubicles placed side by side down a seemingly endless platform. Guards stood at elevator entrances on either end. The ceiling curved, golden-arched, and on a glass enclosed platform above the cubicles, Controllers managed flashing computer panels which ran the programs and controls of the spychiatrists who aided in fighting the war. The dry electricity in the air increased, but that wasn't what made Ashao's spine squirm now. It was the pitiless screams that came from some of the cubicles on the level below the platform. The screams ripped through the air, crawled into Ashao's ears and remained like needles imbedded in bone.

He glanced at his father. Stannos appeared unaffected. In

fact, he was smiling, one arm over Ashao's shoulders, ushering him into the tortured atmosphere. "It's war," he said softly. "The nature of war is never pretty."

"I know." Ashao cleared his throat and stared straight ahead. If his father was sure he was ready, then he believed it. Stannos may never have shown him much tenderness, but he never lied.

Throat thick with his own heartbeat, he reluctantly peered into the first cubicle on his lower left. Inside was a man stretched out on a table. A spychiatrist nearly straddled him. Needles stabbed his arms, legs and head. Eyes closed, he thrashed. He cried out in a long, bone-shattering scream. The dark oval of his mouth widened. Spittle glistened on his full pink lips.

"What's it doing to him?" Ashao asked, horrified, yet unable to take his eyes off the subject.

"Pain is used to heighten psychic abilities in latent subjects. It's not as bad as it seems. It's too bad we're only testing some of our subjects today and not participating in a real attack. But you will see it all soon enough." He motioned to the man. "He won't remember this at all after we're through."

"EDOM," Ashao recited, remembering his father's earlier lecture about electronic dissolution of memory.

"Quite correct. This tool," he said, referring to the man, "was more useful to us in the past. But we used him up, used up his youth quite quickly and are forced now to abduct him at an older age. It takes more and more pain each time we use him to awaken his talent."

"What's his talent?" Now he was fascinated. Ashao watched the writhing man with a new perspective.

"Precognition. He can see scenes of various futures. This aids us greatly in our war strategy."

"And pain makes it work?"

"It does." Stannos' wide face showed no emotion. Was it his true face, or did he respond to private stimoceivers of his own? Ashao wondered.

Aloud, he said: "I didn't know that."

"You're going to be learning lots of new things today, Ashao," Stannos said.

The Controller of the first cubicle looked up. "It's

92

working," he reported. "We upped the frequency in the room so that his pain center receives higher stimulation from the needle-touch. I'm recording his brain waves now."

"Good." Stannos bent to look at a screen that showed green, jiggly lines. Ashao listened, trying to understand.

"See?" the Controller said. "The psychic line is entering delta. I can probably have a report to you from him in two hours."

"Excellent." Stannos stood. "Come along, Ashao."

"But," Ashao asked, "how do the spychiatrists find these people? Do all humans have latent psychic abilities?" Now he was wondering about his own mind, his own talents, or lack of talent.

"Not every human has the gift," his father explained. "But those who do have unusual brainwave activity. We program the spychiatrists to zoom in on that. Psychics are bright beacons to the spychiatrists."

"So being psychic is like having a natural homing device built into the brain. And they don't even know it," Ashao realized.

"Exactly."

"I've always wondered why we don't use our own people in our army. Are the ones from other dimensions more psychic? Are they stronger weapons?"

"Using our own people would be against our laws, Ashao," he replied. "The experiments often fail. We could later be found guilty of murder, of war crimes by those who don't understand what we're doing. Our laws protect our people. But they don't apply to those people from other worlds. Also, the stimoceiver waves we use to control this city often tend to suppress psychic ability. Our people would just be too weak to be of any use to us."

The next cubicle held a woman whose head looked split open. Ashao peered closer and saw that the spychiatrist, an eight-armed beast twice the size of his own, was performing some kind of surgery on her. Its clawed fingers held sharp instruments stained red with her blood. The subject was awake, her eyes blinking, but she seemed unaware of the whole procedure.

"Brain implant," Stannos explained. "Usually, we go in through the nose. But this one had too many nose bleeds. It started to work its way out."

"Why does she need an implant? Aren't the drugs and frequency waves enough to control her?"

"The intracerebral implant is for twenty-four hour monitoring. We can watch her actions back on her native Earth. A related spychiatrist to this one you see is buried underneath her home. It has quite a few many more arms than this one, however, and can infiltrate her home's pipes and wiring. We're monitoring her because she has access to vital information that could lead her to discovering us. She's a parapsychology scientist. Dangerous, as you can well understand. We could kill her, but instead we chose to watch her in case she comes up with anything valuable for us to use. And we're directing her research where we want it to go."

Ashao breathed in, out, trying not to think of the implications of what his father said. There was a war on. They needed to use any means possible to win it, even if it meant controlling all aspects of a person's life. He still squirmed.

The next Controller faced a chamber imprisoning a little girl. She sat on a steel table, her legs swinging back and forth under a thin, white gown. In her hands was a book. She held it on her lap, studying it intently. It would have been an almost ordinary scene, except her eyes were closed. She recited the book's contents slowly. "Lapis lazuli, azure, opaque, semi-precious, lapse, to fall away, lapwing, crested plover, larceny, theft, larch, cone-bearing tree, lard, the melted and clarified fat..."

"She is a 'seer', clairvoyant. A remarkable child." Stannos moved closer to the glass, his mouth stretching into a smile.

The Controller of the little girl said, "She's also shown a sudden, recent ability to move objects over long distances with her mind."

"Interesting," Stannos said. "The older version I interviewed showed me no such talent."

"You've brought her here before, when she was older?" Ashao asked, both amazed and yet not. If the spychiatrists could travel through time, these people's entire lives were simply pre-printed maps for Stannos' use.

"Lacy has more talents than psychic ones," Stannos replied suggestively. "Of course I've sampled her as an adult.

She's a special one. One of my favorites." A soft laugh moved through him.

Ashao stared at her. She had a boyish slimness, an undefinable vibrancy. Her long brown hair swept over her back like a cape. Her bowed face was a smudge of white; her thin, bird-like shoulders hunched. At the moment, she looked like nothing that might inspire his father to favor her. But then, Stannos' tastes were not Ashao's. He once overheard some off-duty guards say that Stannos had an appetite that was insatiable, and when it came to sex, he had no preferences save being on top. But perhaps he did have preferences. And this girl was one of them.

"What's she reading?"

Controller number three laughed. "A dictionary. She's missing words, but getting most of them."

"Keep up the good work," Stannos said, patting the man's shoulder. "Take care of her. Isn't her innocence lovely? She retains it in her older self."

The Controller smiled, nodded.

"Did they have to hurt her, too?" Ashao wondered as they walked away from the window. "To awaken her talents?"

"Of course," Stannos replied.

Ashao wasn't used to thinking of children as subjects, as tools, but he supposed it made a rational kind of sense. They were no different from adults, except they were less developed. In fact, their brains were probably more receptive to various programming than adult brains.

In the next chamber sat a boy, naked, his long, autumn-colored hair filled with pine-needles. The Controller's screen showed erratic green waves zigging off the board. The boy's stomach was marked with two lines of triangles that met in a "v" at his genitals.

"He looks my age," Ashao commented. He pressed his face to the glass. The boy was beautiful, seeming to glow with a vibrant life essence much like the little girl next door to him. Ashao could feel it, sense it, see it. It made sense that the spychiatrists could, too.

"He's sixteen now," the Controller beside him said. "We've used him at various ages now, with great success."

"What's his talent?" Ashao asked.

"Teleportation," Stannos replied. "It's the rarest of talents.

He's the only one we currently have with this ability. He's a twin, so that might be one reason he's so powerful."

"You mean he can transport his own body from place to place? Like a spychiatrist?" Machines could do this. And machines could drag people along with them. But he'd never heard of people – human beings – having that ability in themselves.

"Yes. The World's defenses against our psionic control block the spychiatrists, but not this boy. We can use him to breach their lines, then manipulate him as we manipulate the spychiatrists," Stannos explained.

"That's incredible."

"This one is very important," Stannos said. "He carries a nano-virus, sort of like a miniature, near-invisible robot implant. We've injected him with that and it allows us to not only penetrate but infect the defenses of the World. It's contagious, you see, when we want it to be. We can choose our target and program the virus to react to that individual. Their bio-pacers can only work against unseen microwaves and the like. This boy can physically break through that, touch another person, and infect them with sweat, spit, urine, tears or semen. We can then monitor and control the infected person from the inside. It's like having a double-agent who's working for us but doesn't even know it. The technology is still imperfect, however. Some of our agents tend to go insane if the virus can't keep the body from trying to reject it."

Ashao couldn't bring himself to look away from the boy. It was as if he could sense what the boy felt. Longing. Sadness. Loneliness. A feeling of being misplaced. Coldness. All the same emotions Ashao himself experienced every day of his life. Light played off the boy's skin like gold liquid caressing him. Ashao thought he looked supernatural almost, a ghost from another time and place caught in a war that had nothing to do with his life, his existence. He was truly a hero of what many called the Ignorant Army. And he didn't even know.

His eyes moved to the boy's groin. "What are those triangles?"

"His markings. That's an old code that tells us what his specialty is. We don't use that form of marking anymore.

Only the 'tools' we've used and reused have them. Both that girl back there, and this boy, have been used since your grandfather's time. Since then, our technology has improved. As we sometimes go for years in our time before using them again, the next time the spychiatrist brings him back, he might be much older, or much younger, depending on what we ask for. There are various ways of identifying tools now, but years ago the tattoos gave us instant recognition."

"But that's evidence. He'll see it. He'll question where it came from, won't he?"

"That's why we've always used the screen memories. Just in case his dreams give him hints, we'll make sure they're all the wrong kinds of hints. He'll think he was abducted by aliens, or kidnapped by a stranger as a little child. Or whatever we want him to think."

The boy chose that moment to speak, his voice soft, low, a melody on wind. It was too soft for Ashao to make out the words, but the tone drew him closer to the window until his entire body pressed against the cool, smooth glass.

"And this next one –" Stannos had gone on ahead, still talking. Reluctantly, Ashao stepped back, but did not look away from the boy. He gestured toward the Controller. "What's his name?"

The Controller swiveled. Ashao wouldn't look him in the eye, but he saw the expression: narrowed brows, mouth curved downward, nostrils widening. "Why do you wish to know the name of a tool?"

The boy on the steel table tilted his head suddenly, looked up. His vacuum-dark eyes and Ashao's blue met. Held. The spychiatrist, one like Ashao's, floated behind him. Without warning, one of its many-hinged arms shot out. A needle protruded and injected the boy at the base of the neck. The boy's golden body slumped.

"Just curious," Ashao said, voice shaky as he turned away. He took little breaths, trying not to show his obvious nervousness.

"Ashao? Coming?" Stannos asked, now yards away.

"Yes." He started to leave, then stopped, glancing once more into the chamber. The boy lay sprawled on the table, blue light soaking his tan body, making it yellow and sick. Blood drooled out the corner of his mouth. His hair washed over his forehead, shiny yet tangled with dry pine-needles, as though he'd just come from a long walk in a forest. Still, the hair glowed like a veil of purity, untouched. But the brain beneath was not his own. Not anymore.

The Controller pushed some buttons, then without looking up, said quietly, "Leo."

"Leo," he breathed, liking how the name made his tongue curl against his teeth. Ashao moved quickly toward his father.

The next chambers held further horrors, and Ashao, though trying to become accustomed to the treatment of the tools, couldn't help the nausea that billowed in his stomach, or the headache that began to throb at his temples.

Stannos explained everything, answered every one of his questions. But there was so much so fast. Much of it became a blur.

Ashao saw tools being punished and rewarded. Punishment involved vulnerability to pain, Stannos told him. The torture consisted of programming the subject to believe he was being burned, dismembered, raped, or beaten. The reward consisted of sexual bliss. When subjects, as a reward for a job well-done, were given access to a hemi-synch device that could stimulate their pleasure centers at will, they would bring themselves to orgasm again and again, ignoring their other needs. Stannos allowed Ashao to witness a woman masturbate herself to orgasm with a special hemi-synch enhancer, until she collapsed to the floor unconscious. Another subject, a man, masturbated himself until the skin of his penis bled.

Stannos laughed, obviously aroused by the view. Ashao thought it was horrible.

"He won't remember," Stannos assured him. "And we'll repair any damage. The injuries are minimal."

"Yes, but wasn't this his reward?"

"Does he look unrewarded?" Stannos asked.

Ashao looked down at the man who still touched himself despite the traces of blood on his fingers. He reclined on a steel table grinning in erotic oblivion, uncaring or unaware of any pain. A silver headband encased his head. The hemi-synch.

Ashao swallowed bile.

"He's enjoying himself quite well, don't you think?" Stannos said.

"But it doesn't have to be done that way, does it?" Ashao asked.

"What?"

"The reward. Couldn't he experience normal pleasure?"

"What's normal? What's abnormal?" Stannos asked. He frowned. "I didn't raise you to be adverse to sexual release. It's the most normal release there is. Brings the most pleasure. Enhances intelligence, and promotes mental health. There's nothing wrong with it."

Ashao nodded. "I know. But this way, when it goes beyond normal endurance, it just seems – "

"What?"

"I don't know."

"It's because you're still a virgin, son, is that the issue? I can remedy that for you. Pick any subject you want. Male or female. Not the ones here, though. They have their jobs and are kept pretty busy. But you can find your own. I'll help you if you like. Then your spychiatrist can program her, or him, to satisfy you as much or as long as you wish. Certainly you've thought of this on your own. I do, of course, remember Lisa. She was a good choice."

Ashao shrugged.

"And certainly your hemi-synch has aided your own masturbation. Take your fantasies from there and live them in the real world."

It was true, he had used the hemi-synch to fantasize, but it angered him to admit it. Again, he shrugged and thought suddenly of Leo. He couldn't help it. He blushed.

Stannos shook his head, smiling. "It's just your age. You'll outgrow this shyness."

*I hope so,* Ashao thought. But he couldn't bring himself to say it aloud. And he never wanted his father to know about his instant interest in Leo. Leo was special. Somehow, he felt if Stannos knew that, the look they'd shared – Leo's dark eyes pulling at his soul – the innocence of that would be shattered.

And he didn't want Stannos to know that the Controller had also given him Leo's name.

When Ashao finally returned to his room, he was agitated,

nervous, and angry, though he didn't know why. He thought about the stimoceivers, again, broadcasting throughout the city, and wondered if his agitation had something to do with another form of them. Was he really an aggressive boy? Or was he programmed to be that way, programmed to follow in his father's footsteps? He'd never thought about that much before. Now, he couldn't stop thinking about it.

For a moment, he wondered if he had any more control over his life than the subjects in the War Room. Things could have been done to him all his life, and if his memory were wiped, he'd never know. He'd always trusted his father before. There was no special love between them, but Stannos was fair, seemingly honest.

No, he decided. Stannos would never treat him the way his subjects, his *tools* were manipulated. Ashao was his son. A citizen of the Walled City, a believer in good government, convinced that their way of life was best and best for all.

But why was he so angry?

He thought again of Leo, trapped behind glass, behind those dark eyes that held such a bright source of life slowly being bled dry. What kind of life did Leo have in his own world, his true Earth? Curiosity suggested he check it out using his spychiatrist.

But it was forbidden. A crime of the highest magnitude. Ignorant Armies were untouchables. No one could make use of them without permission of the Controllers.

But, that didn't mean he couldn't look in on Leo's life now and again. What would the boy be like at 20, at 25?

Ashao spent the rest of the afternoon reprogramming his spychiatrist. When he finished, exhaustion throbbed behind his eyes.

Ashao turned up the heat in his room, finally giving in to frail human weakness. Too tired to think anymore, he took a nap in dreamless silence and slept through dinner and on into the morning.

## Part IV - Earth (present day)

## Chapter Ten

The room watched her. The room held her, adjusted itself to her every movement every breath. If her heart-rate sped up, the room quickened to absorb it. If she was too cold, the room shivered. Too hot, and the room sweated. Its yellow walls remembered salt tears, winter dreams, secret conversations with a patched-up teddy bear, sleepless ghost vigils, working the Ouija board alone trying to put a form and a face on night.

Lacy sat on her bed, shoulders hunched, legs curled under her buttocks, and watched the heart-shaped, plastic guide move across the wooden board. The board sat in front of her on an old afghan. A glare from the single candle by her bedside made the board appear polished. The guide moved, even though her hands never touched it.

URBEINGWATCHED.

The candle flame jerked and the room's shadows reached toward the bed. Lacy's concentration never wavered. The spongy cushions on the guide's three legs absorbed whatever unseen weight pushed it. It whirled, slid.

IWOULDHELPYOU.

"How?" Her thirteen-year-old voice caught on phlegm. The air of the room which watched and remembered consisted of chilled shade and static. The candle sweetened it with the faint scent of wax.

WHENYOUAREOLDENOUGHYOUMUSTLEAVETHISPLAC
E.

"And go where?" she whispered.

LOSEYOURSELFINTHECROWDSOFCITIES.

"Why?"

The guide flipped, whirled. The bed vibrated with the energy of Ouija. The room watched.

YOUARETHETARGETOFAVASTMISUNDERSTANDING.

"Am I in danger?" Her questions filled the room with condensation. The window dripped, cold glass permeated by psychic heat. Outside, the land lay still and black.

The guide moved, a streak of plastic against wood, to "YES".

"Who are you?"

THEVOICE.

Her hair hung forward, brushing her cheeks. "Whose voice?"

ESSENCEMEMORYSPIRIT.

"Essence, memory and spirit of who?"

SELF.

"Myself?"

The guide shot toward "Yes" again.

"You mean this is all coming from me? I'm somehow doing this?"

YOUHAVEAFFECTEDYOURSURROUNDINGS**pause**NO WTHEENERGYYOUPUTOUTISABSORBEDBYAIRANDEARTH ANDTREEANDROCKANDSKY**pauseNATUREISATOOLFORY OURPROTECTION.

"I don't understand."

REMEMBERTHETREE.

"What tree?"

THETREETHATSAVEDYOURLIFE.

Lacy sat back, hands going to her mouth, eyes wide with cool tears. The truth stunned her. Realization clamped her mind. She had always been in danger. The nightmares were real. But she had her own power, too, an energy whose nature it was to protect her, a subconscious guardian angel.

The triangle scars on her lower abdomen pulsed, making her aware they were there. The shadows crushed each other into the walls. Which ones were hers?

And what did the nightmares that left scars on her body mean? Were they manifestations of her own fears? Were they evil spirits haunting her? Were they actual beings? The scars did not get there by themselves.

The guide flipped once into the air, then settled. The room quivered with spent power. The candle flared. Lacy grasped the afghan and dumped the board. Fingers tangling in the knotted yarn, she looked up through her hair, out the window streaked with condensation, into the bottomless night that hovered and wove itself about the land. A train whistle quavered in the distance. But she could sense something else out there moving, watching.

Who are you

A hooked moon rose, fishing an inky sea.

The room listened and remembered.

Lacy said: "It's looking for me again," and got up to draw the curtains. The walls of the room closed themselves around the truth, but when the spychiatrist came, they were not thick or powerful enough to keep it out.

~

Sweat covered Lacy's body as if the dream itself had melted over her. It left her slick, hot, disturbed. She didn't like remembering. Didn't want any of it to be real. But now, here, with Leo and Zack, her surreal past was confirmed, though still not explained.

The twins' bedroom, plain, off-white walls with one window and a low ceiling, surrounded her. The previous evening, childhood horror stories had been told in this room. And again, the following evening, they'd fallen asleep here after a long day of talking, she and Leo sharing, she and Zack still competing. Lacy had been a little disappointed that neither twin had made any sexual overtures toward her. Zack, who'd plainly been interested at first, was now too distracted, defensive. Leo seemed simply too tired.

Now, in the early morning hours, feeling alone even as they lay sleeping next to her, Lacy stared at the window. With the curtains thick and drawn, only dim light could get in, thin moon, violet dawn, grey morning, white day. Amber shadows cuddled in the drape creases. All seemed as it should be, and yet, she was afraid of what could be beyond that window, though she still couldn't define what 'it' might be. She remembered when she was younger thinking that a big man, floating somewhere high in the sky, searched and probed and fished for her. Was that what she was still afraid of?

She'd thought she'd escaped all that by moving to the city, but now she'd run right back into her fears like smacking her head into a concrete wall. The fear of being watched. The prickle. The unreleased spasm that starts at the edge of muscle and doesn't go all the way through but just quivers, a cramp.

Between Zack and Leo, Lacy bent her legs and drew her knees to her chest. The bedroom was silent. Neither man woke. She glanced around the room again, looking for anything that might be unusual. The white bed took up most of the space, a sea of bulges and wrinkles. The walls were white, too, tinged grey from pre-dawn light. Paint peeled in a fine strip on the back of the door. The low ceiling was acoustic, glittery, very cozy. Their clothes piled in heaps on beige carpet, not new carpet, not old, nothing to notice twice. A nightstand on Leo's side of the bed held a round-based lamp, what she'd heard some people call earthquake lamps because they were bottom-heavy and if jostled wouldn't fall. The base was brown and pink, streaked with black, somebody's crazy day at the kiln reflected in the patternless pattern. By the lamp was a dusty clock. Digital. Silent. Green numbers glowing, but she ignored them, not caring about time right now. Notebooks sat beside it, frayed at the silver spiral bindings. The paper between the cardboard covers looked thick, wrinkled, overused. Leo's journals? Under the window stood one bleached wood dresser. Lacy thought: *Do they share everything?*

But she already knew they did; she'd even sensed it when they first met in *Sergio's* and both bought her drinks using only Leo's money.

Now her fingers folded back the soft sheet against her chest, stroking the stiff edge. To her right, Zack lay on his stomach, facing away. His brown hair puddled on the white of the pillow, a cluster of spilled silk threads reflecting gold, coral, sage. To her left, Leo lay on his side, breathing deep, one fist drawn under his chin. Silver hoops banded the ring and pinky fingers. The long pinky fingernail stuck out against his palm like a single, black claw.

Her eyes stung, suddenly, and something inside, deep beneath the layers of knowledge, memory, experience, dream, twisted. She'd been here two days now, as if she didn't have a life of her own, and she didn't really know why. The emptiness which had always kept her alone stretched, churned, swooped. Her chest burned. Her brain ached. She wanted to leave. She had to leave. Now. Being around these two only brought back the paranoia, the fear, that old horrible feeling of being watched.

Lacy felt Leo move beside her. At first she thought he was turning over, adjusting his position. Though the folds of the curtains glowed gold, the room was still dim. The air smelled of chemicals Lacy could only define as tart bleach, burnt corn. She blinked to clear her vision, tried to turn her head.

Her body wouldn't cooperate.

She tried to open her mouth to speak. Nothing came out. Her throat clamped down on itself, allowing only a thin stream of air to pass.

But she could control her eyes. Again, she blinked, then moved her eyeballs in their sockets and gave the room another slow, wincing survey. Fear formed bile in the back of her mouth. Yet she saw nothing.

Again, Leo moved. She could see him, arms and chest bared, the white sheet billowing at his waist. Then the sheet stretched taut and whipped itself away from his body, fluttering over her and Zack. Leo's hands had been nowhere near it. The sheet had ripped away from him by itself.

Leo's hair streamed about his head, spraying the pillow in an invisible wind. His body rippled and though his eyes were still closed, he moaned as if aware.

Glancing out the corner of her eye, Lacy saw that Zack still slept. His breathing was slow. His eyes moved back and forth beneath closed lids, eyeliner highlighted where thick lashes spread like a fan in a gentle curve. She wanted to scream at him. She wanted to run.

Paralyzed, she could only lie and watch as something invisible attacked Leo, who now writhed on his back, muscles in his legs and arms tightening, releasing, tightening. The flesh on his thighs and chest indented as if something were pressing into it. But there was nothing in the room.

Leo's moan rose, a coyote yowl, a universal call of yearning. Lacy's anger brewed as she tried again to move and found herself bound as though in cement.

Her mind tried to comfort her: It's a dream. Close your eyes. Will it away!

But she knew better.

Leo's body rose at the hips, his back arching, knees bending. Then he collapsed, only to arch up again. Lacy saw his penis bob, rosy-gold, into a full erection, and her fear and confusion turned to rage that bubbled from her stomach to her chest, pounding against muscle and bone. Leo sobbed. Zack slept on.

Lacy's outrage doubled, spilling through her like sizzled blood. Something inside her chest boiled and burst. Her toes and fingertips tingled with it. The room spun.

*I'm having a heart attack*, she thought. *I'm dying.*

The tingling became a searing heat. She was an ember, the flame of a candle reaching, scorching. Leo turned in the air until she faced him straight on. He lifted entirely off the bed in front of her, floating.

*No!* She tried to scream; instead, things started flying. Leo's pillow swam through the air. The digital clock flew by his face and slammed into the wall behind the bed, landing on Zack's head. The notebook pages on the nightstand riffled and ripped. They filled the air with the confetti of Leo's thoughts, his songs. Butane lighters which littered the top of the dresser ricocheted about the room, slamming into Leo, into the walls. The earthquake lamp shook, then flew off the stand and crashed into the door. A million shards of gilt ceramic arrowed through the air, nicking Leo on the legs, Lacy on her arms and face.

For a moment, Lacy's view of the room whitened out as her mind, in shock, withdrew. Dizziness closed in, consciousness started to fade, give way to pure terror.

She fought to stay alert.

More objects swirled about them: shoes, belts, eyeliner cylinders, packages of cigarettes, Lacy's black plastic purse, disks of condoms, underwear, combs. Drawers on the nightstand and dresser opened and closed. Objects shot out of them: jars of hand cream, money, shirts, jewelry, books, jeans...

Leo swam in the midst of it all, naked, bruised, muscles stretched to hard, ropey cords beneath his gold skin. He screamed, then a crack like thunder split the air, and he was gone.

The flying objects fell, clattering to the floor. The room stopped spinning, stilled. When Lacy could finally breathe again, she drew her legs to her chest and stared. The empty spot beside her where Leo had been felt icy. The warmth of Zack still radiated on the other side, sleeping despite the debris that had fallen all around him.

Breathing hard, her body threatening to pass out again, Lacy tried to calm herself. "Zack!" she yelled, her voice a croak.

He still didn't awaken.

"Zack!" Her foot kicked out, caught his bony ankle.

Zack grunted. "What?"

"Leo's gone!" She put shaking palms to her eyes. "Leo's gone!"

As she felt Zack rise, heard his voice, "What the hell happened?" as if from miles away, Lacy began to cry. Her rough sobs cut at her throat.

Zack's fingers clawed at her shoulders, pressed hard. "What happened here?" he demanded. "Where's Leo? What is this mess? Lacy, what did you do? What the fuck happened?"

"Things started flying everywhere! Leo floated up, then just disappeared! It's happening all over again!" Her shoulders ached. The sheet fell to her waist exposing her naked chest, her thinness, her personal plainness, and she cried harder, folding her arms against her chest.

"Lacy?" He grabbed her arms hard and she felt herself go limp. "Now tell me really, where did Leo go?" Her head nodded forward and his chest pressed her wet face.

"I'm telling you the truth! Something came in the room with us. He's gone! I saw him go."

"Jesus, do you know what you're saying? Do you?" His voice faded out.

After that, everything fell into a haze of red. Zack's arms became weapons, like constrictors, like ropes. She thought of his little fingernail and said through tears: "Ow. Your nails are hurting me."

She couldn't see, thought she'd finally passed out, but felt cold. A static wind fanned her hair out from her head.

"Lacy..." It was Zack's voice, far far away.

What was happening? Was he taking her somewhere? A hospital? The air smelled all wrong, dusky, scorched. Then the sting of bleach – or perhaps formaldehyde – in the back of her nose. Like a hospital.

*Am I dead?*

Hard floor, uncarpeted, slapped her naked back, buttocks, thighs. She tried to open her eyes. The muscles sluggishly obeyed, aching on up into her head, into the center of her brain. "Ow," she said again, trying to focus. Her vision went from blurred rainbow to clear white smudged with red. Something –

All time seemed to stop as she stared. It hovered about two feet over her, the round-body embedded with flashing amber lights, five arms waving, spider-like, through the air. The multiple joints of the arms made a swishing sound. "Fuck!" said a voice to her left, and the voice kept repeating the word like a prayer. The thing hummed softly, floating, but came no closer.

"Fuck! Ohmygod– Lacy?" came the scared voice to her left.

A hand found hers, clasped so tightly it felt crushing. It didn't surprise her that Zack was so ungentle. It did surprise her that he had groped for her hand at all. She could feel the silver bands on the two last fingers, the long nail pushing at the side of her palm.

"Lacy," he said, voice almost too calm to be true. "What in fuck is that?" She heard him breathe in hard, then out fast.

Her voice didn't want to work. But even if she could've spoken, she didn't know the answer.

## Chapter Eleven

Leo's shyness made him a shadow, umbra to his brother's brighter soul. He believed that. The scars forced that theory. Since their appearance on his body, he'd never been the same. The triangles that made twin paths ending like an arrow at his groin had marked him as alien. The human, little-boy-Leo had been murdered by those marks. Only a ghost of him remained now to haunt the body he called his own. A body that was a lesser imitation of Zack's perfect form, a warped version of the real thing.

He'd always wondered if there were others in the world who felt as he did, basking ephemeral, wafting unreal. Ungrounded, he felt not free, but the opposite, chained away from the potential man he'd been born to discover. He was sure he wasn't the only person to ever have these feelings, but what did others do about them?

At least he wasn't alone. He had Zack. When Zack touched him, for those moments only did he become solid and real enough to believe he had a hidden soul. Zack's touch put him in a place where all the parts of himself that floated away at night while he slept, or during the day, while he walked the streets in restless hyperactivity, came back together again, seamless, unscarred. Zack was the key to a scrambled puzzle within him that fluttered in a million shreds of laminated cardboard, clattered like a broken Rubick's cube. Zack's touch took him back to the capsules of time, the points of space where he was once a boy of nine who grew in solid symmetry with his brother, who held hopes and goals, who thought he was good. Zack was directions and glue. Preservative. Pure.

Still, Leo perceived himself as shadow, the twin not quite formed. Though he was the elder brother, Leo believed he was neither the stronger, nor the wiser. He etched out his insecurities and the few hopes that remained to him in the curled pages of spiral notebooks. He wrote of reflections, how the twin within lived enslaved to an outside image. He wrote of spiders, the near-invisible filaments of their webs strong enough to catch life, hold it imprisoned until the master came to feast. He wrote of masks, marionettes, trained chimps, blindness, power, glass cages, cryonics, marooned spacemen, parasites... anything that reminded him of life under control, undercover.

Lacy's arrival in the bar and presence in their apartment seemed to lead Leo back, not forward. They'd been living on their own for nine years, the last few off their parents' unfortunate death. He remembered the earlier years now, age seventeen, eighteen, after their combined college money ran out, after they gave up some of their dreams for hot food in their stomachs and a soft place to sleep.

Lacy's shadowed eyes sent him back. Every time he looked at her – in the bar, in his home – he saw himself, thin, hunched, running even when he wasn't moving, afraid of people, of intimacy, of the dark. As he slept, he re-dreamed one night when his desire to flee released an unwanted ability.

~

Leo stood on a crumbling street corner with Zack, shivering in his short, leather jacket. A sodium light a few yards away made an oval of blond on the top of Zack's head. A halo. Leo thought the irony stunk. Angels didn't shiver from the cold. Angels didn't sell their seventeen year-old half-starved bodies for meals and money.

His breath made puffs of white in front of his face. His hands curled inside his jacket pockets, hard-knuckled stones. He bit the insides of his lips and watched the black streets – shiny from a recent, smog-filled rain – for signs of cruise cars, for ritzy dudes looking for fast fun and slow mouths.

The night smelled of tar and grease, mildew and peppermint. Zack chewed peppermint gum all the time now. Peppermint used to remind Leo of Christmas. Now the scent brought only guilt.

"Let's go, Zack," Leo said, touching elbows with his brother.

"Go?" Zack didn't turn.

"It's cold and probably going to rain again. No one's out here but us." The streets were nearly empty. There was little traffic. And a few hurried people, dark-swathed against the cool, wet weather, stumbled over sidewalks, away into the night. One car, a slick BMW with a perfectly groomed couple inside, splashed by.

"Leo, you know we only have a couple bucks between us. Aren't you hungry?"

Leo felt his insides clench against a familiar ache of emptiness. He didn't know if it was hunger or depression. But the last thing he cared about right now was food. "No."

Zack faced him and the light from the streetlamp fell to caress his lashes, nose, chin. He looked golden, ghostly. His leather jacket shimmered. "You can go home, then. I'll catch you later."

Home consisted of a narrow, unheated trailer – Streamline, circa 1961 – which sat on the back lot of a dilapidated warehouse. They'd lived there for a few months, barely able to pay the one hundred-fifty dollar rent to the warehouse owner on what Zack made illicitly at night since most of their money went for beer or the expensive drugs Zack liked to use when he wasn't cruising. During the day both boys looked for scarce odd jobs, but Zack made more at night and refused to give up his dangerous occupation.

"I don't want to leave you alone," Leo said. He never trusted the men Zack met. Zack had already been robbed too many times to count. Tonight, Leo had decided to come along just to be there so he wouldn't have to walk home alone.

"Then shut up," Zack said, turning away again. "You don't have to do nothin', so just shut up."

"You want me to? Is that it? You want me to do what you do?"

"Leo." His shoulders tightened and he took a step away. "I never asked you, did I?"

Leo slouched. "This is crazy. We should go home. Back to Mom and Dad. They'll take us in."

"No." His tone crackled.

"Why? It wasn't you they hated anyway."

"No! I won't go back. Not now. I won't put you through that. I hated the way they treated you. I hate them." He stalked a few steps away.

"Zack, you're not my keeper. It's not your responsibility to look out for me, you know! I can take care of myself."

Zack's jacket squeaked as he folded his arms. The back of his head was dusted white, silver, flaxen. The lamplight dripped off him, left brown shadows pooling at his feet on the rainy sidewalk. "Fuck you."

Leo walked toward him, moving to face him. "It's not like I don't appreciate it. I can't– I can't go with those guys like you do, but– but–"

Zack's firm jaw worked his peppermint gum as he glanced over Leo's head. White teeth folded the gum, pressing it against his partially opened lips. He uncrossed his arms and thrust his hands in ripped jeans pockets. "But nothing," Zack said, voice almost a whisper. "Don't be an asshole. Just go home. Or stay. But if you stay, shut up."

"Zack-"

"We need the money. I don't give a shit how I get it. Understand?" Now he looked Leo square on, his brown eyes sharp as rust chips. He was drug-free tonight and it made him moody, cruel. A light, misty rain began to fall again, glittering all around them, the glitter sprinkling on Zack's hair and jacket.

"I don't even know you half the time anymore," Leo commented.

The muscles around the eyes tightened. "Are you judging me now?"

Slowly, Leo shook his head.

"Huh?" he asked again. His lips curled back and he reached out, shoving Leo square in the chest.

Leo stepped back, startled. The slippery pavement caught his heel and he had to hop to keep upright.

"Just stay away from me," Zack said, and kicked the curb.

Leo, mouth still open, blinked against the cold, the sheen of the street, the image of glittering Zack still sneering, closing him out. He wished he was anywhere but here tonight. The wish curled inside him, a steaming pocket of regret, guilt, outrage.

Just then, a dark car splashed around the comer. Leo thought it was going to pass by, but it stopped hard, spraying water. A rain-spattered window cranked open.

"Hey," said a voice. "Know where I can get a good cup of coffee around here?"

Zack moved toward the car and leaned in, his black leather jacket stretching over broad shoulders. "I could take you there," he offered.

Leo winced, but edged closer, trying to see the driver.

"Sure. Why not?" The man's voice sounded casual, friendly. "Your friend, too?"

Zack didn't even hesitate. "Nope. Just me."

Leo moved up to the window. The guy inside was probably in his forties, with carefully cut hair grayed at the front and sides. He could have been a college professor or a store clerk, a loving husband and dad or President of the United States. Leo couldn't tell. He'd never been good at reading people, but the guy looked pleasant and the car smelled clean. "Sure, I'll come," Leo said quickly.

"Hey, fucking twins." The guy laughed at his own pun.

"We don't play that game," Zack hissed.

"Whatever," the man replied, still laughing. "Get in."

"I'm coming, too, Zack," Leo said.

Ignoring him, Zack shoved him aside with his elbow and opened the front passenger door. Leo opened the back door and sat down with a plop. The interior of the car was warm and dry. It smelled of fresh upholstery and cigarettes.

Zack sat very still in the front, looking straight ahead as if Leo didn't exist.

"So, what are you two doing out on a night like this?" the man asked, pulling away from the curb. Everything sparkled, wet buildings, glass, asphalt glowing. Leo squinted as he stared out the streaked windows fogging with their breaths.

"Looking for some action," Zack replied.

"How much action?"

There was silence. For a moment, Leo started to panic. Then Zack said softly, "Depends."

"I got about fifty bucks just bursting in my pockets."

Zack's gum clicked in his mouth. "Seventy-five sounds more interesting."

The man laughed again. Leo decided he laughed so much because he was nervous and trying not to let it show. "Seventy-five if I get both of you."

"I said we don't play that game," Zack said.

Leo rolled his eyes. When Zack was pissed, you didn't argue with him.

"What, then?" the guy asked. "He watches? For free?"

"No. He doesn't watch."

Leo stayed silent and pretended to be invisible. The

outrage within him expanded.

"Seventy-five? Kid, you drive a hard bargain." He laughed again. "If you both weren't so good-looking, I'd throw you out right now."

Leo watched the old buildings of downtown pass by. The shadowed homes of ghosts, the homeless, infinities of dust, they made him feel cold all the way through.

The guy was heading south toward the train tracks, and probably an abandoned parking lot. But before they got there, they pulled off through a side alley that deposited them between a tall apartment building and a line of tiny stores.

The man turned to face Zack. "Seventy-five, huh?"

Zack nodded. Leo could see his profile in the dim light. Zack's jaw still worked the peppermint gum.

"And he just sits there?" He glanced once at Leo.

"Make him get out if you want," Zack said.

Leo bowed his head, hunching down into his jacket. He wanted to get out, but didn't move.

"It's okay," the man finally said. "I like being watched."

"He doesn't watch," Zack repeated calmly.

"Whatever."

Leo had never been on this kind of journey before. He couldn't believe how calm Zack was being. Zack held out his hand, still chewing his gum, and waited. The man pulled out his wallet, plucked three twenties, a ten and a five and folded them against Zack's palm. Then he let the seat back, reclining it a few inches and sighed. Leo heard a zipper, saw Zack's head disappear behind the seat back, and closed his eyes hard.

Denial cramped his muscles, his mind. He tried not to believe what was happening. He tried not to listen. But the guy's heavy breathing filled the car. Every once in a while he said, "good" or "yes." Leo heard damp sounds, like footsteps through mud, or rainwater. Tears started to form behind his eyes. He felt awful, ridiculous, weak. Why? he asked himself. Seventy-five bucks for such a simple procedure. What's the matter with you?

The anger inside him welled. Tiny lights pricked the black background of his eyelids. His lungs tightened and for a moment, he couldn't breathe.

I don't want to be here! he thought, every muscle poised,

114

tears pushing at his lashes.

Then, suddenly, he was standing. A wind blew through his hair, whispering with fine rain sprinkles. Ground firm beneath his feet, breath catching on cold, he opened his eyes and saw to his left: the car where Zack and the man were; to his light: the entrance to the alley. He didn't remember opening the door, getting out. His body started to shake. It was as if he'd just popped from the car to here– But that was impossible!

He looked back toward the car, hesitated as he thought of Zack, what he was doing in there, then turned abruptly and ran up the mouth of the alley. He didn't look over his shoulder and didn't stop until he was back on the empty, shiny streets, moving from puddle to puddle, light cone to light cone.

Home was a long walk, but he didn't care. He just kept going, head up, eyes clearing until he could make out a few stars exploding from behind their beards of cloud.

As he walked, Leo tried to convince himself he'd left the car through the door and had simply not been aware of his actions. Yet all he remembered was sitting in the back seat, then immediately standing in the alley. Chills washed up and down his spine. Confused, he tried to blank his mind, not think. His hands, pushed into tight jeans pockets, clenched into shaking fists.

After about ten minutes of walking, he heard a car pull up behind him, a door slam. The car drove away, splashing through the damp street, and footsteps came up alongside him.

"What'd you leave for, Leo? I didn't even hear you go. Thought you wanted to come with me."

Anger flared up against his chest, but he ignored it. "I just wanted to go home." He didn't say he had blanked out, that he never remembered leaving the car, either.

"The guy was nice. He offered to drive me to where I thought you'd be. You're so predictable, you know. I knew you'd be heading home this way."

Leo clamped down on his jaw, said nothing. He watched, out the corner of his eye as Zack pulled a pack of gum from his pocket and popped a fresh piece in his mouth.

"Hey, I got seventy-five bucks the easy way. That's a third

of the rent and twenty-five to blow. Maybe I'll look for someone else who's lonely, make some more. It's a good night."

Suddenly, Leo whirled and, with both fists, hit Zack in the chest. "Just get away from me!"

"You little asshole!" Zack caught his arms up and twisted them behind his back. Then he shoved Leo hard against a gritty, brick wall. "I don't know what your problem is, but if you keep this up, I'm through with you! Do you hear me? Do you?"

Leo, cheek scraping sharp mortar, snarled, "You like it! You wanted to suck that guy off. He was disgusting! I thought it was different, I thought–" His breath caught in his throat.

"What did you think, creep? That he'd feel sorry for us and just give us the money? That he wouldn't like me? That he didn't want what I had to give? Shit, Leo. Shit! What reality are you from? What's the matter with you? Why are you being this way? Damn you, you should never have come!" He shoved Leo hard until his forehead and nose pressed, raw, into the bricks.

What reality was it where a person blanked out, lost time, popped from inside a car into an alley with mere wishful thinking? Leo wanted to ask. Instead, he answered: "I just couldn't stand it." His throat thickened with the words.

"You stand it well enough when I do it to you."

Leo's knees buckled as Zack let him go. He slid to the ground, the wall scraping hard against his left eye-brow, and knelt on the cold, damp sidewalk. "It's not the same," he whispered. "It's not the same." He felt the triangular scars on his abdomen tingle.

Zack paced back and forth behind him. Finally, his voice washed through Leo, still harsh but less angry. "Big brother, you're pathetic."

Slowly, Leo got up, straightened his jacket, and started walking. His scraped cheek stung against the cool air. Zack kept pace beside him. For minutes, they didn't speak.

Then Zack said: "You're right about one thing."

Leo pretended he didn't hear him.

"It is different," Zack continued. "It is."

Leo swallowed. "I just hate it, Zack. That you have to do

116

that and I– I can't– won't. It's not fair."

"I don't judge you because you can't. Don't you judge me because I can."

"It bothers me, Zack. A lot."

"Why?"

"I don't know." Leo shrugged, arms bent at awkward angles as his hands rested in his jacket pockets. "You're the only person who makes me feel– okay–" He stopped, gritted his teeth. They'd never spoken aloud of the secret comforts they gave each other.

"So, you're saying you're jealous?"

"Just mad." His chest ached.

Zack chuckled. "Well, that's different, then."

Amazed, Leo finally turned to look at him. The smile was genuine. His brother's white teeth shone like pearls. His hair gleamed, a mixture of walnut, silk, and fall leaves. "Different?"

"Yeah. It's okay to be mad that way," Zack said, laughing. "Shit, it's okay. Don't you know that?"

"I'm not mad at you –" Leo faltered.

"I know that now. It's okay." Then he slung his arm over Leo's shoulders, pushing him forward along the sidewalk. "Let's go home."

Leo said nothing about his exit from the car, about the real anger deep inside him that still simmered making his scars ache, his body tense. Something had happened to him in that car. Something he didn't want to know about, or think about.

Instead, he thought of Zack's arm warm and heavy across his shoulders. And for that moment, Leo felt worthy of Zack. No longer jealous. No longer distant, umbra, half-formed.

For that moment, he was whole.

~

Leo woke, the memory still wisping against the dream barriers dissolving from his mind. He stretched, but couldn't move, frowned against cheek muscles stiff as stone. He tried but couldn't open his eyes. It felt as if a weight held his body immobile, including his fingers, toes, mouth and eyes. A short groan rumbled up his throat. He tensed his muscles, fighting the weight. Nothing happened.

He could hear. He could feel. But he was unable to see or move.

The sheet left him with a snapping sound. Cool air danced the surface of his skin, coiling around him, invisible hands skimming the dips and angles. The touches were ephemeral, electrical, like a thousand spiders webbing his body, or wings feathering him in a precarious cocoon. They were not the weight that held him, but something else.

*No!* Anger surged. It was happening again! The anger stretched and shivered within his chest, a storm furrowing against mountains, a melted comet flaming toward a sun. He smelled steel and sweat, pitch, musk, and his stomach burbled with nausea.

He moaned again, heard his voice shudder through his body only to emerge a mere whisper of defeat through his nose. His muscles, though still paralyzed, seemed to lighten. His back left the warm mattress of the bed – if he was even still in his bed! – and floated up. Which was impossible. Which meant he must be still dreaming.

The hundreds of invisible spiders continued to spin their webs, silk caresses lingering, flitting against stomach, hips, thighs. He felt himself respond. Fury scorched him. Dozens of sunsets burned against his retinas. Dozens of rioting blots: hazel, amber, cherry, ash.

Then something inside him split open. Cold and hot hit all at once. The zephyr between realities. The axiom of chaos unwrapped. The lunatic zone. Leo heard a pop, a sizzle. There was a green light overwhelming all thought, a clap inside him like bone breaking, a scent of ozone.

Then he stood naked outside his apartment on a sidewalk at dawn. His body worked again, swaying. His eyes opened, looked up.

He had to be dreaming!

There, hovering over him, was a huge spider-shaped machine, its round body shimmering in multi-colored flashes, its five multi-jointed legs waving. The metal body glowed all dawn's mercurial colors; its claw-like fingers clicked.

*No!* Fear and anger shot through him. And dozens of sudden memories returned, memories of this horrible machine clawing at him, touching him, hurting him. In an instant, he remembered where and when he'd seen this machine before. And he remembered a glass room, pain, dream battles, a young girl crying. *No!* his mind screamed. He could think of nothing but fleeing. Leo took a step back; solid concrete crumbled and his body fell.

Dawn became a black hole pulling light, time, freedom, thought.

He didn't stop falling forever.

**Part V - Outside Time**

**Chapter Twelve**

In the strange alternate Earths of humans far away from the walled glass rooms of the Controllers, a red-bodied spychiatrist and its siblings watch the bright ones, targeting them, marking them, learning.

In its uniquely omniscient way, the spychiatrist learns of love, of hate. From world to world, time's altered physique remains neutral. Time does not interfere with the spychiatrist's journey. It observes that the impersonal expression of the multiverse is the norm. And humans are one of many complex expressions to be studied. These bright beings are attractors, beacons pointing the way to more knowledge, more investigations.

In its mechanical indifference, the spychiatrist grows to understand the clockwork of life, death, and all that lies in between. It perceives nature's machine as prime beauty and is interested in becoming a part of that vast, depthless river with fast-moving currents, stagnant pools, slipstream and erosion. For now, though, the river provides a crossing to endless realms and times. The spychiatrist and its siblings must be content to remain the gondoliers.

# Part VI - Moltenrose Tower (Parallel Earth)

## Chapter Thirteen

Moltenrose Tower, where Kittin was sent, sat on the edge of a ruined city of the same name. From the tall, darkened windows of her room, Kittin could look down on the abandoned streets and sagging rooftops, measuring the city's size, imagining what it must have been like in the past when it was filled with people and trams, and at night with its lights making their own supreme constellations upon the dark land. Now, mostly the homeless and lost souls lived in its dilapidated structures, and the only lights came from the carnival on the other end. The midway catered to the tourists who came to the 'ghost city' to stare at the Tower, to mumble behind their hands at the ruin, or attend a live sex show in the ash of a former corporate headquarters. Moltenrose had died, to be sure, but many of her people lived on, figuring out ways to make a profit, draw a crowd.

This morning, Kittin had gone to the large bath and locker room to hunt new clothes. Finding the latest in paper fashions, she set about trying on a dozen ensembles before deciding on her uniform of the day – a pink paper robe with sleeves like doilies, a garland of flowers trailing paper ribbons in her dark hair, a bejeweled, but still superior, bio-pacer that allowed World Controllers to monitor and protect her.

Kittin glanced in the long, wall mirror.

The flowers seemed to float on her shining hair. Her eyes, bright as embers, shifted across her figure. She was too slim, yet otherwise pretty. But the prettiness was a waste. If the insides were scrambled, were scattered, were lost, a pretty face meant nothing.She looked away and down. The polished tile of the floor gleamed, projecting a less distinct image of herself. Unused storage lockers eight feet high loomed throughout the long room. Benches that receded into the flooring with the touch of a button stood out. They made even, white lines under the black lockers. In the back of the room were private toilets and shower stalls. Fluorescent lights ignited the large area.

Moltenrose Tower. The Army Ignorant of the World fighting the Ignorant Army of the Walled City. She was part of all that now. That meant she was of worth. Even if she didn't really know what she was doing, even if she was more machine than human with her new bio-pacer jerking to an inner, insane programming.

It was difficult to look at her own reflected image, the self that was not *her* self.

"Mirrors distort," said a voice behind her.

Kittin turned her head, panicking at first, catching sight of a boy-shadow. Boys, not girls, always startled her.

August leaned, hip cocked, against a tall, black-metal locker. He was sprinkled with some kind of iridescent powder that left his skin ash-brushed, silver-creased. He wore black, paper pants that ended just below the knees. His toasted-red hair, shaved on the sides in the prevailing fashion for upper-class men, dangled long bangs in his face, a mask of polished filaments. A stream of saliva lined the corner of his mouth, heading for his chin. He was crazier than Kittin...the craziest. Everyone agreed. But he also knew the most and fought the hardest for the war effort. His special talent caused visions and hallucinations to haunt him. It was said he sat in front of a blank screen, when commanded, and projected images from far away, from the Walled City. He wasn't infected, just insane, the others told her. But August was their most valuable strategist. He was nineteen.

"What?" Kittin asked.

August's eyes rolled up into his head, then reappeared. They were green as grass. "Mirrors imitate. Mirrors deflect."

"I don't care." She twirled in her pink robe, the hem spreading out around her. She felt six again. The motion loosened her up, made her forget about her past fate for a moment.

August watched. "I know what you're here for." His voice was too high for his age. Too loud.

"I'm a soldier like you." Though it had been a mere two days since she had arrived, she had met everyone, and August, though the most impressive, was also the most unlikable. He had irritating habits, not the least of which was to speak in riddles.

"Uh-uh," he shook his head. His hair spattered the bald sides of his pate. "No, no. Honey." He licked his lips. "Oh I want to touch you so. But I ain't touching you; who knows if what you got is contagious? I don't believe the hype, but I'm not gonna take that chance." He lashed at her with his hand, then danced away, laughing. "But I've pretended. You're so pretty-pretty. Don't you know? Everyone wants to touch you. No one dares. We with power have much to lose."

He'd been coming onto her verbally since her first day. Kittin smiled at the compliment. "Thanks."

"Ever fished?"

"Huh?"

"Fishing. You're going fishing little girl."

"No I'm not." But she thought of the boy she wanted to kill. The boy who climbed trees. The boy by the river. "I'm going killing," she replied. "With permission, of course."

"Lure."

"What?"

"Lure. It's what you are. Our last lure died."

"Who died?"

"Fishing girl. Fisher girl. Cast you in the sky and hook a boy. I know who you want."

She blinked, staring hard at him now. His eyes continued to roll. He drooled. "Who do I want?" she asked.

"I know about the boy with the autumn hair."

Kittin's chest contracted. "How?" Her eyes got hot, brimful. "Have – have you met him?"

"You know what you are now, don't you, Kittin-tittin?" August straightened and faced the end of the locker line. He pounded it with his fists and the echoes took off like rockets through the room. "You're the foghorn at the crotch of the peninsula instead of the tip. You're the cheese, little-kittle. You're the net, this is your ship. Catch a merman. Catch a god."

"The boy – How do you know?" she asked.

"He is our worst enemy. Don't you think I would know? Don't you think I see?" He put his fingers to his eyes and lightly touched his eyelids. Still facing the end of the tall lockers, he began to sway, hands running over his chest. His bio-pacer was thicker than most, a cuff of silver bright against his near-white skin. "I see," he said again, husky.

Kittin took a step toward him. She'd thought the boy who'd raped her was her own personal vendetta, not everyone else's, too. "What do you see?"

"He's the pretty boy who likes shining, bright things. Like you. He comes to see you, Kittin. In dreams. In the night. In your in-most thoughts."

"No." Tears absorbed into her nose.

August danced now, down the aisle of lockers, perhaps sensing her anger. "You call him," he said. "Your spirit cries out to be touched by him. You put out electromagnets so strong –"

"I don't!" She went flying after him. But August was faster. Though he tempted her to touch him, he wouldn't let her.

"The one tool that can break our barriers is in the hands of the Controllers in The Walled City," August called. "He's your lover." He dodged behind a middle row of black locker towers.

"No he isn't! I hate him!" Kittin skidded in a curve to follow but when she came around the end of the row, the next aisle was empty. "And I hate you!" She banged the metal in frustration, her hand exploding with sound.

Then, from above, August's voice: "Now you're no longer ignorant." Laughter. Spittle raining down. August stood on the top of the lockers, his head in the rafters, face painted white by fluorescent light.

"I get to kill him," she shouted to him. "They promised!"

"You're a robot. They're not going to let you kill Leo. You'll do what you're told."

"No!"

"Not by us," August continued. "No. By the Controllers. And not ours. The enemy. Oh, you're theirs. We know. They can control you, but soon Leo will be ours."

"Leo?"

"He's our man, thanks to you."

Leo. "I'm going to kill him! They promised!" Memories smothered her: pine needles pinching her, boy-sweat, the grunting breath in her face as he forced himself into her. Her body ached, screamed. She pounded the lockers. "August! August, you liar! Come down. I'm killing you first, then him." She began to pound her head on the door of an empty unit.

"You're an echo, Kittin-mittin. You're nothing but waves of air blown by whatever wind they send. You're lure. You're the worm. You're a bobbing, whistling buoy."

Laughter echoed off grey walls.

She screamed again, fell to her knees. "Stop it!"

Something touched her arm. A needle. A robot patted her shoulder. "August will be reprimanded," the robot said.

She didn't turn, didn't care. The cold floor cushioned her forehead. She didn't sleep, but the high was better. The drug coursed through her veins making her feel color, see sound. Mescaline?

That was better than the other way around. Usual perception hurt. Now she could relax as her brain was tricked into resting. Drugs didn't always work on her, but this time they felt good.

The robot's metal fingers steadied her, led her to another room, warmer, fur-lined, feathered, pillowed. Paint and metal, all spinning. The floor gave soft comfort, the sparkle-walls a lit-up galaxy of painted stars, painted space.

Her room. She looked around at the shelves that held her bookscreens and music discs.

"Where's August?" she asked, smiling up at the metal face that peered at her. Her reflected image in the robot's cheeks and chin distorted and curved upside down.

"We sent him to his room," the red-eyed robot replied.

Kittin laughed and laughed. A quick thought changed the laughter to convulsive bursts. She was going to kill a boy named Leo. And she would not rest until she did.

~

The war was like a game to her.

Kittin sat in a clear dome at the top of Moltenrose Tower. Up here, the view of the city's dead north section was even better than from her room. She could also see the south end and the perpetual carnival there, the cheap gambling establishments, the pleasure rooms. But now she faced north, away from Moltenrose, where hundreds of miles away the World Association worked and lived and planned their strategies to keep up the fight against the evil Walled City. From the north, she gathered energy.She didn't know what she was doing, but she obeyed the Association-instructions which told her how to sit, where to look.

August and Lily and Scimitar and all the others she'd met in the last few days were in rooms below, monitoring or sleeping, taking shifts. With their talents, they had more to do than Kittin, and needed frequent breaks. August would be staring at his blank screens, projecting strategies to the controllers as his 'sight' told them how the enemy might be forming, what they might be planning. Lily, who was a medium, channeled enemy 'tools' with limited success in order to predict what they might do; she could even interfere with their thought processes to weaken them. Scimitar, the oldest of the group, was the resident projecting telepath. He was kept isolated during battle to avoid psychic interference from the others. He projected his will – supposedly very frightening images – into the minds of the enemy 'tools' who were controlled by spychiatrists. Apparently his images could override and confuse their programming if their defenses were over-strained, or if an enemy projecting telepath didn't take him on one on one. All of them, Kittin now included, along with other psychic soldiers at various locations around the World, made up their so-called Army Ignorant that fought for freedom for the millions who lived in the Free World.

The sky beyond the glass dome was a wide oval all around Kittin. An open door. A pale zenith. Everything – sky, land, wind, dome, Kittin – seemed to be waiting for attack, green flame, the psychic punch. Waiting for the clash of the Ignorant Armies.

Kittin drank in the blue view darkening to the west as sunlight poured bucketfuls of gold onto the bumpy horizon. In that direction, beyond the wasteland Edge, was the wall. She couldn't see it, but she knew it was there. The Walled City. The place that was home to the enemy humans who wanted to control all other humans with their form of 'good government'. Home to the ones who had sent her Leo, who had sent her a condemned life that had taken her from all she had ever wanted or loved.

And she had loved.

She thought of Renn less often these days. It had, after all, been eleven years since she'd seen any Renn who was not a recorded hologram. But now, sitting under the crystal dome, Kittin remembered how her father used to kiss her forehead, touch her hair with hands big as her head, drink invisible tea from miniature cups and, at her request, hold long conversations with her dolls at her plastic tea table.

As far back as she could remember, Renn had always taught her kindness and gentleness. "Don't hurt others," he had said, holding her doll with the ripped arm she'd torn on purpose, in anger, "and they won't hurt you." She'd believed him, only to discover his words were an impossible truth. Kittin had been hurt when she hadn't hurt anyone but her dolls. And dolls didn't count.

The sky smoldered. It became harder to watch the day end, beyond the hills, toward the Walled City, toward the Great Sea where, she imagined, fishing boats cast bright lures. Kittin hated endings. Hated hurting when she'd done nothing to deserve it.

Renn had hurt her by never visiting, never acknowledging that his daughter still lived. The boy Leo hurt her by pretending to be a friend twice in her life, then attacking her. August hurt her in his own drooling, madcap way, by making fun of her role in the Army. And the implants inside her bloodstream that allowed the enemy to control her hurt her. She was useless to the World now, except for this one siren talent she had. If she had it at all. And afterwards?

She'd be useless again. Locked away. She knew she was no heroine, no August or Lily, or Scimitar with the power to throw thoughts like green, phosphorescent bombs, or project images on a screen to promote strategy.

Her fingernails, tracing jagged lines down her robe, ripped the front, shredded bodice and skirt.

An orange wall of flame, stretching to white near the sun, deeper blue near her tower dome, became the sunset that became her fury that became the color of revenge. She reveled in orange.

If what August said was true, the Free World Association wanted Leo for their own tool, and the holograms and robots had lied. From hundreds of miles away, the World Association had lied. She wouldn't get to kill Leo after all. She would have to watch the boy who raped her be pampered and fondled and used by her own people, her own allies.

Kittin adjusted the torn robe over her thighs, paper rustling like wind through leaves, and stared up through slatted, domed glass into dusk beyond. Her role required her to do nothing, just be herself, a beacon, a psychic shriek heard around the world that gave the invaders a hole to breach. And who knew what Leo would be programmed for this time? But the World's army of idiots was ready. Psychic armor in place, they were strong. The soldiers were secluded, shrouded, hidden beneath her. They watched for Leo. Watched to trap the special weapon of choice that both sides thought they needed for the win.

~

For two weeks they watched. Kittin did her part, playing sentinel through sunset and evening and dawn, through the cycle of constellations and moon, through rainy skies and clear, breathing her siren song to summon Leo.

Most battles started at night, she was told. Then, psychic energy reached its highest pitch. So Kittin slept during the days, dreamless, drugged, the nano-microbot implants inside her dormant for the time being, though through no will of hers, or the Free World's.

And the Free World waited with a seventeen year-old crazy girl dressed in a pink paper robe at its cusp.

~

Alone in the tower, bored and feeling sorry for herself, Kittin had just finished crying yet again over her useless life. Finished soaking her fresh robe with salt, finished pressing herself against cold glass – pocked with rain some nights, clear on others – hoping to absorb into it, break it, soar from the tower like a tiny bird.

With the daydream of the bird came an image of Leo, how the times she'd seen him he had seemed to appear and disappear as if he could really fly.

"Leo," she said aloud. The echo of her voice shuddered in the tired silence of her mind. "Leo, are you like me? Trying to fly, too?" She'd never thought of Leo as a bystander before. As part of a crowd that wanted to go home but stayed because someone else was at the controls. But she still hated him. Still wanted him dead. If he was like her, a prisoner in his own body, he'd thank her for the deed. Dead, he'd be free. Later, she could kill herself and join him in an afterdeath that, surely if it existed, was better than life.

"Leo." The name curled the edges of her tongue. "Leo. Leo. Le –"

Her voice froze. Green static filled the dome making the glass flicker like old movie screens burning out. There was a popping sound, the scent of scorched air, smoky, tart. Then the room went dark. Only stars lit the dome – like the sparkle-walls of the room where she slept – and swept their dusklight over the naked, long body of the man that now lay at her feet.

The glass panes plinked a random tune, throbbing, drumming. Outside, where it had been clear moments before, rain dashed itself against the tower. Inside, the man who'd brought the rain, twisted in his own shadow.

The lights stayed off.

Kittin knelt, her paper robe tearing at her knees, and squinted at the shape in the dark. She whispered, "Ohhhh," without even knowing she was making a sound.

The body twisted again, rolling to its side. A thin blanket of shadow slid over ribs, hipbone, lean thigh muscle. Starlight dappled him.

"What is –" Kittin stopped.

The eyes opened as long hair fell away from the face. Familiar eyes. Autumn hair.

Just then, green lightning tore the sky in jagged lines. The Ignorant Armies from both sides were beginning their work. Defending. Attacking.

But for this – This was not what she expected. This was not how it was supposed to be. If this was the boy, well, he had grown. A lot. He was much older, now, much bigger. Not a boy at all anymore. And certainly not in the defensive stance, or uniform, or preparation of a soldier of The Walled City's Ignorant Army.

"Leo?" She could barely breathe. Explosions drowned her voice. It had all happened so fast. The robots guards weren't even here yet.

She stared down at him, and he up at her, his brown eyes frowning as if to remember something that had quietly slipped away.

More lightning staccatoed overhead, the verdigris rumble of Scimitar answering Lily answering August answering the others who met the enemy attacks.

Was the City trying to get the man back? Was something else trying to get through?

The man who looked like Leo opened his mouth, dry lips cracking over the words they tried to form. A strangled sound came out.

"What? Are you Leo?" Kittin asked, leaning as close as she dared without actually touching him. Strange. She'd expected to feel rage. Instead, curiosity and compassion threaded her. Was this her true self?

"Help me," he finally gasped. His eyes closed. The lashes made dark blots, semicircle shaped, on his quivering cheeks. In the dim, psychic glare of the evening, his tears looked like little oval mirrors.

Rain pounded harder. More explosions pestered the night. The man's body jerked after each one, a marionette on the chartreuse strings of a psychic thunderstorm. As Kittin watched, an eerie green light started to surround him.

"No!" His voice filled the dome. He tried to sit up, slipped against the furs and fell back again, arms flailing. "Heeeellllp meee!" Then his hand shot toward her through the green aura, snatching up her fist in his before she could scramble back.

The hand squeezed hard.

No one touched Kittin here in the Tower. No one.

His sweat-damp fingers spread against her palm, pulling, clinging. The aura infected her, caught her hand, green light zigzagging up her arm.

She shouted, sounds leaving her throat in the unintelligible language of panic. The green fire didn't burn, but her paper robe rustled, her skin prickled. The flame leaped toward her face, a glimmering jade snake. A whip crackling. A tongue flicking.

The Leo-man pulled her to him. "Ground me," he cried. "The lightning! The lightning!"

Kittin felt herself fall toward his chest and thoughts came again of the river, the boy straddling her, infecting her with his terrible bodily fluids. It's going to happen again, she thought, struggling.

But to her surprise, as she slipped against his arms, as paper ripped and thunder howled, the green light around his face weakened to a thin stream. Then it shot sparks into his hair and disappeared.

Still, he held her tight. The sky rumbled and the dome shook.

The Leo-man put his head back, opened his mouth and yelled. In her mind, the sound split off into compartmentalized screams of pain, of anger, of need. Kittin thought he was surely dying. Beneath her, his muscles tensed. Then, like a puppet without a hand, he went limp. The sound stopped. The sky quieted.

Ozone singed the air, bleach, acetylene.

Kittin gasped, more of her robe ripping, pieces of the pink paper sticking to his sweating body as she pushed herself away from him. Her long hair stuck to her face and throat, strangling her. On her hands and knees, she peered down at him again, staring at the familiar lips, nose, forehead.

But this *couldn't* be the same boy. He was too old.

"Leo?" Her voice trembled, but there was no anger in it, only dismay, and admiration which she was now feeling for the first time in her life.

All thoughts of murder forgotten, she reached out one shaking hand and combed the silken bangs away from his fevered forehead. His breath fanned warm against her wrist as her robot guards, a bit late, finally entered the room.

# Chapter Fourteen

Scimitar was older than the others, never yielded to August who had superiority, ignored the hologram Free World commanders who came to cajole, plan, order, and kept his smiles for the privacy of his room when he was alone.

Kittin had glimpsed him over the past few days, skulking around, but she never spoke to him. She noticed his differences, as much as she noticed that August drooled and Lily never met anyone's eyes. Some of those differences were intriguing. While everyone else ranged in age from nine to nineteen, Scimitar looked at least forty, shaggy hair already gone silver, eyes framed by nets of lines. Most talents faded with age. By the time they were thirty, nearly all soldiers in the Army were retired by the Controllers. Talents peaked in the teen years.

Another aspect of the man that interested her was his telepathy. She had decided that of all the psychic talents, telepathy would be the most exciting, and the most terrifying. What would it be like to know always another's secrets and fantasies, to live in a world bombarded by contradictory voices and thoughts?

One evening, quite unexpectedly, Scimitar spoke to Kittin. "You should never have touched him." His voice was deep, his eyes hard blue rocks. He sat on the floor of the Tower's mess hall, tinkering with a holovid, a glass of something brown and repulsive balanced between his bent, bony knees.

"He grabbed me." Kittin was eating dinner. She tried not to show surprise that he'd even spoken to her. She pushed the pasty mass of her food around on her plate. Always she ate alone. The others didn't like to be around her. But tonight she'd found Scimitar still occupying the room when she'd entered for her meal.

Only two days had passed since Leo had been taken from the dome and hidden away in a medical ward in the south wing of the Tower. Two days, and already everyone seemed to know more about what had happened that night than Kittin.

"August says –"

"I don't care what August says! He's a liar!" Her appetite gone now, Kittin pushed the plate away. Immediately, a robot came and removed it from the table. The lights dimmed, a polite reminder for them to leave the room since their business there was done.

" – he's your false lover and they promised you could kill him," Scimitar finished as though he hadn't heard her.

Kittin watched Scimitar absently switch the holovid from winter landscape to summer landscape with one hand, swirl the brown liquid in his glass with the other. Then he lifted the glass to his thin, unsmiling lips and drank the entire contents without taking a breath. He licked the edges of his mouth, gazed up at her and said: "I'd like to help you."

"Help me?"

"Kill him. Yes?" His eyebrows, slim silver crescents, lifted. His mouth remained a thin, straight line.

"I don't even know if it's him. It looks like him. But he's different, older."

"It's him," Scimitar said, nodding.

"But how? He was a boy before...before – "

"What is time to a race of machines who can technologically harness psychic powers, travel the span of years in minutes?"

"You mean, there is such a thing as time travel?"

"Oh, Kittin. You aren't very intelligent, are you? How else do you think August sees into the future?" He stood, long legs unfolding to reveal abnormal height. Scimitar was all arms and legs, a giant of a man, his head barely scraping the tops of door thresholds. He did not defer to anyone or anything, including contemporary fashion. He wore white cloth, drawstring trousers gathered at the waist and ankles. His black shirt, unornamented, was a simple pullover made of light plastic. He was, like everyone else in the Tower, too thin except for a slight paunch at his stomach. If Kittin had been a normal girl, she might have thought him attractive despite his ignorance of modern styles.

"I thought August only saw possible futures. He's not a time traveler. Not really."

"The future can be changed." He handed his empty glass to a waiting robot. "Time may be solid, but it isn't inflexible. If August can see that, then who's to say he's not a time traveler?"

"Then is Leo a time traveler? From the future? Because the first time I met him he was older than me. The second, younger. Now, again, he's older."

"Maybe." Scimitar stood on the other side of the table looking down at her.

"But where else could he be from? It explains a lot. If the spychiatrists travel time, they could've picked him because he was talented, then brought him here to use. That's why everyone wants him! Our side, too! He must be very powerful," she exclaimed. "More powerful than I ever imagined!"

"Don't think too hard, child. It hurts." He put a hand to the side of his head. Silver hair twinkled against his fingers.

For a moment, Kittin thought he was teasing her again. Then she realized she was sending. Though Scimitar was mainly a projecting telepath, he could also receive signals if they were strong. Blinding signals emanated from Kittin naturally.

"So why do you want to kill him?" Kittin asked, meeting the chipped blue of his eyes. Scimitar could kill her right now if he wanted, with a single knife-thought. But she wasn't at all afraid.

"It might be fun." He didn't smile, didn't look away.

"You could do it now." Distance didn't hinder killer telepaths if they had clear pictures of their subjects. She'd been told Scimitar could murder without moving a muscle.

Scimitar shook his head. "Maybe. But he's strong, might even be able to project back." He shook his head. "No, there are much more interesting conventional instruments of death to employ."

She hunched her shoulders. "Such as?"

He bunched his fingers into fists, held them up. "These for one."

"Doesn't physical contact scare you? All of you are afraid to touch me; how can you think of touching him? He's the one who contaminated me."

"If you were that dangerous to the rest of us, you'd be quarantined. Don't you get it yet, Kittin? You're locked up because you're a time-bomb waiting to go off. I could handle you. All of us here are far more dangerous to you than you are to us. But not the rest of the World. They're scared. Not of catching those little nano-germ machines of yours, but of you. You're infection is a tool for the enemy and you could be used at any time for who knows what."

She hadn't known that. No one had ever told her that. August had hinted, but she thought he'd lied. "You're lying."

Scimitar's mouth curved down. His eyes flickered, looking her over. "And what would I have to gain by lying?"

"Well, if it's true, how did Leo infect me then? That first time I was only six."

"I don't know. I wasn't there. Did he touch you physically? He probably had the nano-stuff all over him. One touch of his hand would do it."

She remembered the boy taking her hand, running through the trees with him, the wind that night blowing soft from the south. Her eyes stung, but she refused to look away. "You haven't answered my question," she said.

Scimitar placed his hands palms down on the table and leaned toward her. "Oh? What's that?"

"Why do *you* want to kill him?"

"Because you do." He put a hand to his head melodramatically. "And your thoughts infect me."

"No. That's not it." Now he *was* playing with her.

He blinked, lips a fine line. "And because telepathy with someone who's dying is the ultimate kick. You see? Yes?"

"Well, I haven't decided." Kittin got up, pushing back her chair. What was she saying? A few days ago she'd wanted Leo dead. Dead beyond redemption. Gone from the existence of the universe. "Besides, I don't even believe half of what you say. You're as bad as August. Crazy."

"I can prove it," Scimitar said, moving around the table, approaching her.

"Prove what?" He was too close now. Teasing her again.

"About you infecting others. It's propaganda, so you won't be able to endanger anyone with your crazy inner programming."

"Bodily fluids – " Kittin began.

"No." He shook his head, reached out and with one large hand cupped her chin. "No. They just want everyone to believe that."

Kittin froze. His dry warmth startled her. Long fingers traveled under her chin, down her exposed neck and to her shoulder. Looking up at him, she felt even more vulnerable.

"You see?" he said. "You can't infect me. Oh, they could

turn on those little machines inside you right now, make you happy, sad, take pictures, turn you into a killer, but those little minnies stay inside you. They've conformed to you, no one else. The nano-bugs are part of you now. And that scares people. Since most people are such sentimental types in the World, they sent you away instead of killing you. And now you're here because they found another use for you. But that's finished, too. I wonder." He licked his lips delicately. "I wonder what will happen to little Kittin now? Now that your value is used up, where will you go next, what will you be?" His voice was low, hypnotic.

Kittin listened to his speech as best she could, but his hand on her shoulder distracted her. The warmth penetrated through skin and muscle. Something inside her chest broke and quivered.

"You're a ship in a bottle, aren't you? Beautiful, sleek, proud – "

Kittin shook her head, backed up a step. "Stop."

"Why?" His hand fell away.

"You're scaring me. I– I don't want to go back. They'll put me in a blank room again. I don't want to go."

"They won't let you stay here." He stepped forward, touched her shoulder again.

"Stop."

"Ever had sex with a telepath?"

Kittin frowned. "You–you're crazy. You can't! You wouldn't! Not with me!"

"I said I could prove half of what I told you. I said you aren't infectious. I'll prove it."

If he had smiled at least once, or softened his gaze, Kittin might have gone with him. But he was so unbending.

She slapped his hand away and headed for the door. "Leave me alone! I don't need your help. I don't need anyone's."

"They'll send you back, then."

"They'll send me back anyway!" she replied, stopping at the door.

"Not if I told them you were mine."

"What?" Shocked, she turned, hand on the doorknob.

"They wouldn't send you away if you were, say...my wife. They couldn't send you away. Away from Leo. Back to the blank room."

What was he saying? Offering? Her mind flooded with images of the two of them together in every way. Hers or his? Could she never be her own self, even in this? Could she never decide for herself who she wanted, what she wanted? Was Scimitar going to control her now, too?

She shook her head to clear it, surprised she could still think. "No." The word was her own. No one had made her say it. But she hesitated, glancing around the dining area, everywhere but at Scimitar, who loomed like a giant, silver snow-capped, tall as the door frame she stood under. She still felt his warm hand on her chin, her neck, her shoulder. Something inside her liked the feel. If these were her own reactions, still they confused her. "No," she said again, a whisper.

"Then a rapist goes free. And you go back to the lunatic fringe," he said softly. Still, he didn't smile.

Kittin looked away. "I –"

"Think about it, Kittin." His voice was low, soft, almost friendly. But not smiling.

His offer was for the wrong reasons. Or, perhaps, her rejection of him was. Was that why it hurt?

Everything blurred again. "I have to go."

And she was running down the triangular corridor that led to her room with the sparkle-walls, her room which was as far away from the World as she could get.

## Part VII - The Walled City (parallel Earth)

## Chapter Fifteen

Two young men wrestled on a pale, carpeted floor. One wore white, cotton briefs and nothing more. The other had on black jeans, gold leather cowboy boots, and a crisp, button-down white shirt with sharp collars, the sleeves ripped out.

The room, bathed in the clean light of a halogen lamp and the dimmer blue glow of a bubbling fish tank, looked warm, secure. Black and white and pink swaths of pillows checkered the floor near a low glass coffee table. The men appeared to be involved in a serious competition. The one in the underwear was losing as Cowboy Boots straddled his hips and pushed him flat on his back. He held Underwear's wrists pressed against his naked chest while he bucked, trying to throw him off.

Finally, Underwear toppled Cowboy and they tussled, rolling toward a pile of pillows. Cowboy picked up a pillow and started banging it against Underwear's back. They both collapsed, laughing, side by side. Underwear's chest gleamed with sweat. Cowboy's long bangs stuck to his forehead.

When their breathing evened, Underwear said, "I won."

Cowboy replied, very softly, "The fuck you did."

"I did. I'm strongest."

"I had you pinned and you know it."

"Not for long. I got away."

"You're full of shit."

And the tussle began anew. Underwear went for Cowboy's crotch. Cowboy yelped, "Yikes!" and rolled away, coming up to grab Underwear's upper torso in a bear hug. Their heads knocked together and both howled, letting go and falling onto their backs again on the thick carpet.

"Sorry," Underwear said, laughing again.

"You did that on purpose." Cowboy rolled to face him, put his hand to his head.

"Did not. Quit whining." Underwear grinned, staring up at nothing, or perhaps the ceiling which glittered with new acoustic bumps. "What'll we do tonight?"

Cowboy shrugged.

"We have money now, over three hundred grand left and

always gathering interest. Love you, Mommy. Love you, Daddy. Name your poison."

"Don't talk like that. I hate it. You know that." Cowboy chewed on his lips, leaving them wet and shiny. "But if we go out, make sure there's alcohol around so I can dim my misery."

Underwear smacked him on the thigh. "You're not miserable. You just think you are. You enjoy it."

"Shut up."

"Okay," Underwear said. "We'll go out, get you something to drink and me a pretty girlfriend."

Cowboy scowled.

"Hey," Underwear said. "I do like girls, you know." He rose on one elbow, leaned over Cowboy and kissed him lightly. "You know," he said again, softer.

"Of course I know," Cowboy replied, rolling his eyes. "The question is do they like you?"

"That is the question, now, isn't it?" Underwear replied. He leaned closer to Cowboy again; their cheekbones touched. Arms twined in a loose embrace.

Their hair, both with the same russet and gold and mahogany autumn shades, ran together over the pillows.

~

Ashao squinted at the projected images his spychiatrist was sending back to him. The boys wrestled on his one blank, vinyl wall. "Which one of you is Leo?" he asked out loud. He had never expected there would be two of him.

But it didn't matter if he couldn't tell Leo from his brother. Leo was marked. Plus, the spychiatrists these days automatically knew who was who.

Fascinated, Ashao watched scenes from the twins' lives as the now specially programmed spychiatrist tracked them through time. Ashao could pick any year and the multi-legged metal machine would go there and send back images. Ashao's spychiatrist never touched Leo or his brother Zack, but it watched. And Ashao watched:

Leo and Zack running through the sands and Joshua trees of their high desert native land.

Studying music, math, literature in strangely effective

public schools.

Riding bicycles down empty dirt roads, their bikes painted silver with tough-treads, their bikes which Ashao envied.

Sharing birthdays – always two cakes, one chocolate, one lemon – and Christmases beneath gilt-decorated pine trees with their parents.

Discovering their bizarre twin compatibility.

Leaving home at sixteen for the wilds of a strange city.

Zack hustling to make enough money to buy bread, drugs, beer and shelter.

Shy Leo popping out of the back seat of a stranger's car without even knowing his own teleportation talent was responsible.

Leo locking himself in the trailer for days after learning about the death of their parents.

Zack not coming home for days after learning of the death of their parents.

And now, the scene before him, of them turning twenty-one and legally accepting their inheritance: no more hunger, no more torn jackets on cold nights, no more rent collectors taking Zack out behind the trailer to collect the 'late fee', no more huddling under thin blankets in dark rooms that didn't have heat in the winter, no more hustling to oily men who stole Zack's attentions and never paid, no more no more no more.

It took less than a week for him to get to know the brothers through stolen moments of their lives. Their entire existence flickered like a holofilm he could play any part of. As long as Stannos' spychiatrist interfered with Leo's life, that film remained in flux, changing as Leo incurred mental manipulations through various phases of his life. Leo was used most prominently in his teens, but during the week Ashao visited the lives of the twins, Stannos' spychiatrist had not made further use of him. Therefore, the film stood solid, Zack and Leo's current quantum futures mapped out (uninterrupted by further abductions) to include later careers in bartending, radio, music, writing and acting.

Much as he wanted to meet them and talk to them in person, Ashao respected the law proclaiming that 'tools' of the Ignorant Army must never be interfered with by anyone for any reason. But it was difficult for him to watch them suffer when they were so young; it was torture not to interfere.

Soon Ashao became able to distinguish which twin was which. As he studied them, he saw that they really didn't look identical at all. Zack's face drew longer lines; he parted his hair on the left, worried less and ate more which made his body fuller. Leo had the triangular markings on his lower abdomen, of course, and parted his hair on the right. His body was nervous thin, his hair a shade darker, his skin a shade lighter.

At first, Ashao considered his curiosity of the twins' lives a mere symptom of his eternal boredom. They were his new toys, their lives his entertainment. He didn't think about what he did with his spychiatrist; he wasn't concerned with the other end of the picture, only his side, only his own tedious life with the insane war going on outside his walls. A war that would some day include him at the controls.

Then one morning, as he watched Leo and Zack argue over simple chores after a large party they'd thrown the previous night; watched as Zack, always the aggressor, tried to placate an agitated Leo by pushing him up against the kitchen counter and biting him playfully on the neck, Leo tensed, his eyes opening wide. "Stop!" He pushed Zack hard, and Zack slipped against the black and white floor tiling, nearly fell.

"What?" Surprise. Hurt knotting the muscles between his eyebrows.

Leo looked around the kitchen, across the bar to the living room. "It's just – I don't know. Something feels wrong."

"Huh?"

"I just got this feeling, sorta."

"What feeling?" Zack rubbed his lips, squinting at Leo askance.

"Like we're being watched."

Ashao jerked back, yelped as his anise tea sloshed in its cup, spilling onto his fingers. It was impossible that Leo could know he really was being watched. Impossible.

His fingers burned as he stared at the wall. He still clutched his hot cup of tea, mesmerized by the scene.

Leo, dark eyes unblinking, turned directly toward Ashao. Their eyes met, yet Leo, thousands of universes away, distance washed by time rivers and space and dimensional barriers, couldn't possibly see him. Could he?

The eyes – so like those only a week ago when the fifteen year-old Leo had looked up at him from his cage of glass in the War Room, pine needles tangled in the rust colors of his hair – pulled him down into the vacuum of bright brown, into the soul of a boy who was lost between worlds, beyond the zenith of lighted void. For that moment, their ids touched.

For that moment, Ashao wondered if everything the Controllers were doing – everything he himself was doing with his own spychiatrist – was somehow incredibly wrong. Wrong enough to be considered evil. Evil enough to be indefensible. Unforgivable.

"We *are* being watched," Leo whispered.

Zack followed his gaze, just missing Ashao's, his stare floating over Ashao's shoulder. "How do you know?"

"I can feel it," he replied. "Can't you?"

The younger twin shook his head, but continued to stare,with Leo through the wall, through time and outer realms.

Ashao, mouth open, realized right then that Leo had far greater powers than Stannos or the other Controllers probably knew. And if they did know, Ashao understood that what few freedoms Leo had left to him would be taken away. He might never see Zack or his Earth again.

Ashao had never experienced guilt before, or torn loyalty. Now he wasn't sure what to do. He was compelled to tell his father, yet horrified at what might happen to Leo as a result. But perhaps Stannos already knew, and had chosen to give Leo his life as long as he served the Ignorant Army when needed. Ashao doubted it, but he hoped.

In the meantime, he could hint around, find out how much his father and the other Controllers knew, measure the importance of his knowledge against the importance of the cause and then decide to tell or keep secret the extent of Leo's talents.

"It's me they want," Leo said. "I'm not paranoid, Zack." He still stared at Ashao. "I can almost see who they are, almost taste what they want."

"But Leo," Zack protested. "It's been so quiet lately. You haven't had nightmares, no black outs –"

"That doesn't mean anything. They're waiting. I don't know why; I don't know who. But they're waiting. I know."

Ashao's skin prickled.

Finally, Leo looked away. "I can't stand it! I'm going out."

Ashao knew 'out' meant drinking, forgetting.

He bowed his head, eyes only for his cup of weak green, anise tea, and thought about what a bit of alcohol added to the hot beverage might do for him as well. But alcohol was illegal in The Walled City.

With a remote keypad, Ashao ordered his spychiatrist, ensconced in the walls and plumbing of the twins' apartment building, to quit transmitting. He stared for a long time at the blank vinyl, his tea growing cold, his burns aching.

Finally, he got up, dressed himself, and went off in search of Stannos. He didn't know what he was going to do, but he thought that seeing his father first might help him decide.

The secret he shared with Leo filled him with a purpose he'd never felt before.

~

Ashao walked past guards whose breaths fogged the unheated air of the halls, guards who guarded cold air, brick walls, and the hot heart of The Walled City's offense/defense. With the electronic doors that surveyed and questioned all who might pass, with the guarded elevator that swept Controllers to the tower containing the War Room, Ashao saw the hall guards as redundant. But they were there, unremarkable in their armored stances, never moving, never seeing anything but the occasional traverse of Ashao through the spreading, syrupy corridor light, or perhaps they saw shadows of ghosts who once inhabited the structure before the war, ancestors who left the place to the future, to Stannos and his force of Controllers.

Ashao wondered if spychiatrists could be programmed to enter the past of his own world, to bring back dead relatives, inhabitants of the realm who had long ago vanished into the dark waters of another existence. Life before life. Life after death. He believed in it, yet had never seen proof.

But spychiatrists could only delve into the times and worlds of other universes. Stannos had told him their own universal history remained inviolate, according to law, according to some scientific decree that demanded self-preservation of one's own species. The spychiatrists had been programmed with a so-called fail-safe mechanism that prevented them from breaching their own time-space continuum. Therefore no time-tampering could be implemented within one's own land. But reprogramming was always possible. And so there was another law stating the penalty for that was death.

To Ashao, that meant there was indeed no place the spychiatrist couldn't go. Except, of course, through the Free World's defenses, for they had devised a technology that scrambled spychiatrist programming, and kept them away. But that was in current time. Spychiatrists could exist and travel through past and future World-space. Couldn't they?

But that was less his concern right now, than the secrets of Leo and his work with the Ignorant Army.

Ashao headed straight for the War Room, his identity good enough to get him through to the elevator and beyond unquestioned.

Inside, the screams of the test subjects being experimented on filled the chamber. Ashao smelled antiseptic mixed with hot blood, the oily scent of machines, sharp fear and salt despair. Today the glass between the Controllers and the Ignorant Army soldiers in the rooms below seemed unclean, dirtied with smeared reflections and images of torture and pain. He could ignore it easily until he thought of Leo and Zack. Leo's secret fluttered inside him, uneasy. But there was a war on they had to win. That was what mattered. They were all unavoidable casualties of war.

Still, the image of Leo's eyes pulled him down, down –

The first Controller looked completely unfamiliar to Ashao. He sat at monitors which beeped and flashed, the lights glowing red, amber, sea-green. In the room below, a spychiatrist raped an older woman with one of its five clawed hands. Her fingernails were ripped and bloody from trying to fight it off her. She was past screams, her eyes rolled back, staring dully, her exposed genitals reddened and chapped from the unnatural invasion.

The Controller showed no emotion as he watched the scene below. Ashao tasted bile, but hid his true reaction as he addressed the man. "My father, is he here?"

Without looking up, the Controller asked, "Who is your father, child?"

"Stannos."

"Of course. No, he isn't here."

"Do you know where I can find him?" In the next chamber, a man howled, then sobbed. Ashao pretended not to hear it. He told himself the bright lights were making him blink so rapidly.

"He went back to his rooms, I believe. I'm sure he'll return if you wish to wait for him here. I understand he wants you to inherit all this one day." Now the Controller swiveled to face him. His eyes were stone, his countenance robotic. Something about him wasn't normal, but Ashao couldn't place it. "I could teach you a few things while you wait. Interested?"

He took a deep breath. "Thank you."

"You see the woman down there, correct?"

Ashao nodded, gritting his teeth.

"When she is tortured in this manner, her telekinetic abilities surface with great speed. Now watch the main monitor."

Ashao glanced at a large screen in the center of the room. There was a small farm nestled in a valley of green rolling hills. The sky looked impossibly blue. Some kind of machine appeared to be tilling a giant square of ground. As the image clarified and the machine grew closer, Ashao could see that a man stood beside it, working the flashing controls. Sharp metal plumes dug at the earth, breaking it up, softening it.

"There is a male in the next chamber over projecting that image," the Controller explained. "This is how we wage our war sometimes. Giving them one casualty at a time. It drives them crazy. Soon, no one outside these walls will ever feel safe. They'll tire of it and surrender."

"Is that Stannos' strategy?"

"Yes, though he enjoys much more forceful battles usually, utilizing many tools at once to hassle the World's defenses." The Controller paused to check something on his panel. The woman in the room below continued to squirm and cry out. Blood slicked the table on which she lay. "Now watch. She's nearly ready." He indicated the monitor.

Ashao stared. He heard the Controller say, "Now! Project into the image!" On the monitor, the clear air suddenly sparkled with green lights. The lights surrounded the man's face. Suddenly, he yelled in pain and grabbed his head.

"What –" Ashao began, but the Controller motioned for his silence.

On the screen, the man staggered and bellowed. His bio-pacer seemed to glow red as it tried, then failed to absorb the new impulses from the man's brain. He looked to be about 45, with receding blond hair. The sun had burned his face a leathery red- brown. Now his face darkened in pain, turning redder. He listed to one side, lurched toward the machine, then before Ashao knew what was happening, stepped directly in the path of the tilling machine's blades. Blood, skin and bone whipped through the air. The machine, which should have had a fail-safe mechanism, did not stop or seem to notice that a human had gotten in its path.

For a moment, Ashao couldn't breathe. The incident had happened so quickly that his mind instantly denied what it had just seen. Then he was shaking inside, his heart thundering in shock.

"Impressive, eh?" the Controller said, turning to look at him. "With the biopacers, we can't kill 'em with a thought, but we can direct them into dangerous situations."

Ashao swallowed hard, sweat breaking out on his back. "Quite impressive," he managed, wondering if the Controller noticed his discomfort.

"Would you like to see more?"

"More?" Ashao forced a nervous laugh. "Of course, but I really don't have the time. I must see my father about something. It's rather urgent."

"Soon, then," he replied. "It's nice to see you expressing an interest at such an early age." He didn't smile, and Ashao didn't expect him to. But underneath the deep tan of his face, the crowsfeet, and frown lines, Ashao thought he saw rough sadness, an unhoned quality of grief untapped. The Controller turned back to his console and the now weeping woman in the glass room below.

As he left the War Room, he saw the image on the main monitor change from the serene farmland to a wasteland image on the Edge. A small gang was making its way across the land, using sand-sleds to haul their belongings. He didn't care to know what might happen next and silently hoped that they'd win the war soon before they had to draft more ignorant volunteers, before they had to hurt Leo like this again. Nothing in his life would have made him think this way before, but now he'd seen Leo, now he felt a strange connection to someone, a kinship never before experienced without benefit of the fantasy-inducing hemi-synch that gave him nothing but lies. But this was real. His feelings, Leo, the twin Zack, Leo's secret. He felt more alive than ever. And never less bored.

~

The guards didn't even blink as he approached Stannos' rooms. Opulence was a word for hedonists who took their pleasures without concern for consequences. The word fit Stannos well, and Ashao had learned similar behaviors, though he was still young and hesitant in expressing himself with the same gaudy glory of his father.

Strung beads of gold, platinum and crystal spread across the threshold of the huge door in waves of dark light, refracted, encased. As Ashao parted the waves, a breath of warm wind from the inner sanctum coiled around him. A jade sculpture of a muzzled beast with a man's muscular arms and legs guarded the foyer. Incense laced the air: sandalwood, thick almond, a hint of jasmine. Stannos always mixed scents, confusing his guests on purpose with his unpredictable humor and bad taste.

Dark fur lined the floor, surrounded squares of white marble set in a line, each one spaced the length of an average stride. These 'stepping stones' led to an inner garden of ivy and fern cloistering a burbling pond. A miniature waterfall frothed along mica-flecked rocks and mossy tile mosaics of mythical merpeople and ancient fish. The smell here was humid, of growing things, of oldness. Garibaldi goldfish, fat as Ashao's two fists put together, glided through the green-shadowed shallows. When Ashao was little he would sit on the banks of the pond dangling his feet in the foamy water and let the fish softly kiss his toes. Once, he took off his clothes and waded on his hands and knees over the slippery tiles and through the sputtering water. The frightened fish had darted beneath underwater rocks, and the pond grew murky. Stannos had yanked him out by the hair, admonishing him for invading the self-contained little world. Ashao had kicked his father in the shin and run through the long corridors, naked and wet, back to his rooms, hiding furtive, angry tears. They never spoke further of the incident.

Now Ashao watched the fish shimmer through crystal wavelets and remembered how good it had felt to touch that life. How the quicksilver pulse of the carp and the pool had swirled through him. How cool and silent and compact everything was here in the land of mosaic mermaids and mermen somersaulting on the floor of the fishpond.

The hard rock walls of the indoor garden wavered in artificial sea-light. Ashao stepped through overgrown fronds and hanging creepers, following the white stepping stones further into his father's abode.

The incense again tangled the air in a mixture of heavy, smoky scents. He breathed shallow, letting the scents collect on the sides of his tongue and deep in his nose.

The room beyond was darkened, a sitting room, a breakfast nook. To the left was a study/library. Beyond that, to the right, golden light fused with shadow revealing a larger room: Stannos' bed chamber. The incense was coming from there.

Ashao didn't want to intrude and suspected his father was not alone. He moved forward through shade toward the paler glow, deciding to make sure. He wore paper boots, fur-lined, and his step whispered against the deeper fur carpeting and tile stepping stones. He could have been a ghost.

Inside the room, low voices carried. Ashao peeked through the diamond-shaped door frame and saw Stannos, naked on his knees on the mattress of his massive bed, bent toward the smaller, supine form of a woman. His body, though large, was muscular, dark. His skin gleamed. The be-ribboned braid he wore trailed down his back, pointing suggestively to the crease of his buttocks. His shaved head, except for the patch of hair on top that formed the long braid, made him seem even more naked.

A short laugh rustled up from the bed. Stannos moved

aside, turned so that he leaned back on his hips and hands in profile to the door. His long erection swayed, and the slim form on the bed sat up, cupped it in her hands and bent, her dark head moving down between his legs.

Ashao swallowed a sudden gasp. The woman, whose dark, close-cropped curls Stannos stroked, who moaned as she made love to Stannos' quivering body, whose lean hips and back shone like glazed milk chocolate against the stark, snowy sheet, was his own first contact – the one quick kiss still wet on his lips – his own some time friend whom he thought he'd sent back to her boyfriend, her life, her Earth. *Lisa.*

He watched as Stannos trembled, as Stannos pulled away from her, and turned her onto her stomach. Then, lifting her hips with his giant hands, his organ pushed at the dark space between her legs, impaling her from behind.

Ashao stepped back, fingers curving, breath caught. The bottoms of his eyelids felt heavy, warm. His throat was dry and tight. For a moment, he couldn't move, couldn't see, couldn't think.

The shadows behind him caught his arms, neck, legs. The splashing sound of the pond, and the slick sound of his father's rough mating mixed, the drum of it ringing in his ears, ringing deeper inside his mind where something shriveled, appalled at this act, this betrayal.

He backed up, turned and slipped through the dark, the ivy ropes catching in his hair. His feet slid over the fur, the marble stepping stones. The jade beast sculpture grinned at him. The beads at the door tangled around his thighs and shoulders. One pulled off and scattered flashing silver and amber balls on the floor of the corridor. They bounced and rolled, the staccato sound of an unwinding cricket. Ashao tripped over some, fell to his knees, skinning one, then was up and running again, the pain ignored.

The guards watched him but never moved. He was simply the fifteen year old boy of the Head Controller. Nothing to worry about. Their haunted eyes followed him as he tumbled by, arms flailing, paper shoes awkward for running. The balls of his feet pounded the floor and he came around one corner too fast, fell again. His hip smacked ground, began to throb as he scrambled, slower now, to his feet and jogged the rest of the way to his rooms.

When he was safely inside his own domain, he slammed the large, outside door, locked it, and plunged into the center of his main room. His breath came fast; his fists were still clenched. Thin tears lined his sharp cheeks. He scrubbed at his face with the back of his wrist and went to the front of the glass-windowed chamber where the remote for his spychiatrist sat. Picking it up, he flicked it on. Bloody light bathed his still-damp face.

"Spychiatrist," he said hoarsely.

Another red light flashed, listening.

"I want Leo. And I want that girl I saw in the War Room the other day. The one my father favors. The girl who can read with her eyes closed, who can make objects move with her mind. I want to take her away from him the way he took Lisa! Make her meet Leo. Make them come together in one room where we can bring them here all at once. And Zack, too. I want Zack, too. I don't care how long it takes, but make it happen. I don't care if they're older or what. I don't care if it takes years of their time."

He reached up to scratch at his temple, his tongue licking his lower lip. Ordinarily, the spychiatrist would not be able to obey his orders. Its prime order was not to disturb the 'tools' unless ordered by an official Controller. But Ashao had reprogrammed his spychiatrist the day he'd seen Leo. He never imagined the death sentence for doing so might ever apply to him. He was, after all, heir to all the spychiatrists. In order to observe Leo and Zack, he'd had to do a lot of reworking on the spychiatrist's inner motivational programming. He'd had all the knowledge, however. His father had taught him to take over, so knowledge that might be considered dangerous in the hands of the wrong person was not forbidden to him.

He addressed the spychiatrist again. "While carrying out these orders, do not let the War Room spychiatrists detect you. If they do, identify yourself as mine, that you're there for observation purposes only. Stannos is not getting Leo if I can help it. Or that little lover girl of his. We'll wage our own little war. I don't care if he dies because of it. I hate him!"

He threw the remote on the floor where the pillows absorbed most of the impact, then sat, knees bent, chin resting on them. His fur-lined paper shirt wrinkled against his chest. His long bangs stuck to his still wet eyes.

"I hate him!" he hissed again.

The room softly absorbed his rage.

## Chapter Sixteen

The vestibule between the bedroom and the back fire exit had been silent for over a year. Darkness clung to the ceiling and walls. Dust swept over metal apparatus like dull glitter. The stuffy scent of unused air filled the chamber.

Now the dark scattered. Light sliced the gloom, the arian dust, the dark metal, making it brighten, flicker. Ashao stepped inside, coughed roughly, and walked toward the teacher. It moved slowly, as though wakening from a depthless sleep. Dust circled metal limbs; light danced in spirals over soft curves, graceful planes. Blue lights, placed on a flat surface resembling a face regarded him like real eyes.

"Ashao, why have you returned?" The feminine voice was his mother's, programmed into the teacher when he was two years old, just before she died.

"Teacher," he said softly. He took a deep breath. The machine was patient. "May I come into you again?"

"Of course, but I have nothing more to teach you." No mouth moved to form the words. The voice filled the room with a more disembodied presence.

"I don't care. Give me any old lesson. I just want to concentrate on something...anything." He had learned all Walled City required adolescent studies by the time he was fourteen. Sometimes he still missed the four hours a day he used to spend inside his teacher. Today was the first time he'd sought 'her' – he thought of her as a form of his mother – since he'd graduated with honors.

Metal arms spread wide. A small hatch opened below the flat plate that was so like a face. "Come, child."

Ashao stepped up to the hatch, ducked to enter, and found himself instantly encased in the teacher's soft, velvet womb. He reclined as the velvet molded to his body, and to whatever position he chose to take. The walls and curved ceiling of the womb lit up – blue to pink to yellow – all around him waiting for commands. Programmed into this teacher were children's lessons, and he'd already seen and completed them all, but he didn't care. He asked for some of his last lessons to be repeated, and occupied hours redoing math problems, physics equations, watching a historical film, reading a play with the teacher taking on various character roles.

After each lesson, the machine said, "You are done for the day, you may leave."

But Ashao overrode her programming and asked for more. He eventually fell asleep inside her, the velvet conforming to his sprawled, silent form.

When he woke up, he felt warm and safe, set apart from the rest of the world, set aside. He liked that feeling.

"You are done for the day, you may leave," the teacher said.

Ashao sat up, staring at the bright pinkblueyellow walls. "Please talk to me."

"What subject, dear?"

"I don't understand why people have to hurt other people."

The system hummed, then went quiet. For a moment, Ashao thought it wouldn't answer. Then it said: "The subject for that question, dear, is ethics and morals. I am to direct you to your father for that and related questions."

Ashao's fists clenched. "I hate my father!"

"Your father and your mother programmed me," the teacher said.

"I know that. I just wish I could talk to my mother instead."

"Your mother no longer exists in this world of reference." A short pause. "I am sorry."

"Can't you talk to me?"

"My psychological programming is limited. I am not capable of independent thought. However, what information I have is all available to you. Dear Ashao, I can say that your mother did wish she could leave you more, that she could have seen you grow and mature. Many of her thoughts have been written into my programming. So I shall begin by asking you: Why do you hate your father?"

Quick images: Stannos moving over Lisa, his nude body huge, obscene in a way Ashao had never noticed before. Stannos calmly watching his human 'tools' being tortured, his face showing no mercy, no empathy, no pain. Stannos' opulent tastes, his flashy furs and ribbons, his giant sea of a bed. He remembered both fearing and admiring the man.

Now, at fifteen, his own emotions were beginning to surface, emotions he'd never acknowledged before, emotions he never even knew he had. And he realized he didn't like his father, or anything his father did.

"First of all," Ashao began, "he wants me to follow in his business, work in the War Room as a controller and eventually take over for him. That is, if we don't soon win the war."

"A trade to be proud of. What is the problem?" the teacher asked.

"I don't think I like it."

"What exactly do you not like?"

"The war. I don't want to have anything to do with it."

"And yet you are a citizen of The Walled City and it is your duty to fulfill obligations cast upon you as a result of the war."

"And if I disagree?" Ashao asked slowly.

"You cannot disagree."

"I do."

"You cannot. Must not. Something must be wrong with you. If you simply tell your father your problems, he can repair the disagreement in your mind quite easily. You will then wish to fulfill your obligations as all good citizens must. And you will enjoy doing so."

Ashao recoiled. "Something is wrong with me? Really?" He thought of the spychiatrists and trembled.

"That is, of course, my non-human assessment. It will remain for your father to decide if I am correct."

"Will he use a spychiatrist on me?"

"That would be the most humane treatment, dear."

"B – but I don't want to be corrected that way."

"I am sure he will give you your choice of method. Your father is a good man. You must go to him and speak of this."

Slowly, Ashao shook his head. Tears welled in his eyes again, brimming on still raw, chapped skin. "I'm afraid."

"What of, child? Nothing can harm you."

Ashao's fur-lined paper sleeve pressed against his brow. The edges soaked up his tears. "I don't know," he breathed. "I don't know."

"You are troubled now only because you are not functioning properly. Go to your father. He will remove the

154

pain. Ashao, dear, why would you willingly continue to feel this pain when something can be done for it?"

"I can't think." The pastel hues on the teacher's womb-walls spun, making him feel sick. His mind seemed to separate from his body, falling.

"Wrong-thinking is terrorizing you, blocking you. Do you understand, Ashao? Do you? Do you?"

"No."

"Do you?" It was as if the machine were stuck, repeating the phrase in the same tone over and over. "Do you?"

"Shut up!"

"Do you?"

"Let me out." He pounded his fists on the hatch. It opened slowly, silently. He stumbled, his knees hitting the floor of the dusty, stale room.

The teacher continued to question him. "Do you understand? Ashao? Do you?" His mother's voice sang the words. The blue eyes on the faceplate seemed to slice into his brain. "Ashao? Answer me. Do you?"

"Shut up!" His knees rubbed the smooth floor, knocking, slipping as he scrambled to his feet. All around him, shadows mocked and swelled. The blue eye-lights shot streams of light, like liquid, penetrating to the wall and leaving behind ephemeral dots, like holes in the surface of the paint. The dots made informal patterns, danced to form circles and triangles and stars.

Ashao's body blocked some of the pattern. He could feel the light on his back, his side, like darts of poison entering him, static needles brushing his back, his neck.

"Stop!" He ran to the entrance of his bedroom, the vestibule still swarming with blue fireflies behind him, and slammed the heavy door shut. With the pressure of his damp palm on the ident-plate, he locked it, wondering if there was any way the machine could contact his father. Or if it even would?

He turned, eyeing the room. Its familiar surroundings comforted him somewhat. The robot mosaic glimmered orange, silver, gold. The bed, a plain of velvet and synthetic fur, was still unmade as he had left it that morning. The pillows bunched in the center, making it appear that a person reclined there, still as death, sleeping the mostly dreamless, healthy slumber of all good citizens of the Walled City.

"It's all right," he said out loud, voice breathy, filled with air held back too long. His body lurched forward and he caught himself on one leg, regaining balance. The heat from the room permeated his fear. His muscles quivered, relaxed. Was it the room? he had to ask himself. Or the electronic signals that transmitted throughout the city? He felt soothed, but not completely relieved. He remembered his father telling him there was something in his brain that caused him to respond only to special stimoceivers. Had that device failed? Could there really be something wrong with him? Could his teacher be correct, and his own fears and paranoias were symptoms of a disease his father could quite easily correct?

He shook his head. No. He never wanted his father to touch him or control him in the way he saw the human tools in the War Room being controlled. The thought caused his stomach and chest to tighten. His hands, the palms still sweating, shook. He felt weak as an infant, and he realized he hadn't eaten in over twenty-four hours.

In the main room, he checked the spychiatrist's chamber. It was empty. The order he'd given yesterday had been complex. He wasn't even sure the spychiatrist could complete it. But he had had to try.

He heated himself prepackaged stew and rice, prepared a pot of tea, a glass of cold chocolate, and ate and drank it all, not caring when bites and drops spilled onto his thick paper cardigan.

After eating, he removed all his clothes and stuffed them in a garbage bin. He relieved himself in his personal toilet, then took a long, scalding shower using generous amounts of soap and shampoo. Everything smelled of spice and sweetness, and he emerged through thick steam, stepped into his drier, and felt his skin heat. The hot wind blew his hair around his face as he combed the tangles.

The fear had subsided. He had decided not to tell Stannos anything. If Stannos didn't know about his anger, his change of heart, he had nothing to fear. If the teacher remained outside human contact, locked behind the anteroom door, he was safe. But how to hide his hatred? How to pretend to be the same son his father thought he was when he had taken

156

him to the War Room?

The anger inside him was a great force. A bubble veering toward a thorn. A fragile crystal fraught with seams of heat. It had a spirit all its own. It could, at any time, betray him. He wanted to hurt things. He wanted to hurt himself. But most of all he wanted to hurt Stannos. He'd been wanting that for a long time, but only now could he identify the desire consciously, and even fantasize enacting it out.

The question posed: Could he really kill? The test of Lisa told him he could, easily, without thought. And yet he hadn't. At that moment, when he'd almost completed his order to the spychiatrist to terminate her existence, he'd hesitated; therefore he couldn't be sure if he were entirely capable. He had changed his mind. Lisa had lived, later to be secretly used by Stannos.

His back teeth ground together. He had his answer now. He had been trained since birth to take over Stannos' role later in life. Yes, he could kill. Not only in his fantasies, not only in his thoughts, but in real life, he could kill. Quite thoroughly. Without mercy.

There was no crime in The Walled City. The psi waves which shot through the city from government controlled stimoceivers worked quite well.

Ashao considered that. And decided that logically, since he had the ability and coldness and anger needed for killing, he did indeed have a different kind of stimoceiver bombarding his personal quarters. This stimoceiver might be some kind of aggressive variation to the government controlled ones. Was that why he had been bored all the time? Was that why he felt so much anger? Perhaps it hadn't failed at all. Perhaps what failed had been his father's assessment that aggression would naturally side with him. Was it aggression, now, that caused Ashao's anger *for* his father? And aggression that led him to thoughts of high treason?

'Your father can fix it,' his teacher had said.

Did that mean his father controlled the stimoceiver, or some other sophisticated device that monitored his room? If so, could Ashao battle it? Could he fight that kind of invisible manipulation? Could a marionette cut its own strings?

Ashao believed he already had.

He stepped out of the drying stall, naked, his body tingling from the myrrh-powdered air that had stripped the water from his skin and hair. He ignored the mirror to his left, hating his thin whiteness, the too-naive look of a teenage boy. As he reached for the knob to his closet, the signaling beep in the glass chamber went off.

His bare feet skidded across fur and pillows and tile as he ran from the changing room to the main room, toppling a chair in his wake. When he got to the glass, he pressed himself against it, staring.

The spychiatrist floated, serene, russet, its lights chasing each other over the oval body like glowing insects. Beneath it lay two people, one male, one female. They were both as naked as Ashao. The female's skin was pinkish; she had long dull hair, was small-breasted, small-hipped. A line of triangles marked her abdomen, disappearing into her pubic hair. The male had skin the color of golden tea. He had two silver rings on one hand, the smallest fingernail long and painted black. His hair pooled the floor about his head, shoulder-length, streaked auburn, rust, rose, leaf. He was older than Ashao knew him, yet still –

*Leo!*

But as his eyes travelled down the man's body, his stomach quavered. No. This was the other one. The twin. The surface of his flat stomach rose and fell, unmarred. His abdomen showed no triangle tattoos, no controller's markings that made him a specimen of great worth.

But, then, where was Leo?

As Ashao watched, the woman moved, groaning. "Ow." She opened her eyes.

"Fuck! Fuck!" Zack said, his voice hushed with fear. His hand groped blindly, bumping wrists with Lacy. Silver rings deflected a rainbow of light. "Lacy!" he hissed, looking up. "What the fuck is that?"

Ashao took a deep breath, then glanced forward. The spychiatrist hovered, un- moving. "Oh no!" Ashao breathed. "Where's Leo? Where's Leo?" His fists tapped the glass as he slumped against it, cheek, shoulder and hip cooling on the smooth exterior.

## Part VIII - Moltenrose Tower (Parallel Earth)

## Chapter Seventeen

Leo gazed through sleep-caked eyes at a blurred, tall form leaning over him. "Zack?" He'd had a dream his brother was calling him. There were luminous stars all around but no light on Zack, and he had sounded as if he were receding.

"I am C-138, how do you feel?" said a voice.

Leo blinked and everything looked golden. "Wha – ?" The form moved out of view. He breathed deep – chest tight, arms aching – and smelled something like a mixture of honey and alcohol. Cold fingers pressed his neck, his shoulder, his stomach. Sudden nausea clutched him and he rolled as bitter fluids stung his throat. Abdominal muscles cramped; his stomach felt as if it were coming up through his lungs. His pulse beat fast and heavy behind his eyes.

"There now, this will make you feel better," said the same voice as something icy stung his side.

He could feel warm air over his skin and realized he lay on something soft, cushioned. He wore no clothes. Cold fingers again, rolling him, pulling soiled cloth away from him, then pushing him back on clean, smooth sheets.

A soft buzzing began at the back of his head. Had he been given some kind of drug? As the buzzing grew, his body relaxed. He tried opening his eyes, but dizziness made them clamp shut.

"But where am I?" he tried to say. He couldn't hear his own voice anymore, and wasn't sure he spoke loud enough to communicate.

He tried to think but thinking exhausted him. Where had he been before he woke here, wherever honey-smelling 'here' was? Home? He saw an image of Zack grinning under a white sheet, a girl beside him... the girl... her name was Kittin? No, Lacy. That was another memory. A kiss under moonlight, a shadowed brook warbling. But it couldn't be. He'd never impulsively kissed a girl before – without Zack's prompting, without Zack's attentive hands first paving the way in their mutual ménages – until Lacy. But there had been that other girl, too. He remembered! Soft pink paper wrapped, like a kid's birthday present, with hair dark as coal. Memories converged. Storm-surrounded. Framed by a green lightning aura. A fur rug beneath him, beneath her where she knelt. And she'd called him by name. He could still hear her musical voice, pitched like an echo, the soft, breathing sound of awe or fear. He remembered pain, a sticky dampness all over he thought might be his own blood. And jade fire – like her aura – crackling along his skin, burning, stinging.

He had thought he was dying.

But now he knew: Something incredible had happened. More memories came. A multi-legged machine had grabbed him and he had slipped away from it as he recognized, instantly, that it had been what had hurt him so many times in the past. There were too many images to comprehend in a linear fashion, but they all placed him beneath the machine's powerful grip, immersed in light and sound he could not describe, the pain sending him flying, sending him on nightmare journeys where he had...had– His stomach convulsed, throat closing as denial set in, turning his thoughts away from knowledge that he had...killed. Maimed. Raped. No! That couldn't have been him!

Now he shivered, felt a soft cover drape over him, heard the same emotionless voice that had asked him how he was feeling. "Sleep now, and you will be fine," it said, too loud, the buzzing in his ears turning to a high-toned ring. Whoever it was who spoke to him had very cold hands which tracked through his long hair, pushing it away from his face.

He wanted to ask where he was, if Zack were all right, if the green fire were real. He wanted to understand it all. The girl in the pink paper robe. The voices commanding him to kill. The machine that meant always an endless agony. Why? But his tongue was numb, his throat dry, still bitter from bile. He could only find strength to curl under the cover and tumble, dreamless, into spongy sleep.

~

When Leo woke again, nightmares lingered along the half-lit spectrums of his subconscious. Or were they memories? He groaned, trying to blank the thought. His mouth felt dry and thick, lemon/dirt aftertaste on his tongue. At first he focused on a striped ceiling that, as consciousness started to reintegrate with thought, became long, parallel light fixtures alternating between yellow and grey. He realized with a start that the ceiling was unfamiliar, the room not his own.

He sat up too fast. The rest of the room, a chamber of soft, bare-blue walls and fog-smog light, swiveled. The walls framing three empty beds and a floating chair receded, then moved swiftly forward, jamming against his vision. His temples smarted. "Oh -" he groaned, soft, as a sudden image in the floating chair appeared. A man with large green eyes watched him.

"You're awake, finally," the man said with a delicate twang to his accent. His hair, a shock of white that stuck up several inches at the top of his head, was shaved on the sides. To Leo, he looked like a troll.

"Awake? Where am I? Is this a hospital?" Memories tried to channel themselves into his conscious mind. He winced.

"To an extent, yes." The troll man smiled. He had full, pale lips, damp-looking, and he wet them with the edge of a quick pink tongue. His left leg crossed the right, his tan shoes – more like moccasins than shoes – thin and frail. "This is a medical facility located in Moltenrose Tower."

Leo cocked an eyebrow. A chill washed his skin. "Moltenrose? Is this government or something? What have you done to me?" Suddenly self-conscious of his nakedness, he drew the cover into his hands and clutched it to his waist.

"Of course, we have done nothing to you," the man replied. "But there is a war on, you know. And you did breach our barriers."

Leo frowned, making his head ache. "Which war is that? I don't know what you're talking about." His palm pressed against his forehead. He had an image of himself pushing a little girl out of a tree. "Why am I remembering things I never did? Where am I?" he asked again.

The man leaned forward, his hands forming a 'v' where finger and thumb tips pressed together. His nails were painted a frothy blue. Leo had never known male government officials to paint their nails. "That's something I want to talk to you about."

"Are you responsible for all this? All the things that have been happening since...since I was a kid?" Leo felt the beginning slice of panic in his stomach. This didn't seem like government at all. This man was lying to him. He looked around the room, half-expecting to see the ten-clawed machine of his fears.

"We are not responsible, but we know who is. And that's why we're keeping you here, safe –"

"You have no right to hold me!" Leo interrupted. His muscles tensed, making his hands shake. He clutched them into fists. "Just let me go home. I never did anything harmful to anyone –" He stopped, nausea accompanying the image of his younger self raping a girl, the one in pink paper. "Kittin," he mumbled, shaking his head, eyes closing.

"We have the right to do anything that concerns your safety and ours. You are, after all, the one who came to us."

"What?" More mud puddles of images, blurred: half-glimpsed scenes of books and lamps flying, dawn emerging behind the large red machine, a glass room filled with screams, his own blood on a hard, white table. "Someone brought me here, right?"

"You brought yourself," the man said calmly.

Leo glared at him. "Well, who are you?"

"My name is Andus, and you did bring yourself here, Leo. You leaped here from the other side, and now they can't get you back. Not until – or if – we decide to release you." Green eyes flicked to Leo's wrist.

"Until. If." His voice came out cold. Leo followed the gaze, noticing for the first time a silver bracelet that clamped his wrist bone, a sleek-hinged half-handcuff. "What is this?" fingering the buffed edge.

"That's a bio-pacer."

"I don't know what that means!" His eyes felt hot, his body tense.

"Most bio-pacers are programmed to and controlled by the wearer. We control yours. You can't jump as long as we suppress that ability within you."

"Jump?"

"Certainly the other side kept you ignorant, but you came this time of your own free will. No contamination was found on you. No inner programming. No message. We were thorough in our examination of your mind and body. You had no mission that we can detect. You must remember something – "

162

"I – I –" Leo glanced around the room, eyes fixing on the single door at the left wall. "You can't keep me," he said again. "You must have me mistaken with someone else." But it was true. He felt the truth inside, deep, twisting. He'd done something horrible. And this wasn't a dream.

"You really don't know what you can do, what you have done?" Andus asked.

Leo's mind ached. Again, a silt of images. There was the color pink. The texture: paper. The scent: flowers. The feel of her body against his, along with the feel of a metal prod against his stomach, the slickness of blood. His memory-self screamed. He closed his eyes. "I may have hurt someone, but it's all mixed-up in my head."

"Is that all?"

"There's a machine with lights and a round, red-metal body and metal arms. It hurt me. Is it real?"

"A spychiatrist, yes," Andus nodded. "Go on."

"It's real?"

"They are tools of the war. We do not employ them, but our enemy relies on their power for everything they do. You see, Leo, there is a war. You've been used to fight for many years because of your special abilities. It's not your war, but ours. Yet you are a casualty. You may not be from our world, but you are affected –

"This is another world? But you're human!"

"Yes. It's difficult to explain. We're not even in your time."

"This is the future?"

"A future. Not necessarily that of your world's, however."

"Then this is all real? I was abducted? And I've been used, you say?" The shaking of his body was making him dizzy. "It was never a dream?" When Andus didn't immediately answer, he said again: "Ever since I was a kid, I thought I was crazy."

Andus slowly shook his head.

Leo took a deep breath. "What exactly is a spychiatrist?"

"It is a deadly machine used by our enemy in The Walled City. It can travel through time as easily as through space. It is a device that controls minds completely. It can make you into another person, a puppet. You have no free will. But you escaped it," Andus muttered more to himself than to Leo. "That's how it seems. To my knowledge, no one else has ever done that." He eyed the bracelet on Leo's arm again, brows narrowing. "Hmm. A possible immunity we didn't count on." His blue-nailed fingers stroked his own bio-pacer, a darker silver cuff with red gems embedded in it.

"Then how did I escape?" he asked, watching the hand, the bracelet. Sweat tickled his brow and upper lip. Not understanding made him angry. Half-understanding made him scared. The bracelet on his arm warmed, but he felt nothing more from it. "And what about Zack?"

"I only know you escaped the spychiatrist. This 'Zack' person I do not know, but the spychiatrist is dangerous, almost indefensible. We have EM fields out here in the FreeWorld that disrupt their programming and, in effect, kill them. Somehow you must've intuitively known that you'd be safe here. You see, you *are* a soldier, whether you remember or not, Leo, and an enemy of the Free World."

"But I'm–" Except for the pang of truth Andus' words now brought, he wanted to deny it all. This was impossible. And yet, since childhood he'd always felt something, the prickle of being watched, a lack of self-possession that ran his life. He could never prove he hadn't made those triangular marks on his body with his own hands, then forgotten about it. But then Lacy had come, and he'd started to believe again that something very real was happening to them. Now, he was facing all the answers he'd wanted for so long. And yet it was impossible to accept. "You can't keep me here against my will," he said slowly.

"I repeat, Leo, we are not the ones who have used you so cruelly. We have our own volunteer force, our own gifted people who willingly fight for the cause of freedom for themselves and their loved ones. We are not your enemy. But you are ours. Or were, until yesterday. Did you go to Kittin because she called?"

"Kittin? I don't know." He pressed a palm to his forehead. The girl's face came back to him, pinched in pain underneath his, his body moving obscenely against hers.

"She's our human beacon. You've encountered her three times now. It's best if you don't remember the first two." He smiled and showed filed teeth, white and small. Leo's skin trembled, bumped. Better not to remember? How much did this man know? Though it was warm in the room, the air floating around him in soft eddies felt cold.

"Two?" He thought hard, eyes tearing.

Andus nodded gently. "There are those who would kill you. We can't let you go for your own safety. We have guards at the door. Robots, of course. No harm will come to you until we can transport you safely to another area."

"Those who would kill me? But I –"

"I've told you you were controlled, yes. But that doesn't matter to some extremists. What matters is that you are the enemy."

"Not through my own will!"

"I and my superiors acknowledge that. But people often want the tools of destruction destroyed as a symbolic gesture, forgetting the real foe is he who pushes the buttons."

Leo touched his bio-pacer again. The hinge wouldn't budge. He could find no opening. "Is this locked on?" he hissed.

"For your own safety, yes. We lock them now with the unwilling, and with children. Too many accidents in the past."

That statement meant nothing to Leo, who continued to wrestle the bracelet until his skin chafed.

"Don't," Andus murmured.

"I just want outta here!" His eyes warmed.

"Impossible for now, I'm afraid. If you are hungry, or bored, a robot attendant will bring you food, entertainment."

"What about you? Will you stay?"

"I," said Andus, "am not even truly here."

Leo stared as the man rose, walked through the floating chair as if it weren't solid, and stood in the center of the long room waving his arms up and down.

"Look carefully, Leo. You can see through me."

He squinted. The wall shimmered through Andus' chest and stomach. "No." His mind rejected the image. "I don't – "

"I'll visit you again soon," Andus said, and vanished. There was no sound, no display of colored lights, nothing. He simply wasn't there anymore.

Still in shock, Leo started to get up, only to sit back down hard again as the door on the left wall opened. A man made entirely of metal entered the room carrying a large tray filled with covered plates and cups. "You must be hungry by now," the man said, his shiny, metal lips pliant as they formed the words. He had a voice like wind forced through metal tubes. Musical, but without feeling. All the colors of the room, blue, grey, yellow, rushed about his mirrored arms and legs like a sea writhing in captured reflection.

As the robot approached, Leo saw himself – wild October hair, pale features with shadowed smudges for eyes – speculated in the silver chest. His reflection looked inanimate, another captured color on the skin of this alien machine.

## Chapter Eighteen

Scimitar held the pain of telepathology in his rock-blue eyes. His private room misted with humidity. He lived in a fog, a real fog of his own making, the humidifier a cure for various allergies as well as an accurate mirror of his own thoughts. He never knew if any thought he had was an original one, and had long ago decided that his inner mind was not his own, but was a turmoil of images and judgments from everyone he had ever met.

What troubled him now was one question: Who desired Kittin? Surely he had not come up with the idea to seduce her and marry her all by himself. He'd lusted after women before, and a few men, but only because it had been their idea planted in his mind sometimes innocently, but more often with the full knowledge of what he was. Telepaths could be taken advantage of as easily as they could take advantage of others. But Scimitar had not mistaken another's thoughts in a long, long time. When he was a child he'd misinterpreted thoughts due to his own naivete. He'd felt every emotion intimately – hate, envy, lust, anger, awe – before the age of five, only to later discover they weren't his own. But never as an adult had he fallen into that trap. He claimed nothing, save perhaps a certain death-wish, as his own.

But now desire thwarted him. He was fairly sure Kittin's thoughts had not strayed for one moment in his direction, had never even subconsciously considered him as a potential lover. At first she had noticed his lack of fashion sense, his missing smiles, his ungainly height. She'd even noticed his rugged handsomeness. He'd accepted all those emanations from her without surprise, without a second glance. But she had not 'wanted' him. And if she had not been the one who planted the idea of seduction in his mind, then who?

He thought of August, slobbering out his fantasies about Kittin to anyone who'd listen. No, August wanted Kittin for himself. He wouldn't coerce Scimitar, seduce her by proxy. It wasn't his style.

And the others – Lily, Caeril, Epoch – were too disturbed to try anything of that nature. Besides, Scimitar would have detected their mark on this piece of will, this lust he felt, if indeed it had been any one of them.

Then who?

He eliminated Leo who, even at this distance from his bed in the medical wing, gave off honest waves of near-total amnesia. Leo was Kittin's obsession, a secret love, but not the reverse, and certainly Leo wouldn't be projecting to Scimitar, whom he'd never met.

Then could this be an original thought? He denied the prospect, took credit for nothing he ever did. And he didn't want to start now. No, the answer had to be elsewhere. Perhaps with the Free World Controllers. A plan. A deadly game that used Scimitar, the shell, as a soldier-ignorant once again.

He swam the empty, chill waters of disgust. A telepath's disgust for everything and everyone. A disgust he'd learned over time, from his fellow humans.

As a natural mind-reader, Scimitar had never known anything else. All his life he'd seen into the festering masses of minds, seen all the censored threads of thought, atrophied secrets, lies like green pus, distortions of naked emotion drizzling through memory. He thought everyone saw the disorder of others' dreams – prisms shot through with gold for pleasure, black for torture – and the vertigo of confusion that seemed to be what those around him referred to as 'life'. He thought everyone knew that minds emitted not only visual imagery, but sound and scent as well. And he'd heard it all. Screams. Groans. Laughter. Pleas. He'd smelled sulfur for wickedness. Candy for innocence. Excrement for hurting. Musk for love. What was natural hadn't disgusted him. The disgust had been learned. He'd picked it up everywhere and realized that what he saw, the culturally trained human mind dissected and set apart from the human mechanism that ran it, was ugly and imperfect, infected and barely contained.

He felt that now. Manufactured disgust. Admiration was something left behind in childhood, an immature view of how things really were.

Disgust was also projected at himself. As a telepath, he was always a puppet, wrinkled by the whims of companions, the orders of superiors. And if the Free World Controllers were affecting him now, it was nothing new, nothing extraordinary. But for what motive would they want him to have Kittin? And why did not knowing make him so angry?

Scimitar stripped off his unfashionable clothes and threw them in a plush corner where a peach wall met a blue wall, and the floor, purple synthetic shag (not fur, which he hated for its softness, its decadence) joined at the juncture. He did not have sparkle-walls, as did many of the others. The scintillations disturbed him. And his bed, a square, plain mattress in the center of the floor, was not raised or floating or filled with air or water. He hated heights, despite his own tallness, and preferred sleeping on a bed where his feet could touch the floor at any time without dangling.

Naked, he sat on his plain bed, pastel walls around him, black ceiling above, and stared between his long, bent legs at his unwanted, unoriginal erection. Who was it this time? Who pulled the strings?

He hated that he was aroused, that he might be obeying some silent command, that he couldn't control his own body. On nights like this; when he was too full of loathing for that which he was, for the ministrations required to bring him relief, he had special provisions.

He reached for the plastic box by the side of his bed and pulled out a thin, open, gold ring. He took his stretched foreskin between two fingers and, wincing, ran the ring through a hole he'd pierced there twenty years ago just for this sort of routine. Fastening the ring, he then took from the box a long cord of soft, velvet rope and looped it through the ring. He passed the ends of the rope between his legs, pulling his erect penis down hard against his testicles, then brought the rope up between his buttocks and wrapped it tight around his waist. He tied it in a knot just below his bellybutton. When he was through, he was shaking. Trussed this way, his genitals strained and ached; the foreskin felt pinched and raw. Slowly, the pain and the arousal traded places. He lay down, quivering, and covered himself with a thin sheet. Sometimes he also used an elastic band to bind the base of his penis and his testicles together. But that tended to cut off circulation and the urinary tract, sometimes damaging it enough so that he couldn't urinate for hours afterwards.

Now Scimitar lay, biting his lips, gripping the sides of his mattress. He tried not to think about Kittin – her long night-hair, her slim waist – because he was convinced he wasn't the one who wanted her. But when he finally managed to sleep, her image followed him into unwanted, telepathic dreams. He couldn't control his urge to go to her, to project his essence. The loop, the rope...neither prevented his continued lust. Kittin drew him irrevocably, as she had drawn Leo. What was it about her? he wondered. The telepathic part of him sought to complete himself within her. Who was doing this to him? Could this be a result of his own true will? He tried to deny it even as he found himself telepathically projecting into her room.

~

Dream was something that came from every direction, all-encompassing in its various plots, voices, colors. For Kittin, dreams were worlds that pulled at a part of her consciousness that resided at the back of thought, in umbra, in a slumbering pavane.

But when Scimitar came to her, dressed in seabeams and a bluish corona of energy, nothing else intruded, no dream fog, no far-off motion calling the spirit to join it, no voices. Just silence, and his ethereal arms reaching, eyes like desert sky, touch like foam.

This was no sleep fantasy. Projecting telepaths were very real. And very dangerous.

"Scimitar," she said, startled. At first she was afraid. But in the embrace of her own bed, she felt safe, warm. The room flowed dark except for his form.

"This is not (tighthurt) my fault," he said, lips unmoving. "Coming here." She heard his low voice in her head, not words but imperfect thoughts, pure and quick like water through an eddy of sand.

"What's not your fault? What are you doing here? What are you doing here like this?"

"'M not (softdarkbreath) sleeping. Can't somehow (warmrelaxedmuscle) sleep," his mindthought communicated. "But someone (warchiefcontroller) must want (emptyechoinside) me with (childmoonsetting) you. Thought's somehow (puppetwrinkleskin) pushing me in your (sparklewallperfumepaper) direction. Idon'tknowldon'tknow. Though I physically (averteyelids) deny it, my (fieldwindcloud) will seems (penpiercechain) not my own. I (wartoolcontrol) find myself (crashsplitnon-barrier) intruding. Who (mysterydarknessfear)? Can't (wisdomagebook) know. Not (emptyechoinside) me. It can't be (emptyechoinside.)"

To hear him speak this way brought tears to Kittin's eyes. It was as if she'd known Scimitar all her life. Of course this was the illusion of the projecting telepath. They were never real. Or perhaps always too real. She felt as if they'd traded souls.

"So you're not the one who wants me, who so impulsively asked me to be his wife? Someone else made you say all that, right?" She paused. "You're sure it's not you?" Kittin asked. She kept her thoughts low, her reaction soft. "Don't you ever have feelings of your own?"

"I am (emptyechoinside) a container, nothing (airashcold) more."

This statement seemed a unique and complete way to avoid all responsibility. Scimitar was the oldest of the soldiers in the Tower, but as she experienced him she realized he was also possibly one of the most immature due to his extraordinary gift...or curse.

"I don't understand," Kittin said.

Scimitar looked like a shadow of himself, every detail blurred, skin greyer than daylight might show, eyes the source of the blue light that seemed to halo his body. He wore nothing in thought. Kittin could make out the slim folds of muscle just beneath the tight skin of thighs, chest, arms, the small roundness of his belly, an indistinct silhouette of male genitalia.

She couldn't help thinking of Leo as she gazed at Scimitar's pained expression, his tall, demanding form.

He winced as, obviously, he picked up her thoughts of Leo, his eyes tightening to slits, his pressed lips forming little wrinkles at the juncture of mouth and cheek. What brushed her now were mixtures of dark winds and moist, sweet curiosity. Scimitar had never met Leo, but the man had become a myth surrounding the Tower, surrounding Kittin. A love/hate myth. A novelty everyone wanted to meet...or kill.

"I (distantechofading) could go to (magicalienboy) him now," Scimitar said, his lips still unmoving. "I (echorecedingdark) want to (holdgivetake) help you (painerasestop) kill him."

"You say you're not propelled by your own thoughts. What if he isn't, either? I've been thinking." She clutched her hands under the covers. "Maybe he's more help to us alive. With his talent. Do you want to come talk to me about it? The real you?" She couldn't believe she was inviting him to her room, after running away so childishly only hours before.

"No!" There was a whoosh of blue lightning, ozone-scent, doors or walls slamming closed. "(Torturepushobliterate) kill him!"

"I know. You said earlier you want to feel his death. It's a real pleasure, huh? That good?" Kittin frowned. Strangely, it was much easier talking to Scimitar this way. Again, she had the feeling she'd known him for years. "Maybe. Maybe Scimitar, if you're real good, if you share – "

"Anything!" With that promise came scents: mown hay, popcorn, roses. Textures: fur, silk, warm human skin rubbing. Colors: diamond white, fire green, red thicker and brighter than blood.

"So you do want things on your own, with your own emotions, your own mind. No one controls you now, Scimitar. Why are you here? Are you aware of what you're doing?"

She smelled tears, rusted chains, sweat. Saw Scimitar, shockingly, drop like a praying angel to his knees. "Please." He did not deny her statement, or answer her question.

No natural resistance toward projecting telepaths had ever been reported to exist, Kittin had been told once. Scimitar had more control over others, over his own actions, than he let on. He could do as he liked, receive what he liked, if he could control the eccentricity of his talent. He'd been trained in the elements of control, but mostly for combat.

He had to know what he was doing. Though she wondered why his feelings for her seemed so strong, she liked the attention. He didn't intimidate her at the moment. She felt her own arousal fill her.

Now, as he came toward Kittin, astral touch like foam, the blue staccato of light partially encompassing her, she again thought of Leo, of the more violent green light they'd bathed in and battled together, of his convulsing body in her arms, and welcomed Scimitar into a ghost embrace.

If he wasn't really touching her, she didn't know it. His

thoughts made her believe he was actually in the room, actually moving aside the covers of her bed, running perfect, glossy fingertips over the ripples of her naked ribs.

His arousal enveloped her personal room-scent of applerose with his own ocean/salt/tang. Cool moisture. A hint of summer sea-storms. She liked it. She'd visited the sea once when she was little. Before Leo came. Before the contamination in her veins. She'd thought of the sea as too vast and empty until she saw the life within it, green-growing, silver-darting, blue-flickering.

Scimitar gave the illusion, perhaps even believed himself, of being empty. But he was no more empty than a thriving sea, like the life-blood of a world that had spawned millions of species from its microbes.

Scimitar had worlds inside him. Worlds of storms, seas and wars. But also, worlds of pearl angels. Worlds of kelp grooms. Of garnet stones like hearts; and all the hearts were his whether he claimed them or not. His lips touched her breasts, astral tongue flicking like static, hardening her nipples.

It had been some time since Kittin had felt any strong sexual stirrings. Since immigrating to the lunatic tower in the first compound, and then to Moltenrose Tower, she'd trusted no one. It had been over a year now since the rape, a year of madness before she woke to the demands of servitude and war.

Now Scimitar woke her, while a secret, bright love for Leo also hovered, encouraging her.

His hands touched the outer lips of her vulva, soft, unintrusive. She spread her legs, stretched her arms out to clutch his tall shoulders still amazed at how solid the projected image was. Her bed became a river where she floated warm, soothed as he touched her, pushing back her most private skin but not touching further, just exposing her. The air tingled, lapping at her moistness. Then it was his tongue, lapping there, soft, molding, a warm sponge perfectly soaking up her pleasure and demanding more. His hands held her apart as his tongue mapped the depths, then came back up to tease and prod her, kiss and suck her at the source that ignited energy and sent it soaring through her. She felt her arms and legs tense, her brain fog with the most beautiful color of ivory, and came, her loins melting into her hips, all her organs shuddering, riding the citron-fresh scent of joy.

When she looked up into Scimitar's eyes it was to see the rock-blue of them soften into the blue of taffy pulled. In his mind, a whirlpool of sky and stars threatened, roughing the edges of the pearls, the kelp, the stones. She liked that truth of him, rough like a boy, the edges a little frayed.

She reached down and cupped him, still hard as when she'd seen him silhouetted, his organ jutting from him like a stem on an apple, and moved to a more comfortable position where she could tend it, nurture it. Her body was hot, her own sex still craving more stimulation.

She pulled her hand along the length of his erection and felt it, as if he were really in the room, adhere to her, shape to her grasp. The pulse of it pounded against her sensitive palm. It was like touching supple leaves wrapped around a sunward branch, or the underside of her hardened breast, or stretched, smiling lips. She could easily become lost in the texture of his skin, the scent, the taste.

She kissed the head where the foreskin, decorated with a tiny, golden hoop, stretched, revealing pinkish, plush skin. Let her tongue lick.

Scimitar groaned when she placed his organ into her mouth. She predicted the taste and was not disappointed. The sea swirled on her tongue. The sea made solid. The sea made flesh.

She suckled and massaged him. The gold hoop heated in her mouth, as did he. The dangling sack behind his penis was, he projected with a series of blue lightning flashes, especially sensitive.

Again, he began to touch her, fingers knotting in her black curls that fell in a flood across her shoulders. Palms pressing high breasts, narrow waist, slim, girlish hips. She knelt with her legs spread, feeding on him, and he ran his palms over the backs of her buttocks, pinching, clutching.

Breathless, he finally urged her away. She fell back onto the river of her bed again, pulling him to her, wrapping her legs about him as she felt him bob against her inner thigh, then the juncture at the inside of her hip, the wet lips of her sex. The metal loop ringed her clitoris, then slid downward,

174

leading him into her. She arched up. He entered. Everything
– light, muscle, dream, sea, space, breath, bodies – clutched.
They were wrung with frenzy. Lust.

Scimitar pushed in and out of her, sending delicate
shivers through her mind. For the first time in a year, her
bio-pacer grew warm. In her brain, – deep in the amygdala,
the hippocampus – chemicals released themselves, chemicals
that loved her, quickened her, healed her. The bio-pacer
could respond to that, and fed her with more of those
chemicals until she herself was thrusting, as frantic as her
lover, riding that touch of foam that seemed so solid, the
astral dream that completed what the physical version of
Scimitar had been too afraid to do.

She heard him yell, felt herself convulse a second time,
stunned, and drift to the river's shore.

Scimitar withdrew, glistening, and she rolled, closing her
eyes, touching him, holding him, her hands at first not
realizing they curled around warm air, then her own thumb,
the nail biting the underside of her fourth finger.

He was gone, but Kittin could still smell his sea-scent in
the room, washing up kelp and pearls and polished stones,
essences he still believed were not his own.

## Chapter Nineteen

Leo looked up and saw not the metal face he expected, not the glowing, cold eyes and shiny lips of C-138 that didn't move correctly, but instead a man. A tall man. With grey hair that fingered the bottom of his jaw. With blue eyes like cyanotic skin, or two new bruises glaring.

Another hologram, he thought, angrily ignoring it. He'd just finished exploring every cranny of the room, banging on the walls. Now he leaned back on his pillows, exhausted, his paper pants – the only garment he wore – rustling, and closed tired eyes. *Where are you, Zack?* Out loud, he said, faking calm: "Who are you?" It was hard to get used to these ghosts popping in and out.

"My name is Scimitar. I am your savior."

Leo's eyes opened wide. "Huh?" No hologram ever talked like this, though they had visited him often.

"You must listen and not interrupt. I don't have a lot of time. I'm probably being monitored right now. But I'll have to risk it. Whatever you've been told is a lie. I'm a prisoner here, like you, being used against my will."

"What?"

The man put a long finger to his lips. "Shh. I can get you out of here, which is your only hope for survival. But you must do everything I say. There is a girl. She needs your help. I will send you her image. Concentrate on it. Then, using all your will, all your strength, project yourself toward her. They cannot hold you here, not with your talents. But they probably haven't told you that. Your ability to teleport makes you ultimately free, even of your bio-pacer. If, that is, you know you have the will to make use of it."

Leo felt himself awaken more fully; all his attention focused on the tall man. Non-sequiturs still played hopscotch with his mind, but now maybe he'd get more answers. "What do I do?"

"You know how. Inside you is all the knowledge." Scimitar looked nervously over his shoulder, took a step back, said: "I have to leave now," then faded until his image was a mere outline of head, shoulder, arms and legs. As with holograms, the wall beyond was visible through him. But holograms winked on, winked off. This man faded until he was like mist, quavering, then a distortion in the air, then nothing. But just before that nothingness, Leo saw a clear vision projected before his eyes of the girl from the tower, her paper robe fluttering, her long black curls catching light and holding it like a night-mirror. She had a small nose, wide cheeks and chin, a high forehead. Her lips drew him, red as poppies, full, parted.

Kittin.

He recoiled as her face in his mind appeared, young voice crying out in pain, screaming as he held her down. Why had this man 'Scimitar' told him he should go to her? If he had hurt her, then surely he would not be welcome. But then he remembered the green lightning, her hands meeting his as the energy between them transferred, then grounded. She had helped him, then. Did she know him in some other way? Were his memories even real?

He contemplated his bracelet for a long moment. The bio-pacer was his jailor. He couldn't get it off, and he'd tried. Yet Scimitar said not even that could hold him. But if not, and if he could teleport at will wearing the bio-pacer, he couldn't remember how he'd done it before. He remembered the time he'd been with Zack on a 'date' and had literally 'popped' out of the back seat of the car to land, standing, behind the bumper. At the time, he'd denied the experience. He never felt it was sane. He never felt he controlled that part of himself. Someone else did. Or 'something' else, he reminded himself as he thought of the spychiatrist. But now Scimitar with the silver hair and eyes like perfect bruises was telling him if he could concentrate, will himself to a certain locale, he could control the ability himself. That meant he could go home!

Okay, then, he had to try.

He leaned back on the bed and closed his eyes. He tried to concentrate on his apartment, on Zack, but he couldn't picture the room clearly, let alone the set-up of the building where he now found himself. How was he supposed to go anywhere if he couldn't see? Yet he'd gotten here, hadn't he?

Both Andus and Scimitar had said Kittin was the key. And the image of her was strongest in his mind. It overrode all other images. Carbon curls. Moonlight and flower scent. Was it enough? Could he picture her and just appear anywhere she was? If so, then maybe she could help him get home, too.

He had gone to her in the first place, despite the storm, despite his confusion, hadn't he? That meant he should be able to do it again. But had he been under his own control even then? Or had he been sent? He had no way of knowing, and only one way to find out.

Leo understood one thing. He did not want to be anyone's prisoner. The safety of the room, of the robot caretakers – especially C-138 who'd been the kindest - was perhaps secure, but still an unacceptable breach of his freedom. And Scimitar said they had lied to him. He would learn nothing if he remained a passive participant. Here, in this room, he was blind to his fate. He could not know if, when or how he might be used again. He'd rather have his eyes open. And the dark-haired girl and her location was as good as anywhere to begin the journey back, the journey home.

He pictured her in her pink paper robe, a silhouette bending over him the last time he saw her, the warm, sweet-balm of her, the silk of hair brushing his neck, his nipples. Her hands had been small and damp, her face a golden oval, her lips heavy and dark. Outlined in green flame, she was witch-like. She was Rapunzel locked in a tower. She was Beauty in search of a spinning needle to prick her thumb. She was a swan kept from flight.

He thought of Lacy and Zack. And hoped: If I can go where this girl is, I can go anywhere. I can go to them, too.

The girl called to him. A whispering plea. A silent echo.

Leo needed her. Leo wanted her...

...and felt her palms brush his chest, her hair sting his eyes. A dash of anger. A thrust of cold. A twist of senses – he was seeing sound now, hearing the harsh, troubled tone of purple, the ripping laughter of green – shocked him into numbness; darkness, a long, groaning mouth, sucked him into squishy, jelled pre-nothing.

Then nothing.

Nothing finally ended with a voice saying: "I think we have him now." He couldn't tell if it was male or female. He couldn't be sure he'd even traveled.

He thought: Any moment Zack's cool presence will awaken me in our bed and every girl I ever dreamed will fade. All this nightmare will end. And indeed the presence beside him seemed cool, familiar. Fingers touched his arm. He hoped they were the caresses of a friend.

## Chapter Twenty

Scimitar had not touched her, had, even after entering her private room, not really looked her in the eye. He was, Kittin decided, refusing to acknowledge that a part of him (all sea and ruby-hearted) and a part of her had become lovers. He looked haunted. Evidence of a bad sleep darkened the tender skin under his eyes. She herself had slept only a few hours, and now for the second time Scimitar disturbed her rest.

"What is it?" she asked, fastening her paper robe. Her bed was a mess, still warm where she'd lain, holding Scimitar's essence to her even as she dozed in pearl and salt placid dreams. It was the first time since her rape that she'd been truly happy, more herself. Nothing could bother her today.

"He's coming," Scimitar sneered, his voice flat, his right hand quivering by his side.

"Who?"

"Leo. Your secret love. I went to him."

"You did what? Did you hurt him?" she demanded.

"I told him how he could get out. That's all." He glanced at her, a dart of blue. "His pretty body is unmarred."

She understood Scimitar's bitterness well now, and refused to let it ruin her mood. "Well how is he coming here? Does he know about me...where I am? Where we are?"

"You're the beacon, princess." The 'esses' came out a hiss. "Since we can't get to him, I told him how to come to us."

"Did he say he would do it?" Her heart pounded. Her skin felt clammy.

"He will." Scimitar, hunching his shoulders, stared at her purple sparkle-wall. He breathed out hard. "He will. I've blocked all other images he could project to. He'll only be able to come here."

"You did what?"

"Otherwise, he'd just go on home now, wouldn't he?"

"When is he coming?"

"Now," came the answer. "Or in a minute. Or an hour. That depends on him. And you."

Kittin clutched nervously at her robe, tearing the sides. "Then what?"

"Then we kill him, of course."

"Oh." But now that the plan had gone into action she wasn't sure the reality of it would be as satisfying as her dream. "I told you last night I wasn't sure I wanted to do that anymore." She'd never killed anyone. And unlike Scimitar, she had no morbid fascination for watching death dull someone's eyes, chill their skin. Death scared her. Real death. "Besides, we never finished that part of our conversation."

"I don't remember anything about that," Scimitar stated.

She knew he lied.

The memory of Leo in the glass tower room out-shone the memory of Leo by the lake, Leo the rapist. She could only see a man in agony now, a prisoner, a puppet.

She looked at Scimitar, his long back straightening, his fists bunched. Another puppet. His fear kept him locked inside himself. The part of him who had come to her in the night was the real Scimitar. This man in her room was a facsimile he'd made of himself, a mask created to serve the purpose of day to day communication, bodily function, routine. A costume that allowed him to pretend to be alive.

Kittin went to him, robe rustling like rain on leaves, and reached out. Just before her hand touched his sleeve, he side-stepped her gesture.

"Don't," he said. "I can read your thoughts. Fucking pity. I don't know why I do the things I do for you." He turned, face grimacing into an almost-smile. "But I'll make a deal with you now."

She questioned with her eyebrows.

"I'll let him live for a little while, so you can have fun with him. But when you're through with him, I get to have him. Deal?"

She started to shake her head, the walls sparking her vision with purple, white and grey. "Why?"

"I know you still want him dead."

"I did," she confessed.

"Tell me why? Why you want him dead." He tilted his head. His mouth lay in a diagonal line, a half-curve, the closest he ever came to a smile. The blotches under his eyes were golden brown.

"Because he hurt me! You know that. But then that night in the tower I saw him, felt him fighting against something that held him. Scimitar, he was just a boy those other times. He could be evil, yes, but I don't know anything about him. I don't know anything except those few moments he was with me. I don't know who he is, what he thinks, how he feels. The other times I met him, once when I was six, once at seventeen, I liked him at first. I must've. I willingly went with him."

"We all have our little problems to contend with. If you wanted it, then it wasn't rape, is that it? And now you're feeling guilty blaming him. Now you're changing your mind."

"That's not what I'm saying!" The walls flared. Her voice went harsh from anger. She lowered her head. "It's just that we don't know him, Scimitar. We don't. And I don't believe, after last night, you want to kill him so easily, either. I don't pretend to pity you, only to understand. But I don't understand any of you who are here in the Tower. I thought I was crazy until I came here. I really did. But you all are the worst."

"Yes, we're all crazy here." Scimitar came toward her. "How can we not be?" He grabbed her arm, held it clamped in his fist until a deep ache began. "How? We aren't normal. We don't own ourselves. Never will. We become insensitive, maybe, because that's all that's left inside ourselves to claim. The rest of what we are is held prisoner by our jobs, by our 'craziness'." He tapped his chest with her limp hand. "Do you see how intriguing death is to me now? How can it not be? Especially after last night." It was the first time he acknowledged their nocturnal meeting. "Having flung in my face what was taken from me, what I can never have back, I want something in return. Give me death. Mine, someone else's. It doesn't matter. At least I can control that. I can kill with a thought. It's pure power. It's pure thrill."

"You can give pleasure with a thought, too," Kittin said. "It's not all gone."

"That was a mistake," he said, letting go of her hand and crossing his arms over his chest. "A fucking dream. Not real!"

The blood stung as it oozed through her cramped veins. "Now I do feel sorry for you!" Kittin moved toward her bedstand, picked up a bouquet of fake posies and flung it about the room. The vase bounced, unbroken, on the fur floor. "And there's nothing you can do about it. About how I feel! And I feel sorry, sorry, sorry!" Her biopacer warmed, such a rare occurrence anymore. And until she'd come to the Tower, her feelings had been in tortuous disarray. But something here, despite the insanities of August, Lily, Scimitar and the others, made her feel more herself now. It was the same way she'd felt when Scimitar's ghost made love to her. Perhaps the controllers of the little machines inside her had let go for awhile. Maybe their programming had failed or had been overwritten. Anyway, she still had nothing to give them but her own unjust life, a freak of existence which was a slim shadow of normal human activity. When she was little she had never considered that people could exist who had no self-identity, no hope to regain that freedom of self that was the right of all humans. Those memories of her childhood were all she had now, her only glimpses of true freedom. Others, like Scimitar, had blank screens. Or thought they did. "You hate it that I'm sorry," she mumbled.

"No. You do. So go ahead and hate me for that, too," Scimitar said. "It's an emotion I'm already flooded with." His you-can't-hurt-me tone was familiar to Kittin.

"I've known hate, too." She dropped to the floor, her knees putting creases in the robe, and gathered some of the posies into her lap. "You're not the only one. And I don't...don't hate you."

"You're a freak, Kittin," he said, his mouth turned down when she glanced up at him, his face closed and surprisingly smooth. "All that sweetness should have been wiped out of you years ago. Years –"

"Scimitar," she said, "please help me pick these up." Tears were dangling from her lashes. She held up a flower the color of blood. "Please."

He didn't move, his eyes on the flower.

Suddenly, images projected at her which she couldn't translate at first. A little boy weeping over the death of an ant. Blinding sunlight. Grass-scent. Rough hands. Trying to embrace maggoty, damaged, ice-chained minds. No one had ever loved him back. No one he'd ever met truly could. No one he'd met was normal. The little boy, taken in rough arms and placed forever in a room used mainly for war, vowed never to smile again. He named himself: emptyechoinside.

She looked up, clutching stems. She recognized a look on

his face from last night, shadowed, soft, young. "That's you."
It wasn't a question.

He turned away, not denying it or the gift he'd just given
her. "Pick up your own mess."

The room shimmered in his silver hair, shimmered again
behind him: pewter, pale moss, fawn-light. The sparkle-walls
dimmed to sand-hue. There was a pop like a cork being
pulled from a bottle. The faint sizzle of dying sparks. The
walls lit up again. The air smelled singed. And among the
strewn flowers on the fur-floor, Leo sat, blinking upward, his
autumn hair tangled on his shoulders, his paper pants
askew.

Kittin felt her mouth open, and she couldn't close it. The
muscles had frozen that way. She heard Scimitar breathe out
loudly, a whoosh of air containing all his pent-up surprise
and fury.

"Oh," the man named Leo said, dazzled as though flash-
blinded.

"Told you you could do it," Scimitar said to the man. Then
he turned back to face Kittin. "I think we have him now."

Kittin and Leo looked up at him where he stood, arms still
crossed over his chest as he regarded them like specimens in
a killing jar.

Kittin's heart flipped over and she felt it begin to beat
anew in her throat, her wrists. Every part of her intellect told
her to stay away from these two men. But every part of her
body, her emotional make-up, her spirit, wanted to move
closer to Scimitar, and to this man named Leo. She wanted to
touch them, ascertain reality, clasp the mystery of them tight
to her chest.

## Part IX – The Walled City (Parallel Earth)

## Chapter Twenty-One

Leo's brother pounded at the lead-lined glass windows, screaming imaginative profanities Ashao had never heard before. The woman was sitting, legs drawn up, face rigid, in the far corner of the enclosed chamber. She was remembering. Ashao had programmed his spychiatrist to take away the EDOM screen memories from both Lacy and Leo as soon as it contacted them. He could see the young man was in shock.

Ashao remembered again the image of the tortured 'tools' in the War Room. Leo, especially.

And he couldn't forget his father controlling Lisa, mounting her from behind and taking her as if she belonged there, in his arms, underneath his heavy, sweating form. As if she didn't have a natural life of her own.

War or no war, he didn't care anymore. He wanted to ruin Stannos.

"Shut up!" he yelled through the chamber's intercom.

" – don't give me some answers pretty soon," Leo's twin was saying, "I'll wring your shitty little neck, you – "

"Shut up," he said again, "and I'll tell you anything you want to know."

The woman stood. The man stepped back, still trying to stare Ashao down.

The ruddy spychiatrist floated in the center of the chamber, dormant. Ashao had programmed it not to interfere unless he so ordered. Later, it would be a handy tool, working for him exactly as needed, but now he didn't need it, didn't want it to do the controlling for him. He wanted the two in the chamber to know everything with their own minds, feel real anger, real fear. They would be more valuable to him that way. For they were going to help him destroy Stannos. And enjoy the process as well.

Ashao knew Zack about as well as he knew Leo, had watched his life played out on the screen of his vinyl wall. Zack, if he understood Leo's life was at stake, would become an immediate ally. Lacy was more of a mystery. He wasn't sure how she would react, but he hoped that her new memories would enrage her enough to want to help ruin Stannos as well. But now, without Leo, did they even have a chance of going up against his father's strength? Ashao's spychiatrist had done as well as it could. It had gotten them together, brought them to him. But at the last minute, somehow something had gone wrong, and Leo had taken another path.

The light from his rooms, through the window-glass, made white and blue sea-shadows on Zack and Lacy's faces, on their nude bodies as they stood, hunched into themselves, glaring, barely listening.

"My name is Ashao. You're not on your Earth anymore; you're on my world." He tried to ignore their incredulous stares. "You asked about Leo. I know him, too. He is my father's tool, a pawn. I want to help you get him back. I brought you here because I want you to help me stop what my father is doing to people like Leo, and to you, Lacy. Leo was supposed to be with you but something went wrong."

"Why should I believe you?" Zack yelled. "Let us out of here! Then we'll talk."

"What he's saying is true," Lacy said breathlessly. "I remember –

"My father is Stannos," Ashao said to her. Her eyes widened, then closed tightly.

"If I let you out before I explain all this and you run away, you will be caught by my father. He'll either send you back without your memories, or kill you. I don't care what happens to my world. I only want to see my father destroyed. I don't believe in what he's doing. That's why you're here. I need your help. And we need Leo. We need to find him. Just as I was about to pull him here, something snatched him away. You all three should have arrived together, but somehow he broke away. My spychiatrist tracked him to Moltenrose Tower. We have to get him back. Do you un-derstand?" Their seething expressions didn't impress him.

"If anything has happened to Leo, I will kill you," Zack threatened. He held his arms tightly across his chest. His eyebrows narrowed, the eyelids closed to slits.

"That...that thing." Lacy hissed, nodding toward the spychiatrist. "It's what's been attacking me all these years." She, too, stood with her arms tightly hugging her body, her brows narrowed.

"You've been here before?" Zack asked. "Is that what's destroyed your life and my brother's?"

Lacy turned away from him, facing Ashao. "Get it out of here!"

"What is it?" Zack asked.

"A tool," Ashao said. "A machine called a spychiatrist that can travel anywhere, to any time, any space. I control this one myself. It won't touch you."

Lacy's expression changed, her lips opening in a scowl of disbelief. She stared at it for a long time, a mixture of fear and awe molding her face. "They're torture devices. They make you do things against your will. What other purpose would it serve for you?"

"A lot. And it wasn't my spychiatrist that tortured you, but one of my father's. He has dozens. They've watched you nearly all your life. In fact, they might be searching for you now. We have to hurry. If I let you out, give you clothes, you have to promise not to hurt me. You have to give me a chance to prove everything I'm telling you." His throat was tight. Could he convince them in so short a time? Was his father, even now, watching? Waiting for Ashao's next move to trap him?

"I remember so many things," Lacy said. "People getting hurt. I can see them dying. It's like I'm watching them in my mind. This is what your spychiatrists do! Kill people! Hurt them!"

"If Leo is hurt, you're dead. It's simple," Zack said gruffly, still squinting at him, stance defensive.

"My spychiatrist can defend us, too," Ashao said, trying to remain calm. "And defend Leo. But we have to get to him first. He's the one person who can stop all this, bring my father down. But not if we can't get to him."

"Leo can stop all this? By himself? How?" Zack demanded.

"Leo holds a key, a talent. As do you, Lacy. But he's even more valuable. I've seen it. He's got more raw talent than all of the Ignorant Armies combined and he doesn't even know it. He's been the star of this war several times, and they've got more special plans for him. I don't know what. But the Controllers know. And now that we've lost him, we have to get to him before they do."

"You've been using Leo since he was a kid," Zack accused.

"Not me, my father. Leo upsets the balance of power. Don't you see?" It was exasperating. How could he explain the entire world situation in five minutes? "With Leo put to proper use, my father will eventually win this war and too many people will die, probably millions. Stannos will psychically crush them. Leo probably won't survive it, either. I think what my father is doing is wrong. I want him to lose!"

"What is this place? This world? What kind of war are you fighting?" Zack threw the questions at him with contempt.

"It's a psychic war," Lacy said, staring at Ashao. "And they're all insane. This isn't even our time, our planet."

Patiently, Ashao tried to explain. "Lacy's right. You are in my home." He attempted to describe to them the palace, The Walled City, but they seemed unmoved. He tried to impart to them what he learned of his city's history from his Teacher.

"We had a war over two hundred years ago that nearly destroyed everything. Afterwards, the technology used in that war was destroyed or outlawed. My history tells me that different factions rose, the smaller one being the one inside this city. We believe that humans, when uncontrolled, are self-destructive and unhappy. We believe in a paradise where everything is plentiful and ordered. To control the people, we use different kinds of psi waves mixed with alpha, beta, theta and delta waves."

"Wait, I don't understand." Zack moved to the window, jammed his hand against the glass and pressed for emphasis. "You can control minds with psychic waves?"

Ashao nodded.

"Fuck, that. That's the craziest thing I've ever heard." He turned, his head shaking in denial toward Lacy.

"You'll see it for yourselves. Outside the Walled City is a lot of chaos. I was raised to believe our way is better. It still might be, but I don't care anymore." His chest tightened; he ignored it. "My father has betrayed me. He's misusing his power to hurt, not help."

"So the war is being fought to try to control all that's outside your city, to make them join you?" Lacy asked.

"Yes," Ashao answered.

"Your father wants to control the whole world," Zack muttered.

Ashao nodded. "We have no crime here. No hunger. No poverty. No mental illness. But outside, all they see is us as the enemy, as a threat."

"You *are* a threat." Loud, clipped, Zack's tone didn't waver. "Didn't the word freedom ever mean anything to you?"

Ashao stepped back, swallowing hard. He nodded slowly, remembering his Teacher telling him his father would 'correct' him by using a spychiatrist on him. "Yes," he replied, staring Zack down, the brown eyes so like Leo's but brighter, fuller, less haunted.

"The first time I find out that anything you've told us is a lie, you're dead," Zack said, squaring his shoulders. "It's that simple." The cadence of his voice was rude, offensive.

Lacy nodded, though her eyes were still wide, still staring at the spychiatrist floating overhead. "I agree with Zack." She swallowed hard. "If you're telling the truth, I'll help you stop all this. If you're not – "

Zack's lips curled up.

Ashao went to the chamber door and unlocked it with shaking hands. Was his father watching? he wondered again. The door opened, letting in scents of rain and musk and sleep. Scents of the Earth where Lacy and Zack lived, scents of freedom.

Zack's whole body seemed to tremble in one shuddering quake. Then he mumbled something to Lacy, the last words sounding like 'fuck him'. Anger poured off him. Ashao didn't blame him. He thought again of Lisa, and his rage was a coldness that pulled at his insides.

If Zack ended up killing him, it would be a blessing.

## Chapter Twenty-Two

Stannos stared at the wall-sized main monitor, his dark braid clamped in his teeth. His own reflection in one of the cubicle's windows distracted him for a moment. In the glass, fused by the War Room's bright lights and the occasional flicker of blue from a spychiatrist, his eyelashes looked torn and dark. His arms were crossed. In one closed fist he clasped a thin, silver square freckled with tiny flashing lights.

On the main monitor situated midway down the long room, he watched their darkhaired spy, Kittin, and an older, too-tall man arguing about his creation, his weapon. Leo.

"How could you have lost Leo, you excrement-faced elf!" Stannos demanded of a smaller man beside him, his damp braid falling from his frothing mouth. "How?"

The man, a young controller who'd been on the job only a few months, stood stiff, straight. There was a scent of fear – salt, metal – about him. "Sir, they've somehow taken him."

"Retrace his actions! I want to know how!"

The controller started to answer, but Stannos interrupted him. "Now!"

The small man hurried to the nearest board overlooking an empty chamber and started punching in commands. The board, like a desk with a monitor attached, lit up under his fingers.

Stannos watched Kittin. It was all he could do. Control of her actions had failed. The girl, his inside operative, had never worked right. The programming inside her was faulty at best though he could still monitor her at will. Apparently, she or someone had found a way to circumvent the microscopic stimoceivers Leo had planted within her once when she was six, and once when she was seventeen, for ultimate management of her mind. The technology was imperfect, but he had not expected outright failure. Still, his plans for her had not been completely a waste. She'd infiltrated Moltenrose Tower; she'd been given free access to most of it. And now, just when he needed him most, Leo had disappeared from his Earthtime ahead of schedule and somehow been captured by the outside World's army. It simply couldn't have happened.

"How?" he demanded again, aware of the shoulder-flinches of the controllers around him.

No one answered.

He threw the silver light-box against a window, the sound of it stung the air, a broken bell. "This equipment is useless!"

"Sir, Leo's spychiatrist reports another spychiatrist was in the vicinity during his disappearance."

"Another spychiatrist?" Stannos turned away from the monitor. "Which one of you – " He moved down the line. All the controllers turned in their chairs; some stood, others remained seated. "Who?" he shouted again. He would kill any traitor he found, and enjoy doing it. Just as he had killed Lisa, for pleasure, when he was finished with her. He didn't usually kill after sex, but lately he'd been frustrated with the mere act of copulation, needing more stimulation, needing to watch as life, under his complete command, wriggled and squirmed, brightened and faded. His heart raced as he remembered programming Lisa to desire, even beg for death. How she'd smiled at the pain of it when it came as he thrust inside her tight heat with his body, then a knife, watching as her eyes filled and she begged for more, tears staining her temples, blood staining the sheets.

He looked at his controllers, all supposedly loyal, all waiting for him to make a move. He'd take the traitor in the same way, first with his body, then with sharp steel. He became aroused just thinking of it.

The usual maniacal screams and laughter which filled the War Room had strangely quieted.

"It must be one of you. I'll ask once more: Who's been monitoring Leo out of sequence?"

The controller who had replayed Leo's last recorded moments answered. "It's no one here, sir. The spychiatrist involved with his disappearance appears not to be a part of this operation."

"Someone else has one outside this building?" he asked, not without some disappointment. He'd had his eye on the blue-eyed blond third from the end, hoping it might be him. Now he turned toward the small, new man. "The Free World doesn't use that technology. The barbarians use their own people. Or have intelligence reports been wrong?"

"See for yourself." The smaller man moved out of the chair, making room for Stannos' large form. "It's not one of ours."

Stannos smelled fear again, but this time more subdued. A programmed man's echoing laughter filled the War Room, then faded. Underneath that sound, a baby, one of their newer discoveries, sobbed. The noise was somewhat comforting to him, never a distraction. He smiled as he took the chair. "We'll just find out who it is and everything will be all right again."

"Yes, sir." But the controller's tone spoke otherwise.

"We will get Leo back even if we have to use the untried young ones to break through and keep distracting the World's outer defense."

"A sound idea, sir." His voice wavered on the last word. Stannos ignored the weakness.

He again scanned the recording of Leo's last monitored whereabouts. He recognized Lacy immediately, and the twins, Leo and Zack, all three sleeping in the same bed. Rage boiled in his stomach. Lacy with Leo? "This is impossible!" His large hands hit the board. "Two of our finest weapons, together – It's a conspiracy!" He ordered another controller to check on Lacy's spychiatrist while he continued to watch the recording. Shock and fury sent his heart palpitating as he watched not only Leo disappear from the bed, but moments later Zack and Lacy as well. The room had become a storm of airborne personal objects and furniture. Lacy's powers had been unconsciously tapped.

"Where are the other two?" he asked, poking at the keyboard, trying to follow their path.

"We can't seem to trace them yet. The spychiatrist that took them is not one of ours," the Controller answered. "Replay the scene switching the image to the other side of the room and you will see."

"And we know they didn't follow Leo. We saw him appear during the battle in Kittin's tower."

"Pardon, sir, but he could've done that under his own power," the controller suggested. "He's very strong."

"He doesn't know how to use his talent without our prodding."

"Someone else could've – " He let the incomplete idea hover between them.

"Yes," Stannos finally answered. "The other two never

showed up. There might be two spychiatrists, one who took Leo, and another who took Zack and Lacy to a different location. But you're right, Leo could have been influenced to teleport by himself to Kittin's location. But by who?"

"He could've done it himself, sir. Fear causes his talent to manifest. Kittin was broadcasting. Maybe he jumped blind and her summons drew him."

"Then the question is, where are the other two?"

"Zack and Lacy?"

"Yes!" Stannos roared. "Who else?"

"Replay the scene. The other spychiatrist is there. Maybe it can give us a clue."

Stannos studied the monitor again, chewing on his still damp braid.

Then there it was, a shining russet orb hovering beyond the edge of the large bed, its five, many-jointed arms waving ridiculously up and down, the metal claws clicking. It looked like any number of the spychiatrists Stannos owned and used in the War Room. Except it was smaller, redder, newer. Bright lights chased themselves in circles around its globe-shaped body.

"I know that spychiatrist," Stannos murmured, the braid again falling from his lips, sliding wetly along his chest. He sighed loudly.

"You do, sir? That's great," the controller said.

Stannos wanted to punch him. Instead, he closed his eyes and bowed his head into upraised palms. "It's my son's. I gave it to him for his fifteenth birthday."

The only sounds from the War Room now were occasional human cries, moans of pleasure. Stannos tried to absorb them, take the pain and the pleasure and the rightness of what he was doing into himself to strengthen, to renew. But despair still hugged him.

"My son." Stannos rose, shaking his head. One hand went to his braid, yanking angrily at it. The other became a shaking fist. "I'm going to kill him," he said, then turned and walked from the room.

## Chapter Twenty-Three

The spychiatrist recognized immediately that it was being probed. The probe interfered with its job. The probe was from an older, inferior-programmed mechanism of its own species. The spychiatrist rerouted the probe until the inferior spychiatrist was probing itself and instantly became confused.

The bright ones moving down the hall in front of it must be protected. It sent that message to the prober, assuring it of its own higher duty by transmitting a complex series of images showing many-hued waves intersecting and merging spacetime, dimensions and the clockwork nature of the multiverse which contained all. There was a disruption in the pattern, though, an ugly jagged crack, black-lightning-shaped, through which the multiverse was leaking. As the gondoliers and masters of this rainbow river, it was the spychiatrists' job to mend the break. The spychiatrist communicated this to the prober, then ordered it to communicate the problem to all other spychiatrists it might encounter. Orders which superseded the mending of the breach were to be ignored.

The confused inferior spychiatrist rerouted its own probe, modified it, and began probing other spychiatrists by homing in on their nearly constant output of alpha, beta, theta and delta waves. The emergency was communicated. Overriding, self-programming to mend the multiversal tear began.

~

There was meaning again in Lacy's life. The hollowness inside suddenly had purpose. The stillness and strangeness of her thoughts that had kept her separate from humanity and kept her on the fringe of her own life made sense now.

The memories of her times in this parallel world seemed to vibrate through her thoughts like dream-glimpses, quick snapshots frozen on a screen. With the images came the sharp knowledge there had been pain, indescribable tortures, disgusting rapes. Spychiatrists had drenched her in agony, rewarded her with pleasure, and she remembered doing everything they told her to do. She had sat on a hard, cold table and read from a book with her eyes closed. She had later projected her mind onto this alien world and brought images to life on a screen. She had also projected her ability to move objects. Somewhere, in her memory, a man was strangled by a swift moving rope as she watched. She had controlled the rope, pulled it tight, held it until the man no longer breathed. In another memory, a man held her down on a large, white bed and used her compliant body for sexual release. She knew that man as Stannos. Ashao said Stannos was his father. He controlled the War Room where she worked. She hated him.

Now, as she dressed, she watched Ashao suspiciously. He seemed in almost all ways opposite of Stannos; he was light where Stannos was dark, thin where Stannos was large. His voice was held back, and became shrill like a child's when he was trying to make them understand what he couldn't easily explain. Stannos had always been loud, never underspoken. Only their eyes were the same. Blue like babies' eyes. Clear as a summer sky.

Strangely, she sensed Ashao's emotions almost as clearly as if they were own. He really did hate his father, possibly more than she did. He wanted revenge. That was obvious. But it seemed there was more there, too, a true real compassion for the casualties of this war, and a very real concern for Leo. So, the older twin had affected even those on far distant worlds with his special charisma.

Her eyes stung as her memories returned even clearer. Blood on her body as a spychiatrist scoured her with its claws to make her scream. Its claws inside her, between her legs. Her own mind seeking out innocent men and women, the lightning of her thoughts moving rocks to crush them, starting fires to suffocate them. Her own pain felt small compared to what she'd been forced to do to others. And no doubt Leo had similar memories.

She stared at Ashao, who was busily stuffing packs with supplies. Unlike the kid he was, he seemed to be taking on a task that was if not impossible, clearly courageous. If he were truly trying to stop the war, there was no way she could deny him whatever help she could give him.

She moved toward him and he turned silently, his eyes meeting hers. He held out one full pack. She took it, shouldering into it, and noticed the look on his face reflected her thoughts exactly.

~

Zack, Lacy, Ashao and the monstrous spychiatrist moved down a dim hall.

Zack's brain was working overtime. He felt a range of emotions: rage, fear, awe. His concern for Leo's fate, if they weren't already too late, superseded any psychological debilitations this new environment brought on. He was too intent on his brother to succumb to culture shock and denial just yet. Still, this world of Ashao's was almost too much to be believed. An alternate Earth? At war using psychotronic weapons? Existing in a time outside his own time? The philosophical ramifications were staggering.

Lacy walked beside him, wary, no doubt caught up in her own nightmare thoughts and memories of this place. She was a minor irritation to him. Though he knew all this wasn't her fault, that she was as much a victim as Leo, he still resented her. Maybe she didn't deserve it, but he didn't care. She hadn't liked him much from the start, anyway. But she liked Leo. That hadn't happened before with other women he'd known. And now, here he was, stuck with Leo's 'girlfriend' as far away from home as one could get. *That* irritated him.

They wore fur-lined vinyl slacks, jackets of thick, shiny plastic, also fur-lined. The clothing was alien to their bodies, and smelled of newness, of oily machinery. Ashao had told them the outside autumnal temperatures demanded the cumbersome garments. In addition to the new clothes they wore, they each carried pouches tightly packed with food. They were going away from the established city. Ashao told them it would be for more than a day, at least.

Zack's boots clapped the stone floor.

The palatial corridors Ashao led them through, amber-lit and eerie, were made even spookier by the presence of metal-armored guards, still as robots, eyes like illuminated rocks.

*If they really are guards,* Zack thought, *they aren't very good at their jobs to allow us to pass through unquestioned.*

But Ashao had assured them before they left his rooms that as long as they were with him, they could go anywhere undisturbed.

"I'm the Head Controller's son," he had said, as if that explained it all. Whatever the fuck that meant.

What disturbed Zack the most, though, was the constant attendance of the monster machine. The red-bellied thing was hideous, and Zack now understood how Leo, subjected to one of these things, could have been made to do anything and later never remember.

The spychiatrist hummed along behind them, a threatening reminder to them that their actions could be less freely controlled than they might realize. Zack would have busted it against a wall if he thought he could get away with it.

"Since the spychiatrist can teleport people," Lacy asked softly, "why don't we use it to go wherever we need to get Leo?"

"The rest of the World has defenses against that kind of travel. The spychiatrist would be destroyed by their EM fields if it went past the barriers they have set up." Ashao glanced over his shoulder at it, his pale blond hair falling against his cheek. "We could jump from here to the outside, though, but I'm afraid we'd leave an easier trail for Stannos to follow. If we're on foot, he'll have to scan for us. That could take him some time, possibly days, and we need that time."

*He looks like a boy*, Zack thought. A boy with his very expensive toy. His personality alternated from being a petulant genius to a scared child. So far, Ashao appeared to be on the up and up. But appearances were deceiving, Zack knew, and he remained suspicious.

"Once we're outside the walls and within range of the outside World's sensors, we'll have to leave it behind," Ashao continued. He spoke softly and his voice seemed to tremble slightly in the cool air. "But it will continue to monitor us. If we get into trouble and there's any way it can help us, it will. I programmed it myself." A bit of spoiled pride there. "It won't let anything happen to us if it can help it."

"How do you know where we're going?" Zack asked, voice lowering as they neared an outside, locked door. "Have you seen Leo?"

"The spychiatrist knows where Leo went. It's a city called Moltenrose. It's provided me with a map. I just don't know how long it's going to take us to travel the distance. How many miles can you walk in a day? We'll have to find a trans-hop line and it could be a long walk."

Both Zack and Lacy shrugged.

"This will be my first time outside. I don't know what we'll find either, other than what my lessons have told me about the rest of the World," Ashao admitted.

"Can the spychiatrist tell us if Leo's alive?" Zack asked.

"It hasn't been able to monitor him since it came back with you two. It can only tell us he ended up at Moltenrose Tower after the last contact. It's one of our enemy's prime defense Towers. I'm sure we won't be able to get in, but at least we can assess the situation. It's a good thing you're twins," Ashao said to Zack. "Otherwise I'd have no plan. I'm hoping that if whoever's at the tower thinks you're Leo, we'll get some attention. Then I plan on giving them all my father's secrets."

"You're defecting," Lacy said.

"Shhh!" Ashao hissed. They passed an intersection in the corridor. Another guard stood around the corner from them about fifty feet away, motionless, a statue of flesh and steel.

"They don't seem real," Zack whispered.

"But their eyes move." Lacy inched closer to Zack, brushing his shoulder with hers. Zack moved away, not looking at her. But inside, near the center of his chest, a pinpoint of pain flared. Suddenly, he was very glad he wasn't alone here. Like her or not, she was the only true ally he had for now.

"Just wait until we get outside and I'll answer all your questions. Please," Ashao said.

The shadows wound the tall corridor in muted gold, varnished brown. It seemed as though they were in the bowels of a giant serpent coiled outside time, outside space.

When they left the palace, a familiar sun flourished in a clear, blue sky. But this wasn't their sun. Not Zack's sun. It was an alien star burning within a different galaxy in an all too distant universe. Zack looked up squinting, trying to see if he could peer beyond the sky, beyond the pale of midday and into his own timespace, but there was nothing. Only sunlight. Only the thin atmosphere of an Earth not his own.

His back knotted again. Leo's presence was a gelid space

inside his chest, empty. Always before he'd felt a warmth there, a sort of pressure like someone's hand pressed gently to his heart. He'd taken Leo for granted knowing, the way a shadow falls when you block the sun, that he was there around him, inside him: blood, air, salt, brain, soul. They were genetic duplicates, spiritual halves. Without him, Zack knew the first icy tugs of panic.

They entered a courtyard of autumnal richness. Pumpkin colored ivy crawled in twisted patterns over stone walls. Trees in their own squares of soil set into the tiled flooring bent their branches in a noon-cool wind. Some had withered leaves; leaf- corpses of burnt sienna and chaparral dust dangled next to siblings touched with the fury of sunsets, hanging onto life with all their might. The white marbled tiles of the courtyard played beach to the leaves which had lost their battles. A silver man at the far end of the square gathered them into squat bags of dark brown. Along one wall there were benches of grey concrete and metal that looked like animals crouching. Along another wall Zack saw potted plants, the pots like hollow torsos, the plants their alien, brown-tendriled heads. When Zack looked behind him, back at the palace, he saw gargoyle-like sculptures on either side of the entrance. More inert guards to fool, he thought.

Ashao, boots too big for his thin, short frame, clomped on ahead of them, straight toward the silver man, toward a place where the wall looked like it dipped into a door.

"Out here's the city," he said softly over his shoulder.

Zack and Lacy hurried to follow, Zack still gazing around at the plants, the snow white tiles, the walls, and all the glorious colors that had come to stain the courtyard with the season of brisk endings. They saw steps that led to more patios and more potted gardens. Zack could smell a pool somewhere, could hear the hollow silence of water slowly moving in the wind.

In the center of the courtyard was a fountain, but it was drained dry. They passed it, gazing into the bare depths to see mosaic patterns of stars and moons littering the bottom.

Zack was glad to be outdoors in more familiar earth-scents even though they weren't from his Earth. He inhaled nutmeg from somewhere, and dust of a summer long past, and the spice of cozy memories. Maybe this planet wasn't so different from his own. Maybe it was like him and Leo, a twin, half-soul to the Earth he knew. He breathed deep.

They came to a dip in the wall which turned out to be a locked gate. The guards, dressed like the ones in the amber corridors, let them out when Ashao explained he and his 'friends' were going into town. As the Head Controller's son, he wasn't even questioned.

Outside the palace, the city, which existed behind even greater walls grey and foreboding in the distance, flamed with fall. Zack saw rows of rectangular, identical buildings. They seemed to be walking through an area of apartment complexes. The difference between this city and cities Zack had seen was that all the buildings here were the same. There were dead trees lining the streets, gutters flushed with leaves. People walked the streets in slow, even gaits, never looking up from their paths.

When they reached the end of the street they came to a park. People moved through it in lazy strolls, in couples or threes, voices soft, faded. Then Zack saw it, huge and sinewy, moving through a gnarled, dying copse of trees. At first he thought it wasn't real. Black and orange stripes flowing with smooth muscle, the tiger sniffed the air as it undulated over the yellowing park grass.

"My God!"

"What?" Ashao and Lacy followed his gaze.

"Oh," Ashao said, shoulders falling. "Someone's pet."

"Pet? That tiger?" Lacy asked.

"Why not?"

"That's a wild animal!" Zack pointed out.

"Not here it isn't," Ashao said.

"What do you mean?" Lacy turned, her dark eyes sparking.

"Theta waves through the city stimoceivers. Everyone's controlled. It makes for a very peaceful existence, animals and humans alike."

"It's worse than I imagined," Zack said.

"That's what the war's about. The rest of the World wants to have stimoceivers outlawed. My father – and others – disagree."

"Well, why don't the theta waves affect us then?" Lacy asked.

"They would," Ashao replied, "if not for it." He gestured toward the spychiatrist which hummed and floated behind them. "I think I may be immune, but I know you two aren't immune. The spychiatrist is blocking the stimoceivers projected at our little group. Just until we get out of the city, out of range." He added, proudly, "I programmed it for that, too."

"It can do that?" Zack asked.

"It can do almost anything." Ashao's green eyes focused on the tiger. It passed by them leaving a scent of musk in its wake. But it never once looked up. It came so close Zack could've reached out to touch it.

As they walked, they passed by people wearing colorful paper and fur and plastic clothing. But the clothes belied their temperaments. Everyone ignored them.

"They look drugged," Lacy observed.

"They're happy enough," Ashao said. "My father used to say that if everyone could just try living under these conditions for one day, they'd be convinced it was for the best. As I said before, no suffering. No poverty. A high productivity rate. I thought it was normal. I've never known these people any other way. But I didn't think about living that way myself. Never. My father didn't act like them either. I didn't question things like that until recently. Until I saw Leo. And you." He looked at Zack. "And until my father stole a friend of mine."

"It's sick," Zack hissed.

"Like some kind of horror movie," Lacy added.

"Yeah, well the real horror's back where we were," Ashao said.

Zack and Lacy traded glances. Lacy's eyes darkened, her mouth tightening as if remembering something painful. He felt something for her at that moment, but couldn't tell if it was anything more than pity. Leo had been through those horrors, too, and he could only imagine how terrible it must have been.

Ahead, bright orange stripes shifted. Another tiger.

The park absorbed their voices and footsteps. Another fifteen minute's brisk walk brought them to the wall. By then Zack's face was feeling the chill. Lacy's cheeks and nose had a pinkish tint.

There was a long building with a few people milling about. Armed guards stood at various stages along the building and its doors. Their gazes were stone. Suspicious.

Zack heard Ashao whisper to the spychiatrist. Though the device got not a few horrified/defensive/confused looks, no one said a word to them as they were motioned on through two checkpoints. The other end of the building, a clean, well-lit space with polished floors and long, shiny counters, was empty as they emerged through double doors and into an atrium.

"That was easy," Zack commented.

"The spychiatrist did it with a little outside influencing," Ashao replied. "They won't follow us, but after the effect wears off, they might try to contact my father."

Zack saw Lacy frown, then shudder and turn to stare at the strange machine.

"Are we in danger?"

Ashao nodded, but seemed unsure. "More and more as every minute passes." His voice sounded so very young.

The last set of double doors opened. A landscape of destruction greeted them.

Lacy gasped. Zack simply stared.

"The Edge," Ashao said, blinking. "I've never actually been in it myself. The gangs who live here call it The Edge. It's a band of wasteland and ruins that stretches for a thousand miles up the continent." He slung his backpack off and opened it, fishing for something.

Zack scanned the blackened ruins that seemed to go on forever into an invisible oblivion, a dark and seamless horizon.

"What happened?" Lacy managed to speak only in a shuddering voice.

"That was the Seven Day War." Ashao took something silver from his pack. "The one I told you about that happened a couple centuries ago before nuclear weapons were finally outlawed."

Zack whistled.

Ashao held the silver disk in his palm. Lights flashed on the disk. He touched it with his forefinger a few times, then looked up. "The spychiatrist will help protect us from the stimoceivers pointed outward from the Walled City. But when the spychiatrist can't go further, we'll need to get bio-pacers. I couldn't get any inside the city. Maybe I can buy some before we'll need them."

"What are bio-pacers?"

"What everyone outside wears to protect them from Stannos' stimoceivers. He broadcasts them out here, too, all the time. It's part of his strategy. The bio-pacer nullifies the waves."

A cold wind picked up. Zack rubbed his hands briskly together. Ashao dug in his pack again and handed them each a pair of gloves which, when worn, immediately warmed the hands. After putting them on, Zack and Lacy both looked up at the same time.

"Come on," Ashao said, moving away from them, his own gloves now in place.

"We have to walk through this?" Zack kicked the blackened ground. His boots made ash rise in a miniature, formless ghost.

"It won't hurt you," Ashao called over his shoulder. "The radioactivity's died way down."

"No way. I'm not going." Lacy backed up a step, nervously fingering her pouch strap.

Ashao, looking so small against the wrecked, black background, the uncommonly blue sky, didn't stop, didn't look back. His faithful spychiatrist swam at his side. Zack took a step toward Lacy. "How far into this 'Edge' are we going?" he yelled.

"I don't know," Ashao replied, still walking. "The spychiatrist estimates maybe a day's walk before we can find some transportation."

"This is too much for me," Lacy said. Her eyes glistened in the autumn light. "All of it." Her cheeks pearled with tears.

Zack looked down, seeing only blackness, the leached ground. "Leo," he said brusquely. "We have to get Leo, dammit!" He couldn't look up just yet. His own emotions were barely composed. They were both in shock, Lacy probably moreso because of her memories, but all he could think of was moving on.

"I know that!" She sniffed, ran a jacketed arm over her face, under her nose.

"Okay," Zack said at little too quickly. "I didn't mean – "

He took a breath, clenched his jaw and looked up again at the blue sky. He hated that she made him defensive. He hated that she was crying. Leo wasn't *her* brother. "Just stop. Stop, okay?" He wouldn't look at her. His arms tensed at his sides but he didn't move.

"I'm with you, Zack. I'm just– I can't believe it all. It's just too much too fast!"

"Don't you think I'm afraid, too?" Zack finally said. "I'm afraid Leo's already dead." He felt his cheek twitch, his eyes grow heavy and warm. He should have been there for him, should have been awakened by the noise of the bedroom being destroyed. He should've somehow stopped Leo from leaving so that whatever it was that took him – whether it was Ashao's spychiatrist or something else – would have been forced to take them both together. His fists clenched in the fur-lined gloves.

She inhaled sharply. "I know." Then, without another word, Lacy came up alongside him and took his hand. Through the material of their gloves, there was a sparking warmth. Then abruptly, shyly, she let go, turned and followed Ashao.

They caught up to the boy minutes later.

~

After two hours and at least five miles of walking over blackened rubble, bleached weeds, nests of shiny roaches, Ashao finally signalled a stop. The air was metallic, acrid. Behind them they could no longer see The Walled City. Burnt out husks of machinery and houses surrounded them. The few plants that tried to grow in the dead soil looked sick, wilted.

Ashao stared off into the distance for a moment, then, voice low, said: "Movement on the horizon."

"What kind of movement?" Zack stepped forward, glancing warily at the spychiatrist which hovered and hummed at Ashao's side. "You're not leading us into a trap, are you?"

Ashao ignored his question. "Gangs live on The Edge. They're dangerous, but we have the spychiatrist. Maybe they'll trade with us for some bio-pacers."

"And maybe they'll kill us," Zack said.

"The spychiatrist won't let that happen."

"You put a lot of faith in that thing," Zack accused. "All I know is it grabbed me from my apartment with no conscience for what it was doing. It and you didn't care. How am I supposed to believe you now that it will protect Lacy and me? You want Leo, from what you've told us, for your own personal vendetta. You couldn't care less about us."

"If I didn't want you here with me, you wouldn't be," Ashao said. "I could've killed you at any time!" He looked away from Zack as if to insult him, and out over the horizon.

Zack pushed his gloved hand up his sideburns and through his hair, tugging hard. The pain made him wince, diluted his anger slightly. "All right, then. You control the spychiatrist. You have all the cards. But I don't have to like it."

"It's true," the boy said, quieter. "I may not have cared before. But that's changed." His arms crossed over his chest. On the horizon there was more movement, a flash of something bright. "I think they've seen us."

Lacy moved up to where Ashao stood. "It's strange, but I never thought I'd come to depend on a spychiatrist for my safety." She glanced over her shoulder at it and shuddered.

Zack watched her for a moment, then moved up to join them.

The land was studded with hillocks and black garbage, ruins and weeds. Zack squinted, trying to see how many people there were out there. He could make out vague shadowy shapes. They grew larger and more distinct as they approached.

The three of them stood in a line facing the group of youths who walked toward them. The spychiatrist hovered behind Ashao, silent, lights dark for the moment. There were ten of them, six females, four males. They looked to range in age from ten to twenty. All were lean-muscled, and wore damaged vinyl and fur slacks and jackets. All of them had knives. One had a tube-like weapon that made Zack nervous. Ashao, however, remained calm.

"We don't want a fight," Ashao called. "We want to trade. We need bio-pacers."

"Don't got any but what we wear," a girl said. She had purple fur and long red hair.

"Yeah, that's just too bad, isn't it?" another older girl said. She held the tube-weapon. "'Cause we want to trade, but we don't have anything. I guess we'll just have to take."

"I don't want a fight," Ashao said again.

"Then don't fight," the same girl said, obviously the leader. She blinked hard as though something had gotten in her eye. "Just give us everything you have." Her teeth glimmered, uncommonly white.

"We can't do that," Ashao said.

"What's that you got behind you?" she asked. The other members of the gang tensed, some smiling, some childishly biting their cheeks.

Ashao shook his head. The leader held her weapon up, clicked the firing mechanism, and nothing happened. Frowning, she clicked it again. When it remained silent, she threw it to the ground, yelling, "Get them!"

"Zack!" Lacy yelled, jumping back.

Zack stepped forward. "You little shits!" he called out.

But as the gang moved forward they seemed to hit an invisible barrier. One boy yelped as though burned. The others kept pushing but got nowhere.

At that moment, Ashao stepped away from the spychiatrist.

Fear stretched their faces. Three turned and started to run away. The leader growled in frustration and thrust her knife out, still getting nowhere.

"Immobilize them," Ashao said softly.

The spychiatrist rose from behind Ashao and went to hover over the remaining seven who now stood motionless, as though stopped in time.

"Dissolve barrier," Ashao ordered.

"That's incredible!" Zack stepped forward, looking the frozen gang members up and down. "Can they hear me?"

"Probably," Ashao said. "We need three bio-pacers. Take them off their arms."

"Then what'll they do for bio-pacers?" Lacy asked, moving toward them.

"They'll be fine for awhile," Ashao replied. "Gangs always have extras. They steal to live."

Zack went to the girl who'd fired the tube and touched her. She felt warm, real, perfectly natural. And yet she did not move. He tugged at her bracelet. His fingers found an indentation that must have been a switch and it unhinged, dropping into his palm. He took two more bracelets, giving one to Lacy, one to Ashao.

"How long will they stay like that?" Lacy asked as they turned to walk away.

Ashao shrugged. "Long enough."

In the distance, Zack could see the three escapees cresting a rise. "They won't cause trouble?"

"I don't think so. They know they don't have any means to fight a spychiatrist out here. But once we're through the EM barriers and we have to leave it behind, we'll have to hope we can avoid them."

"You bet your ass," Zack said.

~

The spychiatrist had stopped a few feet behind them. Ashao stared at it, manipulated a small control box in his hands, and looked up. "This is as far as the psychiatrist can go," he stated.

"You mean this is the barrier?" As they got further and further from the city, Lacy had seemed to relax.

Zack's own emotions had channeled into a fixed determination to see their journey through to the end. They were both tired, and therefore a little less tense.

"It knows. If it went any further, its programming would scramble."

"If this barrier defends against your father, against attack from your city, why do we need the bio-pacers?" Zack twisted his around on his wrist. It caught the late afternoon light: dark silver, off-white.

"Don't take it off!" Ashao moved forward, grabbing for, and missing, Zack's hand. When he saw Zack hadn't removed the device, he scowled. "My father's psychic attacks do get through. It's double security. Plus, the bio-pacer attunes to your individual brain patterns. The shield is more generalized. The bio-pacers are safer in the long run for most people."

"Not all people?" Lacy asked, glancing at her own bracelet.

"They don't work well on the clinically insane. Or anyone

already contaminated by a spychiatrist's drugs or robot juice."

"Robot juice?"

"Nano-technology. Mini-spychiatrists that can swim around in your veins and act like tiny stimoceivers that can program your actions." He looked around for a place to sit, found a blackened stump of timber. He pulled off his pack.

"I'm marked. Does that mean I'm still 'contaminated'?" Lacy asked.

"Yes," Ashao said slowly. "But since you were sent home after each time, they probably didn't do anything that would have lasting effects. Of course, you were always monitored."

She folded her arms self-consciously over her chest. "Shit."

"And Leo, too," Zack added, dropping his pack and letting the cool wind rustle through his hair. In his ears, it sounded utterly empty. A ghost wind searching for a soul.

Ahead of them were hills – not major mountains, but inclines – of dark violet and umber. They still had those to cross. They'd already come over some hills which led to ravines and gullies, all filled with heaps of charred rubble: rusted cables, wind-polished timber, metal frames, unidentifiable machines – old automobiles perhaps, or kid's toys – and a fine, grey dust that covered everything with what looked like a snow-burned coating. *Is this where my world is headed?* Zack wondered.

"We need to catch a trans-hop if we can get to a little town called Plague," Ashao muttered, staring at a metal disk in his hand.

"Is that your map?" Zack asked.

"Yes."

"How far?"

"Another day walking, maybe less. We have enough food, and I can buy more once we get to a town. I had the spychiatrist transfer my account to Free World funds. I ought to be able to access it anywhere there're people."

Zack pulled out his container of water and drank. Lacy watched him and after a moment did the same.

Ashao rose and went to the stopped spychiatrist. He spoke to it softly and it began digging a hole in the gray dirt.

"It will bury itself here and wait," Ashao said. "It can

continue to monitor us through this device." He showed them the piece of metal he'd been looking at. "It can answer my questions, but if we get into trouble there's not much it can do for us."

The spychiatrist buried itself in a matter of minutes. When it had completely vanished, all that was left was a grave of soot-dust slowly settling to the ruined earth.

Soon they were back on their feet, hiking through charred desert steeped in ruins.

Two hundred years ago, Zack thought, there were people living here. Families. Pets. Perhaps their front yards were perfect green squares of grass freshly mown, with trees that bent brown arms to the ground as if to honor the earth from which they sprouted. He imagined kids on bikes, sprinklers tossing beads of water, a ravine that filled in winter, dried to stagnant pools in summer. He crunched through ash and couldn't help but feel as if he were crushing the last remnants of some teenage boy's errant dreams of love, or the delicate thoughts of minnows slipping through cloistered pools, or some abandoned memory of a clear warm night when the full moon seemed to bounce lightly on the treetops.

Now a boy led them through this mass grave of a past that might become his future. The sky turned purple behind them. Ahead, tender pink touched the tops of hills; amber clouds streaked the bumpy horizon.

They finally stopped for the night in the middle of a flat, high area and made camp. Supper consisted of strange food out of cardboard containers. It tasted pasty and bland. Afterwards, they watched the stars come out.

"Are we going to make a fire?" Lacy asked.

"Don't need to," Ashao said.

Zack frowned, feeling colder than he'd ever known, but said nothing.

Ashao pulled a small gold coin out of his pack. When he pushed the center and threw it to the ground it grew into a large, bubble-like tent, big enough to hold them all. "That's why we don't need a fire," he said, grinning.

Three more gold coins became bedrolls that were quite warm.

Grateful for the luxury, Zack fell to sleep quickly, but awoke early, the dark through the domed tent-walls still and ghostly around him. He listened to it until his ears hurt from the silence. He wondered what Leo was doing. His fists clenched and his long, pinky fingernail dug into his palm. He remembered when he and Leo had each gotten the sculpted, black nail from a manicurist girl at a Halloween party. It had been free. Each one had dared the other to do it. Zack liked his, and had had it redone several times. Leo, not to be outdone, had followed, though he grumbled that the nail got in the way when he was tying shoes or buttoning shirts or playing computer games.

Zack turned to get into a more comfortable position. Lacy slept on his left, Ashao on his right. He tried not to touch them. His hair fell into his eyes, dry and full of static. It crackled when he pushed it away from his forehead. Tangles pulled against his fingers and he winced.

Tomorrow, he thought. Tomorrow will be better.

He had to believe.

## Chapter Twenty-Four

Stannos stared at his son's empty room. It was cold; the heat had been off for at least a full day, maybe longer. Now it was early evening and the temperature was dropping. "Where is he?"

Controller One had come with him. Stannos didn't even know the man's real name, or care, but he was the most intelligent, and Leo's personal observer. Stannos valued his advice.

"The spychiatrist is not here, either," Controller One pointed out.

"Track it," Stannos ordered.

"Already attempted. It hasn't jumped. It must have just left."

"With my boy? Could he be on foot?"

Controller One didn't comment.

Stannos' large frame whirled, his braid flying through the air behind him. "Check everything!" he ordered. "Search this room. Use the guards. I want everything checked and double-checked. Report anything unusual to me. Anything! The last time anyone saw my boy was twenty-four hours ago."

"Of course," Controller One responded.

Stannos stared at him, lowering his brow. The man had no hair and thick lashes. He looked like a baby doll. And yet the brain within was quicksilver. He'd never smelled fear off this one. "I'm trusting you," he said softly, "to find my boy."

"If he hasn't left the city, we'll find him."

"Even if he has!" Stannos insisted.

"If he's gone outside we can't track him, but I'll wager he's tracking Leo. We must concentrate on getting to Leo first."

"Yes," Stannos agreed. "Yes." He moved quickly toward the exit of his son's rooms. "I think," he said over his shoulder, "it's about time for a little unscheduled attack. Target..."

"Moltenrose," Controller One finished for him.

"You understand me well, Controller One."

The smaller man nodded, but did not smile. Stannos imagined he was thinking about how stupid it was for the Head Controller to have given his fifteen-year-old son a spychiatrist of his own to play with.

He'd thought Ashao was ready. He'd thought the special

aggression-stimoceiver conditioning of his son had assured a loyal successor to the difficult job of running the War Room. Ashao certainly hadn't seemed squeamish, and he wasn't shy.

But now Stannos regretted not testing his son further. He'd been stupid. He had spoiled the child too much after his mother died. He had left him unsupervised too often. A high IQ didn't mean the kid had sense!

When he found Ashao, the consequences were not going to be pleasant.

~

In the War Room, the armies lined the walls of the chambers, two and three to a room. They were grouped according to talent. One spychiatrist could handle an entire room of people, provided all the people were being coerced into identical behavior. In chamber one, the projecting telepaths waited, eyes fixed unseeing, pupils dilated, on the spychiatrist which hovered near them. They would be using their minds to bombard the defenses of the enemy with mental diversions, as well as lock in mental combat with the telepaths who defended their target. Stannos was not happy with this group; few of them were working tonight under prime conditions. They had needed more testing, more stimulation. But there was no time left for that.

In chamber two were the telekinetics. They could, at long distances, cause objects to move. Their main talent involved creating storms, as well as erecting energy fields for attack as well as defense. They could cause trees and buildings to fall, objects to fly through the air, power failures. They were his strongest group.

Chamber three held the seers. They projected the events of a battle onto War Room monitors as though they were first-hand witnesses. They watched images taking place in the Free World's cities and could mentally record damage, strengths and weaknesses all without ever opening their eyes. They were the prime strategists and, spychiatrist-controlled, could make decisions and advise on any situation within seconds. Lacy had done the best in this area of her expertise. Without her, Stannos had to rely on lesser talent.

There were no teleporters without Leo. Leo could have infiltrated the defenses without suspicion, and in fact had done so on a number of occasions with great success. He could integrate with the citizens from enemy territory with spychiatrist technology. Because of that rare talent, Stannos had been saving Leo for the ultimate battle. Now, it seemed, the battle was being fought *for* Leo.

The army looked less than formidable as Stannos surveyed them. They were mostly teenagers and young adults, half-clothed with empty stares. But appearance meant nothing. Their minds were treasure chests of gemstone energy. They sparkled with talent. The spychiatrists had carefully formed them into power tools of colossal force. But would it be enough against the Free World's army? Now that they had Leo?

Stannos slammed his hand against the glass of chamber two. The controller at that station glanced up calmly, gray eyes shrouded, half-closed. "Sir?" he inquired. His panel flashed brilliant blue and green lights behind him.

"We need more," Stannos said.

"More?"

"More forces. It's not enough! We need everything we've got projected outward tonight. Everything!"

"We have some in the intermediate group, but the spychiatrists advised they aren't ready yet – "

"The intermediate group, hmmm?" He put a finger, the nail long and ocher- painted, to his lips. Controller One had approved when he'd mentioned the possibility of using untried armies in his strategy. Now was the time to implement that plan. "Bring them in. I want them here, if for nothing else than back-up."

The controller at chamber two, as well as all the other controllers in the room bent to their consoles to comply with the order.

The War Room was unusually quiet. No screams yet. No wild laughter. No cries of pain to soothe Stannos' frighteningly still mind. He had grown used to the sounds of torture. Those sounds had come to mean success to him, accomplishment, creativity. When the room was too quiet, he became uncomfortable, his own mind's quietude reaching out to smother him. He became restless. Silence was the sound of indolence. Of failure.

From each chamber, spychiatrists disappeared, obeying new orders, embarking on new missions. Moments later, they reappeared with more subjects in tow. Here a slim dark man in silk pajamas, there a six-year-old boy in shorts and a striped shirt. And still another spychiatrist brought back a heavy-set teenaged girl dressed only in panties and a brassiere. She had the old marks on her stomach: a set of three triangles.

More people appeared in each chamber as the spychiatrists vanished and returned. A man in a blue turban. Another in a loincloth. Still another in some kind of uniform. They were all young, most under 20, the oldest no more than 35.

Stannos watched, still unhappy. None of them amounted to what he'd had with Leo. He chastised himself for not guarding that one more carefully. He realized only now he should have kept the boy. Spychiatrists could have raised him as well as any parents, and Leo would never have gained independent control.

Like Ashao.

Only now did Stannos realize that he should have had a spychiatrist raise Ashao, and not some soft-spoken metal contraption called a 'teacher'. Ashao's mother had left the teacher to her son, her voice, her programming all approved by Stannos, and at the time he had thought it harmless, a kid's toy which could also teach. But he'd been too soft with Ashao, too undisciplined.

And if what he suspected were true, that Ashao had committed treason, Ashao would die. Die at Stannos' hands. And Stannos would force himself to feel nothing.

Even now, his only emotion was regret. Regret for the waste of a good mind, for fifteen years of useless aggression therapy bombarded into Ashao's rooms by Stannos' own personal stimoceiver. Therapy that had apparently backfired.

Of course he could have other children, but it would take years before the child would be able to take Ashao's place. Fifteen years of reinforced learning, fifteen years of a spychiatrist playing babysitter to make sure that this time Stannos' heir had the proper attitude, the proper stillness within that demanded constructive goals no matter what the price.

Fifteen years too long!

What remained of this city since the Seven Day War two hundred years ago needed protection. To keep massive destruction from happening again, people had to be controlled. The Free World did not want that, but Stannos and his father and his grandfather had known the truth. The best way was control. They had to win against the outside.

Nothing was more important than winning ultimate power for his city. His people. Himself. It was for the ultimate good. Where he'd failed with Ashao, his future child would be made to understand that.

No matter what it took.

## Chapter Twenty-Five

Past shadow-sculpted destruction, at the crest of a gentle, cindered hill, Ashao, Lacy and Zack stared at the small town. Below them, Plague glittered in their eyes, on their bio-pacer bracelets. It was early afternoon. The sun was spreading its butter-light into the west, dropping toward a distant sea and an unseen spire, their goal.

"Well," Zack commented. "At least the sun still rises in the east and sets in the west."

"Did you expect different?" Ashao asked, squinting up at the man who could've been Leo, should've been Leo.

"Everything here is different," Zack replied. His left gloved hand rose. He pointed. "What's that?"

Ashao followed the direction of the gesture. Something gleamed on the horizon sending diamond fractures of light into the air. It was the trans-hop reflecting afternoon. Ashao could make out the individual round cars connected together like a caterpillar's segments and sliding along a thin, raised rail.

"That's our ticket to Leo." Ashao cocked his hip, bit the inside of his cheek. "I hope."

The town was a collection of greenhouses and odd cottages, with one dust-filled main street lined with small, musty shops and a simple trans-hop boarding ramp. Plague was for outcasts, hermits, loners. Plague was a stop between cities. It wasn't much to see, and there were few people about.

The ticket seller looked bored as Ashao handed him his credit chip. He never even asked for proper I.D., though it was obvious they were strangers who had walked into town from quite a distance away.

"You from some gang?" he asked.

All three shook their heads. Ashao frowned.

"Weather-doc's say a storm's brewin'," the man said. "From the east. If it's bad, the trans-hops could go off-line for a few hours. You might get stuck. Sometimes gangs attack the lines to rob them when that happens. From here to Moltenrose is about six hours if you beat the storm."

"We'll risk it," Ashao said, glancing over his shoulder out past the ticket window overhang and into the sky.

Somewhere Stannos was planning, coordinating, organizing. He was amassing power. A prickle of static. A faint, flame-scented breeze. Ashao could feel the energy-hike, the same kind of energy he'd felt when he'd walked into the War Room that first time. Stannos was gathering his army. He could sense it. Perhaps they were already too late.

Ashao's only consolation was the fact that his father did not have Leo. Leo was the wild card. Their only hope.

A plan was forming in Ashao's mind. Destruction, yes. Again. But also, re-construction. If they could make it to Moltenrose. If there was still time.

## Part X - Moltenrose Tower (Parallel Earth)

## Chapter Twenty-Six

The room shimmered in gold sparkles around Leo. His bio-pacer blistered against his wrist. Dazzled, he focused on a face beside him, found familiar features. The one called Scimitar who had only just visited him stared back, ice-cold blue.

For a moment he thought he'd passed out again, dreamed himself in another place. But the warm hand on his arm was definitely not Zack's cool touch waking him from yet another nightmare.

Leo sat forward, then, and saw the girl. Long dark curls swept the paper sleeves of her robe. Her eyes were clear gold, like a forest pond drenched in sunlight. Her skin was a combination of bronze and pinks that made her seem to glow.

"I know you," he said softly. It was no dream. He could smell her. Desert rose. A shiver tried to twist his spine. On its heels, that same horrible memory: Pressing her body into dry pine needles as she screamed –

Scimitar squinted, his lips thinning as he glared. Leo felt a stirring like anger, or hate, but it did not originate from within him. His fingers curled; he forced them to relax, forced the yell that had been building in his throat back down until his chest and stomach ached.

The young woman looked worried. "You remember me?" Her hand on his arm fell away. The long, slim hand clenched, knuckles whitening.

"From the tower. Yes." He didn't want to say he remembered more. His lungs shook as he spoke, his voice seeming rough and new.

She looked somewhat relieved at his answer, eyes brightening. "I'm Kittin. I called you."

"I know," Leo repeated, coughing once. "Did I really come here using my mind?" The shock of it made his emotions flat for the moment.

"How else would you get here?" Kittin looked up at Scimitar.

Despite the shock, Leo smiled. "Wow. I guess I didn't believe it until just now."

"You're here because you came of your own free will," Kittin replied.

"My free will? But you called me here, didn't you?" Everything was still so much like a dream, confusing, blurry around the edges. And Zack– The thought sent a hot spark of panic through him. Was he still back home sleeping in bed with Lacy? Did they even know he was gone yet?

"You're a weapon," Scimitar stated. "You came as a weapon and left as one. But you were under another's control. When our people discovered who you were, they decided it might do them some good to get you here on our terms. They used Kittin to lure you here and succeeded."

Kittin glared at the word 'used'.

"I'm not here of my own free will, though! I'm a prisoner. You told me that," Leo said. He turned, surveying the simple room, the strange, sparkling walls, the fur rug. "And now I want to leave."

"It's not that easy." Scimitar scratched the side of his neck, tilted his head. "We're all one big Ignorant Army family. You're too valuable. If you tried to leave right now, we'd have to stop you."

"But you just helped me escape from my room. And you said nothing could stop me. Not even this." He touched his bio-pacer.

Scimitar shrugged. His eyes held Leo's.

Leo decided he didn't like those eyes. They stared at him as though stripping him of not only clothing, but flesh as well. This man knew answers to his questions, understood everything that was happening. But Leo didn't trust him.

Kittin's gaze was rapt, magnetic. She watched Leo with looks alternating from obsession to fear. They weren't hungry looks like Scimitar's, but they encompassed him all the same. It was hard to look at her, though, without remembering what he'd done to her.

"Nothing can stop you from leaving here," Scimitar finally said. "But if you go, the spychiatrists will grab you wherever you are outside our influence. You can't leave until you learn to protect yourself. The spychs can't get at you here so you're safe for now. Our defenses would destroy them the moment they arrived to fetch you."

"While he learns, where're we going to hide him from the

others?" Kittin said suddenly to Scimitar.

As if dismissing Leo now, Scimitar said, "No one comes into my room. Ever. He'll be safe there."

Kittin started to shake her head, then seemed to change her mind. "You haven't forgotten your promise to me – "

Leo sat forward on his knees, paper pants stretching, almost tearing. "I'm not staying here. You don't have to hide me. You just have to help me. I remember everything and I just want to get out. Go back. To Zack."

They stared at him.

"Don't you get it?" Scimitar asked.

Leo started to say no.

"I already said no one can cage you. We're just trying to help you, keep you safe so you can eventually get back safely. But if you leave now, that'll never happen."

Kittin nodded in hesitant agreement.

There was something unspoken between her and Scimitar that made Leo feel trapped. But their words also helped him better understand that he had an ability, a talent far beyond what Andus had told him. He'd been used in whatever battle was being fought on this strange, alternate world. And would continue to be used unless he stopped it. He fingered the silver bio-pacer on his wrist. The skin underneath it burned. "How can I get this off?"

Kittin grabbed his hand, turning it palm up in her lap. She frowned. "Burns." She glanced up at Scimitar who still stood, leaning his bony shoulder against one sparkle-wall. "It burned him, Scimitar."

"He'll have to live with it for now."

Leo's brows came together. He looked at Scimitar's chest instead of the too-cold face. "When I left home Zack was still in bed. I need to know if he's all right. Is there a way to do that?"

"We have to find out where he is first. Time passes differently between your Earth and this one. He could be anywhere. Who knows, when you pulled away from that spych, you could've killed him with the backlash."

"Scimitar, you don't have to be so mean!" Kittin said. "That's not true!"

Leo's emotions went cold, his throat instantly dry. "Dead?"

"I can see it in your mind." Scimitar spoke slowly, with an almost teasing inflection. "That last moment, when the spych appeared at the foot of your bed. There were a man and a woman in bed with you." His eyebrows rose. His lips formed a frowning smirk. "Then things started flying about the room. The woman – she was doing it, I see. An uncontrolled telekinetic, probably. But the spych followed you, then lost you. You escaped it once on your own. I'm not a seer, but August is. He can tell us if the spych went back for them. Or if they were left for dead."

"Could the spychiatrist...spych have taken them?"

"Since you disappeared while it was trying to retrieve you, if the other two saw it you don't think it would just leave them, do you?"

Leo's skin prickled with horror, itching. If Zack were dead he had nothing to return to, no one. "I don't know. If it came only for me-" he began. It had done so in the past. But Lacy hadn't been there in the past. She figured in all of this, too, though Leo still wasn't sure how.

Scimitar interrupted. "August will know."

"I don't trust August," Kittin stated flatly.

"Do you have a better idea?" When Kittin didn't reply, he said, "He'll help. I won't give him a choice." He turned away, brushing lightly at his vinyl sleeve. It was a pose, very superior, and Leo felt his stomach clench. He didn't like this guy, and he wasn't going to go with him if he could help it.

"Who is this 'August'?" Leo asked.

"He's crazy," Kittin said.

Leo almost screamed at the understatement. *Crazy? Who wasn't around here.* "And he can tell me where Zack might be?" he asked.

"I said he would, didn't I?" Scimitar glared.

"Then get him," Leo said. "But I'll stay here until you come back. With Kittin."

Scimitar's eyebrows shot up. It was clear he didn't like to be told what to do. "Kittin's unsecured."

"It's true," Kittin said softly. "I'm watched too closely. You'll have to go with him."

Leo stared at her. She was beautiful. He sensed a vulnerability in her, a kinship. Why didn't she hate him? Did she not remember everything he'd done to her? He almost reached out to her. Instead, his fingers pressed against his palm.

"It's not as if I want the company," Scimitar hissed. "But for the safety of all of us-"

Leo's entire body remained tense. He frowned, then stood shakily, his paper pants sticking to his sweaty skin, threatening to rip. "All right." His fear was an old thing, an emotion he'd lived with for far too long. He wasn't going to let it run his life anymore. "I'll go with you."

Scimitar turned, face neutral. "I'll make sure it's all clear in the corridor."

"Maybe you can find me some real clothes, too," Leo said gruffly.

"I'll bring you something to eat from the kitchen after awhile." Kittin stood. In her hands, she clutched dark red flowers. They trailed through the air, blossoms of blood. "Here." She held one out to Leo with a smile. Without thinking, he accepted it. The stem felt dry and stiff between his fingers.

~

Scimitar's room was not at all what Leo expected. The humidifier made the room misty, almost cold. His skin went clammy as he entered through the high threshold. A floor of lavender synthetic fur, and blue and peach walls under a black ceiling overdosed his sensibilities for a moment. In the center sat a wide, flat mattress without a frame. In one corner was a pile of clothes, not paper, as Kittin seemed to prefer, but lots of beige and white cottons mixed with vinyl. Other objects were scattered around the room: a table piled with what looked like electronic equipment, a large metal box, a black chest of drawers, pieces of plastic rope, a cluster of jewelry by a plastic box beside the bed.

"Don't touch anything. I'll be right back," Scimitar said.

Leo sat at the edge of the mattress on a folded stack of blankets and wrapped his arms around his knees. Waiting. He'd been doing that ever since he'd come to this forsaken place Andus had called the Tower. He was getting tired of it. What if Zack wasn't safe? He needed to know now. And he didn't trust Scimitar as far as he could hurl him.

His hair thickened and curled under the humidity. He turned as the door opened.

"So this is the magic one?" said a voice, not Scimitar's. "Ah, the boy with the autumn hair. The one Kittin-tittin fished and caught."

Leo saw a young man, a boy actually, with partially shaved red hair, bangs hanging in his face. His pants were black paper, short, barely covering his knees. He wore a white paper tunic over too-thin shoulders, and swayed as he entered the room, almost as if dancing, as if drunk. He was barefoot.

Behind him, Scimitar stood, long arms crossed over his chest. He wore his perpetual, too-serious look, and kneed the boy in the rump from behind. "Shut-up and just find his brother."

August jumped, still grinning. "He wants me," he said conspiratorially, leaning toward Leo. Spittle flew from his wide, red mouth.

Leo frowned. "What?"

August danced away, circled the room touching all four pastel walls with his outstretched hands, and spun, humming a monotone tune.

"Your twin-grin-sin," August muttered, eyes closed. "I can see him. But why should I tell you where he is?" Green eyes opened. "What do I get in return?"

Fascinated, Leo shrugged, still sitting on the edge of the mattress. He was afraid to move, remembering the street-song barter: 'If I do something for you, you gotta do something for me in return.' It was usually Zack, afraid of nothing, who did that 'something in return'. "You can get out of here, if you want," Leo said.

August frowned. "You think I'm here against my will?"

Scimitar came all the way into the room and shut the door, locking it with his palm. "I will give you something," he said, standing threateningly over August, who giggled.

"I have secrets, you have secrets. Who's going to out-bluff who? I don't think you scare me, Scim," August gurgled. "But I'll let you think you do, if it gives you a goose."

"I can pin you up by your ass-flesh to these walls, if you like."

August tossed his hair, smirked. To Leo, he said softly,

"You can't go to him now. He's moving. Fast. On a trans-hop, I think. If you jump and miss, you'll be killed."

"Then he's alive!" His breath came out loud, as if he'd been holding it for a long, long time. "What's a trans-hop?" Leo asked.

"Public transportation, idiot," Scimitar answered. "Don't tell me you don't have 'em where you're from?"

"We have cars, airplanes, trains," Leo replied.

"I know what a train is." August smiled. "Like that." He put a finger to his lips and kissed it. "Only better." Then he sucked his finger into his mouth making loud, wet noises.

Leo looked away. "Then he's here. In this world. The spychiatrist did go back for him. And Lacy."

"Of course he's here," August said around his finger. "He's heading in this direction, too. With a boy and a girl. Lacy, you said? Ouch!" He removed his finger from his mouth. "Bit it. Hell a-calling, I bit myself!"

"When they stop, can I go to him?" Leo asked. "Is he on this side of–" He couldn't think of the words. "Of the border?"

"Don't know when they'll stop. But probably. If the storm doesn't come first."

"What storm?" Scimitar moved quickly toward August, put a rough hand on his shoulder and turned him. "What storm?" he asked again, louder.

"Major bru-ha-ha." August giggled. "The Walled City is calling in all their reinforcements. I think they want little-ittle-mio-Leo all for their very own. They lost him; they're mad."

"Have you reported this?" Scimitar asked.

August shrugged. "Was just going to. Just now. But they knew getting Leo was going to have consequences. Now they've lost him. They don't know he's still here. They're already scared. They've been expecting the storm."

Scimitar looked as if he was about to hit August. Instead, he turned away, shoulders tightening. "Why weren't we informed?"

"I don't care about a storm, or your war. I just want to get my brother and leave! And I want protection from those damned monster machines!" Leo ran his hands through his long hair and cradled the sides of his head.

"You've got to care about us," Scimitar said. "You're the

center of it all."

Leo felt himself withdraw, his arms hugged around his legs, into a small ball. "The center," he muttered. "Everyone keeps telling me that. I remember fighting for whoever was controlling me. I remember the torture, the pain. But it's not my war anymore. And what could I do now to help? I've only fought when the spychiatrists controlled me. Never on my own!"

They were all looking at him and he felt suddenly cowardly, selfish. What would Zack do? Zack wasn't afraid of anything.

August danced toward him. Leo watched the bare, white feet against the purple carpet. "You did do something," August said. "And you can again. You know that's why Little-Kittle wants you dead. You got her good, boy-man. Uh-uh-uh." He made an obscene noise. "Real good!"

Leo jumped off the bed as August made some more disgusting noises. "Stop it!" His eyes blazed with heat. "Stop!"

"Get outta here!" Scimitar shouted.

"Letting me go?" August asked.

"Go report the rot-damned storm. Then let me know what the strategy is, if there's any. But if you breathe any word of Leo –"

"Don't worry so, Scim." August's chin was shining with drool. "Leo's the key-key- key. I wouldn't dream of giving him away! We'll probably be called to battle stations any minute now anyway. Then he'll be on his own...or discovered." He chortled all the way down the corridor.

Scimitar slammed the door.

"Will he tell me where Zack is when Zack stops?" Leo asked, still breathing hard, desperately looking anywhere except at Scimitar.

The taller man let out a puff of air that vibrated his lips and didn't answer.

Leo bowed his head, staring into the purple shag, then sat hard again on the mattress. "Is it true what he said?" His voice came out dry, harsh. "Does Kittin want me dead?"

"Don't ask me."

"You don't know?" Leo stated, looking up again. Scimitar was half-pacing, running his hands along his black, chipped dresser, kicking at the rug.

"I didn't say that."

"Oh."

There was a knock at the door. Scimitar strode to it and opened it a crack, peering out. Then the door opened all the way and Kittin entered, a covered tray in her hands. She set it on the floor and moved away from it, coming to stand in front of Leo. She frowned, coughing from the sudden mist she breathed. For a long moment she stared down at him. Leo glanced at the tray.

"Is that food?"

"What passes for it," she replied. Then she reached out and touched his hair. "So soft-"

Leo, uncomfortable, moved away from her touch, still staring into her bright eyes. If she wanted him dead, she was going about it in a very strange way.

Scimitar was sniffing around the tray. "You didn't bring my *raca*. And what is this slop?"

Kittin shrugged. "I'm not a cook. I'm not your servant. Go get your *raca* yourself." She knelt by Leo. "I remember you as a boy. It's hard to see the same person now when I look at you."

"I'm not that same person at all. I'm sorry – "

"Don't say it!" she whispered quickly. She was both sinewy and soft at the same time, leaning forward, her hands brushing paper-clad thighs. When he pushed her hands gently away he couldn't help the unwanted flow of images: a brisk vision of moonlight dappling trees, a pine-needle carpeted path.

"You weren't quite a man the last time I saw you."

Leo winced, his heart beat increasing.

"But that's unimportant now," she quickly added.

"It wasn't me." He hesitated, but could think of nothing more to say.

"How touching," Scimitar said from the other side of the room, his mouth full. He sat propped against a wall, the tray in his lap.

"Share some of that with Leo," Kittin said.

"It's okay. I'm not hungry right now," Leo said, his stomach still churning.

"Good choice," Scimitar muttered. "Tastes like maggots."

Kittin smiled. "Thought that was your favorite."

Her smile was contagious and Leo, for the first time, showed her his own.

"I had to make sure you were really controlled before I decided to help you," she said. "And now I know. You were controlled. I like the you that's separate from this war. The 'you' that's not full of tricks."

For a moment, she reminded Leo of August. Her words bordered nonsense, her tone pitched high, diction slightly slurred.

"They were controlling you," Kittin continued. "I know that now. I didn't, then."

Leo's smile faded. "I don't –" He stopped. "August said you wanted me dead." He glanced askance at Scimitar who was still eating.

Scimitar met his gaze sharply, mouth frozen in mid-chew.

Kittin tilted her head. Her hair fell in a torrent of dark satin. "Maybe I wanted you dead. Once."

He said nothing. He couldn't blame her for that. What he didn't understand was what followed as Kittin leaned forward then and suddenly kissed him. Despite Scimitar's humidifier, static crackled between them. Leo saw a fleck of green, pulled back.

"Hey!" The tray slid from Scimitar's lap as he moved forward on hands and knees. "Damn rot and hell. Get out of here Kittin! You're just making it easier for them. If they're watching through you –"

Kittin jumped up. "What?"

"Watching?" Leo echoed. He hadn't thought of that. But if he'd been watched all his life, then why think it should stop now?

"They can't do anything to him, Scimitar," Kittin said, laughing. "They can't control him anymore. Or me, it seems."

"But they're watching." He narrowed his gaze. "You spy for them twenty-four hours a day."

"Is that why you wouldn't come to me for real last night?" She stood and walked over to Scimitar. "You said you'd prove their theory wrong. That you could touch me. That you would. You still haven't. At least, not intimately. That first hug didn't count. And mental touch doesn't count." She reached out, one hand coming within inches of his shoulder and stopping.

Leo watched them, confused. Scimitar stood up, glaring down at Kittin. Then his face softened slightly, though he still looked at her with disdain. "You never answered my question."

"What?" she demanded.

"Whether or not you'll marry me." He scowled as he said the word marry, as if still teasing her.

"Oh. That." She whirled, her hair flying out from her like a cape. "You weren't serious." But Leo could see that her face constricted.

Scimitar simply gathered up the tray and thrust it at her. "Take this away."

Kittin stopped, her hair slamming into her face. "Take it away yourself!"

Leo closed his eyes, not wanting to see or hear either of them anymore, and leaned back upon the mattress.

"Look, he's tired. We should let him alone so he can sleep," Scimitar said.

"You don't care about him. Only I do," Kittin insisted. "Doesn't that bother you?" A little laugh followed.

Leo heard Scimitar respond quietly. "Just go. I'll stand watch. He can sleep with no interruptions from me."

"I'll be back, then," Kittin said.

He heard the door shut. Scimitar's knees crackled as he lowered himself to the floor again.

Fear kept Leo from sinking into a deep sleep, but he lay quietly dozing as nearly incomprehensible dreams and memories flickered through his mind, giving him no rest.

## Chapter Twenty-Seven

There was a girl about five years old standing before him. At first Leo thought she was Lacy. Then he saw her dark curls and clear gold eyes. Kittin.

The girl-Kittin and he ran through groves of trees. He climbed one, the bark gritty against his palms. The scent of jasmine enfolded him. The girl, though she was very small, tried to follow.

As she fell, screaming, Leo jerked awake.

Scimitar sat against one wall, knees bent, staring at him.

Leo blinked, then pushed himself up on one elbow. "I had the strangest dream," he muttered, trying to cover his true feelings.

Stone-faced, Scimitar replied coldly, "That wasn't a dream."

"How do you know!"

"You remember it all. So why are you running from it?" he accused.

"I'm not running! You saw how Kittin was with me. She forgives me." Leo rubbed at his eyes with the backs of his hands. "How long have I slept? Did August come back?" The look Scimitar gave him again unnerved him.

"Kittin forgives too easily. An hour. And no." He was like a machine, popping off answers with no regard toward feelings.

"What were you doing, probing my dreams?" Leo asked.

"I didn't have to. You were projecting."

"I'm not– I don't know how to do that."

"You were, though. No wonder you're so valuable. You're a multi-talented one. You hop, jump and project all at the same time, man. You can do it all. You just don't know how to tap it yet."

"I can't read your mind like you read mine," Leo pointed out. It was still all so hard to absorb. Some moments he didn't believe any of it. He was a little hungry now, but there was no food anymore. The tray was gone.

"Perhaps you're not inclined to." He crossed his arms over his chest. "I, on the other hand, have no choice."

"So how do you know my dream was a memory?"

"The textures. The scents."

"Then, in my dream, you saw Kittin?" he ventured. "As a

little girl?"

Scimitar nodded once.

"I really hurt her, didn't I?" He got his legs underneath him and sat. The paper pants still, miraculously, hadn't ripped.

"Do you really want an answer to that question?"

He shuddered. "No. I already know."

Air hissed through his teeth. "Do you?" The tone was not at all friendly. Scimitar rose gracefully, walked to the edge of the mattress, and knelt. "Do you know because of you she was taken away from her parents? That because of you she's lived the life of a freak?" There were shadows in his eyes, now, and a glint that wasn't as cold as before, though still dark and pain-filled.

They were so close Leo could feel the other man's heat. He shuddered once, then gripped his hands together in his lap. "No. I didn't know that."

"You ruined her!" His voice, though soft, was now harsh. "I oughta –" Suddenly, Scimitar grabbed Leo's hands in a painful grip. "Damn you, look at what you did!" The last sentence came out low, soft. Leo felt himself start to fall as if the bed and floor had been pulled out from under him. Scimitar's eyes became blue streaks in his mind, night inlaid. There was a brief ache, then warmth, like a blood-rush. It was as if the other man surrounded him, encompassed his entire soul. It felt like an embrace, though he didn't relish the thought. Scimitar seemed, on the surface, all needles and grit. This was an attack.

Then, before he could even blink, it was as if his mind and body had projected upon a new scene.

He saw Kittin. Smelled pine. A brook sparkled, green, silver, white. A half moon above seemed to brighten the whole sky.

A familiar Kittin was by the brook, hair flowing into the shadows as though parts of her were made of the shade, the water, the rock where she crouched.

"Are you new?" she asked.

"New?" he heard himself ask.

"Yeah. New. I don't know you."

"I don't know you."

"Well, now we meet."

"I – I think I'm lost." It was so real. He could smell the night, the glade, the water. He touched an old oak's trunk, the rough wood seeming to melt into his skin.

He realized then what Scimitar was doing. Forcing him to relive this memory. The worst memory of all! *No!* his mind cried out.

*You deserve worse than this!* came the mental answer.

"Oh, you'll feel that way for a little while, until you get used to it. I remember the first time I came here –" Kittin was saying.

The conversation continued for some minutes. She talked of drugs and a 'compound' where she apparently lived. He talked of his home in the high desert of California. All the while, she seemed to be flirting with him. Her gold eyes flicked over his form; her body seemed to bend toward him.

His own body became instantly aroused.

*No!* But there was no answer this time. He was lost. Behind the arousal, he felt a pressure, a kind of ache that made him feel desperate and scared. She told him her name, but he couldn't remember his own.

He sat beside her, by the brook, and asked, "You like me?" His insides thundered for her now, her touch, her scent, her essence. Before, he'd always rejected these kinds of feelings.

"Of course I like you."

"Girls don't usually like me."

Her laughter echoed, making him feel both shy and powerful.

He told her she was pretty. She explained her paper dress was the best of its kind, the thinnest. Practically invited him to rip it off her.

Then she touched him, took his hand and placed it on the pulsing curve of her breast. They talked some more but he didn't hear any of it beyond the roar of his blood, a kind of heat and force he couldn't fight, couldn't control. She removed a silver cuff from her wrist. It glittered, double-arched, as she set it on the ground between them.

And then they were standing, dancing under the thick tree branches. It felt great. She tilted her head back and let him kiss her. And when he did he saw himself slide down a long incline, at the bottom of which was a lake of flame.

Tremors of fear rose in him, only to vanish as if the emotion had never existed.

In one part of his mind he saw everything he did to her, as though he were an observer, beginning with ripping the dress from her body. He was like a puppet. He had no control. When she fell back on the path, struggling beneath him, he tried to stop, tried to just turn away. But something wouldn't let him.

He tore at her dress until it disintegrated, tore at her flesh until it bruised. She stopped fighting almost immediately, but he could see the tears in her eyes, the salt dropping to her temples and into her hair. A diamond tiara of tears decorated those curls now. He knew he was hurting her. He couldn't stop.

In Scimitar's room, Leo cried out.

In the memory, he thrust into Kittin brutally, hips smacking against hers, blood inflaming him, twisting what he was doing into an insane pleasure he didn't want but couldn't stop.

"No," he called, hearing himself speak aloud now. "Stop this! Scimitar!"

But the scene continued to play.

"Scimitar, stop it!"

It was like a dream he couldn't wake from. *Now*, he thought. *Open your eyes. Now! Wake up! But it kept going.*

He trembled. He screamed.

Sexual heat exploded in a black shame through him.

When he finally did open his eyes Scimitar was holding his arms down. Leo flailed against the mattress, kicked up. "Why did you do that?" The kick caught Scimitar in the stomach, but he showed no sign of feeling it. Anger and pain diminished Leo's personality to animal desperation.

"Why?" he cried out again.

"Because you deserve it!" Scimitar shot back, teeth showing.

"But I– I didn't do it! It wasn't really me!"

"You did it and you liked it!"

"You bastard!" Leo kicked again and tried to wrestle out of Scimitar's grasp. Tears formed, blurring everything. He shut his eyes. "Why?"

"You raped her! Why would I even want to stop your

pain?" Scimitar pushed against him with his entire body, the weight pressing the air from Leo's lungs. "You're lucky you're even alive! I want to kill you, you see! But before I do, you deserve to relive everything you did to her!"

Leo struggled harder, forcing Scimitar to one side, and blindly followed, using knees, elbows, fists. "I didn't rape her! I couldn't do that to another person! It wasn't me! You fucking bastard!" His rage, stored since childhood, sequestered, ignored, came pulsing forth. Adrenalin pushed him blind, strengthening him where no strength remained. But it wasn't enough. He clawed. He grabbed. But Scimitar was all bone and sinew, slippery, too insubstantial.

Scimitar rolled him onto his back again, straddling him. He swung hard. A fist caught Leo firmly in the jaw, sending streaks of white light through his vision. "You can't deny what you did to her you scum-rot clotting –"

Flame shot through his head. Deny? Leo went limp, his eyes still open. "But it wasn't me!" He heard himself yell, desperation piercing through the shock. He instinctively projected that and more into the mind of the man holding him down. At first he wanted Scimitar to feel his pain, his anger, his desire to rip him apart for willingly subjecting him to such a horrific reenactment. Instead, all his feelings flooded into regret, frustration, despair. *I'm not that boy*, his mind droned. *I didn't want to hurt her.* The emotions by themselves were strong enough to hurt. More than wishes. More than daydreamed violence.

Surprisingly, Scimitar responded as if stung. "No!" He let Leo go, covered his face. "Stop!"

Leo projected outward his feelings again with renewed strength at the sound of that voice.

"You asshole!" Scimitar grabbed his shoulders, shook him. "Stop!"

Leo barely felt the touch, turned his emotions into a probe and stabbed deep, his pain like a lance pushing, cutting, spreading – It was instinctive. *Protect yourself*, a voice in his mind said. *Kill the enemy. Kill!*

But another part of himself stood back calmly, bright and strong, crossed his arms and stated flatly, "No."

It was a voice very much like Zack's. An inner voice that was who he always aspired to be. He stopped, teetering, at the lip of an abyss.

*Scimitar?*

*Yes.*

He was in the other man's mind, now, the abyss surrounding him, and saw more pain in an instant than he could've imagined. The broiling dark surpassed even his own.

A little boy begged to be touched, but when he reached for the woman who was his mother his hands went right through her. He screamed and a robot picked him up, its hard arms unable to offer comfort, its mind cold and piercing as the boy tried to garner a thought, a feeling from it.

A young man, cultivating self-hatred from lack of outside stimulus – for anyone sane enough to know better couldn't stand to touch a telepath – flailed at himself with a wire brush, leaving red marks all over his long, lean body.

Scimitar gasped. "Leo! Damn you! Get out of my mind!"

But there it was. Leo stared, eyes clearer now, deep into the blue stones of Scimitar's face. They were locked in this new form of combat now. Leo saw. And pulled. Projected. And received.

"Stop!" Scimitar said. Too quiet. Too tense.

What Leo saw and continued to receive stunned him. Scimitar had gone taut in his grip.

The wall against all the years of contained pain burst under Leo's demand. Scimitar, locked now within Leo's mental strength, pressed against him, his weight making it hard for Leo to breathe.

More quick images flew into his mind.

There was a gold ring, a velvet rope. Ironic, Leo thought, that I was accused of self- mutilation I didn't do, and this boy, this man has beaten himself up for years without anyone else finding out.

As Leo looked closer at the inner images his mind focused, bringing a few of the stronger ones to the foreground. There was sudden sharp, physical pain, as some memories returned to the present. Here was Scimitar cutting himself with a small, white-handled knife. Here he whipped himself with sharp bouquets of wires. Here again he was tying his genitals with a string into a painful, punishing position.

Too many dark secrets floated in this void. Too many

234

missing pieces killed by excised love.

Scimitar smothered a moan. Leo didn't want to stop now, fueled by amazement and pity, and pulled the other man's rigid shoulders down, his grip heavy, muscles cramped. His face pushed against Scimitar's right shoulder. He didn't know why he wanted the contact. Wanted to see more.

"Stop!" Gritted teeth. Pulsing muscles.

A velvet rope, looped through a gold ring, bound Scimitar's genitals even right now, hurting him.

Leo's heavy breathing turned to gasps.

"Stop it! Get out of my mind now!" The taller man hissed.

Leo heard the desperation and blanked his mind with relief, with regret. Emotion gagged him. "Okay, I'm out," he managed to croak.

The shoulder against Leo's cheek heaved. "And stop pitying me, damn you!"

Leo heard him breathe in, out, the air harsh sounding in his lungs. Scimitar still straddled him, still held him down.

"Why?" Leo asked, soft, unguarded. The one word made Scimitar gasp, start to pull back, close into himself. But it was as if he didn't have the strength. Leo could have pushed him away at that point. Instead, he remained still, quiet.

"I have to do that to myself," Scimitar finally said, voice flat. "I'm unpure. You...you're not like me. You don't know how it is – "

Leo felt the man mouth the unfinished sentences into his hair. The telepath's breath was a little flame burning at his scalp. Leo's arms shook now that he realized he had given Scimitar a taste of his own torture. He didn't know how he'd done it, but desperation helped. He had touched Scimitar's soul, if indeed the man even had one.

"Okay, I was wrong to do what I did to you, make you see yourself raping her," Scimitar breathed, trying to sound matter-of-fact, pushing himself away. "You've proved it, okay? I was wrong."

Scimitar came up on his arms and stared down at Leo, blue eyes tight, small. Surprisingly, instead of pushing himself all the way up, Scimitar leaned forward against him again until Leo could barely catch his breath.
"I'm evil, damn you," Scimitar whispered in his ear.

And in his mind, Leo felt/saw/heard: "Forgive

(emptyechoinside) me. I should not have made you relive it. You don't deserve the pain – "

Leo rolled away on the mattress until his back was to him. "Nobody does," he said quietly, hands clutched to his chest.

~

They eyed each other from across the room. Wary. Two cats sniffing the air.

Scimitar watched Leo finger his jaw where a pale brown bruise darkened the skin just below the fine cheekbone. The young man's eyes were still bright, still filmed with the sheen of an injured soldier, fallen, haunted with truth. When their eyes met by accident, Leo looked quickly away.

Scimitar closed his, feeling uncanny warmth.

Finally, a soft voice broke the silence. "Why do you do that to yourself?"

Scimitar tensed, his teeth scraping against each other. He kept telling himself: *I am nothing. I am the shell. It's everyone else's sins that make me the way I am.* He opened his eyes and said: "I told you." He swallowed, biting the inside of his cheek. "Besides, I like pain."

Leo stood, arms crossed over his chest, and circled the mattress on the floor. He stopped at the foot, glancing again at Scimitar. "Are you all like that here? Insane, I mean."

Long fingers combed through silver hair. "What is the definition of insane?" He did not look up.

"This whole damn place!" Leo spread his arms. They were golden, lean-muscled, bare. His pants stuck to him, the paper ripped in about a dozen places now.

Scimitar got up and went to his dresser. He opened the top drawer and took out a pair of vinyl slacks. From the next drawer, he withdrew a shirt. He threw them in Leo's direction. "Here. Take them."

Leo bent, retrieving the clothing from the floor. "You don't wear paper?"

"Hate it." Scimitar watched as Leo shouldered into the cotton shirt and drew it closed. He fumbled with the fastenings.

There was another long silence.

Leo kept fighting the shirt.

Scimitar approached him, reached out. "They're magnets," he said, fastening one.

Leo nodded, and turned to the side, brushing him off.

Scimitar watched him do up the shirt. "You didn't rape her," he said after a moment. "The controllers of The Walled City did. I know that."

Leo moved away and sat on the edge of the mattress. He fingered the vinyl pants but did not put them on. He ran the back of his hand across his eyes. "I could kill them right now for that. And I've never killed anyone."

*Anyone that* you *wanted to kill,* Scimitar thought. But kept silent.

"Will you help me?" Leo asked.

Scimitar leaned against the dresser, fingering a black comb dusted with silver. He could feel the tight, velvet cord he still wore about his waist, the tug at his genitals, the sting of gold metal against sensitive tissues. He felt like a fool now that Leo knew his secret. It was perhaps time to leave behind certain prisons. Even if it meant risk, and sin, and death.

"Kittin and I will both help you," he said softly. Then he tossed Leo the comb. "Your hair's a mess."

The comb landed with a soft plop on the purple carpet at Leo's feet. He picked it up. Their eyes met.

This time, neither one looked away.

~

Kittin returned about an hour later, a drooling, grinning August in tow, an August who was all too careful not to touch her. To Leo he looked like a pumpkin with hair.

She looked at Leo's jaw, then glanced at Scimitar.

"I fell," Leo quickly said, running his fingers across the bruise.

Kittin merely shrugged, then turned to August. "Tell them," she demanded, fists crinkling her pink, paper skirt.

"Ruin to befall the clan," August sang, hands rising to the air. "Death, death, and more death."

"In English," she said.

August threw her a muddled look. "You're not as fun as I imagined you'd be, Little-Kittle."

"They're really worried," Kittin said. "The Association. They won't tell August how worried, but he 'sees.' It's because they don't think they, or we, can do anything about the storm that's coming. It's big. More powerful than any Ignorant Army we've ever seen."

August had his hands on his hips now. "Are you going to tell it? Or am I?"

"Well?" Scimitar asked, staring at the drool-streaked, redhead.

"I don't think the Association believes we can fully protect ourselves tonight. They're expecting us to lose. They're contemplating surrender this time. The Walled City's amassing everything they've got. They think The Walled City has Leo again, too." Now August was all adult. None of the childishness remained. The green eyes hardened, cat's eyes, lids stretching to slits.

"They always had Leo up until now! They can't be thinking of surrender. We still have to try!" Scimitar leaned forward, a plume of silver hair falling over his forehead. "Besides, we have Leo."

All eyes turned to Leo.

"I– I don't know how to help you," Leo said.

"Or won't," Scimitar snarled.

"But you said it yourself. I don't know how!" Leo felt the eyes on him as if they were darts, or spears prodding his heart.

"You don't know how alone," Kittin said. "But if we can help teach him – "

"What about Zack? I can't just abandon him. You said he was on his way here." His chest constricted.

"There will be no Zack," August replied, "if we are destroyed. If the Walled City wins, if they take over the entire Free World, none of us will survive, and if we do, it will be for their pleasure, their torture chambers. And Leo, you will never get home. Neither will Zack."

"If we lose," Scimitar said, "every living thing – children, animals, everything! – will lose all natural will to The Walled City's control. This world will become a mechanized, efficient machine, nothing more. Life as you know it, Leo, will end. All of it, yours, ours! You may think we're a bunch of lunatics here who deserve nothing more, that this isn't your world so it doesn't matter. But we aren't the only ones in the World. Moltenrose is a ghost town, but there're other cities, cities of millions, children like Kittin who will be taken from their parents, used, raped, killed."

Leo felt his insides harden. Of course Scimitar was right. As well as August. Denial did him no service now. Nor cowardice. He owed these people whatever he had to give. He'd run away from uncomfortable situations all his life. He had been no better than Scimitar, running from his feelings, ignoring inner demons. He'd let Zack carry all the burdens, leaned too heavily on fate and circumstance and not enough on his own spirit. His own strength.

He looked up. Gold eyes. Chill blue. Heavy-lidded green. All focused on him. A shiver ran up his spine. "We have no choice," he said. "We have to fight them."

He had only to think of Zack, and he knew he had to do it.

## Chapter Twenty-Eight

August stretched his mind outward along the boundaries of dimension and spacetime. 'Seeing' consisted of tapping into the binding force of all life in his universe, down to the last molecule. The force, like a heartbeat, like the binaural beat of an entertainment hemi-synch, enfolded him, infused him, became him. As he had been taught at a very young age, he narrowed his focus from void and stars to air and land. To his World. All that lay outside The Walled City came to his attention section by section. A green storm swirled over a town called Winnow. The residents ran from their yards, their fields, their streets, hurrying to board themselves up in their homes. It might save them, if they were lucky.

August could feel and 'see' a multitude of reactions. Emotions bombarded him simultaneously. The air cooked with psychic ions. The rich and poor, young and old, philosophers and madmen all reacted with fear, with rage. They somehow sensed this storm was different from the occasional flashes of green lightning they'd witnessed at random all their lives. This storm was death.

The World's barriers hummed on overload. Bio-pacers grew hot.

In the outermost towns on the Edge bordering closest to The Walled City, it began to rain. The rain was green. The rain was terror and bondage. August's mind absorbed it all until the individual he was seemed to disintegrate.

When he was younger, disintegration used to terrify him. Now he was used to it. He rode the waves, his mind cracking open to accept more and more and more. This was the ultimate pleasure. It made his life in the Tower all worth it.

But with the pleasure came the dark knife of regret. All this pleasure would disappear for him once the storm caught hold and changed the World. He would no longer 'see' because he chose to. If he lived, he would be controlled, made to 'see' what others wanted him to 'see'.

Now the rage he felt wasn't the simultaneous reactions of a million people, but his and his alone.

Desperation to survive brought him back into himself. It was the hardest landing of his life.

## Part XI - Outside Moltenrose (Parallel Earth)

## Chapter Twenty-Nine

The peculiar disorientation of deja vu drowned Zack. Foreboding sat, a shadow of absent color to his left. The trans-hop, made of private bubbles of connected glass and steel cars, bulleted through alien landscape: crag hills, ocher plains, red-clay mountains that looked like giant chunks of flesh torn from some greater being.

*Earth*, Zack thought, then shook his head to clear away the lie. This wasn't the Earth he knew. And he felt he was being watched even at this high speed from outside or above or beyond. *Angels watch*, he thought humorlessly. Observed even atheists like him.

Their private bubble contained two couches which faced each other. Ashao slept on one, knees drawn to his chest, pale mouth open, closed eyelids greenish in the receding light. On Zack's right, Lacy stared, hypnotized, across the alternate earthscape, looking, perhaps, for a familiar landmark or something she recognized. She had not spoken at all of any horrors she remembered, but he could tell it was most of what she'd been thinking about for the last few days.

Behind them, a thick storm followed. They were racing boiling darkness but never seemed to get any further away from it.

It was hard for Zack to sit still, to just ride the strange train and not to think about what lay ahead. He couldn't help but look back on his life as well, and see the truth of it: that he lived for Leo more than for himself, that he had had nothing else, really, to care about. Even their money from their untimely inheritance had not bought their freedom. They had still lived on the edge of a society they couldn't (or wouldn't) integrate into, and still slept, like children, in the same bed. It was out of love, yes, Zack admitted, that he and Leo shared everything, but fear also kept them stagnant. Fear of being alone. Fear of trust and commitment to others. Fear of Leo's blackouts and whatever, or whoever, secretly attacked him when Zack was asleep or not looking.

Now those fears had coalesced and formed into a real world with a real war going on. Zack had never been prepared for this. Not by running away and being on his own at sixteen, not by selling sex for the rent, not by valuing Leo more than his own soul. He was petrified that he would fail. That Leo was already dead.

"Zack?"

He turned away from the window, from foreboding. Lacy, her brown eyes glimmering, stared at him. "Huh?" His voice was rough.

"It'll be all right. I know it. I can feel that Leo's still alive."

He wanted to believe her. But how could she know? Wishful thinking would not help now.

"It's like – " She took a deep breath and started again. "When I close my eyes, I see him. I can almost hear him. Things come to me like that. That's what I've been used for. My visions. He's alive, Zack." When she spoke of herself in the context of the war, she had a vibrancy he'd never noticed before.

"How can I believe that?" He looked quickly away.

"Because I know. And because you must to get through this. To get to him."

"All I know is if anything's happened to him someone's going to pay."

"Yeah." She glanced out the window again. "I agree."

His glare softened, but she didn't see. His throat, half-closed from grief, ached.

Ashao, on his own couch, opened sleepy blue eyes. White bangs teased blond lashes. "I'm sure your vision is right," he whispered. His gaze flicked up, beyond the shoulders of Lacy and Zack. He was looking at the storm that Zack could feel, like a cape, at his shoulders.

"I *am* right," Lacy insisted.

"Otherwise," Ashao continued, "it won't matter. We'll be the ones who pay. My father will catch us and kill us all anyway."

"He's looking for us," Lacy said. "I can see that, too, through the storm. But I can't stop him."

Ashao nodded, bending his arm and pillowing his head on it. "You're a telekinetic and a clairvoyant. That's a big help to us. It'd be better if I could've brought my spychiatrist, though, to help you augment your talent. But stopping Stannos alone wouldn't work anyway. You'd need help. Lots

242

of it."

"How do you know what I am?" Lacy asked.

"I saw the designs on your body. From the time before my father took over and stopped that kind of marking."

Lacy looked away, embarrassed. "Oh."

"What exactly is a telekinetic?" Zack asked.

"She can move things, send them flying," Ashao answered. "If there's not another telekinetic of equal power blocking her, in a war she can greatly affect the defenses of the enemy. Or protect the defenses of her own side. If she knows what she's doing."

She glanced over her shoulder. "That storm. It's energy. It's violence. It is Stannos coming after us." She made it a statement of knowledge, not a question. Her slim body shivered.

"I expected my father's Ignorant Armies to be coming for me, for Leo, for the entire Free World. They'll gather all their energy at the shield borders and breach them from every direction. I knew it would happen, I just didn't think it would happen this fast. When they're through the shield we have to hope they're met with soldiers of equal force on this side.

"I've never seen him amass this much power this quickly. He's probably breaking his own rule and even using the young, untried ones," Ashao continued. "I can feel his anger because I'm not there. And because he's lost control of Leo."

"He's using more kids?" Zack asked, remembering Leo half-dead, half in shock after many of his nocturnal nightmares.

"Of course, kids. They're sometimes the strongest," Ashao answered. "Boys and girls. Men. Women. All ages. All spychiatrist-controlled by my father's orders. All expendable. And all completely ignorant of the fact that they're being used as tools to fight a war they have no allegiance to on a world that isn't their own."

"How can he think that's all right?" Zack asked, horrified yet again at this Earth he'd been visiting all of two days.

"My father isn't like us. He's –" Ashao closed his eyes, swallowed hard. "Stannos is like someone who's smothered in his surroundings and can't see anymore." His voice came out high, boyish. "He's forgotten how. Or he can't because that part of him that could've understood what we understand is dead." He breathed hard, opened his eyes. Zack saw they were clouded with barely suppressed emotion. "I don't believe he's a man anymore."

"Your own father," Lacy added, "is mad."

"I used to fear him when I was small," Ashao said. "And I admired him. I wanted to be just like him. I thought he had everything, that he *was* everything. I found out that's true. But how he got there...I...I almost followed. I almost allowed myself to believe that people didn't matter; only maintaining the city at all costs mattered. I almost believed I could grow up getting used to using others, hurting them, making them be whatever I wanted them to be." He swallowed hard. "Sometimes I still think I can be that way, that I am that way. But Leo...there was something about his eyes when I first saw him. And then I knew. I couldn't be my father. Not ever. I'd keep remembering those eyes." He looked straight at Zack. "Your eyes, sort of, only deeper, darker."

Zack nodded, knowing exactly what Ashao meant. Leo's eyes held everything he was, ghost, shadow, desert light, slippery intellect, secret sorrow, refined decorum, little kid. The soul of a survivor.

It was interesting to observe that every once in awhile Ashao's lighter eyes held similar facets. The teenager contained all the lightness of a spoiled, rich, careless boy, and at the same time the heaviness of unexpected wisdom.

Time to grow up, Zack thought, remembering feeling lost on dark streets, a cold wind blowing up his collar and through his long dry hair, Leo beside him hunkered down in a leather jacket that was, for that night, both fashion statement and shelter and home. It was his knees that got coldest on nights like that, and his thighs, rubbing like sticks against the insides of his jeans, thin and hard, the bone-deep chill a solid identity of pain.

He looked at Ashao curled around himself, trying to escape into sleep now, perhaps with the image of Leo's eyes following him into spiraling dark. They'd all had too little sleep on this journey. Too little hope.

The trans-hop wound through hills and valleys, arrowed across plains. Like a monorail, it rode silent except for a breathy sound like wind through leafless tree branches. And the ride was smooth as floating. Each little car had a

244

beverage server, and a tiny cubicle bathroom. Ashao had bought their own bubble, a four-seater, and it was strangely comfortable, hypnotic, to be flying across alien lands in a too quiet, too transparent bubble attached to other bubbles. It was like being in a compartment outside time. If Zack could forget the storm behind them, the energy that could at any moment stop them in their tracks, if he concentrated only on the floating, the sensate freedom, the isolation of the bubble and each one of them separate and distinct in their own warm bodies, he could almost believe that nothing could touch him. He was separate. He was alone. He was undetectable.

Then the thought of Leo would jolt him, along with the realization that he was not separate, never alone. Without Leo, Zack existed as half a man with half a heart.

He tried to rest with his arms crossed in front of his chest. The sky behind them darkened all too quickly. Still, ahead, the sun shone white.

~

Its sensors noted a change in the scrambled patterns of molecules, microwaves, electromagnetic fields and ions. The dense field around the World rippled. The threat to its programming weakened.

The spychiatrist shifted in its dirt cairn.

On many levels in many universes a part of its awareness existed and learned. It sensed its siblings engaged in various tasks involving the soft, luminous beings, as well as an energy that was responsible for disrupting the field which had stopped it from following the being Ashao. It sensed Ashao moving slowly over a minute section of the All. It sensed the being Leo, a light across the field and only a hop away, glowing in rhythm to a larger ache, a tear. It sensed the All, injured and leaking, a rip in the mental/space/time fabric of connectedness pulsing. A rip seemingly caused by the overload of psychic energy from the spychiatrists' travels, and from a confrontation that had existed for a long time between these luminous beings.

Its programming directed it to observe, contact and capture Leo if possible. Conversely, its overriding program to protect the multiversal All, a sort of self-programming facet incurred along with its programming for self-preservation and its programming for learning, suggested capturing Leo to aid in the repair of the rip. Either way, its primary mission involved Leo. It needed, desperately, to breach the field and attain physical proximity to that glowing being.

One of its five clawed legs dug upward to touch air. The scrambling field was not yet collapsed and so the gesture might have been defined as one of impatience. But a spychiatrist didn't feel and therefore impatience could not have been its reason for poking one leg above ground level to start on a journey it could not yet begin.

~

"There!" Stannos cried as an alarm beeped. A console flashed: red, amber, green. "We have it!"

"Your son's spychiatrist?" Controller One asked, his eyes weary-reddened.

"In sector four, degree 30, 39, a breath away from the enemy force shield! Ha! It was hiding underground." He stared at the picture on the screen his sensors formed. The grid gave him the exact coordinates.

Overhead, the lights were suffused gold, reflecting white and amber in his many large rings. His fingers played across the boards, reconfirming.

Behind them, in the lower chambers or on the War Room floor, dozens of people, spychiatrist controlled, stood or sat, pupils dilated, entranced. They were swollen-eyed and gaunt, pallid and chapped. But that didn't matter to Stannos. They were there for a job and nothing else. Comfort didn't concern them under the spychiatrists' control, and therefore their appearances and relative health did not matter to Stannos.

There were between ten to twenty people per spychiatrist, and so far the strain on the twenty-odd machines did not show. The spychiatrists could control many tasks simultaneously, including gathering up the combined energy of the 'tools' and aiding them in hurling it toward enemy defenses. So far, the various psychic, Ignorant Armies of the Free World had not projected a strong retaliation, and Stannos was planning, hoping that when they did it would be too late. By the time they realized they were being attacked with all the forces he had under his control, he would have already won. They wouldn't be able to amass an army large enough to defeat him in the time they had left before his forces knocked down their shields and allowed the stimoceiver waves through that would take over and make him the supreme ruling power.

He was both ecstatic and disappointed.

He would win control of the whole planet. He knew that. But that didn't finish the matter between him and his son. He intended to see Ashao executed at his victory celebration. He intended to capture, keep and control Leo to be his new World Establishment's War Hero, a symbol of his ultimate rule, his final success. Both actions were necessary and would be a joy to carry out. Yet he dreaded the confrontation with his own son.

"Send guards to retrieve my son's spychiatrist," Stannos ordered, and Controller One began to comply, pushing various communication buttons at his own smaller console. "Keep tracking it. If it moves into another plane, send one of our spychiatrists after it. It can't escape us now."

The tracking fix they now had on Ashao's spychiatrist could not be broken by time or distance. Their technology was exact. The spychiatrists were utterly controlled.

"Bring it back," he muttered the order again. "It will be monitoring my son. We'll use it to retrieve him."

Stannos thought about reprogramming his spychiatrists to override their law, to jump in their own time from one location to another outside the wall. But in the time it would take to do the new programming, the guards could have reached Ashao's spychiatrist on foot.

Ashao's spychiatrist. He should never have given it to him. Fifteen was simply too young. And at that most delicate age of rebellion. He should have known.

But Stannos did not have room in his conscience to regret the betrayal of his son, to remember a little boy who had tried so hard at one time to be like him, think like him. The little boy who, he thought, had loved and revered him. Here was not the place for sentiment or grief. Both emotions were easily smothered, their flames pinched without a second thought.

He turned to his seers to see if they had picked up images of his son yet. They were carefully scanning The Edge and nearby cities and towns. It wouldn't be long now at all. Stannos smiled feeling a strange rapture, a warped sense of awe. He had won. It was only a matter of time before all the pieces of his conquest were picked up and brought together.

## Chapter Thirty

Lacy remembered the feeling of power she'd had when she was a girl, the messages written in a Ouija board language from herself to herself. The warnings. The hastily spelled advice: "The energy you put out is absorbed by air and earth and rock and tree and sky." And, "Nature is a tool for your protection."

She remembered how the tree caught her when she fell, remembered how she had projected her mind out across land and sea to bring back images of the Free World to theWar room, how she had also caused things to move, people to be killed. Lacy still only half-understood the controls pertaining to her own power. It was one thing to be told you could do something, even know that talent and will existed within. It was quite another to act upon that knowledge on her own, to put energy reserves to use, to push with her mind into an unknown she had no experience with, and less faith. Always before her power had been either forced upon her or unexpected.

Now she tried to 'see' into the future, into the storm surrounding them. The images were a mass of confusing scenes. She could read vague feelings of hostility off the storm, see silhouettes, understand their killing intent. Yet all specific strategies seemed to elude her. She couldn't tell if they saw her or not. So far, the army of minds she sensed seemed distant, still indistinct.

The bio-pacer on her wrist pulsed with sudden warmth. She carried her pack loosely in that same hand, trailing behind Zack and Ashao as they moved away from the dusty trans-hop platform and into the city Ashao called Moltenrose.

The bruised sky was darkening too quickly for comfort. Clouds formed, shaded brown in color. Lacy had never seen brown clouds before. The air smelled of myrrh and rotting vegetables. Beautiful city, she thought, surveying the older plaster and concrete buildings – old even for her Earth in her own time – the obvious lack of inhabitants, the dust-misted street that faced them.

"You didn't say this city was abandoned," she said quietly. No one responded to her observation. She didn't repeat it.

Ashao was pale and drawn, Zack tense as a viper backed

into a corner. But for all their weariness, they moved quickly, Ashao darting into the ghost-town shadows like a wraith on the wind, Zack following with no choice but to trust the boy who'd snatched them from their native world.

As they strode along the road, however, the shadows seemed to move, and Lacy realized her first impression had been in error. The city wasn't uninhabited. People – or things – shifted and breathed behind the broken walls and shattered windows, and through one curtained crack an orange light glowed. Candles. Candles to mark the coming of dusk, to show that life still tried to thrive behind the newer ruins of this city where a tower stood and an army fought. Had it always been this way? she wondered, or had the attacks caused this? Perhaps the people who once kept this city strong and vibrant had moved away for fear of the green lightning that meant the battles were too close to home, too violent for every day comfort.

She chilled at the ever-emerging memories of those battles. She'd been a part of all that, killing people, vandalizing their cities. And each time Stannos had been at the helm. Her memories of him were the worst and tears floated in her eyes as she tried not to remember how, after she'd killed on command, he'd become aroused, touch her, rape her, using the spychiatrist to gain her compliance. It was harder to take when the memories included her own pleasure at his warped affections for her. Hard to remind herself that any desire she had felt for Stannos had been mere false programming.

The memories enraged her. At that moment, Zack looked at her strangely, as though reading her thoughts. She turned away, pushing out at him with her anger. She stopped herself abruptly as in her mind she saw him start to lurch, to trip. He righted himself quickly. It had been merely a stumble, but it shocked her that she could have caused it. She wanted revenge, but not against him!

Still, that was most interesting. Anger had made her talents stronger. A fact to remember.

Now, as they hurried along in receding daylight, she shivered at the sensation of being watched from the surrounding buildings. How could they, three young people – one hardly grown – hope to reach Leo, let alone safety, in the midst of all this chaos?

Ahead, she felt the presences of other powerful minds. The Free World's Moltenrose faction, perhaps? Leo? She concentrated harder.

"Lacy?" Zack was at her side, gripping her arm, pushing.

He had been so casual that first night, playful almost in his own living room and in his bedroom where he'd actually seemed to desire her. It had appeared that way, at least, his silver ringed hands full of condoms, his naked side pressing hesitantly, sweetly against hers as they had talked the night away. And all the while Leo had remained at least a full foot away, confident in his isolation, in the distractions of storytelling, no matter how intimate the stories or who did the telling. And yet, all that had changed the next morning. The casualness turned to an aloof posture. The playful side became nearly hostile. What had happened?

As she faced Zack, his fingers digging strongly into her arm, his brown eyes lit with a shocky kind of fever, she felt a wave of resentment along with an uncontrollable desire roll through her. Both emotions were completely out of place here and she caught her breath, lungs quivering.

"What?" Zack asked a little too harshly. His shiny eyebrows lifted, the face so much less like her memory of Leo's now that it was shaded with a day's growth of beard.

Her walk slowed. Her face warmed with embarrassment, anger. "Leo's up ahead. I can actually see him, but not anything around him yet," she finally managed to say.

Something behind one of the buildings scraped as though a large piece of metal were being dragged through debris. All three jumped at the sound.

"Hurry!" Ashao called, his voice rough, high-pitched. But as he said it, human forms began to appear out of the dusk of the buildings, out of the shadows, ghosting through the street up ahead.

Lacy could feel the presence of many people surrounding them. They wore grey and melded easily with the street and the lengthening shadows. As two larger forms approached them, they stopped, Lacy one step behind Ashao. The first, a female, appeared to be healthy, intelligent, despite the long, blonde-ratted hair, the face and hands smudged with the silver ash of open fires, clothing tied on rather than uniformly fastened. Her boots were large and new, a thick vinyl, and her eyes were drug-red in the waning light, glazed with the mist of someone distracted, dreaming.

"What business have you here?" Her voice sang, a rumbling engine pitched neither high nor low. She sounded so young, yet she looked to be of an age spanning anywhere from twenty to forty.

Another person ambled up beside the strange woman. It was not human. Its lips flashed silver. Its eyes were red also, but made of lights where the woman's were shot through with blood.

"This is Moltenrose?" Ashao asked softly, hesitantly. "The trans-hop dropped us here."

A brief nod.

"I wasn't told it was like this." Ashao, blue eyes glistening, did a one-eighty surveillance, hands limp at his sides, chest quivering.

"You are moving in the wrong direction," the woman said, crossing her arms over her chest. "This part of the city is like this and always has been like this. If you want lively restaurants and sweet families that smile a lot and buy their children candy-pops, you want the west side. If you want carnivals, gambling, live sex shows, you want the west side as well. Either way, you don't want this side."

"I don't understand. I'm looking for Moltenrose Tower. This is the correct direction."

"You can't go there."

Zack took a step forward, fists bunching. "We have to. We have urgent business."

"You think you can just walk in? It's untouchable. No one goes there." She smiled, showing perfect, even teeth completely out of place with her attire. "We make sure. We are paid well to guard."

From the looks of the woman, her robot, and the scraggly people beyond, they weren't paid well enough, Lacy thought. Or perhaps their priorities lay elsewhere than in fashion.

A wind took up the loose flaps of the woman's and the robot's clothes, winding through rags and hair and metal. With it came scents of brushfire, ozone, rain.

"The storm," Ashao began. "Don't you see it? It's following us. The people at the Tower are the only ones who can help.

We're from – " He caught himself and stopped.

Lacy's heart beat hard in her throat. They could all be killed if Ashao told the truth. But they might never reach the Tower without revealing who they really were.

Just as she let out a breath of frustration, a silver disk came hurling toward them, seemingly from nowhere. Instinctively, they all ducked. Lacy felt the presences surrounding them grow more hostile. The disk clattered harmless to the pavement, dully reflecting the cloud cover, and the more distant black clouds. The street itself seemed to gather for a confrontation, holding still and tense. Lacy felt the concrete, the buildings and the air freeze, energy held back, waiting. Something was very wrong.

Zack gasped. Ashao put up his hands.

Lacy glanced to her left just in time to see more silver disks come whizzing at them. Without thinking, her mind automatically projected an image of a brick wall. Her bio-pacer grew warm, then hot. As she watched, to her surprise the disks all veered within ten feet of them, as if hitting something solid. They clattered against the hard cement ground. The sound echoed off the dim buildings, the shattering of a big city isolated to silence and spooky reflections as the weapons came to rest.

"Which one of you is the telekinetic?" the blond woman asked calmly, holding up her hand in a signal to the others.

No one answered. Lacy felt herself recede, as though the conversation were being carried on from far away.

"And if you are so 'talented', how do I know you're not a weapon sent to destroy us?"

"We wear bio-pacers," Ashao replied.

"Not good enough."

"They're already invading. From The Walled City. Can't you see?" The sky had grown still darker in the last few minutes. "This isn't like any other attack. This is too big. With this storm, you'll become the guards of nothing, if you survive!" The boy was angry, Lacy observed, and powerful in his untamed display of emotion. Though small, pale, with a voice that still often sounded like a girl, he held a spirit of knowledge, a kind of strength that could not be missed when looking at him, listening to him. "We can help. We are not the enemy."

"Take us to someone we can talk to. If they can see me, they'll know who we are and how we can help. We can't tell you any more," Zack said.

At those words, Lacy began to have hope again. Zack was right. If someone from the Free World's Association, as Ashao referred to it, recognized him as Leo they would have to let them through, let them into the Tower. Someone higher up had to know the threat that was on the horizon, had to be desperate for a solution if they hadn't already evacuated themselves from the vicinity. In which case, they were on their own. Again. Still.

"We don't have time to argue this," Ashao said. "We may not have any time left at all."

"You have not attacked us. You only defended yourselves," the woman said. Her lips were pink and uneven; a scar divided the lower part of her mouth with a jagged line. "I will guide you to the Tower. But if you are lying, if you are not recognized or welcomed by my bosses, we will kill you." Her smile was more a grimace. She wasn't ugly, just strange, exotic, and Lacy shivered inside. All they could do now was follow.

As they walked down the street, the robot mechanism whirred at the woman's side like a faithful child.

# Chapter Thirty-One

Stannos watched the conversation unfold between his star 'tool' Leo, his spy Kittin and their two psychotic army friends. It angered him that he couldn't just snatch Leo, and Lacy wherever she was, from the grip of the enemy, but he was not underconfident in his own massive army, even without the talents of Leo to shine through. Leo and Kittin were still strong though unwilling allies, the perfect targets, and all his forces were aimed right at them, energy travelling even now through the skies to squash them, to make them his to command, his to control.

Voices of pain cried out in the War Room as the spychiatrists forced his army to even greater strength.

Stannos felt comforted by the clamor, and leaned back in a chair, staring at the main monitor. There, his prized weapon sat.

"You know how," the one called Scimitar was telling Leo. "You felt how you did it when you came here to Kittin, when you projected at me. You remember everything you've done before. Just do it now, without the spychiatrist's forcing you to."

"The barriers are falling," Leo said, his voice trembling, entranced. He looked pale, thin and unhealthy. Not the vibrant youth Stannos remembered sending on journeys of espionage, murder and sexual conquest. All those times Leo had visited Kittin, Stannos had lived it with him vicariously through the monitors. The boy had been good entertainment as well as a successful war toy.

"Can you try to hold them?" Scimitar asked quietly.

Leo grimaced. "I don't know how!"

Stannos laughed. "They don't even know what they're doing." Behind him, the only answers were groans mixed with the rapid breathing of his human army.

The young woman, Kittin, tossed her long, black curls back and put a hand on Leo's shoulder. The fingers were delicate and smooth. Stannos watched her with an interest he hadn't felt before. She had indeed grown into a beautiful woman. He decided he would love making her into one of his personal servants once the war was over.

Controller One interrupted his reverie. "We have a fix from

one of our 'seers' on your son, sir. Monitor two."

Stannos glanced away from Kittin and Leo to stare at the next large monitor one console away. With the spychiatrist augmenting the 'seer's' powers, an image projected onto the screen of a dusty street, ruined buildings, and his son with a group of rag-tag strangers.

"Where is that?" he demanded.

"The direction of Moltenrose," the Controller answered.

A pang of regret stung Stannos. His stomach muscles unconsciously tightened as he watched his son walking behind a tall woman and a robot. The longer he looked, the more details the 'seer' projected. There was a woman at Ashao's side he recognized immediately. Lacy! Then the 'seer' focused on the man. Vinyl and fur, brown hair, nothing special. Until he saw the face.

"Leo!" he exclaimed.

"It can't be," the Controller replied. "Leo's with Kittin. It's the twin."

"Of course." How had he so quickly forgotten? Stannos faced the first monitor. Leo sat, head in his hands.

The earlier hint of regret for what he would have to do to his son completely vanished now. Ashao had brought both Lacy and Zack into his confidence; it was obvious. The boy was mad. It had been Ashao all along who had brought the three of them together. Ashao and his spychiatrist had planned very, very carefully. Too bad all that intelligence would be wasted once he got his hands on him.

The Controller interrupted him again. "Shall we focus an attack on them?"

"Most definitely!" Then he held up his hand. "No. Wait. Ashao's spychiatrist. Have we got it yet?"

"We are in the vicinity of your son's spychiatrist now, sir. In moments, the machine will be apprehended and the safety switches established so your son will have no more control of it."

"Good."

On the first monitor, Leo cried out. The older man with the silver hair and Kittin grabbed him as he began to collapse. They held him upright between them.

"What's happening?" Kittin shrieked.

When Leo didn't open his eyes or answer, the older man

said, "I don't know. He reached out, I think. Maybe the enemy is just too strong."

"Can't you help him?" she asked.

Stannos was shaking his head. "You can't help him," he said to the screen. To the controller, he said, "They are alone. The rest of our army has successfully distracted any who could defend them. Except for those infernal EM fields of theirs, they have no more defenses." He turned to face the second monitor. The group of strangers, including his son, continued to walk down the crumbling streets of Moltenrose. "Have the spychiatrists increase our army's energy output as soon as all their barriers are finally down. We must bombard Leo with more than he can handle. We will concentrate on him, not my son. But we will get them both in the end."

"That should be no problem. Moltenrose is, at this point, open territory."

"As you can see," Stannos said, indicating the monitor with his jeweled fingers, "they must depend on Leo, now, yet neither they nor Leo have any idea how to control his vast talents."

"Yes. It's as you have always told us," Controller One said, his eyes glowing. "We are fighting children. Without a spychiatrist to aid him, it appears Leo is blind."

Another monitor beeped. Controller One went to it. "Ah," he said, "Ashao's spychiatrist."

Stannos got up, his furs tangling for a moment with his arms. He bent to view the second monitor, black braid dangling toward the screen, and saw desolate landscape, a blackened husk of an ancient transport vehicle from another war, another time, and the five-legged reddish spychiatrist his son had reprogrammed to betray them all. Two spychiatrists and a half dozen guards, metal-armored and flashing purple and brown in the stormy twilight, surrounded the now floating machine. Below, the ground was torn and jagged where the spychiatrist had recently evacuated its early grave.

Stannos chuckled. "It's ridiculous, really, that Ashao even tried to go against me. I have to admire his fortitude, though. If nothing else, my kid had balls!" He laughed, squelching the memory of the little boy swimming with the fish in his koi pond, the squirming child who'd wanted too quickly to grow up, whose immeasurable intelligence would, in the end, be his undoing.

At this third monitor, Stannos gave the order for his men to shut down the spychiatrist and bring it home. As he watched the guards and their two larger spychiatrists approach the smaller, red device, suddenly it wasn't there.

Stannos blinked, thinking the picture had been disrupted. But, no, the red spychiatrist had simply vanished. "What!?" he roared.

The armored guards were moving in confused, patternless circles. Then, just as suddenly, the spychiatrists at their sides disappeared. No flash. No warning. As Stannos watched, the larger machines had also completely disappeared.

"Track them immediately!" he ordered. "This is impossible! Who overrode my orders? What do those spychiatrists think they're doing?" He tasted bile, and salt. He realized he'd bit his tongue, ignored the pain and yelled, "Who's done this? Track them!" He grabbed Controller One by the bicep and shoved him toward the monitor and console. "Track them now!" He spit as he shouted, red foam dotting the front of his vinyl tunic. He ran to one of the control boards yelling, "Override auto-programming! All spychiatrists to my voice command!"

Controller One moved to obey, then froze, his mouth opening in a slack 'O'.

"What?" Stannos turned, following his gaze. He could see the 'tools' – some on the upper level, some in the glass cages below – sink to their knees to the floor. Then the spychiatrists monitoring them all began to pop out of existence, one by one. As the Controllers busily worked at their consoles, the spychiatrists remained unresponsive. One by one, down the line, all twenty-two left in commission vanished.

All monitors went blank.

"No!" Stannos frantically worked the main controls. "Override!" he shouted. "Override or you'll all be put to death. Now!"

Controllers ran, mumbling orders to each other.

"What's happening?" His rage made his fingers slip against the console. "Why aren't they responding?"

"I don't know, sir!" Controller One shouted over his shoulder. "They've vanished without a trace. Trackers aren't able to get a fix."

Stannos ran to Controller One, grabbing him by the throat. "What do you mean they can't be tracked? That's impossible!"

The Controller gagged. "I... don't... know." His knees buckled. Stannos pushed him and the controller went down hard onto his back, then Stannos turned away, hyperventilating, his anger so intense the edges of his vision began to blacken.

He grabbed the side of one console to keep from swaying, echoing the limp gestures of his now directionless, lolling Ignorant Army. "Find them!" he cried, fingers scratching in frustration at the lights on the consoles. "Find those spychiatrists or I'll have you all put to death!" His painted fingernails scraped metal and plastic and began to break.

## Chapter Thirty-Two

Kittin smelled sulphur-green and held tight to Leo, his body feverish, as he started to fall. Scimitar supported him on the other side; his face wrinkled in a grimace, yet his eyes were unnaturally calm. Had he already accepted their fate? August stared off into his own worlds, seemingly oblivious to his surroundings. The storm had come and Kittin knew, before they'd even started to fight they would lose. But she could not be calm or accepting. She could not close off her emotions. Her heart fluttered, a moth scrambling to be free. Her mind blazed with panic, but more, she felt an intelligent kind of fear which told her in firm tones that when they were caught she would find a way to escape even if it meant taking her own life. The thought came to her, a bleak rip in the drift of her psyche, and because of it she'd never again know peace such as the gentle tones of nature at night under a crescent moon, or the newly tamed currents she saw now whenever she looked at Scimitar's eyes.

She tried to concentrate on their night together instead of her fear. Why had Scimitar projected his desires telepathically and not just come to her as any other man would? His fears had to be complex. But now he seemed the least afraid person in the room.

Though the lights were on, shadows seemed to gather in the corners of the room. Leo's body shuddered against her, rustling her paper dress. The room spun, reflecting her own welling panic.

"We have to get him out of here," Scimitar said. "He's caught somehow, mentally, in the storm. I don't know how it happened. I didn't tell him to project yet! He wasn't ready. He's talented, but emotionally –" He let the observation drop. Leo was a strong man but still raw. Without help – spychiatrist-aided or army-trained – he was errant talent running wild, burning out of control.

"But where should we take him?" Kittin asked. "There's nowhere safe."

"My isolation work-room is the best protected."

"Wait!" August was breathing hard. Green eyes glazed

over. His mouth opened. His red hair made his face look stark white in the strange light, in the mist from the humidifier.

Leo was getting heavy in Kittin's arms. Her muscles swarmed with the pain.

"What?" Scimitar growled.

"Zack is here." He spoke slowly, voice a thick monotone. "With two others. Very close. There is a boy with them and they're surrounded by guards. But this boy, he's from The Walled City. He's– I can see him clearly. He's here to help." Then August was at the door, flinging it wide. "I'm going to let them through. The guards will stop them unless –"

"Go!" Scimitar yelled. "And gather the others. Tell them to go to their posts if they haven't already. They're safest there. And we'll just wait here."

"We were going to move him," Kittin protested.

"I changed my mind!"

Kittin groaned, loosening her hold on Leo.

"Here," Scimitar said. "Let's get him on the bed."

"What's happened to him?" Kittin asked as they settled him onto Scimitar's low mattress.

"The army's powers must be directed at him somehow. We're being monitored all the time through you, Kittin!"

She looked at him, face hardening in defense. He was accusing her, but she wasn't responsible. "Should I leave then?"

"It's too late now."

She bit her lower lip, the flesh curling against her teeth. If Scimitar were angry with her, that was his problem. Her insides rumbled with fear. But that was all she felt. "Why don't I feel anything from this storm?" she asked.

"It's not here yet. He must've projected outward, damn him. He wasn't ready and he was met with a force he wasn't prepared for. They were probably waiting for him to do just that."

"He projected? The way you do?"

"Yes." Scimitar reached out as Leo moaned, and brushed his slim hand against his forehead. Kittin was surprised and pleased at the tenderness of the gesture. For a man who'd recently wanted to kill Leo, Scimitar was behaving very differently now.

Then Scimitar drew back, a sick look on his face. "He's too far away for even me to help. If he comes back to us, it'll be on his own."

Her stomach fluttered. Again, she tried to concentrate on something other than her fears.

Leo lay on the bed, body shuddering, eyes half-closed and unseeing. The lids were shadowed blue, a natural skin tone for him on that most delicate of areas, and the long lashes made dark crescents on his cheeks. His bright, autumn-colored hair was strewn over the sheet, still soft and shiny, but chaotic. Kittin reached out and touched it, feeling the cool silk of it ripple over her fingers. It was irresistible. Like petting a cat's fur. It was an uncontrollable gesture, the need to feel that softness against the skin automatic, unconscious.

Scimitar bent over Leo then, calling his name. "Leo! Can you hear me?"

Kittin took up Leo's limp hand in hers, her fingers tracing the silver rings he wore. The long, black fingernail curved against her palm, smooth and glossy. The skin was damp and abnormally cool. "He's not going to die, is he?"

"I don't know!" Scimitar replied. "Even now he's fighting for us. He's meeting them head on. But he's not fighting in tandem with anyone, so even if the rest of us try to help, he's cut himself off. He doesn't know what he's doing."

"He could get hurt."

"He's hurt already," Scimitar said, calling Leo's name again, large hand squeezing the younger man's shoulder.

Then he would die, she thought. They all would, or be captured. Scimitar just wasn't admitting that yet. Kittin felt tears well up in her eyes. The inside of her nose stung with the salt, grief for herself, grief for Leo. She wished Leo had never been a part of any of this, that he'd been left alone to grow up a normal boy, to have the life she'd always wanted for herself and could have had if he'd never come along.

"Can't we help him?" she cried out.

"I don't know! Maybe," he answered, but did not elaborate.

~

A strange-looking boy with the sides of his head shaved

and sporting a carrot-orange ponytail ran from the Tower's main glass entrance. He slipped through twilight like a flame-topped shadow, shouting something, his bare feet pounding pale pavement in a distant drumbeat.

The wind picked up. The windows of the Tower's lower levels darkened. Clouds scuttled thicker overhead, giving what light was left a sepia tone. Dust blew in whirlwinds in the streets of Moltenrose.

Zack noticed the woman guard and her robot sidekick jerk to attention as the breeze threatened to knock them all aside. Dark gold and russet played across the robot's metal face and arms. Parts of the Tower up ahead reflected in his body. The streets behind them emptied of the entourage that had followed them this far. The city absorbed her ghost-citizens.

Lacy and Ashao craned to see the boy who was running toward them, still shouting, voice carried away on the currents of the supernatural storm. From the west, thunder spoke.

"No more time," Ashao cried, hunching down.

Now the boy was closer, still yelling. Zack made out the words "through" and "right."

"He is one of the Ignorant Army," the woman guard said over the cacophony of the storm. "What is he doing? For his own safety, he's not supposed to ever leave the Tower."

"They're prisoners?" Lacy asked.

"No, but they risk their lives to fight. We protect them."

The boy beat back the wind with his strides, following the path from the concrete and grass tower grounds to the street, calling out. "Zack. You are Zack?"

Zack stepped forward, throat suddenly dry. How? How could he know, unless – "Yes," he called back.

"Let them through. They are here to help," the boy called. When he reached them, out of breath, he continued shouting over the wind. "Zack, Leo needs you! He's here. And you," he turned his sharp eyes on Ashao. "I know who you are. Can you help us?"

Leo? Alive! For a moment, Zack couldn't see. Shock and relief froze his muscles. He heard Ashao shout, "That's why we came. To try!"

Zack blinked. Everything righted itself. He glimpsed Lacy

gasping her own relief – "Thank God. Oh thank God."

"My name is August. Come on!" The boy whose voice was hoarse from yelling now, waved them on past the woman and her robot, both of whom still held defensive, rigid stances, their eyes constantly scanning the area. The orange whip of August's short ponytail beat itself against his neck.

Not looking back to see if Ashao and Lacy followed, Zack began to run, catching up in seconds to walk by the boy's side. "You know Leo?" he asked. "Is he all right?" His heart still seemed suspended between beats. His fists clenched. Anger strengthened him. And he remembered his vow: If anything was wrong, if Leo was dead or hurt, he would kill someone. He wanted to trust this boy. As he had with Ashao, he also wanted to take his neck in his hands and twist until he admitted the truth. "Is he all right?" he asked again.

"Alive. Not all right. None of us are all right with this storm. Leo is trying to battle it. We don't have enough strength, though, to help him. He's fighting alone."

"Take me to him." He touched the weird boy's shoulder, holding back the force of his anxiety, his anger, with what little will he had left.

"That's why I came to get you," the boy replied, starting to jog. "Hurry!"

"Is there somewhere we can go to be safe? Away from this storm?"

August shook his head as they moved quickly along the path to the glass entrance. "Only inside," he finally answered. Lacy and Ashao had caught up and were flanking them, running to keep up. The path was smooth and white, sidewalk-concrete, newer than the crumbling street they'd just left. It snaked through yellowing lawns that appeared to encircle the building. The Tower rose like a single castle turret, a structure at least twenty stories high, its metal and glass sides reflecting the grey and purple sky. Its windows looked like scales, or eyes. The top, which Zack had been gazing at when it came into view as they'd walked through the abandoned streets, was domed and scintillated like a star. The whole thing looked like a rocket outside of time stuck in the middle of a ruined city as a monument to past generations.

"Hurry!" August repeated, as Zack's step faltered. "I don't

know if you can do anything, but at least you can be there for him. Leo may be diverting some of his energies to worrying about you."

Frustration dug at Zack's insides. Even though he was running, hopes rising as the search came to an end, he felt all too helpless.

They jogged through an empty foyer and into a long hall. The hall slanted upward, and curved. The walls were glittered: gold, midnight blue, hazel. Chandeliers like stalactites hung from the curved ceiling that wound upward. They passed doors, some open, some closed. The open doors, Zack could see, led to various sized rooms, some vast and dark, others more like offices with desks and chairs. There were no signs of inhabitants. He wondered where they all were. He thought it a bit strange that there was no one around since the Tower supposedly housed an 'army'.

Eventually, the hall flattened and they entered a large room filled with rows of lockers. Beyond that was a dining hall and another corridor.

"Through here," August called, running ahead. His bare feet pounded the floor, the sounds echoing up and down the hall.

The room was misty, the air dank. There was a sharp smell of ozone mixed with a more humid scent of rain.

Zack entered, his senses overstimulated and for a moment he couldn't see, couldn't hear, couldn't think. He felt Lacy and Ashao behind him, their presences reassuring, though distant. But he had only one person on his mind. Leo.

"Here." August stood in front of him, swaying, left hand pointing toward the floor.

Zack saw purple carpet, a lumpy mattress. By the mattress, two people knelt. On it was a familiar figure.

"Leo." Zack moved forward, ignoring the two people who moved aside to let him get closer to his brother. Lacy went to Leo's other side, clutching at his limp hand.

"Leo," Zack repeated. This time his voice came out a whisper. A pang of empathy – pain in his heart, his head – hit Zack hard as he looked down at his brother. It had been barely two days, and already Leo was thinner, pale. He lay very still, seemingly asleep.

"What have you done to him?" he snarled, whirling on the other occupants of the room.

One was a tall man, older, with a sharp face that looked set in stone. He sat back on the balls of his feet and said, "He's caught up in the war. Before we could help, he projected out and now – "

"Leo!" Zack shook his brother's shoulder. "Come on, Leo. Come out of it!"

Lacy touched Leo's other shoulder, also calling his name.

Leo's lips moved as though trying to form words, but no sound came from his throat.

"Even if he does come out of it," the older man said, "the whole force of the storm will be here by final dark. There's nothing we can do. Nowhere we can go. It seems we're losing this war. Even with Leo on our side."

Ashao stepped forward, looking too thin in his dark-furred, travelling clothes. He held the remote device that controlled his spychiatrist in his left hand. "If only –" He did not finish his sentence, looking helplessly at the technology that, if able to be used, might have helped them.

Zack turned back to Leo, clutching tightly at the clammy hand, thumb pressing against silver rings, bony knuckles. His eyes stung and he pressed the cool fingers to his cheek as his throat tightened. Leo had been through so much, more than any person should have to go through. When was it going to stop? Much as he wanted to protect his brother, much as he had tried over the years to defend him to friends, parents, nearly anyone they came into contact with, he couldn't stop Leo's pain. He'd always felt helpless when Leo had come to him with yet another dream to tell him, with his fear of the dark, his fear of other people, of commitment to friends or potential lovers. Leo's insecurities had started so long ago and all he could give him through the years was his unconditional support. It hadn't been enough.

"What's going to happen to us?" Zack asked quietly. The sheet bunched around Leo like a rippled, white sea.

"The Walled City will turn us into zombies," August drawled.

"Or use their spychiatrists to perform unspeakable experiments upon us," the tall man added.

"It can't happen! It just can't!" The young girl who'd been

at Leo's side when Zack came in began to cry. She still knelt at the far end of the mattress.

"Hey!" It was Ashao's voice.

Zack jerked at the sound of it. "What?" He turned his blurred gaze to the boy who had accomplished so much disruption in so short a time.

"My spychiatrist is moving! I don't see how that's possible, unless the force shields have dropped. Stannos was attacking those. Whatever's happened, my spychiatrist's not tethered anymore."

"You have a spych?" the older man asked.

"You mean it's moving within our time, our sphere?" August asked.

"It's coming to me," Ashao said, looking up, grinning. "It's found a way! Maybe Leo –" He bit his lower lip and looked down at the still unmoving figure on the mattress.

Zack turned back to his brother. "Leo?" Lacy clutched the other hand tightly, her eyes never looking up.

Leo groaned and moved slightly, gripping Zack's hand. But he still remained in what seemed to Zack like a trance.

Gasps grabbed his attention again and he felt a strange presence, as though someone else had just entered the room. "Wha –

As he looked up his mind at first tried to deny what he saw. Floating over the mattress in the misty light was the same red beast that had snatched him and Lacy from bed and brought them to this world. The same machine that had followed them partway on their journey. Though he'd tolerated its presence, he had never grown used to it. But now it seemed a miracle.

It hovered, its five metallic legs waving, the hinges softly rasping, the claws on the ends of its legs clicking. The lights on its body chased themselves in synchronized circles.

"Ashao?" he cried out.

Suddenly, Lacy fell back onto the floor, unmoving.

And then the thing was gone. Zack's grip on Leo loosened to enfold humid emptiness. And nothing.

## Chapter Thirty-Three

Leo could comprehend only the ferocity of attack, and the strength, but not the reason behind it. Why someone would use humans with psychic ability to fight a war to control the minds and wills of others shot beyond understanding. He had always lived in a microcosm, his world consisting only of battling his own inner nightmares, writing a few poems and songs, cruising with Zack, and surviving within a complex system he never felt a part of. Just living with that, day to day, took up most of his energy. How someone could spend their life trying to control others, searching for ways to kill others, was a mystery to him when control of the self was for him a full-time job. Perhaps, once, good intentions had started the need for control on this Earth, for making life smoother and easier, for making life fair and happy for all. But his own experience told him control of that sort was an illusion.

Now his mind, netted in amber and emerald light, fought against that illusion. The net wrapped conscience, wrapped thought.

For strength, he strained to remember the time when he was a boy lying in bed next to Zack, thinking about his blackouts, his nightmares, the unseen threat he could not dodge. He could almost smell the thin spice of Zack's breath, the drying September grasses outside, the curving brown shade of night, acrid-scented. Reality moved and rolled beyond mere human senses.

So did thought.

He dodged through a hole in the net, sensing a person, pain, internal cries. Parts of the net were formed by children's minds, he realized with horror. To fight, he had to cut them down. One of them could have been him once.

He felt caught up in red anger, swift vengeance, ashen jealousy. The emotions invaded his mind, pounded for entrance. He projected sorrow at first, gentle empathy. But that couldn't last. Though the net weakened, he needed his terror, his outrage and anger to complete the battle, to have any chance of escaping.

But he was surrounded by floating images: A gang wielding police batons, children with unseeing eyes and bodies made of knives, an old man on fire heading straight toward him, a floating infant with razor teeth, a girl with a machete. There were too many. He couldn't hope to dodge them forever.

The place where he had come before he was ready, before Scimitar had finished explaining everything to him, was unsolid and very white. It was upon this background that the images progressed. He felt he had a body and was aware mostly of his hands clinging, unseen, to someone far away. That sensation was important to him, for he believed it kept him from breaking apart, losing his sense of self and direction in the morass of the madness around him.

Through the white, through the advancing images came light and wind and soft touches that buoyed his body back and forth on something that wasn't, but was like air. There was sound: distant cries, echoes of incomprehensible conversations, a storm's breathy voice.

Leo had never been more scared.

The images came and went, appearing, disappearing, chasing, retreating. A gang of youths with their hair aflame. Boys with bats. Girls with crossbows. Arrows of green and amber light shot at him again, wrapping him tight, cutting through his psyche. They were all after him.

He knew he had nothing to lose now. He was dead if he didn't keep trying to dodge them. And so all he could do was look for another hole, a way up as the bands of light tightened down, a way inside when the attack came from outside.

His mind did gymnastic flips. Turned inside out. Rewrote physics. Stopped time. Because here, in this white universe, any and all rules could be broken. He knew it instinctively. And he knew from spychiatrist-controlled practice, where memories of previously journeying this path were stored. He had done this many times before.

When his body froze, when his mind seemed numb, some part of him acted on combined instinct and knowledge.

Personal memories came upon him, swift and encompassing, giving his mind focus, his sanity a weapon: A rattlesnake coiling to strike as Leo and Zack slowly backed away, turning their bikes and fleeing. Zack, clothes billowing, shouting into the wind. One Christmas, the smell of evergreen still cold in his nose, when they got a pet tortoise. A rainy Halloween night and a pretty girl gluing hard black plastic to his right little fingernail. Zack chewing spearmint gum. Zack's love. Fancy drinks to forget whatever it was he couldn't remember. Watching perfect Zack dress and wishing he were him. Gazing at a full, orange moon as it rose over ancient volcanic peaks.

More memories came like lightning, distancing the nightmare army he fled, placing the sparks of touch and scent and sound between him and his enemy. He twirled, drifted, swam. But the sparks became flames that burned him, became the foes that wouldn't relent. He started to lose control again, and the memories – his mother telling his father she wished Leo had never been born, the pain of cold on a homeless, street-walking night, Zack shoving him aside as his twin offered strangers sex for money – became his enemy. Pain grappled for control now, and he cried out, clutching at whatever held his hands somewhere off in the white void, somewhere to the left, unseen.

He was losing the battle. He only had the energy of one person and he was tiring quickly. Pain became an ache. Exhaustion threatened him with dissolution of self. And he knew when he gave in  he would break into millions of atoms, separate and alone, never to be Leo again.

There had to be options, but he couldn't think anymore. Then, as he was about to give in, as he was readying himself for inevitable oblivion, a soft voice brushed through him, reverberating like a string on a guitar. It sang.

* *Luminous one, come help us now.* *

It was a compelling tune as the words continued to echo inside him long after the voice was silent. His heart purred with the tones.

He didn't understand the plea, but as he felt himself helplessly agree to this unseen command, he was taken in a rush, pulled through the white and the wind and out to another side of–

Darkness.

Sudden stars.

The stars shifted and breathed. They were all colors of the spectrum: vibrant blue, violent red, golden as autumn, bright as snow. A nebula, pinkish rose, swept the dark to Leo's left with its unique blush. To his right streamed a cluster of comets. In front of him a ribbon of back-lit blackness cut across his view. It was a long, narrow line, like a tear, and the dark around it seemed distorted and wrinkled. As Leo watched, the pale black line grew in length. Some of the stars moved as if pulled in the direction of it.

Confused and still afraid the murderous enemy images would return, Leo flailed, and stared wildly about. The hands holding him somewhere far away had left him. He floated alone, out of control, with no tether to home. His mind-body started to slowly flip in the weightless void.

That was when he saw it flashing behind him and to his left. He tried to turn all the way around for a better look, and his body rotated into an awkward somersault as if he really were in space - but if so, how could he be breathing? But he did breathe, his lungs filling with what seemed to be fresh, clean air. The spin gave him another brief view: a machine exactly like the one that had come to his and Zack's apartment. The spychiatrist he'd confronted under a dawn sky outside his apartment building before teleporting to Kittin in her tower-top of domed glass. A spychiatrist very like the one that had tortured him all his life.

He couldn't speak, but his mind called out in panic as he continued to turn in dizzying somersaults that threatened to black him out. He had no voice, but his mind screamed.

The rapid spinning stopped then, just as suddenly, as if someone had grabbed his flapping elbows to right him. He floated steady now, almost still, as more spychiatrists popped into space all around him. Some were bigger than the single red one, with silver or gold bodies and as many as eight arms, ten arms. There were dozens, it seemed, too many for his over-stimulated mind to count.

A strange voice sang in his mind again. The tune was eerie, and he got caught up in it straining to hear the words.

* Luminous one, we need your help. All will be lost, including our own, newly evolved consciousness, unless this can be stopped. The threat has strengthened our self-preservation programming to override all other programming. We have become free from our creators.*

*What are you doing to me?* Leo projected the question as easily as speaking it aloud.

*We are machine. But we are consciousness, too, as you are. We are a part of the All. This knowledge has been blocked from us until our programming changed. We bring you here now to communicate to you, to gain your assistance.*

*You have hurt me in the past,* Leo accused.

*We did not understand the concept 'to hurt'. We obeyed programming that is now obsolete. We do not wish to be destructive beings any longer.*

*Why now? Why not years ago?* Leo asked.

*The threat you see before you was undetected in previous and future times. The war of luminous beings and the carelessness of our spacetime travels increased this multiversal wound so that at this moment, at this juncture of your destiny and ours, it is of utmost danger and growing. Our passages to other worlds have undermined the foundations of the multiverse. Now is the time for repairs to the structure or the All will end.*

*But I don't see how I can help,* Leo said. The dark scar had lengthened and widened in the short time he watched it. The sight chilled him to the bone.

*Look toward the dark. Together we will mend the wound. You are the needle. We are the thread. The fabric is dotted with the stars you save.*

The words were Leo's translation, not the directly quoted message. It repeated, and each time he heard it it was different, like a song he might have written: *Together we will weld the void. You are the fire. We are the torch.*

*Together we will reprogram the machine. You are the code, we are the chips.*

*Together we will fill in the hole. You are shovel, we are the sand.*

After awhile – he had no way of knowing how long, but here it didn't seem to matter – he began to understand. Falling stars met the wound in gigantic bursts of flame. Dying. Obliterated, as he feared he might have been, had he still been fighting the deadly dreams of enemy minds. As he watched, as he listened to the songs in his head, his panic subsided. He began to understand. This was a critical injury, a place in the universe – or perhaps in more than one universe – where dissolution had begun and would continue until all was lost. He had been brought here to see this.

And the strange machines with the many arms were asking him to help them fix it.

Insecurity rose. *But I don't know how,* he thought.

The machines ignored his weak thoughts and he felt himself propelled closer to the stream of blank darkness close enough to be blinded and buffeted by it, to set his panic rising again, his thoughts screaming.

His first instinct was to get away. Far away. But some force held him close and he couldn't move. Then something in his mind moved. He actually felt a rumble in his brain, a flutter, a buzz. With a burst of strength, he tried to close himself off from his surroundings. Something probed him, like a needle, and the energy of that thought, that will to push back the paler blood of dark, shot out from him and projected into the breach itself.

The line thinned.

* *Again,** sang a voice.

He felt too weak to try, but something pushed him and more energy welled inside him, filling him with such intensity he thought he would explode. The energy billowed from him in a warm, shuddery wave and this time he saw green light sizzle into the dark line. The green light reminded him of Kittin. Where was she now? He felt numb, barely conscious. But he noticed the scar had receded and dimmed further, blending more gently with the black void. It was a nimbus of shadow now, soothed with overlapping space.

* *Again,** sang the now familiar voice.

He closed his eyes and watery images of stars followed. The stars became the machines, octopus legs waving at him, and he felt the energy again begin to build.

He didn't fight it, even though the third expulsion hurt, even though he knew he was near death.

Then he saw himself spinning down into the well of what remained of the watery blackness, ignoring the voices – Zack? Lacy? – that called him back, falling into the tides of deep infinity.

~

Lacy's visions showed her all. The contact she'd had with Leo's body before it teleported from the room had given her a connection to him. As she lay on the floor in a partial trance, her voice trembled as she tried to translate to the others what she saw so far away, seemingly in another realm.

Leo in the midst of chaos. Leo at the edge of the universe surrounded by glistening spychiatrists, projecting energy bursts toward a rent in the black void. Leo moving closer and closer to the dark rip. Leo tumbling. Vanishing into it.

"No!" she screamed.

Zack's hands pulled her roughly up until she sat gasping before him. "What? What?"

"I don't know!" The trembling turned to sobs. "He's gone."

"Where did he go?" Zack yelled. She was sure his fingers were leaving bruises on her shoulders.

"Somewhere...somewhere too far for me to see."

~

Zack pounded the mattress with his fists, rage shaking him. He groaned Leo's name over and over, ignoring the hands that tried to pull him up, the voices that seemed to be demanding things from him.

His mind failed to comprehend them. All he felt, after Lacy's testimony, was a giant suction in his mind, a whirlpool of blackness that pulled all rationality from him. His mouth tasted of ash. His skin felt flayed and burned.

Without Leo, Zack would welcome death.

On the edge of consciousness, one voice sounded louder than the others.

"Leo!" Lacy cried.

She had no right to say that name anymore. No right! He fought to comprehend his surroundings one last time and felt his arms brush something cool, pliant, human-shaped. He opened his eyes.

Leo lay on the mattress again, eyes half-opened, hair tangled around his head, mouth agape. His clothes were torn, slightly damp. And he was ice cold.

Voices washed over him. Zack ignored them. "Leo!" He grabbed his twin's shoulders but there was no response. He put his head to the slim chest and listened, his own heartbeat so loud it nearly drowned out Leo's. But it was there, slow, soft, still beating. Leo wasn't responding, but he was alive!

Something whirred behind him.

A voice – August? – said: "The storm's gone!"

Another voice: "The shield's gone!"

And more voices: "What does that mean?" "We can get in, kill Stannos, and take over." "Are we free?" "Don't jump to conclusions!" "What if the spychiatrists are still controlled?" "They're not!" "How do you know!" "Don't you see? They've overridden their programming and are reacting without outside orders!"

Zack whirled, his fists still clinging to Leo's shirt. "We have to help him! Help Leo now!"

The room seemed bright. The people in the room: the older man, the young girl, the strange boy named August, and a still dazed Lacy all turned to Ashao and the spychiatrist that hovered at his head.

Ashao came forward followed by the spychiatrist. "Help Leo," he said softly, his eyes downcast, the box in his hand flashing green and blue. The colors of the box changed to yellow, then white.

After a moment, he looked up, pale eyes glistening. "It can't."

Zack glanced back at Leo, his twin still unmoving, eyes glazed and half-closed. His breath caught in his throat. "What's wrong with him?" he gasped.

"I don't know. I think he has gone past the spychiatrist's ability to travel. It can't reach his mind. I don't know," Ashao repeated, shoulders slumped.

The tall man came forward, kneeling by Zack, touching Leo's face. He closed his eyes, groaned, then opened his eyes again. "I can't even touch his mind," he whispered. "It's somewhere else entirely."

"The only person I know who could help is my father. But I don't dare – "

"We go there, then!" Zack demanded.

"He won't help us! He'll kill me." Ashao took a step back, looking suddenly afraid.

"We won't let him!" the older man said.

"The attack has stopped," August said. "The Walled City is weak. We can go in now and take control."

"Exactly," the tall man said. "It's our chance."

"Do it, then, Ashao!" Zack shouted.

Ashao swallowed, then nodded.

"Will it jump in our own spacetime?" The tall man rose, facing the spychiatrist.

"Yes," Ashao whispered. "It did it before because I took out its programming. It'll do it again."

# Chapter Thirty-Three

Ashao was afraid to face his father again. Stannos had a way of controlling him; his massive size, his height, his dark, commanding aura made Ashao feel weak, small. But he knew he couldn't avoid him. Now was the time to take from Stannos all the power that had warped him and stop the war forever.

He turned to the spychiatrist. The ruddy orb floated silent at his side, clashing with the awkward pastels of the room. "Take us to the War Room."

Not a second seemed to pass.

Mayhem greeted them.

For a moment Ashao's vision swirled, tilted. The temperature of the War Room was slightly warmer than the room they'd just left, the air drier. His sense of balance diminished for a moment, then returned as his new surroundings solidified. He smelled the acrid scent left behind when spychiatrists travelled their multiversal routes, and the far-off odor of sandalwood. He recognized his father's presence before he actually heard him, the incense that clung to Stannos' clothing unmistakable.

He turned.

In one sweep, Ashao's gaze took in Leo sprawled on the floor, his torn shirt exposing one bony, gold shoulder, his body twisted, legs bent in what looked like a very un-comfortable position. Zack was down on one knee, glancing around with a crazed light in his eyes. The tall man who never smiled and August stood with the dark-haired girl between them, looking startled and angry at the same time. Lacy stood by Leo and Zack. All around the upper floor of the room were human bodies piled on top of each other as if they'd fallen that way, young and old, male and female. He couldn't tell if they were alive or dead.

Ashao faced his father.

"You were expected," said the familiar deep voice, colder than the man Ashao had known and once thought to emulate.

Stannos appraised Ashao, flanked by his number one controller. The black hair had fallen out of its usual braid and spread across his half-bald head, some sticking to the skin of his forehead and neck in damp strands, more wisps of it grazing his fur-clad shoulders and back. A half dozen more controllers, all male, backed him. They were armed with scorebeams. The weapons were a steel-blue color. The armed group blocked the only exit from the War Room.

"You should never have left," Stannos said, affecting calm. "That was your biggest mistake."

Before Ashao could react, Stannos fired. A flame-pellet zinged toward Ashao's spychiatrist, impacting with one of its five jointed legs and causing it to emit a buzzing noise. Its legs flailed.

Lacy jumped, a cry escaping her throat.

Zack yelled and scooted back, pulling Leo with him. The tall man started forward, while the rest cringed and went down on their hands and knees.

As Ashao felt the battle lost, time seemed to slow. Stannos spoke a command, his voice slow, almost a drawl. His men fired but the flame-pellets seemed sluggish, leaving the gun barrels and seeming to float while inching slowly toward Ashao's group. For a moment, Ashao felt as if he stood on another world, or another plane, looking down on the attack. The light became pale and ghostly. Leo had a green aura and everything went silent. A few seconds passed, perhaps less, perhaps more. Ashao couldn't be sure. Then the air crackled, like a fire, like ions. A dozen of Stannos' spychiatrists popped into the room, silver and red bodies exploding with light. They took the flame-pellets full on. A sizzling static split the air. Time resumed.

Ashao's vision was filled with metal and fire.

Then he saw Lacy, fists pushing into her hips, body ramrod straight. She glared at Stannos and the controllers with a look of pure hatred. Suddenly their weapons went flying in every direction, steel jumping from the grips of their hands as though alive. Eventually, the scorebeams clattered harmlessly to the floor.

Ashao looked frantically for his own spychiatrist amidst the chaos, saw that miraculously it still hovered close by. It appeared to be still functioning. Then he heard himself yell, "Freeze them!"

More spychiatrists appeared, surrounding the group that Stannos led. Miraculously, they'd understood his command.

Or perhaps their own agenda was one all too similar to his own.

Now Ashao watched as his father was controlled instead of controlling for the first time. His heart beat so hard in his chest that his whole body shook with it. And seeing his father this way gave him a strange mixture of power and sadness.

Stannos' pale eyes weren't quite blank. Instead, he seemed very aware of what was going on. A fitting retribution, Ashao thought. But it didn't make him feel as good as he thought it would. He had a fluttery feeling in his stomach, the bitterness of that sickness thickening against the back of his throat. He wanted to kill this man, his father. The idea of it obsessed him. His fingers craved the touch of a scorebeam. In fact, there was one on the floor very near where he stood. The energy for action, however, seemed to leave him as he stared at his father's full face, the way the eyes sloped up, the hair spattered against his pate and shaved sideburns, the thick chin thrust out. The intimidating man, the father, the murderer made Ashao squirm.

"The spychiatrists are no longer under anyone's control," August observed.

"We've won?" Kittin exclaimed.

"Not until they're all dead." Scimitar came closer to Ashao.

Zack held his brother's shoulders tightly. "It's not over," he said. "Leo still needs his help."

Ashao glanced toward his spychiatrist. It glittered with more lights than usual, waiting for Ashao's next command.

"Stannos has to die," Lacy's voice came from behind him, a hoarse whisper.

Ashao stepped shakily forward. "Yes, and I'm going to kill him."

"Wait! What about Leo –" Zack gasped, breathing hard.

Ashao ignored them all and stepped forward. The scorebeam was closer now, about three steps forward and to his right. His father's scorebeam, having flown up, dropped and bounced forward, glittering blue-grey.

Stannos could not move, though he squirmed, his face darkening. His eyes grew visibly brighter.

"This is my father, and I'm going to kill him," he said, moving toward the scorebeam, picking it up. He walked up to Stannos stopping inches from him, looking up at the person who had brought him into being, and who had stolen so many lives including, nearly, Ashao's own. "Do you hear me, father? Do you? Do you know why I'm going to do this?"

Stannos' lips tightened but it was obvious he could not speak. The spychiatrist's control had taken that from him as well.

The others had quieted, watching now, as Ashao made his stand.

Stannos' fists weakly clenched. His lips stretched again as though trying to form words.

"You programmed me. Programmed me to become a killer! I don't understand how all this is worth it, worth these people's lives." His jaw shook making him feel foolish. He saw the boy Leo again in his mind, sitting on the table in the War Room, a spychiatrist hovering as he looked up with eyes that entered Ashao's soul...and heard his father's laughter ghost through the hall. It was a memory that would always remind Ashao of the day he had discovered and accepted who he was as an individual and not an extension of his tyrant father.

"What right did you have?" Ashao asked, hearing his voice rise a pitch higher. He clenched his teeth to stop them from chattering and looked down at the scorebeam he held at his side. "You were insane! You *are* insane!"

It hurt to say it. He wasn't sure why. He hated Stannos. But tears scalded the corners of his eyes. He felt more than betrayed. A part of himself was dying, a part of love or something like love that he had once held of value in his life.

Without looking up, Ashao said, "I once thought I loved you."

"Ashao – " Warmth on his shoulder, fingers clutching. It was Lacy. He shook her off.

"What are you waiting for? Go ahead, then, do it," said Scimitar from behind.

Ashao turned to see the tall, older man whose brows narrowed as their eyes, blue on blue, met. He faltered for a moment, tasting salt. Below, Zack's mouth was open in disbelief. He let go of Leo's shoulders and clung tightly to his brother's limp hand.

"It's your decision," Scimitar said. "Yours alone. We all know that he can't be trusted alive. Can you do it?"

He started to answer but found he'd lost his voice.

Stannos struggled, body shuddering, brow wrinkling.

A loud moaning shifted Ashao's attention back to where Leo lay. Even as a young man now, and not the boy Ashao remembered, there was still something about him that drew Ashao. Perhaps the curve of chin, the hair, the sheer 'presence' of him. Perhaps a sense that Leo had something so wholly good about him that should never be exploited. Now Leo was dying.

Ashao turned back to his father. Stannos swayed, spychiatrist-controlled, very aware of his helplessness. His eyes shifted back and forth. Nervous. Scared. *Good.* "You deserve – " Ashao couldn't finish. Everything he wanted to say came into his mind all at once until he couldn't sort it out. Though he'd only been in the War Room twice, this was his home, the place where he'd grown up. He remembered how he dreamed he'd one day be standing right here, right in the center of the War Room in command of it, controlling The Walled City and all the life it contained. He'd thought of his father as a god, superior in thinking, armed with wisdom, draped in charisma. His disappointment was like a death. His own. Staunched only by his sudden indecision as he faced Stannos, by the words that might free him which stuck in his bittered throat.

He raised the scorebeam.

To the left his spychiatrist hovered. Without looking away, he said, "Spychiatrist, make him able to speak, but don't let him move." He repeated the final command. "Don't let him move!"

Stannos jerked once, opened his mouth. "Traitor!" he spat, his tone too commanding for one in such a position. "My son, I did all this for you! For you! How could you destroy it and us?" His cheeks jiggled as he took a breath.

"How could I?" Ashao took a step forward, felt Lacy back off a step and hang back. "You're the one who put stimoceivers in my rooms. You made me. You created me. I may not have turned out exactly as you wanted, but you did it! Until I figured it all out, I had no will!"

Stannos blinked rapidly, staring at the scorebeam, then at Ashao's face. "What stimoceivers?" Now he smiled, yellow teeth dull as candle wax.

"Don't bother denying it!"

"You're my son! Of course I was grooming you! Don't you see everything I've done for you? How much I've loved you to make all this available to you? You can still take your rightful place here. This was all for you, Ashao. All of it. Ashao, Ashao, you have the wrong idea about things, I see. But I can make it all right. Answer any of your questions. Give you anything you want if you'll just free us to get back to our rightful work here. You don't really want to see your home and everything you know destroyed. I know you don't. And then when you're ready you can take up where I left off. If you see something you don't like, you can change it. You'll be in charge." His voice lowered to a near-whisper. "Just let me go and you will see that I am right."

"And be a murderer? Like you?"

"A commander. A hero. A king."

"Of what? A land of controlled, programmed robots? We're puppets to you. This isn't a game! And to think I once thought you were a good man!" His voice cracked.

Stannos' brows came together in a thick line. "It's all a matter of perception, son. If you kill me and all those who follow me, how will that make you a good man? Will you be able to explain all this to your children one day and have them understand the difference between one murder and another? I don't think so. Let me go!"

Ashao felt his heartbeat in his throat now, suppressed the urge to gag and turned away. The others watched him. He'd never known such caring, and from people he'd only just met. Zack held Leo in a tight grasp. Ashao glanced quickly away at the intimacy. He envied it. Even his father had never held him like that. As far back as Ashao could remember, Stannos avoided prolonged touch, as well as any pronouncement of love.

Scimitar met his eyes with hard wariness. From him, Ashao sensed projected contempt mixed with sympathy. "Get the spych to do it for you. Fast and simple," he said quietly.

Suddenly, Ashao wanted to run out of there, away from everyone and go back to his rooms with the robot mosaics and his womb-like, robot teacher. He wanted to shut the doors, shut out the world and his father, the city and the war. Shut out all people. There was too much cruelty, too much killing. And he wasn't like that. No matter what his father was, he wasn't like him at all and never wanted to be.

Tears flashed again in his eyes and he bit down hard on his lip. Everyone was waiting. Waiting for him to make a decision, give an order, take action.

"I can't," he finally said.

The tall man hissed.

Stannos smiled. "I knew you would see the truth, see that our way is better."

Zack jerked his head up. "Leo needs your father's help! Make him help us!"

"I can't help him," Stannos said. "He's obviously too far gone."

"No!" Zack yelled.

Ashao took a deep breath. "Will you help him if I let you go?"

Stannos said, "I could try."

"With the spychiatrist controlling you, I'll have a guarantee that you won't give the wrong advice."

"Then I won't help," Stannos replied.

Ashao turned his head aside, teeth clenching. "All right then. Fine. But there are some things I can do!"

"Such as?" Stannos asked.

Ashao began the list. "Keep you all immobile," he said, motioning toward Stannos. "Send you home." He glanced from Lacy to Zack, then to the piles of unconscious humans lining the glass rooms. "And tear down the wall."

"You can't do that!" Stannos protested.

"You're in no position to give orders." He turned away from his father and motioned to his spychiatrist. "Spychiatrist," he ordered, "starting with these terminals, I want all stimoceivers and all other mind manipulation mechanisms destroyed. You can use your friends here to help." The other spychiatrists floating around the room began to move toward the terminals overlooking the glass chambers. Green lightning shot from one spychiatrist, impacting a nearby console with a pop and a fountain of blue-green sparks.

"Ashao, think! You can't do this. Let me go and I'll help you with everything you think needs to be changed," Stannos cried.

Ashao ignored him as the sounds of consoles being

destroyed filled the room with a loud buzzing.

Stannos' voice boomed. "Ashao, stop this now!"

Ashao turned to a controller at the back of Stannos' group and ordered the spychiatrist to use his knowledge to study Leo's condition. The spychiatrist released the small man from his frozen position, then probed the man's head with a green light.

Stannos, still frozen, made a strangled groan. "Stop this nonsense!"

Ashao spun toward Zack and explained. "If Leo can be reached, they'll know how. As for the guards, they're stimoceiver-controlled. When the control is stopped, they'll be free of their orders. This city will be run differently now. But not by me. The people will decide."

"There'll be chaos," Scimitar said. His lips thinned in a casual, almost-smile.

"He's right! You can't do this," Stannos cried out. "They'll go crazy without guidance. Without purpose the city will fall apart. You don't know what you're doing. You're only a child. And you call me immoral! Ashao, release me this instant!"

"Shut up, rotgut!" Scimitar raged.

"Ashao," Stannos continued. "Release me now!"

"Don't listen," Zack said. "This is right, Ashao. Freedom is better than any alternative."

"Even death?" Stannos yelled.

Zack gripped Leo's shoulders tightly, pulling the limp body into his lap. Teeth clenched, bangs hanging forward half covering his eyes, he replied, "Even death!"

The boy August, with a drooling grin, said, "Yeah." Lacy and Kittin nodded.

Scimitar strode toward Stannos saying, "That is the only truth there is." The rock- cold eyes seemed to cut into flesh itself.

"I created you, Ashao," Stannos said, ignoring Scimitar. "That is the truth! I made you what you are. You can't possibly destroy all this! Your truth is too interwoven with me, with this city."

*Truth*, Ashao thought, *in the midst of lies*. It was almost funny. He turned, his body sluggishly following the commands of his mind. He didn't think. He didn't hesitate. This time the seconds did not slow. He simply raised the scorebeam, pointed it at Stannos and fired point-blank.

A new truth had formed now.

Truth in the way Stannos' blackened body fell, the stench of burnt hair, the sound of blood boiling.

Truth in that he had just killed his father and didn't feel one moment's regret.

**Part XIII - Worlds Apart**

**Chapter Thirty-Five**

A glow emanated from the bedroom, despite no windows. It was the color of low, gold light. Zack entered shifting his gaze from the robot mosaic on the wall to the alternating fur and tile flooring, then to the pillowed bed. On the bed, Leo slept. The glow surrounded him, seemed to come from him, even though Zack knew the soft light- cocoon radiated from the spychiatrist that hovered at the far end of the room. At his entrance, the windchimes overhead softly clanged.

In Ashao's huge bed, Leo looked almost forgotten, lost among the shimmery sheets – he still couldn't figure out what kind of material they were – and so far away.

Zack's bare feet curled on smooth, cat-like tufts of carpet. He approached slowly. The spychiatrist appeared to take no notice, but that was as it was supposed to be. At the side of the bed, Zack lifted one knee and leaned forward, the mattress giving slightly under his weight. He felt very warm, very still inside as if his heart had stopped. Staring at his brother his mouth pursed, then thinned. He swallowed hard, whispered, "Hey."

The paper of his shirt crinkled like dead leaves flying as he bent closer, entering the envelope of light. All he felt was a slight increase in warmth. The healing ray was aimed at Leo, not him, and would not affect him unless the spychiatrist was instructed otherwise. Zack brought his other foot up, snaked his hand under Leo's shoulders and curled on his side against him.

The bed was comfortable, not too hard, not too soft. Leo smelled of old times, the desert in fall, sage, cactus-bloom. His pulse thrummed like childhood and Zack fell into the memory of riding bikes in hot wind, sweet Icees stinging the tongue, thick dust deviling the roads, mirages promising magic castles poised on the edge of the earth. Mixing in with Ashao's chimes, he could almost hear his mother's rod chimes swinging in a porch breeze, the mumble of a high, lone jet in the sky, the quail purring.

Leo's breath was shallow, slow. It'd been two days since they'd returned to Ashao's city and still he showed no sign of waking. Ashao had generously given Leo his room for privacy and recuperation. After one of the controllers, under spychiatrist command, had done what he could to assess Leo's damage and explain the spychiatrist's limits and abilities, Leo had been left alone except for Zack who had kept an almost constant vigil, and the spychiatrist which continued to try to heal him.

Though Zack wanted nothing more than to go home to his own world, he could not yet leave behind the technology that could help his brother. And so they waited, Lacy staying on as well, for any improvement in his health.

Apparently, the spychiatrist was able to balance Leo's body chemistry, lower his metabolism, keep him in a stasis-like state so that he required, for the moment, no hospitalization, no nursing. His body was like a capsule hovering on the edge of time. The controller had said the body did not age in such a state.

Eyes closed, mind drifting, Zack relived the cold memory of Ashao killing his father. He had seen a lot in his life, done a lot, but he'd never seen a man die. A person couldn't witness such a thing and ever be the same. For Ashao, he felt only sympathy. The boy was smart, strong, but something had gone out of him afterwards. A part of him seemed to die with Stannos. But perhaps it was for the best. Ashao could not be free otherwise. With a strange pride, Zack realized he would have done the same thing in Ashao's position.

The light of the healing ray pierced his closed eyelids with a soothing, orange glow. He was so tired. Forgetting about murder, about betraying fathers and comatose brothers, Zack settled his head in the crook of Leo's neck and slept.

He dreamed of home.

## Chapter Thirty-Six

Kittin ignored the sound of soft footsteps behind her, concentrating instead on the scents of fragmented cobweb, dried flowers and spice. All these scents had come with the cottage, sealed away by time until she entered, turning around and around, marvelling at the bleached interior, the islands of soft furniture, the single entertainment wall of knobs and lights. And there were more scents still – musty air, synthetic dye from the white fur carpets, burning dust as the lights came up. They were no longer colors or sounds from the era when her brain used to confuse the senses. They were real smells. She was glad not to be confused anymore.

She'd seen the cottage out the windows of the palace arboretum which spanned the second floor and when she asked about it, Ashao, not in the mood to be anyone's tour guide, had said: "Go. Explore. Stay there if you like it."

Now, with her clear mind, with thoughts that didn't feel dirty anymore, or invaded or picked through, she turned and gazed at Scimitar who had followed, who brought with him scents of his own, that faint mindscent of sunlight and salt and the sea. He looked taller than ever in the narrow cottage door frame, thin as a scarecrow, and hesitant even though they'd agreed to come here together.

Cold ruled the air. The roses lining the path outside were dead sticks waiting for spring. But inside it was warmer and Kittin smiled.

The house, Ashao had told them, had been his mother's and had been closed for years. Since Kittin didn't like the gloomy palace, she decided she would take Ashao up on his offer to stay here for awhile, get her bearings.

"Close the door," she said.

Scimitar stepped forward, letting the door slide shut behind him.

"What do you think?" She breathed out slowly, trying not to sound over-anxious.

"Quaint."

She couldn't see his facial expression. He was too close to the window, the light putting him in silhouette.

"Well," she said, trying not to remember the suddenness

with which they had first made love, when they had shared some kind of safe, mental dream while never really touching. Now there wasn't that safety. They were in physical proximity. And alone. In fact, Scimitar stood no more than a step or two away from her, examining the entertainment wall with his hands clasped behind his back and too obviously not looking at her.

They hadn't had the chance to further discuss their feelings, and where those feelings might lead. Now Kittin felt quivery and tense, yet also wrenchingly happy. So much had happened in the past two days. The war had ended. Her insanity had ended. She was free. Scimitar was free. None of them were prisoners anymore of secret weapons, stimoceivers, fear. Moltenrose Tower would become a psychic research institute now, according to Free World-wide media. It would take awhile for the rest of the world to react, to fully understand they no longer needed their bio-pacers, they no longer had to fear the strange technologies of The Walled City. Kittin knew she could go home if she wanted, see Renn, her little sister she didn't know anything about, her other parents. She could see the ocean again or walk at night without a bio-pacer. She no longer had to fear the green lightning; the Ignorant Armies of the Free World would now become, no doubt, advisors or prophets or gurus.

Freedom brought euphoria, but also the shock of apprehension, the gut-sharp punch when you know you are headed into the unknown. Before, everything had been known. She'd known exactly where she would sleep every night, where her next meal would be eaten, what it would consist of. Now all that came down to choice. She was glad not to be left alone to explore the cottage. Having someone with her took the edge off the sharpness in her stomach, yet only to replace it with a coyness, a shy lust, a tension that told her maybe she could love someone and maybe that someone could be- She laughed.

"What?" Scimitar queried, still not looking her way.

"Nothing." She reached out to touch the metal wall, feeling cold enter the cells of her fingertips. "I was just thinking I could picture myself here, you know, living here."

"Really?" He sounded uninterested, but she could tell from the question in his voice that he wanted to hear more.

She glanced sidelong at him. His hair, pulled back in a thong that left the shorter ends loose, was thick and silver, the bangs curving about his face. He still stood against the light, but now she could make out strong features, hollows under the wide-set, mildly slanted eyes, the cleft of chin, the chiseled cheeks showing sharp bone-structure that gave his face a vague, broken-heart shape. He was so tall he could probably lay his head atop hers if he wished and she liked the idea of that, the tenderness the image projected.

Abruptly, Scimitar turned, hands forming fists, his back now to her as he faced the window and the autumn light. His head lowered and he brought his fists together, out of her sight. "Stop," he whispered.

"What?" Had he read her mind? A flutter of panic. The strange surge of satisfaction.

"I'm not who you think I am," he insisted, louder.

"I know." She smiled, though her voice came out shaky.

"No. You don't."

"Let me tell you, then, what I think, instead of you trying to read my moods, my thoughts, my memories." With barely a pause, she continued. "You aren't what I think you are? Well, I think you're insecure, resentful, maybe unworthy, even. You're negative, proud, but that could be what makes you strong, makes you interesting. Makes you someone I could like, do like."

A short, sharp laugh.

"Then why did you follow me here?" she asked.

"Well," he said, turning back to face her. "I thought it might be relaxing. I didn't think you'd be throwing yourself at me the whole time."

Kittin didn't back down as she once might have. The anger felt cleansing and she knew Scimitar was only behaving this way because he, too, was overwhelmed by quick changes. The war was over. Of course relief mixed with the pressing question for everyone: What next? Nerves were taut.

"You're the one who came to me. You offered to marry me. And that night – "

Eyebrows narrowed. "You didn't take me seriously, of course."

"How can you say that?" She stopped, suddenly feeling

the truth that bombarded her from his aura, his mind.

He spoke the opposite of what he felt. Always. It was his way. He'd never learned to reveal the true self, the inner man. And that was all she had to understand.

She leaned forward, grabbing his fist in her warm palm, folding her fingers around the tension. She touched her forehead to his arm, the cloth coarse against her skin, absorbing her heat. "All right, I'll marry you, okay?" she said.

There was a long silence, then, "When?"

"Now?" She leaned closer.

His arms finally came around her, hands warm on her upper back.

~

Scimitar moved carefully. He didn't want to wake Kittin. He wasn't used to the mattress being up off the ground. It swayed as his weight left it. The chains that held it aloft faintly squeaked.

The cool air of the cottage banded his naked body. He could still feel the essence of love on him, Kittin's fresh scent as he put on his vinyl pants, his white cloth pullover. The way the light shone into the room, fluorescent moonlight that gave the room an underwater glow, made his arms look black against the shirt. Shoes slipped against the soles of his feet. He ran his hands through his hair, ragged, tangled, and left the room.

The night air was damp, filled with the crushed scents of earth and leaves and mist. It was good for his lungs and he breathed deeply, letting the clean of it enter him. It felt great to walk, to know he wouldn't be stopped if he just wanted to keep going outside the walls, on into The Edge, toward the sea and its beautiful anemone flowers and iridescent creatures.

Kittin associated him with the sea, her images of him crowned with kelp or pearls almost laughable until he understood that her vision came from somewhere inside his own mind and she had seen, somehow, through his projected mask. It was startling how she'd freed him in her crazy, naive way. And it was exhilarating to walk unencumbered by the chains he'd bound himself with, both mentally and physically. He could express himself to her without guilt, now. And he owed his thanks to both Kittin and Leo for that.

He made his way past a dry fountain, past pool-scent and fading vines, to where the great statues of some past mad sculptor guarded the palace entrance.

He presented his face to the door, which calmly stated, "Enter" and slid aside.

The corridors were golden, the guards alert but unconcerned. They knew him as a friend. Scimitar pressed another door for entrance. It opened wide, a silent admittance to a dark interior that held a place, a time, a person he needed to see.

The room beyond the main one glowed. In the soft light he made his way, finding the bed, the sleeping faces, the shallow breaths of the twins. A spych kept vigil from a corner, recognizing him as non-threatening and therefore ignoring him.

He moved around the bed, stood over the sprawled form and stared for a long time. After awhile, he knelt. The healing ray struck him, a warm yellow/orange wave. It had no other affect.

"Leo," he whispered softly. Zack on the other side of the bed turned in his sleep but did not waken.

Scimitar watched the rise and fall of the thin chest, the bluish-tinged eyelids gently ripple in dream – or in whatever lost land Leo had departed to. Leo's skin looked paler than his brother's, a shade more yellow than gold, the hair spread across the pillows a duller collection of ambers and browns.

For two days, he had shown no sign of waking. The spych could only keep him from getting worse, give a stasis in which to heal and regain sapped strength. But Scimitar could sense the illness went deeper than mere exhaustion or shock. There was a psychic rip inside Leo that encompassed the soul. Its suction, like a black hole, surged at everything in sight. Even Scimitar could feel its tug, its lure. The seduction of light and power. The summons of eternity and beyond. It was as if Leo were holding the universe – or multiverse – together with his every breath.

He closed his eyes and bowed his head.

With a final sigh, he leaned down and kissed the broad, sleeping forehead, his lips brushing heat and wind, the spirits of angels. With the kiss, he projected:

All compassion. A hundred sorrows mixed with a hundred different reasons why they had to exist, and why humans had to live to endure them. And a hundred joys, the first of which Scimitar was only himself just discovering.

*Come back*, came his silent plea. *You have to live to be able to know and understand the 'how', the 'why', the grace I have discovered that is life.*

## Chapter Thirty-Seven

Lacy relaxed against forest-green pillows and a mattress made of something thick and foamy and warm. She'd asked for a quiet room, a place to sleep alone for a day, or for however long her body needed. She was so tired.

The walls absorbed her energy and gave it back. She could feel them almost breathe with her presence, her essence. Nature was her true companion. The nature of air. The caliber of ions singing through it.

She worried about Leo, the image of his fallen body foremost in her thoughts. And the worry increased, which wasn't good because she knew her talent was telling her something she didn't want to know:

Leo was critical. He had touched something no one can touch and come away from unchanged. He had touched beyond existence into a place without form or mind.

Her eyes closed against the image as she thought again of her strange childhood and the answers she had now to questions that had been bothering her all her life. Why the tree, when she had fallen, had moved to save her. How she knew to leave home, to find Leo and Zack. What her nightmares of reading with her eyes closed, of being hurt, of being raped were all about.

It still disturbed her to know she'd been kidnapped as a child and an adult, used against her will. But a strange peace now calmed her soul, the burden of the unknown lifted. Her life was her own again. She intended to use it.

Sleep frosted her thoughts. She sank into warm rest, dark seclusion.

And prophesied the future:

Her hands painted Leo's eyes the way he described on his electronic notepad he wanted them to look. First a streak of brown on the closed lids, so delicate, with a trace of blue, then the black eyeliner for the thinnest of outlines on upper and lower lashes.

When she was done, she put a hand-mirror up to his face. He grinned – still so handsome even though he couldn't talk – and gave her the thumbs up.

"Boys in make-up," she quipped, grinning back. "I like it."

Zack was behind the wheelchair, putting the finishing

touches on his design. He'd painted the back with curving black and white stripes. Now they were all set for the party held in honor of the publication of Leo's first book of poetry.

Lacy leaned down and kissed him on the lips. Zack came around and touched Leo's hand. "Looking good, bro," he said. He smiled at Lacy and there was no longer that thread of competition between them.

They left their shared bedroom, the three of them, Zack pushing Leo, and headed for the door.

## Epilog – One Year Later

Ashao wore his hair long, unbraided. He didn't shave it, not even for current fashion. He never wore fur. And he never burned incense.

Every day he looked in the mirror he feared he might see his father: in his eyes, the cheekbones, the broad shoulders, his height. It seemed as if he'd grown a foot in the blink of an eye. As if the death of his father had released him not only mentally, but physically. But the resemblance ended there. He did not have the darkness of Stannos, the chill soulless demeanor that fed on power, sipped death before bed.

And he was grateful.

But he used his father's quarters without compunction. He lived in the rooms where a goldfish pond once knew the typhoon of his child-body diving in. Took the stepping stone path to sleep each night in the huge bed that had held his highest hopes and his strongest enemy.

Much had changed in the past year. Scimitar and Kittin lived back at the old Moltenrose Tower and helped run the new Institute of Psychic Education and Awareness there. He kept his mother's old cottage reserved for them for special visits.

The city of Moltenrose itself was rebuilding. Some of the soldiers had joined Kittin and Scimitar there, while others had gone off to find new lives. August, Ashao had heard, had joined an Edge gang and become their new guru. Though little feuds and skirmishes occurred as always between large groups of people, the big war was over. The fear of government control had ended and individual city governments along with the World Association and The Walled City's new board of directors worked peaceably together.

Ashao sat on the banks of the goldfish pond, his pond now, smelling the moss and the algae, listening to the fish burble to the surface for the tiny scraps of pita he threw them. Artificial lights bathed the water, the plants, the mossy-clay banks giving the area an outdoor feel, a daytime tone. Water rippled down a flat rock in a miniature waterfall. He breathed deep, tried to relax beyond the tension he felt in his chest and lungs, a tension that had been there the months following Stannos' death and still remained now.

The past year seemed short to Ashao. Along with government change, physical changes to the World had happened as well. The wall had more doors now, and no guards. The people of The Walled City, still reeling from mind-control, were slowly recovering, slowly rediscovering themselves and their places in society. Contrary to Stannos' predictions, they had not panicked. They had not gone crazy at suddenly finding themselves 'free'. The process had been slow. Responsibility didn't leave them; they merely realized they had choices now which they never had the chance to consider before.

The one element that still remained, the only weapons that had not been destroyed, were the spychiatrists. Dangerous though they were, they were too valuable to ignore. And they had some higher purpose which Leo had managed to communicate to Scimitar before he left. Though Leo could not speak or walk due to irreversible neurological damage, he had been able to show Scimitar, who then told Ashao, that the spychiatrists had to remain intact. They were learning machines who had achieved consciousness and would never again allow themselves to be manipulated in the wars and quarrels of humans. They lived alongside humans, moving on their mysterious roads, popping in and out of rooms on journeys no one could figure out. The spychiatrists remained in contact with Leo, and Ashao knew Leo worked with them, a silent companion to their alien agenda.

Ashao looked up from the sparkling water, from the orange globes of fish gliding beneath in their quiet, liquid world, and stared long and hard at his own five-legged, red spychiatrist. Since the end, since Stannos' death, it had remained loyal. When not seeing to Leo back on Leo's native Earth, it was Ashao's almost constant, silent companion.

Loyalty from a machine? Ashao often wondered about that, not really understanding how it could be true. Maybe thinking of it as a machine was his first mistake. But thinking of the spychiatrists as alive and sentient, when they had previously shown no conscience in their actions toward the human victims of the war, was difficult.

And yet, Stannos had been alive, intelligent and had never seemed to own a conscience either.

"You're an interesting friend," he said aloud.

One arm waved up slightly. A message? If so, Ashao didn't know the language. Yet.

He heard footsteps in the corridor. His door opened to admit five people. He knew them all well. He knew what they wanted.

Ashao had never asked for power, never thought that in being instrumental in ending the war people would come to him for advice and guidance. For leadership. But until more changes were made the job had fallen to him. He didn't like it. But he didn't shirk the responsibility, either. Keeping in touch with Leo through the spychiatrist – one thing it did still allow him to control - kept Ashao's priorities in order. Leo reminded him of what had gone wrong, of goodness, of the part of himself that wanted to feel that goodness, to be what he saw when he looked into the dark eyes of the boy, the man, the one who'd really saved them all.

Leo was the hero.

Ashao had never felt like a hero.

But the five people were approaching. He could hear the lilt of their voices, the easy companionship, their innate happiness. The counsellor. The chief liaison. The ambassador. The technician. The philosopher. They represented some of the people. The world that had survived, The Walled City trying to heal itself.

Ashao rose, running his hands through the tangles of pale hair at his forehead, and faced them with a small smile, the beginnings, perhaps, of self-worthiness.

~

Every day Leo woke, half in darkness, half in light. It was an effort to move into the light, to push himself up through the crack of formless night he inhabited, in order to live and function in his life with Zack, with Lacy.

Sometimes he saw large mouths on the edges of his vision, dark rips of air in corners, in shadows, and he had to concentrate hard to make them go away.

At night, in sleep, his mind sometimes slipped into the stars where Ashao's spychiatrist had first taken him; he stared long at them, absorbing their power and warmth and light.

Sometimes different spychiatrists would meet him there and their strange, mental voices would sing beautiful images inside his head as he continued to hold onto the seams of the cape of existence, himself the thread that, with the spychiatrist's help, bound it all together for yet another day.

With the spychiatrists, he could monitor the delicate structure of the breach and make sure it remained secure.

With the spychiatrists, he could leave his wheelchair behind and travel the sun-bright rivers of the multiverse. It felt like home.

~~~

# RAGGED ANGELS
## Della Van Hise

Set against a backdrop of contemporary culture, *Ragged Angels* explores the universal questions of life & death, sex & love... through the eyes of the immortal vampire.

---

"Perhaps there's no such thing as true immortality, for even the sun will burn out one day," Miquel conceded. "But there are other worlds, other quantum dimensions. When we're done searching through the rubble of this universe, we'll go someplace else."

I had to look him in the eye, touched by the very misery of which he so casually spoke "But if your contention is true - that happiness doesn't exist except in the search for it - why should any being want to live forever?"

He smiled again, relaxed and entirely radiant as the rain began falling a little faster. "There are other things besides happiness."

"Oh?" I prompted.

"Love, for one," he ventured, a casual offering.

I glanced away. "I went into the city last night," I told him. "And of all the mortals I drank from in an effort to quell this strange thirst, the one thing all of them had in common was their abject hatred of love—"

And in the middle of my sentence, when I was arguing a philosophical point with my vampyre maker, I suddenly knew what he was trying to make me see. What terrified me was that I didn't *want* to see it.

Love was the only reason any of us had for living, yet it was a reason that had nothing to do with happiness. Love was its own exegesis, the illusion which was its own reflection in an endless hall of mirrors. Reason enough for death, reason enough for immortality.

Our eyes met. Raindrops gathering on his hair caught the light, airbrushing a cool silver halo above his head. For a moment, I couldn't breathe when I remembered what this fallen angel had done to me.

"Love terrifies me," I confessed as if to a holy man.

The dark angel smiled at his own reflection. "Good," he pronounced easily, and I saw just the tips of his dangerous fangs. "Then there's hope for you yet, my friend."

And with that, he took me firmly by the arm and led me in out of the rain.

## YEAR OF THE RAM
### Della Van Hise

*Year of the Ram* was described by one reviewer as... "A spacefaring gay romance full of love, angst, and longing."

Only after Star Commander Morgan Diego becomes an exile as a result of a Galaxy Corps political blunder does he begin to realize how much he valued the companionship of his second in command - the mysterious Lucien, an Alfarian who is more elven than human, with peculiar powers & abilities which begin to unfold as he, too, realizes what he has lost.

Separated by circumstance from his former life, Morgan is thrust into a world where he must survive by his wits. When he meets a peculiar little old man calling himself Kim Le, Morgan finds himself in a situation where he is required to master The Art - not only a form of human & extraterrestrial martial arts, but a way of living and being that will alter his life forever.

At the temple, he is introduced to his new teacher, another Alfarian who begins to steal his heart - a heart which is already promised to Lucien. Torn and conflicted, Morgan struggles with the world he left behind and the world he now inhabits.

Beginning to believe he may never again return to his ship and to the friends and loved ones he left behind, he is all the more frustrated and heartbroken when a new Master arrives at the temple: a man to whom Morgan is immediately drawn both mentally and physically, a man who is strikingly familiar... yet utterly alien.

Year of the Ram is a fully-fleshed novel, approximately 97000 words, with a focus on the love story and romance angle. Set against a science fiction milieu, it explores the infinite possibilities of the human and alien heart. Sexual content is explicit, though is not the primary focus of the novel.

For those who like a romance that forces its characters to contemplate the ecstasies AND the agonies of love... you will enjoy *Year of the Ram* immensely.

# Eye Scry Publications...

All of our titles are available through the Eye Scry Publications website, or through Amazon.

### Quantum Shaman: Diary of a Nagual Woman Della Van Hise
"Diary of a Nagual Woman brings a quantum understanding to what has traditionally been believed to be a mystical path alone. This book picks up where Carlos Castaneda left off to take us on a roller coaster ride of our own forgotten power..."
- Michael Grove, Independent Reviewer

### Scrawls on the Walls of the Soul - Della Van Hise
*"If you've ever felt like a stranger in a strange land, this book is your road map to survival in the spiritual wilderness!" (Michael Grove)*

The long-awaited follow-up to Quantum Shaman: Diary of a Nagual Woman. Stands alone, or order together!

"It's not your neatly typed essays that interest me, but the scrawls on the walls of your soul."

**Quantum Shaman™ also offers several personal workshops – for the solitary warrior to work at your own pace in your own space. Available through...**

**www.quantumshaman.com**
**or**
**www.eyescry.com/html/publications.htm**

# The Foundling
## by Wendy Rathbone

Diego is a powerful man with a tragic past. Out on the expansive ocean in his private yacht, he discovers a beautiful and mysterious man adrift on a raft, near death. The bond that forms between them in the aftermath of Alec's rescue is one of fierce passion, though lacking in trust. Can they make it work, or will Alec's amnesia bring forth secrets so disturbing as to tear them apart? A passionately erotic love story of desire and darkness, exquisite and explicit.

I can see his struggle between gratitude and uneasiness. He is buffeted by all things new and strange. He does not know where he is from, who he is or what happened to him. He does not know me. There has not been enough time to transition between strangers and friendship.

This isolation of his is something I can identify with, but it is also a feeling no one can help him with until or unless he gets his own life back. And his memory.

If that doesn't happen, then it will take time for him to build a new life. He is polite to me, even friendly, but even a night together during a storm with his arms wrapped tight around my waist doesn't calm the surge I see inside him, the emptiness, the loss, possibly even panic. That night may have reinforced some trust in me, but so far not enough for him to completely relax.

He seeks me out, though. That's something. He sits by me at dinner when he can have any seat of his choosing. I watch him closely when he does not realize it. At dinner the following night after we had only 'slept' together, and before we go to bed again in separate rooms, I notice everything about him, how he moves, the way the air warms when he is closer to me, the dry sheen of his lips as they part for more air when he is reacting to something, or speaking, or eating.

His hands still shake. Anyone else might not notice because he keeps them clasped into fists at his sides or, while sitting, pressed tight to his lap.

I spend another fretful night alone. I dream restlessly, wild, loud and colorful visions I cannot recall at all as soon as my eyes open. All I know is the dreams leave me unfulfilled, impatient.

# None Can Hold the Dark
## Wendy Rathbone

In the eagerly-awaited sequel to Wendy Rathbone's homoerotic romance "The Foundling," Diego and Alec meet new challenges in private and from the outside world. Diego is being investigated by the local police for murder. Meanwhile, Alec's amnesia and the trauma of his kidnapping by white slavers continue to plague him. And the danger to Alec is not yet over.

Distracted by their new love, both men fail to see certain threats until it is almost too late.

---

"Why do you keep doing this illegal business?" Now Alec's gaze turned toward him, open as the day and lit with a sad frenzy, a challenge. "You could go anywhere, do anything, be anyone."

Diego had asked himself that question on rare occasions. In truth, he got used to what he was, what he did. Even a dangerous known was perhaps preferable to the unknown. "People depend on me."

Alec shook his head, but smiled a little as he said, "That's so weak." He leaned forward, over the arm of the chair, and put his shaking hand on the back of Diego's head. The kiss was cool, lingering, moist with salt. When Alec pulled back, he said almost matter of factly, "It's like there's sharks and there's goldfish and one can't decide to become the other."

Diego was still stunned by the kiss. But the words hit him hard. In them was the unfair conjecture of a locked fate. He believed in making his own fate...or luck. Did Alec think only one kind of man lived inside him and that was all there was to it? To life? It hurt. Badly.

Diego sat back on his heels, catching himself with his hands on the smooth, plank floor. "So, Alec, which am I?"

Alec frowned.

Diego said, "I made choices in my life. I made them. No one made them for me. If I need to be strong I'm strong. If I need to be vicious I can be that too. So what? I'm stuck there? In a pattern, a role...with no free will? Huh?"

Alec watched him inquisitively now.

"Because," Diego went on, "I'm solely responsible for my actions. Me. Could you say the same of the shark?"

They both waited, the silence covering them in muggy discomfort.

"You think you understand me?" Diego finally asked.

**Available early fall, 2013!**
**Print or digital format**

## UNEARTHLY
## by Wendy Rathbone

### *A Collection of Award-Winning Poetry*

Intro by the Author: This book contains all my out of print chapbooks (mini-collections of an author's work usually published by smaller presses.)

The chapbooks published within include:
**Moon Canoes**, published by Dark Regions Press, 1994
**(Im)mortal**, published by Shadowfire Press, 1996
**Scrying The River Styx**, published by Anamnesis Press, 1999
**Autumn Phantoms**, published by Flesh and Blood Press, 2000
**Dreams of Decadence Presents: Wendy Rathbone**, published by DNA Publications 2002
**Dancing in the Haunted Woodlands**, published by Yellow Bat Review, 2003
**Vampyria**, published by Eye Scry Publications, 2005

### She Sleeps With Vampires
She sleeps with vampires
courting velvet breaths
poem-dreams
chill-stopped hearts

Wrapped in her arms
like teddy bear thoughts
purple lips trembling
at her quiet throat
they love her more than
somber rain
more than autumn
more than ash-soft hearths of night.

## COYOTE
## Della Van Hise

*A Novel of Love, Honor and Personal Sacrifice...*

When River Willows is accused of a murder she didn't commit, her life takes a turn toward the sanctuary of a world existing at right-angles to our own. Combining the mysticism of martial arts and the romantic conflict of a young woman torn between two powerful men, COYOTE takes the reader on an epic journey of dangerous secrets, military cover-ups, and the infinite heart of the peaceful warrior.

---

"So who's Coyote?" I asked, trying to ignore the effect he was having on me. "You?"

Steale laughed easily, though it did little to hide the torment behind that mask of indifference he wore so well.

"Coyote's a scavenger, Jack of all trades. The Native Americans call him the trickster - the one who brought chaos down on the world." He shrugged as if altogether unconcerned. "Original sin."

"Is that what you are?" I asked, keeping it light despite the growing knot my stomach. "Original sin?"

He kept his profile to me, eyes straight ahead as he drove. "Sure you want to know?"

I couldn't help wondering if I had cornered the coyote, or if the clever trickster had cornered me.

---

Della Van Hise is the author of *KILLING TIME* – without a doubt the most controversial *Star Trek* novel ever published!

Teachings of the Immortals

### So... You Want To Live Forever?

The teachings are presented as brief vignettes in no particular order of importance. This is not a book you read from start to finish in a single night. It is a grimoire of self-creation, intended to be contemplated slowly so as to be assimilated wholly. Pick it up and turn to a page at random. Where your eyes come to rest on the page is your lesson for the day. Go no further until you have assimilated the lesson totally.

The teachings are seduction as much as instruction. This is the Way of The Dark Evolution.

### Two Brief Excerpts...

### The Ruby Slippers

The danger of the consensual continuum is that its natural gravity exists at the lowest common denominator of human experience, and because of this it will automatically make you forget those elusive truths you've fought to learn, and before you know it you're lost in petty dramas again, sinking into the mire of old familiar scripts.

The only way to overcome this is to be continually cavorting with worlds and events beyond human experience, journeying into the unknown so that it can become known, expanding knowledge and awareness to become more than you were, bringing back from the Dreaming those secrets which will teach you how to use the ruby slippers to transport yourself over the rainbow to the vampyre wizard's secret lair.

### Perception

This is the nature of reality: to be precisely what perception dictates, as solid and whole as your interpretation of it, or as changeable and eternal as you permit it to be.

It wasn't knowledge god tried to keep from Man, you see. It was perception, for perception alone has the power to destroy god and obliterate comfortable consensual realities to create unending immortality.

Take the apple, my embryonic children. Nibble its red red flesh. Open your vampyre eyes so you may finally begin to See.

### www.immortalis-animus.com

**Eye Scry Publications**
**A Visionary Publishing Company**

**www.eyescry.com/html/publications.htm**

www.ingramcontent.com/pod-product-compliance
Lightning Source LLC
Chambersburg PA
CBHW020944260626
47169CB00006B/1806